Tempest

The Raveneau Novels, Book 4

Cynthia Wright

Please Note

Published by Boxwood Manor Books
Copyright 2012 by Cynthia Challed. All rights reserved.

ISBN: 978-1483971674

Cover by Kim Killion
http://thekilliongroupinc.com
Print design by A Thirsty Mind
http://www.athirstymind.com

Thank You

DEDICATION

To my readers with gratitude and love!

ACKNOWLEDGMENTS

Special thanks to those who contributed their time and
talents to make TEMPEST a reality:

fellow authors and editors extraordinaire,
Lauren Royal and Ciji Ware;

cover designer, Kim Killion; formatter, Pam Headrick;

my family, especially my husband, Al, who didn't know
he was going to be living with a writer
when he fell in love with me;

my wonderful beta readers;

and my sister authors and cheerleaders,
the sparkling Jewels of Historical Romance.

Part One

Chapter 1

Newport, Rhode Island
July, 1903

"Is it possible that I see monkeys, *in costume*, frolicking on this lawn?" Adam Raveneau's tone was edged with sarcasm as he stopped just inside Beechcliff's enormous scrolled gates. "Tell me that I've drunk too much cognac and that none of this is real."

"What's so terrible about a few dancing monkeys?" Byron Matthews countered. It had taken hours of persuasion to get Adam to not only visit Newport, but then to come with him to this lavish eighteenth century costume party. Now he feared that his friend might not continue on to the arched entrance where horse-drawn carriages were disgorging their richly-garbed occupants. It was true enough that Raveneau wouldn't care for these wealthy, status-conscious Americans, but he had problems he could scarcely admit to, and Byron felt certain that solutions could be found here at Beechcliff.

Of course, Raveneau would probably not behave properly. His very costume was an indication that he did not intend to behave properly. Clad entirely in black except for a white stock deftly knotted round his strong, tanned neck, Adam was the image of a rakish eighteenth century pirate. He wore a tricorne hat over thick dark hair drawn back into a queue, and he'd grown three days' worth of stubble to heighten his look of danger.

Byron sighed. "You could have chosen a more appropriate costume."

"Appropriate? How dull." He flashed a momentary smile, then stared off into the distance, listening to the ocean waves. Beyond the procession of carriages, the torchlit grounds, and the marble façade of the American chateau, there were cliffs that plunged to the starlit ocean. "I don't belong here, you know. I ought to be out there…"

"Of course you belong here. You may have gambled away your fortune, but these people don't need money. They'll be more interested in your title."

He snorted. "I'm merely a viscount, a title which Queen Victoria bestowed on me out of pity when I lost Thorn Manor. The greatest success of my life may have been charming the queen."

"Queen Victoria was only one of your numerous conquests." Byron wondered why he always felt as if he needed to persuade Adam to find a solution to his dilemma? With no money, and only a modest title and a tumble-down estate in Barbados to his credit, shouldn't the answer be obvious? In the past, Adam had joked about marrying an heiress, but now he refused to consider the subject more seriously. Byron tried a lighter tone. "My friend, you are standing next to a fellow with a much shorter list of accomplishments than your own. The only reason I'm clutching an invitation to this ball is because my sister married the Duke of Aylesbury. I'm a penniless artist from South Dakota, for God's sake!"

"Perhaps you ought to look for a bride for yourself and forget about me, hmm?" He knew that Byron meant well, but he didn't want his help. As a monkey wearing a green coat with gold epaulets capered toward them, Raveneau drew his rapier and pointed it. "That animal's clothes are exquisitely tailored."

Byron wondered if he'd made a mistake, bringing Adam here tonight. All the signs were there: the undercurrent of irony in his voice, the twitch of his fine mouth, the flicker in his eyes. "You may be disillusioned with the upper classes in Britain and America, but I've seen the gleam in your eye when you talk about Barbados—and Tempest Hall…"

He purposely misunderstood. "Are they dispensing gold ingots as party favors tonight? Unless the answer is yes, I fail to see how this ball can benefit Tempest Hall."

Light poured down Beechcliff's wide steps to welcome them. "Adam, stop being so thick-headed." The younger man caught his sleeve. "I'm talking about heiresses, with fortunes beyond imagining. There will be throngs of them here, and their mothers are seeking husbands with British titles. That's the one advantage you still possess—"

"God's blood!" Raveneau cut in with a piratical grin, "I b'lieve I've been insulted!" Then, looking toward the chateau's upper stories, where lights burned in every window and mysterious shadows moved, he mused, "What devil stuck this insufferable notion of *heiresses* in your brain? I can't imagine marrying an heiress, not even for the sake of Tempest Hall."

~ ~ ~

"Carriages are turning down the drive!" Catherine Beasley Parrish announced as she peeked out her bedroom window.

"Come over here, my dear." When her daughter had joined her in front of the mirror, Hermione lifted her pince-nez for a last look. "If the Duke of Sunderford doesn't propose to you after our housewarming ball tonight, then I just miss my guess!"

"But Mother, I don't want the duke to propose." Even though Catherine knew it was futile to argue, she couldn't suppress the words. "He is a toad."

"You have been taught better manners than those." Hermione was beginning to have her own doubts about Sunderford, who seemed no closer to declaring himself now than he had upon his arrival three long weeks ago. "Any other girl would be thrilled and grateful to have an opportunity to become an English duchess!"

The porcelain clock on the mantelpiece chimed ten, and the sound of servants' footsteps came to them faintly through the walls. Guests were arriving, eager not only for the spectacle of an eighteenth century costume ball, but also for their first look inside Beechcliff. The opulent summer "cottage," patterned after a French chateau and set on fourteen acres of oceanfront property, had taken nearly two years and three million dollars to complete. Although the Parrish family had moved in late in 1902, Hermione had saved her triumphant housewarming for the height of the Season.

"I'd better see that your father has powdered his wig properly," Hermione murmured. "We mustn't be late."

She remained by her daughter's side, however, surveying her critically in the gold-framed mirror.

Catherine's Marie Antoinette-style costume was a confection of lace-trimmed rose silk over an embroidered ivory underskirt. The bodice was cut low, but Catherine had insisted upon covering her breasts with a fine lace fichu. Diamonds shone at her throat and ears, and her hair was dressed in a cloud of upswept powdered curls.

Hermione found no fault with the costume, but she did wish that Nature had bestowed more generous gifts. At twenty-one years of age, Catherine was little more than five feet tall and frequently mistaken for a schoolgirl. Her rounded face was piquantly pretty rather than Gibson-Girl-elegant. Large expressive eyes, exactly the same shade of golden brown as her mass of hair, were her best feature. Hermione privately suspected that men were more apt to remark on Catherine's wealthy father than her physical charms…

"I feel like a trussed chicken," the girl complained softly.

"Nonsense. Perhaps you'd be more comfortable without that fichu constricting your bosom…"

"No! It's hard enough to be paraded around at these marriage marts without being undressed, Mother!"

There was a knock at Catherine's bedroom door and Isobel, her lady's maid, admitted Jules Parrish. Ever-distracted on such occasions, the steel magnate enjoyed the pursuit of Italian studies rather than socializing during his leisure time. Tonight, in his Louis XV finery, he looked especially uneasy.

"I feel like a trussed chicken," he muttered, "diamond-studded and powdered and completely humiliated."

Laughing, Catherine lifted her skirts and ran to kiss his cheek, while Hermione checked her tiara in the mirror before joining them. "She's just like you, Jules. You both delight in making my life difficult."

"Doesn't seem to get us anywhere, though, does it?" he murmured to Catherine as they started off down the marble corridor.

Their houseguest, the Duke of Sunderford, was emerging from his rooms at that very moment. He had managed to add considerably to his five-foot-five-inch frame by choosing a costume that included high-heeled blue shoes and a tall, sausage-curled bag-wig, but Catherine thought that he looked more preposterous than ever.

"Ah, it is the lovely Miss Parrish, is it not?" The duke, leaning heavily on a jewel-encrusted walking stick, looked her up and down as they approached.

The orchestra had begun to play in the ballroom downstairs and Catherine clung to her father's arm, suddenly overcome by a sense of doom. As they prepared to descend the white marble staircase, Hermione gave her a penetrating smile.

"Dear Catherine, won't this be a magical night? One can only imagine how it will end!"

The Duke of Sunderford was oblivious to the meaning of his hostess's words. He was staring at the lavishly decorated foyer that lay below, wondering how much the exotic flowers, food, champagne, and the two orchestras had cost the Parrishes. There were expensive American Beauty roses everywhere one looked. Outdoors, flickering lights lit the grounds, musicians played on the lawn while pet monkeys scampered about, and an orange grove decorated one of the terraces. That sort of wealth could heat his bone-chilling Sunderford Castle in the winter…and much more.

He suppressed a sigh as he glanced at Miss Parrish. If he were going to marry an American, he'd hoped for a great beauty. Catherine didn't have a swan's neck like Consuelo Vanderbilt or the honey hair and blue eyes of Jeannie Chamberlain from Cleveland, Ohio. She was too familiar with everyone from the servants to her betters. Her opinions and laughter were both offered too freely. In short, Catherine Parrish was very *American*.

Feeling the duke's eyes on her, Catherine looked for an excuse to escape. Guests in glittering period garb were entering the foyer, and the illusion that they were all at Versailles was becoming more real by the moment. "Mother, I would like to see if Elysia VanGanburg has arrived yet. She wasn't feeling well yesterday."

Hermione gripped her soft upper arm, smiling down into her eyes. "Don't be silly, dear. You must stay with us to greet the guests as they arrive. We'll stand under the archway of roses, and you *will* have a lovely time!"

Chapter 2

After greeting what felt like a thousand guests, Catherine's face hurt from smiling and she felt unbearably restless standing in the reception line for so long.

"Do stop tapping your foot," Hermione warned softly. "Ladies are composed and gracious."

There was no time to reply, for Alice Vanderbilt was approaching, radiating the sort of calm composure Catherine lacked. Soft air wafted in from the flower-scented grounds, beckoning. What fun was it to have a wealthy father if one could never do as one pleased, or even make one's own choices in life?

"*Who* in heaven's name is *that?*" Hermione hissed the moment Mrs. Vanderbilt had left them. Tapping the arms of her husband and daughter with her fan, she gestured toward the entryway. "I believe those people may be strangers!"

Catherine focused on the two men who had just entered. The auburn-haired fellow, costumed in a perfectly proper blue satin Louis XVI suit, consulted with the liveried footmen at the door. When she turned her attention to his companion, her heart literally skipped a beat.

Clad all in black, the man appeared to be costumed as a buccaneer, with leather jackboots, a simple white stock, and a stiff coat with turned-back cuffs and gold buttons. He carried a tricorne hat set off by a white cockade centered with a blood-red ruby, and his raven hair was drawn back in a queue. In the gilded setting of Beechcliff, surrounded by satin-clad, jewel-encrusted peacocks, this unadorned renegade radiated an aura of danger.

"I am *not* amused by that man's costume," Hermione decided. She lifted her pince-nez for a closer look.

Catherine stared in fascination. His skin was darkened by the sun. His eyes were hooded, perhaps bored or cynical, and there was a rather harsh edge to his good looks. He was very tall and powerfully built.

"Papa," she whispered, "please don't send them away."

"Of course not." Then, as the two strangers approached, Jules Parrish put on a welcoming smile and extended his hand. "How good of you both to come."

Hermione murmured, "I'm terribly sorry, but I didn't hear the major-domo announce you…"

"I am Byron Matthews," said the fellow in the satin suit. "Mr. Parrish, you and I met at the casino."

Jules was nodding. "Of course! You recently became the brother-in-law of the Duke of Aylesbury." He glanced toward his wife, whose lips were puckered with doubt. "I had my secretary take an invitation to Matthews at his hotel. Such a fine young man."

"How nice." She forced a smile.

"The pleasure is mine, I assure you. I would like to present my worthy friend, the Viscount Raveneau."

"Viscount…?" Hermione perked up visibly. "Welcome, my lord! What a unique costume you have chosen. You appear to be quite…wicked." She gave a nervous titter, as if she feared she had overstepped propriety.

"I am Stede Bonnet, the pirate," Raveneau explained, and watched her blanch under her powder. "Wicked indeed."

Catherine felt giddy. What a dashingly romantic name he had! And his eyes were breathtaking: marbled gray and blue, with hints of gold dust. Voices and time blurred until he appeared directly in front of her and she stared as her hand went into his. His fingers were long and handsome, but his hand wasn't soft like those of the men she knew. It was dark and strong like the rest of him.

"Miss Parrish, I presume?"

Jules leaned over, quite taken with his new friends. "My lord, this is my daughter, Catherine Beasley Parrish."

"It's a pleasure to meet you." Raveneau's eyes crinkled slightly at the edges. "Are you supposed to be an historical character? That fichu reminds me more of a Colonial Quaker than a contemporary of Marie Antoinette's."

Hermione gasped. "My lord, is such a remark entirely *proper*?"

"Probably not," he replied easily, then turned back to Catherine. "Are you a stickler for propriety, Miss Parrish? If so, I apologize."

Dimly, she realized that he was still holding her hand, waiting for her to speak. "I—I am glad to meet you, Lord Raveneau…"

"My name is Adam," he corrected. "That title's just a useless ornament. Nothing to do with *me*."

"I couldn't possibly call you 'Adam,' my lord." Her face was hot. She noticed that the hair curling behind his ears was flecked with silver.

"Of course you can." He leaned closer and spoke in hushed tones. "Tell me about your honored guest, the duke. Are the two of you betrothed?"

She gasped. "No!"

Hermione leaned across to admonish, "Catherine, more guests have arrived!"

"I mustn't keep you," Raveneau said, and released her hand.

She wanted to go after him, but could not. Francine Pembroke appeared on the arm of her brother. Clad in white satin trimmed with gold, a wide diamond stomacher pinned to her bodice, she was ravishing. Her blue eyes wandered over the hall even as she spoke to Catherine.

"Who were those two men? Are they newly arrived in Newport? The pirate is divine! What is his name?"

Hermione intervened. "Dear Francine, would you like an introduction to the Viscount Raveneau? Catherine will be occupied with our guest, the duke, but I should be happy to present you to his lordship."

And off they went, leaving Catherine with Sunderford. "You Americans do things rather differently than we do in Britain," he remarked. "I have never met so many outspoken guests. But then, there is so much over here that I don't understand. Ever since my school days, I've been puzzled by the war between North and South America. Considering the distance between you, what could you have fought about?"

"But—we never had a war with South America!"

"Of course you did, in 1861." He glanced away, as if appalled by her ignorance. "Perhaps you might be forgiven for not knowing, since you weren't born yet, but it was an awfully famous war. Abraham Lincoln, and so forth."

Catherine wanted to inform him that he was the idiot, not she, but her real concern was Adam Raveneau. Had Francine, with her invitingly low décolleté, already gotten him in her clutches? "Let's go into the ballroom, Your Grace. My mother intends that you shall dance with her to open the cotillion."

Berger's Hungarian Orchestra had already begun to play softly as guests milled around the ballroom and accepted glasses of champagne from servants in eighteenth century livery. The enormous room was set off by ornate mirrors and a series of crystal chandeliers. The wainscoting had been taken directly from a Loire Valley chateau. Hodgson, the florist, had brought in drifts of silver-ribboned white hydrangeas and orchids, and the ballroom overlooked the main terrace, which was massed with more flowers.

"Ah, there you are!" Hermione Parrish cried as she bore down on them. "I was just about to send Jules in search of you two naughty lovebirds. Your Grace, I suspect that you have been waiting for this magical night to spin your web of romance around my daughter."

"Eh? Spin my *what*?" he shouted over the din.

"Don't tease me, Your Grace!" Her huge frozen smile gave her the look of a dragon. "Will you kindly come out with me to lead the dancing? Then you may have your turn with Catherine." She gripped her daughter's hand and came close to whisper, "Don't be difficult. Tonight, of all nights, I would have you behave properly."

Catherine felt as if the walls were closing in on her. All the years of training, overseen by her mother, crowded her memory. She'd never been allowed to go to school with other children, but had been strictly tutored by governesses, not only in French and German, but also for dancing and all forms of etiquette. How many hours had she spent perfecting her English accent and learning to pour tea, all the while wearing a steel rod to improve her posture? This was the night for which Hermione Parrish had groomed her only child, just as surely as Jules's horses had been trained to win at the racetrack.

Now that Catherine's moment of truth was at hand, she wanted only to escape. Even the enticing distraction of Adam Raveneau didn't matter now. She didn't need to hear what her mother was saying to the duke as they began to dance; the determined expression on her face as she spoke was enough.

"Papa!" Relieved to spy her father amidst the guests, Catherine tugged at his sleeve. "I—I am feeling rather ill in this terrible crush—"

He frowned at the champagne glass in her hand. "You shouldn't be drinking, angel. You're not used to it."

"Perhaps that's it. I'm just going to go and get a little air…and cool off."

"Your mother won't be happy. She has certain expectations for this evening…"

"I'll be back before she misses me!"

He felt her brow. "You are a trifle pale. I'll explain to her."

"I knew you would understand, Papa." Their eyes met for a meaningful instant.

"I may understand, but we mustn't countermand your mother's wishes."

Catherine could scarcely breathe as she slipped out one of the glass doors and hurried down a staircase to the terrace. The scent of orange trees floated on the balmy night air. She was free! There were only a few guests wandering on the grounds and even the musicians and the chattering monkeys were quiet. The cadence of her heartbeat changed as anxiety gave way to euphoria. Suddenly it occurred to her that she could keep on running. There were no guards or walls to keep her prisoner here!

Her silken slippers were awfully fragile, however, and her boned bodice pinched when she moved. Approaching a Chinese teahouse that overlooked the surging ocean, Catherine decided to rest inside until she could gather her thoughts. Torches had been placed on either side of the door, illuminating the roof of green tiles and dragons with their tails in the air.

"Do my eyes deceive me?"

She cried out in surprise. She didn't recognize the deep, ironically accented male voice, and the sight of a tall figure standing in the shadows frightened her. Hermione had always warned her to beware of strange men. "Who are you?"

He came out into the torchlight and gave her a rakish smile. "Have you forgotten me so quickly?"

"Oh!" Catherine couldn't believe that she was alone in the teahouse with Adam Raveneau. "Of course I haven't forgotten you. You're Blackbeard."

"No, my beauty. I am Stede Bonnet, the wicked Barbadian pirate." His eyes danced as he lifted a bottle of champagne and drank. "Blackbeard's whiskers grew all the way up to his eyes. He liked to twist them with ribbons into little tails, then light them like fuses. I don't think your mother would approve of that, do you?"

"No, but she doesn't approve of you, either, even without a be-ribboned beard." She felt daring. When he held out the bottle to her, she accepted. It was shockingly crass to drink champagne out of the bottle, especially one that had already touched a stranger's mouth. After trying a tiny sip, then a gulp, she licked her lips and beamed. "You are a bad influence, my lord."

"Adam," he reminded her. "And soon you'll be 'Your Grace,' if your mother has her way."

"No!" She frowned at him. "My name is Catherine."

"Like the heroine of *Wuthering Heights*?"

"Exactly! In fact, I was named for her, and as a result, it's now my favorite novel." The truth was that Hermione disapproved of *Wuthering Heights* and, at sixteen, Catherine had bribed a housemaid to bring her a copy. Heathcliff had made an indelible impression. "But enough about my name. What has brought you outdoors to the teahouse?"

"Truthfully, Francine Pembroke asked me to meet her out here. Is that acceptable, Cathy?"

"I certainly don't mind," she lied, "but of course it's not *socially* acceptable for Francine to go off alone with a man at a ball like this. If anyone should see the two of you, her reputation would be ruined."

"And what about your reputation, Cathy?"

Her blush deepened every time he called her Cathy, and she knew that was the very reason he did it. "I don't think it's quite the same thing, is it? Francine was scheming to be alone with you, just minutes after your introduction, while I came upon you here completely by chance!"

"But anyone seeing us here would not know that." Adam drank some more champagne and passed the bottle to her.

"I really don't care what they think. I've spent my whole life learning a lot of silly rules and I'm sick to death of the entire business. Perhaps if I do something scandalous, Mother won't be able to make me marry the duke." Her chin trembled slightly.

"Aha! I thought so. I saw it in your eyes the moment we met." Gently, he took her hand and led her over to a green marble bench. "Have another drink and tell me everything. You'll feel better."

The torchlight flickered over her winsome face as she hiccuped, took another swallow of champagne, and said, "I ought to divulge to you that there is another teahouse exactly like this one at the other end of the sunken gardens. Francine is probably waiting for you there."

"Good. Then we won't be disturbed." He traced her cheek with a fingertip. "Go on, Cathy."

She tingled all over, more intoxicated by his nearness than by the champagne. "I think you already have guessed most of my story. It's embarrassing to think how many daughters of American millionaires have been pushed by their mothers into prestigious marriages; it's embarrassing to think that I'm a character in one of those melodramas."

"It's not a melodrama. It's your own life, and you have to stand up for your rights."

"That is so much harder than it sounds! My mother has been trying to bend my will since I was a baby and I am weary of the struggle." Catherine sighed, leaning against the hard strength of his arm. "She was raised in the South, and though her father made a lot of money, he was considered a social upstart in New York. The Parrishes didn't think Mother was good enough for their son but he married her anyway. I think Mother was so bruised by the rejections she suffered that she decided to get even by molding her daughter into a royal who would be above the touch of New York society."

"Lucky you," Adam remarked sardonically.

"I thought I would be able to ease my way out of this situation until my brother died in a sailing accident, four years ago, when he was only twenty-one. Mother hasn't been the same since. She's always been single-minded and stubborn, but Stephen's death broke her heart."

"But what about your heart? He was your brother, after all."

She wiped away tears. "I was very attached to him; he was the only person who really knew and understood me...and our unusual family. I've felt terribly alone since Stephen died. Mother and I were bound together by our grief for a time, I suppose. I went with her to England and let her dress me up and take me to parties." Catherine looked at Adam and sighed. "A mistake, probably."

"Probably," he agreed drily. "I suppose you met Sunderford then?"

"Yes. We visited Sunderford Castle in Dorset. I realized how dire my situation was when I applied to Radcliffe College and was admitted, but Mother forbade me to go. I had dreamed of becoming a teacher, but she was horrified at the notion of me aspiring to something so 'common.' It was clear then that the purpose of my lifetime of studying had been only to form me into a worthy bride for a nobleman."

Raveneau stared at her as she spoke, trying to fathom how a lively, intelligent girl like this could have suffered her mother's machinations without fighting back. "Why are you still under the same roof with her? How old are you?"

"I'm twenty-one." Catherine straightened her back. "You're a man so you can't possibly understand how different it is to be a woman in these times. I've been raised to follow a strict code of behavior, to never even leave the house unattended. Are you suggesting that I simply run away from home and turn my back on my parents?" Her spine sagged a bit as she sighed. "Well, I've considered it myself, as recently as this evening. Perhaps I would have done so by now if Stephen hadn't died. It's a terrible burden to be the only child, the only source of joy for your parents. I love Papa very much and he certainly doesn't want me to stand up to Mother."

"God, this is giving me a headache."

"We should go back now. My mother will be livid when she realizes I'm missing!" She took another sip of champagne before rising from the bench. "Can't you help me think of a way out of this coil? The duke doesn't show any inclination to propose marriage, but Mother is determined, and I'm afraid that he may take me, just to get his impoverished hands on my enormous dowry."

In spite of himself, Adam felt a guilty pang of interest as he walked Catherine back to the brightly lit mansion. "Did you say…dowry?"

Chapter 3

Hearing footsteps in the corridor, Catherine opened her door a few inches and peeked out. It was her father, striding along in his flawlessly-tailored suit, looking through his spectacles at a slim volume of Italian poetry.

"Papa!" she whispered urgently.

"Ah, I was just coming to tell you goodbye," he said as he reached her door. "Better get out of that nightgown and into your riding clothes, angel. Your mother will have you stewed for supper if you don't make up to her for last night."

"Are you going back to New York City already?" Clearly, he did not mean to aid any further in her rebellion and yet he was the only person to whom she could turn. "Mother was so angry at me last night, when I didn't return until midnight supper. I worry that she means to lock me in this tomb until I accept the duke's proposal."

"Sunderford seems to be a good fellow." He patted her curls. "You're getting older, and I confess I'd like to be a grandfather. Lord knows your mother would be over the moon with a wedding to plan, and then grandchildren to dote upon. Ever since we lost Stephen, she hasn't been the same. Be good to her."

A burning tide of despair welled up in her. "Safe journey, Papa."

"Yes. I'll be going by motor car because your mother has plans for the yacht today. She means to have a luncheon for you and Sunderford and a few friends. I'm sorry I can't join you."

Catherine kissed his cheek, loving the familiar smell of his shaving soap. "I'm sorry, too."

"But, there's one thing I'm good at and that's earning the money to pay for this new house and all the trimmings. I'll see you in a few days, angel."

It was past eight o'clock and Catherine's lavish breakfast was waiting under silver covers on a window table in her bedroom. Her father was right; she hadn't much time before her morning's ride. The Newport schedule was strictly regimented and today of all days, Catherine would be expected to adhere to it. She'd never seen her mother as angry or determined as she'd looked last night. To make matters worse, Adam Raveneau hadn't come back inside for the midnight supper and she hadn't seen him since he'd given her a little nudge, back into the ballroom. Then, he had vanished as mysteriously as he'd appeared.

Sitting down at the table, Catherine found that she had little appetite. Her thoughts were all of Raveneau. Until her first sight of him, Catherine had believed that truly compelling men existed only in novels...like *Wuthering Heights*. Now that she knew better, it was even more dismal to contemplate the match her mother was engineering.

Just then, Isobel, her maid, popped into the room. "Miss, you're going to be late if you don't hurry."

"Will you bring my riding clothes? If you help me dress, I should have enough time to write a very important note."

"I've decided that the Casino is the best thing in Newport," Raveneau remarked. "Alice agrees, don't you old girl?"

Byron leaned down to pet the ancient yellow Labrador retriever Adam had taken into his care upon the death of his mother. "Alice has agreed with everything you've said since she was a puppy. Now it's only worse. She's as besotted as every other female in your orbit."

Adam pretended not to hear as the trio stood together near Bellevue Avenue and admired the multi-gabled, shingle-clad façade of the Casino. Beyond the exclusive shops facing the avenue sprawled an assortment of pleasure-spots, including an opulent theatre, a tennis court, a billiard room, piazzas decorated with spindle-work screens, and a grassy interior courtyard.

"At least, by praising the Casino, you've said something positive," Byron observed. "You were a cynic last night."

"Not completely."

"No?" He noticed that all the young ladies who were passing in carriages were staring at Raveneau, who looked even more striking with Alice's expressive face resting against his leg. Byron was used to the fact that women didn't notice him if Adam was present. "You didn't dance once, and then you insisted that we leave before supper."

"I didn't dance because I was in the teahouse with—"

"God, no—not, ah, I've forgotten her name—the woman with the lovely breasts—"

Adam laughed, and more young ladies stared. "You're thinking of Francine Pembroke. I was supposed to meet her, but I got the wrong teahouse and ended up with Catherine Parrish instead."

"Wh—what?" Byron goggled. "But, that's fantastic! She's the *heiress*, for God's sake! Worth millions! Why didn't you tell me?"

He shrugged, enjoying himself. "Nothing to tell. Cathy's excruciatingly loving mum is determined that she shall become the Duchess of Sunderford—the biggest title money can buy. They may be betrothed as we speak."

"You call her Cathy?"

He rewarded him with a sharp stare. "How much longer must we stay here? I'm ready to return to visiting my cousins in Connecticut."

Byron fell silent, quite aware of the tension emanating from his friend. At length he braced himself and said, "See here, I know that something happened in your family that has caused you to become so adamantly opposed to love or marriage in your own life, however—"

"You are outside of bloody enough, broaching such a topic!"

"I am your friend. Perhaps if you can share whatever it is with me, we can sort it out together. I have always suspected that it might have to do with your father's death in that avalanche…"

Raveneau turned and spoke in a deceptively calm voice. "I cannot imagine why I would *share* any unpleasant memories with you or anyone else. The past is over; nothing can change it."

Just then, a particularly fine sociable rolled toward them along the elm-lined avenue. The carriage was so named for the ease of conversation its opposing cushioned seats afforded. Under an umbrella-like covering, Catherine Parrish was seated across from her friend, Elysia VanGanburg, a tall, willowy girl with flaxen hair. Byron waved and the fine pair of greys pulling the sociable slowed to a stop.

"Good morning, Miss Parrish," Byron greeted her, walking toward them without a backward glance at Adam.

"Hello, Mr. Matthews. May I present my friend, Miss VanGanburg? Sadly, she was too ill last evening to attend the costume ball, but I've been assuring her that it was not half as festive as it sounded."

Alice had suddenly heard the call of nature and was pulling Raveneau toward the grassy courtyard beyond the entrance to the Casino. Catherine felt a pang when she saw him go, but her doubts were overcome by the simple joy of seeing him again, in broad daylight. The night before hadn't been a dream after all, and Raveneau looked just as devastatingly attractive in his light trousers, blue serge jacket, and crisp shirt and tie as he had in his wicked Stede Bonnet costume.

"That's Adam's dog, Alice," Byron was explaining a bit awkwardly. "She's very elderly. Her needs can be…pressing. I'm sure he doesn't mean to be rude."

"She's lovely," Elysia observed, staring all the while at Adam.

"I won't keep you, Mr. Matthews," said Catherine. "But I did want to deliver a note to you…and Lord Raveneau." She plucked it from her pearl-encrusted reticule, blushing, and handed it to him. "It's an invitation to a lavish but tedious luncheon my mother is having on our family yacht, the *Free Spirit*. I thought it might not be quite so dull if you and Lord Raveneau could attend."

"They have the best French chef in Newport," Elysia said brightly.

"We'll be there," Byron assured them.

Catherine went pale, then pink again. "Oh! Well, then, that's lovely. We'll see you at one o'clock."

As the sociable started forward, Elysia whispered, "Both of them are divine, but I can see what you mean about Lord Raveneau. He's utterly…"

"Splendid," Catherine supplied with feeling. "I think he's trying to avoid me. I could sense last night that he'd begun to back away. No doubt he's pursued constantly."

"Why do you think that you'll be luckier than the others?"

"I don't—but with Mother thrusting me at the duke, what have I to lose besides a little pride?" She paused, chewing at an uneven fingernail. "I saw a glint in Lord Raveneau's eyes when I mentioned my dowry. Perhaps he can be bought?"

"Catherine!" she cried, horrified. "I am shocked."

"Don't be silly." Her eyes were dancing as she added, "And, I'd like you to call me Cathy from now on, just like the heroine of *Wuthering Heights*. It suits me, don't you think so?"

Chapter 4

"I hate this," Adam pronounced through clenched teeth. "I'm going back to Connecticut in the morning."

"I think you're afraid of her."

"I don't know what the devil you're talking about."

"Catherine Parrish," Byron supplied lightly. They had just boarded the *Free Spirit* and his tone grew increasingly distracted as he took in the surroundings. "Good God, have you ever seen anything like it?"

"You have lost your mind." He regarded the magnificent yacht with dread. "Alice needs a walk. I'll just give her a turn around the deck."

As he watched Adam go off with the dog, Byron felt relief. It would give him a chance to do a bit of business on his own. Through the glass walls of the upper saloon, he could see Catherine Parrish and Elysia VanGanburg holding crystal goblets and chatting quietly amid the other guests. Hermione Parrish hovered nearby with the Duke of Sunderford, who resembled a tortoise more than ever in his yachting togs.

For a moment, Byron wondered if he were doing the right thing. Excessive wealth brought its own set of problems. However, when Catherine Parrish spied him and began to wave, his doubts melted under the unaffected warmth of her smile. Truly, she was perfect.

"Mr. Matthews!" Opening the teak-edged door, she handed him a glass of champagne. "Won't you come in and join us? Where is Lord Raveneau?"

"Walking Alice in the fresh air."

"Alice?" Her brow puckered, then smoothed prettily. "Oh, yes. The Labrador! I do hope she is yacht-trained, so to speak. Mother would be terribly unhappy if Alice damaged any of the antique carpets."

Byron decided not to make any assurances he couldn't prove. The dog was thirteen, a great age for her breed, and anything was possible. "Alice has a history of unwavering dependability, and our innkeeper trusts her enough to allow her to share Adam's lodgings."

"Innkeeper?" she repeated in surprise. "I assumed that you were staying in a private home."

"We could have, but Adam refused. He prefers the Whitehorse Tavern to a palatial summer cottage."

"Have you and Lord Raveneau been friends a long time, Mr. Matthews?"

He nodded. "Several years. We've shared many adventures and we understand each other very well." He gave her what he hoped was a meaningful glance. "My friend is at a cross-roads in his life."

Suddenly, Catherine stopped minding that Adam was off with his elderly dog. "A cross-roads? Now you have piqued my interest. What do you mean?" She nudged Elysia, who obediently wandered off. "Why don't we sit down?"

He followed her to the afterdeck, which featured an aviary of exotic birds, and a grouping of rocking chairs set among potted palms. Overhead, the sky was clear azure. Newport harbor glittered in the sunlight, set off by the green foliage of nearby Rose Island. Without even tasting his champagne, Byron felt euphoric. "You lead a charmed life, Miss Parrish."

A cloud seemed to pass over her face. "Perhaps it may seem so to you, sir, but not to me." She touched the band of lace at her neckline. "My life is not my own."

"Your parents have named their yacht the *Free Spirit*. Doesn't that speak to their philosophy of life?"

She gave a short laugh. "Would that it did. It refers to my brother who drowned at sea four years ago. Stephen was only twenty-one. He is free now and I am imprisoned more securely than ever." Looking into Byron's eyes, Catherine added, "I told these things to Lord Raveneau last night. He seemed to understand immediately."

"Did he?" His heart beat faster. "I can imagine that he might. He regards the traditions and responsibilities that attend even moderate wealth as burdens."

A steward appeared with a tray of *hors d'oeurves* and they accepted plates which were then set aside. Catherine leaned closer, studying Byron intently. "I have confided a great deal to his lordship about my own situation but it wasn't until this morning that I realized how little I know of his. I don't think that's quite fair, do you?"

He drank from his fresh goblet of champagne. "Adam guards his privacy."

"I mean no harm, Mr. Matthews." The breeze loosened a light brown tendril from the mass of hair pinned up, Gibson-Girl-style, atop her head. "I am merely curious to know where Lord Raveneau comes from, and why he makes light of his title. He's very different from the noblemen I met in England—and there must be a reason!"

"Adam's a renegade, descended from French pirates. His great-grandfather, Andre Raveneau, was a privateer captain during our Revolutionary War, and later settled in Connecticut to raise his family. He built ships and traded with the West Indies, and his son, Nathan, wound up buying an old sugar cane plantation on Barbados. It's called Tempest Hall."

"How romantic!"

"Yes, quite true…the Raveneaus are a romantic lot." The warm sun, the fine champagne, and Catherine's encouraging smile kept his story flowing. "Nathan married a beautiful spitfire called Adrienne Beauvisage and they had a son called Robert. He was educated in England and, after he married, became a don at Oxford. Robert and Arabella had one child— Adam. He's been a real fire-eater since birth, a throwback to the wildest Raveneaus. Growing up, he visited Barbados often, staying with his grandparents at Tempest Hall. He has told me that he always felt more at home in the West Indies than England."

Catherine was wide-eyed with fascination, trying to keep all the characters straight as the story unfolded. "I haven't heard a word yet about the family title!"

"Well…that's a rather recent development." He cleared his throat. "Robert and Arabella Raveneau owned a magnificent estate in Kent. To make a long story short, both Adam's parents have died, and in recent years Adam decided that Thorn Manor was wasted on him. He donated the estate for use as an orphanage, which filled a great need for the neighboring villages. Just months before her death, Queen Victoria rewarded Adam for his generosity by making him a viscount."

"That's because he's proved his nobility through selfless deeds." Her eyes shone. "It's all so much more exciting than my...confining existence."

A steward appeared to pour more champagne. "Miss Parrish, I have been asked by Mrs. Parrish to inform you that luncheon will be served in ten minutes."

Around the corner of the glass-walled saloon, Adam Raveneau lounged against the rail and watched. His eyes narrowed with a mixture of suspicion and humor as Catherine leaned toward Byron, hanging on his every word.

"Alice, my love," he murmured to the dog, "what do you think Byron is plotting? Has he designs on the fair Cathy?"

Guests were wandering downstairs to the mahogany-paneled dining room. Many wore faintly disdainful glances as they passed Alice and she greeted each stranger with a hopeful pink-tongued smile. When no one stopped to pet her, Adam's lean hand moved down to stroke her ears, slowly.

His attention was on Catherine Parrish, who looked quite different to him by daylight, out of costume. She wasn't beautiful by any means, but there was something about her that he found beguiling. Her face was rounded, not elegantly sculpted, and she had a little snub nose. In contrast, her eyes were very large, announcing her every emotion. Her rather unruly brown hair was starting to come loose from its tortoiseshell pins. Finally, Cathy's form was delicately petite rather than womanly, with a waist he could have fit his hands around. She needed more curves to fill out the priceless lace of her blouse.

What were they talking about? Why was she gazing at Byron that way? Adam moved closer, until he and Alice were positioned behind a cluster of potted palms, near enough to catch bits of the conversation.

"I don't think I've ever heard a more romantic tale," Catherine was saying. She tipped up her goblet to finish the last drops. "To think that Lord Raveneau gave up his family estate so that orphans might have a better life! My mother should hear that story; it might teach her that one cannot always judge a person by first impressions!"

"Certainly not," Byron agreed gravely. "Shall we toast to Adam's sterling character/"

She clinked her empty glass against his, watched him drink, and frowned. "We should have kept the bottle. That's what his lordship did last night."

"Did he?"

"Yes. I drank out of it, just like a lady pirate. I vow, it's so romantic to think that he really means to live on Barbados—and that the family estate has been waiting for him ever since his grandmother's death. It must be a spectacular place!"

"Tempest Hall?" Byron repeated, looking doubtful. "It's historic; nearly three centuries old!"

Unable to remain silent a moment longer, Adam sauntered over and tapped Byron's shoulder. "I do hate to interrupt, and I know it's a bore to challenge your highly entertaining tale of my life, but you have left out all the disreputable bits."

Catherine suddenly began to glow. "I think you are modest. You don't want people to know how noble you've been, giving your estate to the orphans…"

"You've been reading too much Dickens, Miss Parrish." He paced in front of their rocking chairs while Alice sat down beside Byron and rested her chin on his knee. "And, my good friend Matthews has whitewashed my character, though I can't imagine why!" Adam sent him a dark glare. "The truth is that I am riddled with defects, not the least of which is a fondness for gambling. I was so deeply in debt that I couldn't afford to keep up Thorn Manor any longer. It only became an orphanage because I didn't want it to fall into the hands of my equally disreputable creditors. Do you still find my circumstances romantic, Miss Parrish?"

She wanted, more than anything, to hear him call her 'Cathy' again. "I don't deserve to be treated so harshly, my lord."

"And that title is just more gammon! The queen was old and nonsensical and she took pity on me when she realized that I'd lost everything my parents worked for. I think she thought I might be able to snare a rich wife if I had a title." Now Adam stopped, turned, and gave Catherine a piercing stare. "It's really all I have in the world, besides Alice, and she means a lot more. So you see, I'm a destitute libertine with a trivial title that's less than a decade old." He sketched a mocking bow and added, "Hardly dashing or romantic. Shouldn't even be here."

Before Catherine could reply, Hermione Parrish came into view on the arm of the Duke of Sunderford. The pearl combs in her blue-gray hair shone in the sunlight and her eyes were keen as she assessed the situation. "Well, Lord Raveneau, we couldn't help overhearing your confession."

Sunderford looked sleepy. "Nothing I didn't already know. Surprised you dared to show your face among these beacons of American society."

"Just so, Your Grace." Adam gave him a fleeting glance that spoke volumes. "I don't fit in at all. I told Byron so, but he wouldn't listen."

"We are not so inhospitable as you surmise, my lord," Hermione said in starchy tones. "You are our guest for luncheon, are you not? I have seated you beside Miss Pembroke, who has expressed an interest in becoming better acquainted with you. Shall we join the others?"

Adam wished it were easier to get back to shore. Avoiding Catherine's intent gaze, he stroked Alice's brow. "Lead on, Mrs. Parrish."

"Ah, my lord, I'm certain you'll understand that we aren't able to accommodate that animal in the dining room. Space is limited, and I would fear that one of the stewards might not see it and trip."

"In that case, *she* and I will wait here." His expression was grim.

Watching him, Catherine thought that Adam, not Alice, was the animal. There was a wildness about him that seemed even more pronounced today, in the sunlight and salt air. "Couldn't one of the servants stay on deck with Alice?" she suggested.

"No, thank you," he replied. As Hermione glided past him, nose elevated, he added, "Alice and I prefer this open air to the stifling pretension in the dining room. No doubt your menu is handwritten in French, even though none of the guests is French—?" His tone was a deft rapier. "*Petit poulet grillé au cresson, possiblement?*"

Hermione's mouth puckered, but she said nothing until the duke had led her inside the saloon. "That man is odious! I wish he would disappear!"

That afternoon, Hermione Parrish got her wish. By the time Catherine and the other guests had finished their *crepes belle angevine* and dispersed to relax on the deck or return to shore, Adam and Alice had gone. Nor was there any sign of him when they went later, by carriage, to the obligatory polo match.

Back at Beechcliff, Catherine decided on a bath before tea. Isobel warned her that Mrs. Parrish and His Grace were expecting her to join them on the terrace, but she could not face them and their scrutiny.

"Tell my mother that I am very dusty after watching polo. I'll try to join them later."

Her private bathroom was magnificent. Painted shell-pink to match her suite of rooms, it boasted a floor of inlaid Italian marble in varying shades of pink, a pedestal sink carved of marble, and a massive bathtub perched on claw feet. Isobel had run the bath while Catherine undressed, and the entire room smelled invitingly of violet bath salts.

"I used the rainwater," Isobel said. "It's soft and lovely."

She was alone then, lounging in the tub that looked out tall windows over an expanse of blue ocean. Her toes came up to play with the array of taps. She could choose from seawater, hot or cold, piped from the ocean to a tank in the attic, or pure rainwater, collected in cisterns under the terrace. It was just one more extravagance that was commonplace for Catherine.

Yet, she knew better than anyone that money didn't bring happiness. No amount of Worth gowns or jewelry from Tiffany's could bring the sort of joy she'd felt standing next to Adam Raveneau in the tea house. That fluttery feeling commenced again in her stomach as she remembered the low sound of his laughter as he called her Cathy, and the simple pleasure of drinking from a bottle that had touched his chiseled, sensual mouth...

She knew that he was trying to scare her away with the talk of his gambling and disgrace. The good girl in her was a little frightened by such revelations but the woman in her wanted him more. From the first moment she'd seen the reckless, laughing pirate, she had felt vibrantly alive. How could she return to the empty existence she'd led before Raveneau?

As the water cooled, she reflected that it was folly to imagine that such a man could choose a mousey girl like her...but she did have something he needed.

Just then the door swung open and Hermione Parrish appeared. "I'll have a word with you, my girl! Dry yourself immediately. I will wait in your bedroom." Her heels clicked on the marble floor as she proffered a towel to her daughter and made her exit.

Clearly, Isobel had been dismissed, which was an ominous sign. As Catherine dried off, she steeled herself for an argument.

She found her mother pacing in front of the cold fireplace. In a tone that brooked no argument, Hermione said, "At long last, His Grace is ready to propose marriage to you, Catherine. You will dress and meet him in the Gothic Room and, of course, you will graciously accept."

Chapter 5

Suddenly, Catherine was freezing cold in the July heat. Shivering, she clasped her arms around her slim body. "Sunderford proposing? Mother, you can't be serious."

"I have never been more serious in my life. As you well know, this is the goal toward which we have worked for many years. Quite frankly, it has taken all my patience these last weeks to jolly His Grace along and your attitude has been no help at all!"

Her legs were shaking, so she dropped down on the edge of a Louis XIV chair. "But, Mother, I have told you that I don't care for him in the least."

"Catherine Beasley Parrish, might I remind you that you are speaking of His Grace, the *Duke* of Sunderford?"

Was it all a terrible nightmare? Catherine stared at her mother, who was impeccably clad in a tea gown of lace and velvet. At her throat, she wore sapphires set with pearls the size of filberts. Hermione Parrish's first priority was an impressive appearance, brushing off whatever might be hidden beneath the surface.

Catherine knew a sense of doom. "Just because he's a duke, that doesn't mean he's better than other men."

"Of course he is. Sunderford is one of only twenty-seven English dukes, and his title dates back to Tudor times!" Her face was set as she bore down on her daughter and bent near. "Catherine, you are not thinking properly. Have you forgotten how magnificent Sunderford Castle is? And that, as a duchess, the king and queen will be in your social circle? You'll wear ermine at coronations and have a crest engraved on your writing paper! It's one thing to go out and purchase grand things, as we do, but quite another to know that one has a right to them by blood. Your offspring will have that right. Your own son will be a duke!" She gripped her daughter's cold hand. "You do understand now, don't you?"

"And what about Sunderford himself, Mother? He's hardly grand."

"He is English," Hermione said dismissively. "He's been brought up to pretend to be aloof, but he's merely saving his displays of affection for his duchess. Don't you see?"

"And for whom is he saving his displays of intelligence?" She knew she shouldn't go on, but the floodgates were open. "Do you know that he believes the Civil War was fought between North and South America? Clearly His Grace is hopelessly dull, pretentious, tactless—and physically repellant!"

Hermione took the chair facing her daughter and her face was white and frozen. "I did not raise you to insult your betters, my dear. Furthermore, might I remind you that you are hardly a great beauty. What right have you to expect to marry a man who is not only a duke, but also a paragon of good looks and intellectual prowess?"

"Is it so wrong to dream of marrying someone who can make me laugh, and be my friend—and perhaps make my heart flutter when he kisses me?"

"Don't be nonsensical. Your heart might flutter for a few weeks, and then you'll find that the husband of your dreams is turning portly and tedious and you'll wish that you had a marriage founded on real substance—a title, estates, and social position!"

Tears welled in Catherine's eyes as she realized that nothing she said could penetrate her mother's armor. "I have always given in to you, Mother, to keep the peace, but this time the stakes are too high..."

Suddenly, Hermione lifted her pince-nez and stared. "It's that Raveneau person, isn't it? You are nurturing some ridiculous fantasy about that libertine."

"I barely know the man." But she could feel the blood rushing into her face as she spoke.

"Ungrateful!" She averted her face. "To inflict such a wound on your own mother who has dedicated her life to you and your welfare—" Wincing, Hermione put her hand over her pouter-pigeon bosom. "It *hurts* so desperately. Send for the doctor, child!"

"The doctor?" she repeated in disbelief. "You aren't serious, Mother..."

"Indeed I am serious! It is my heart! I may be dying!"

An hour later, Catherine hovered uncertainly near her mother's bed.

Dr. Frank felt Hermione's brow again, waggled his thick dark eyebrows, and gave a curious sigh. "Mrs. Parrish, can you hear me?"

Her lids fluttered but she did not speak.

"Her color is fine," he remarked.

Alva Vanderbilt Belmont, Hermione's friend, scowled at the physician. "How can you say such a thing? Clearly, Mrs. Parrish has had a health crisis!" She turned and fixed Catherine with a menacing stare. "We want only the best for our daughters, and yet they brush off our efforts!"

"Ohhh..." Hermione moaned.

"You see?" Alva, a formidable woman in any circumstances, leaned over so that her face was mere inches from Catherine's. "You must do your duty, child, and trust your mother to know what is best for you."

Catherine felt as if she might be sick. She hurried from the palatial bedchamber, back to her own rooms, and huddled near the fireplace in the wing chair where she had spent so many happy hours reading. How could she ever extricate herself from this terrible coil? Even her hopes for Adam Raveneau had been real only in her romantic imagination. Today he'd made it clear that he wanted nothing to do with her. He wouldn't even take pity on her and engage in a flirtation! Catherine had been flicked aside like an annoying mosquito.

A knocking came at her door and Alva Belmont entered. "I must say that I am shocked that you would run away without even a word of reassurance for your dear mother. Are you not aware that her very life is in your hands?"

"Dr. Frank didn't seem to be very concerned."

"You are shockingly impertinent. Dr. Frank realized that your mother is much worse than he thought. He has warned that one more scene between the two of you could be fatal!"

"This is absurd. Would you sacrifice me in marriage to a man I don't love just to rouse Mother from her sickbed?"

"You would be the Duchess of Sunderford," she replied coldly. "It is a title to rival that of my daughter, Consuelo, Duchess of Marlborough."

A chill ran down Catherine's spine as she remembered the stories she'd heard about Alva's campaign to force poor Consuelo to marry the duke. Since Consuelo had another suitor, Alva at one point threatened to shoot her daughter's true love, declaring that Consuelo would then be responsible for her mother's trip to the gallows! There had been an assortment of other ploys and, in the end, Alva Vanderbilt Belmont had gotten her way.

"Perhaps, my dear Catherine," she said more sweetly, "you might try to think of others, rather than yourself. Not only have you your mother to consider, but there are countless people you'll be able to help once you are a duchess. Have you considered the social services you will be able to perform?"

"No. I hadn't." She had to get this woman out of her bedchamber. "I'll try to improve my outlook, Mrs. Belmont."

"You will?" She blinked as if startled that it was going to be so easy. "Well, then, that's good. Of course, until this matter is resolved, it won't be possible for you to have callers. You'll want to sit with your mother and pray for guidance, hmm?"

"Of course." Smiling, Catherine rose and walked over to open the door. "I am grateful for your advice."

"The duke is still waiting in the Gothic Room to speak to you, you know."

"I shan't keep him waiting another moment."

Alva's face puckered as if she didn't quite trust the girl. "Have you heard the latest tidbit of news about the Viscount Raveneau? Your mother confided to me that you are a bit infatuated with him." She put a finger over Catherine's mouth when she tried to protest. "Of course you are, my dear. Perfectly natural. But he's a notorious black sheep in England. No person of breeding would let his daughter near Lord Raveneau. And, word has it that he was recently embroiled in a love affair with a married woman…"

Catherine feigned horror. "Oh, my!"

"I'm sorry. But, that should make it easier to forget about him, hmm? I'll go back to reassure your mother that you have gone to meet with the duke."

"Yes, do tell her that." As they parted and Catherine headed toward the stairway, her mind was going a hundred miles a minute. What a predicament! Not only must she reshape the events of her own future, but also avoid the clutches of her mother and Alva Belmont. They meant to keep her prisoner in her own home!

Just before reaching the Gothic Room, Catherine slipped into the rococo- style library. There was a cellaret in one corner, and from it she removed a bottle of Napoleon brandy, pulled the cork, and took a few burning sips. Her father was fond of saying that brandy gave him courage and she hoped it would replenish her own supply. The liquid coursed through her veins like fire, then her eyes felt blurry and her nose got warm. Was this courage? Suddenly, it didn't seem to matter very much.

There was a set of double doors connecting the library to the Gothic room. Catherine pushed them open and, spying the duke sitting stiffly in front of the fireplace, called, "Hello! I've come, like the proverbial lamb to the slaughter." The word 'proverbial' sounded slightly garbled to her own ears.

He stood up, looking embarrassed. His hair, which was already very thin on top, was slicked down with a lot of oil. "You Americans speak much more openly of private matters than we do in England."

"I suppose so." She smiled broadly. "Don't you hate this room? It's so dark and depressing."

He pursed his lips. "The stained glass windows and the collection of Gothic crucifixes must be frightfully valuable. And the fireplace is magnificent, though one doesn't like to think of such treasures being ripped from their ancestral origins."

"Especially by vulgar Americans." Feeling rather giddy, Catherine sat down in a hard Gothic chair.

The duke looked perplexed. "See here, if you think that I share some of the notions my countrymen have about Americans, you are mistaken. I think that you people have many good qualities."

"Thank you!"

His face was flushed and he began to rub his hands together. "Which brings me to another matter. I—ah— believe that you and I might deal well together….and I hope that I might make you a good husband."

They were sitting half a room apart and his discomfort was so evident that Catherine got up and moved a few chairs nearer. "Your Grace, I am honored by your proposal, but I must beg you to be frank with me. Am I truly the girl of your dreams?"

He blinked. "What a question! No, of course not. One doesn't marry for so frivolous a reason."

"Do you find me at all appealing?"

He frowned. "I've never cared for short girls. And, I happen to prefer fair hair and blue eyes. Or auburn hair and green eyes."

Catherine wanted to laugh. "Almost any combination but my own?"

"Not to insult you, of course."

"And my manner and character? Do they appeal to you?"

"Well, of course, you are American." He cleared his throat as if he needn't say more.

"Your Grace, I'm not certain we would really suit. What is your honest opinion?"

He heaved a sigh. "Suit? If that's what it were about, I'd've married a certain young lady in London."

"One has to live with this arrangement a lifetime. Perhaps you ought to consider marrying that lady after all."

"But, there's Sunderford Castle to consider. It hasn't got any heat or electric lights. The roof's a veritable sieve. The grounds are overgrown and there's only one gardener…"

"Mustn't there be another way to solve those problems? Perhaps, at least, you might meet another heiress who is taller and fairer and quieter than I, someone who will make you a better lifetime companion."

"That is possible," he agreed, brightening.

"In the meantime, my mother is ill and we don't want to shock her. Let's pretend as if we're going ahead with our plans and then, perhaps tomorrow, we can break the news gently."

"I have planned a journey to Wyoming in two days," Sunderford announced.

Catherine grinned. It was amusing to think that her would-be bridegroom had intended to go off to Wyoming so soon after becoming engaged. "You may still go to Wyoming, Your Grace. I'll sort everything out before tomorrow evening, all right?"

"I'm looking forward to seeing some authentic red Indians in your Western regions," he confided. "And grizzly bears and cowboys."

"I'm sure you'll have a much better time than you've had here."

"No doubt," he agreed, nodding gravely.

The echoing sound of the bell from the front door made Catherine pause on the stair-landing. She waited as the butler went to answer the summons. Dimly through the wrought-iron grillwork outside, she discerned the figures of Elysia VanGanburg and her maid. The butler was shaking his head, sending them away. The great door swung closed and the visitors departed.

Catherine realized that there was no time to lose. She went directly to Hermione's room and perched on a velvet chair near her bed. "Mother? I have some news that may revive you…"

The older woman's eyelids fluttered. "Did you speak to the duke?"

Fixing her eyes on a ceiling mural of cherubs, she answered, "Yes, His Grace and I had a very cordial conversation, Mother, and you'll be glad to know we reached an agreement."

Suddenly alert, Hermione pushed herself up against the peach damask pillows. "We must have a dinner party to make the announcement. Only think, my darling, soon you shall be Her Grace, Duchess of Sunderford! Isn't it too wonderful for words?"

"It takes my breath away. In fact, I think I'll go to my room and rest for a bit." She stood, then turned back to add, "Mother, you will wait for Papa to return for the announcement party?"

"Word shall be sent to him immediately." Hermione pulled the bell cord next to the bed. "I can scarcely wait to see the expressions on the faces of my friends when they hear the news. This is truly a coup! We'll put Consuelo Vanderbilt's wedding in the shade. Alva will be outdone once and for all."

"Very exciting." Catherine scurried to the door and was about to turn the handle when her mother's voice stopped her.

"Until the betrothal is finalized, we'll just continue our current arrangement, staying quietly at home."

"Do you mean I still can't go out? Or have visitors?" She tried to suppress a tide of panic. "Not even Elysia?"

"No." Seeing the housekeeper, who had appeared in response to her mistress's ring, Hermione shooed her daughter away. "Perhaps you ought to look after the duke."

"He's going to Wyoming to explore the Wild West."

She rolled her eyes. "Well, at least those plans provide us with an excuse to announce the engagement quickly. It isn't altogether proper etiquette, but when one has a duke proposing, one mustn't dawdle."

Catherine was only too happy to return to her own rooms, but then she found herself at the window, staring out at the ocean while nibbling at a fingernail. Now what? She was a prisoner in the palace!

Just then the door opened and Isobel entered with a stack of thick towels. "Oh! Sorry to disturb you, miss. I didn't think you'd be here."

Turning, Catherine smiled reassurance, then stared at her from head to toe. "I never noticed before, but you and I are about the same size, aren't we?"

"Yes, miss."

"Are you aware that they have locked me in this house until my engagement is announced? I am not even allowed to see friends!"

"Are you really getting engaged to the duke?" The girl's eyes were like saucers. "I don't know if I think that's a good idea!"

Catherine hurried to her side, beaming. "You are the one person I can trust because you truly want what's best. No, I won't marry the duke, but I can't put my alternate plan into effect unless I get off the grounds of Beechcliff—just for tonight. Isobel, would you think I'd gone mad if I asked to dress up in one of your uniforms…?"

Chapter 6

As the clock on her mantel struck eleven, Catherine lay in bed, fully dressed, waiting. The huge house was quiet at last. She'd peeked into the corridor at intervals, watching to see the bars of light extinguished under doorways. The last one, from the duke's room, had gone out a quarter hour ago. Had one of the servants been assigned to watch her? It would be horrible to be caught, but that was a risk she must take.

Slipping out from under her covers, Catherine stood in a beam of moonlight and donned an embroidered lawn apron over her dove-gray gown. Her heart was pounding. Isobel's frilled mobcap nearly hid all of Catherine's hair, and she liked the streamers that went down her back.

Reaching under her bedcovers, she arranged to pillows to resemble a sleeping person. This scheme was quite mad. It was the most rebellious thing she had ever done; more than mere folly. If her mother found her out, there would truly be hell to pay.

She carried her shoes and padded into the corridor, inching the door closed. Fortunately, there was a door leading to the maze of servants' stairways just a few steps away and as she crept toward it, she felt safer already. Sheer nerves guided her down to the door leading into the kitchen garden. Outside, the moon was luminous and waves pounded the rocks below Beechcliff. Catherine donned her shoes and headed through the trees toward the grand brick stables. There were lights upstairs, where the coachman, grooms, and other stable help lived, and she could see silhouettes and hear laughter.

She smiled at the memory of her pleas to Isobel for help. The maid had been so fearful that they'd both be caught and punished that Catherine had been forced to get down on her knees and cling to the maid's skirts in order to break down the last of her resistance. Finally, she'd agreed to everything: the uniform, the unlocked door, and even to opening the stable door to allow easy access to her bicycle.

There was a pathway through the trees that led right out to Bellevue Avenue, the thoroughfare that would take Catherine directly into the center of town. She had to hitch up her skirts to ride the bicycle, and it was hard going as she rolled bumpily westward, away from the sea. Once, a policeman stopped her and she explained that she was going to fetch a special nurse for her employer. Her brown eyes were so wide and earnest that he merely cautioned that a female had to be very careful at that hour of night.

The heart of Newport still consisted of a hodgepodge of eighteenth century buildings, homes, and shops, harkening back to the town's golden age as a thriving seaport. Catherine received her share of curious glances as she guided the bicycle onto Touro Street, past Washington Square, and finally rolled to a stop at the intersection of Marlborough and Farewell Streets.

Rising up before her nearly at the edge of the sidewalk was the Whitehorse Tavern. The gambrel-roofed structure had welcomed travelers for more than two hundred years, and Catherine smiled to herself as she leaned her bicycle against a picket fence and walked through the pedimented doorway. As a little girl, she had loved to wander these streets with her brother, enjoying the games he invented about the Revolutionary War. Once they'd sneaked into the Whitehorse in search of a British spy...

"And what can I do for you, miss, at this late hour?" The rotund tavernkeeper strolled toward her, wiping his hands on a wine-stained apron. His expression was kind but concerned.

She smiled. "I've come from the Osseltrom home, on behalf of Mrs.Osseltrom herself. She's sent me in search of a family friend, whom we believe to be one of your guests."

"Ossel...trom?" he repeated with a furrowed brow.

"I can't spare much time, sir. Please direct me to the room of the Viscount Raveneau. Is he in?"

"Yes, but I'm afraid that I can't let you go up there, miss. It wouldn't be seemly—"

"Sir, I am Mrs. Osseltrom's personal lady's maid, and I am here on her business. I have been instructed to deliver a private message to his lordship. Would you have both of them angry? I thought not. Kindly direct me."

"All right then, but I don't like it."

Catherine made a point of flicking the streamers on her mobcap as she ascended the ancient staircase. She could feel his puzzled eyes on her, but then new patrons entered and the tavernkeeper was distracted.

Outside Adam Raveneau's door, she paused, suddenly panicky. What she was doing flew in the face of all convention. Catherine squeezed her eyes closed, her heart pounding, and imagined herself in a marriage bed with Sunderford. That was enough to give her courage, and she knocked at the paneled door.

"Bloody hell, Byron, can't you allow me five minutes' peace?" shouted an all-too-familiar voice from inside the room. "I'll never finish packing at this rate—"

The door flew open and she came face to face with a stormy Adam Raveneau. He wore only light trousers and a starched white shirt, open halfway down the front to afford a glimpse of a dark, muscular chest. His feet were bare and his black hair was tousled. Her heart began to pound in a rather different way. She gave him what she hoped was an engaging smile.

"You must be wondering what I am doing here at this hour."

Adam could only stare in disbelief. Leaning out into the corridor, he checked for passersby then pulled her into the room and closed the door. "Wondering?" he repeated hoarsely. "Just because an elite Newport heiress appears at my door at nearly midnight—gotten up like a serving maid?"

"Lady's maid," she corrected. "I borrowed my own maid's uniform, and I'm beginning to like it." Spinning around, Catherine let the streamers work their magic, but Raveneau did not seem to be impressed. "I wish you wouldn't think of me as an heiress. You know how burdened I feel by that nonsense."

Alice the Labrador, who had been sleeping on a pillow near the fireplace, rose very slowly and tottered over to greet their visitor. Catherine crouched down to pet her. "Aren't you sweet? If only you could talk, girl, you could tell me how many other ladies have visited your master late at night."

He pulled her to her feet by her apron strings. "Are you drunk?"

"A little, but not the way you mean. It's intoxicating to be out of Beechcliff, away from my mother, and to be pretending to be someone I'm not." She wanted to add that he was the most intoxicating element of all, but his expression was too forbidding.

"How did you know where to find me?"

"I surmised. The Whitehorse suits you. It used to be a great haunt of pirates, you know, before the Revolutionary War, and at heart you are a creature of the eighteenth century."

Raveneau wondered if he were dreaming or going mad. "I couldn't possibly be more confused by this conversation, Miss Parrish."

"Please," she interjected. "If nothing else, won't you call me Cathy again? That name suits me, don't you think so?"

"I'll call you Cathy if you promise *not* to call me Heathcliff," he replied in edgy tones. "Now then, as diverting as this visit may be, I must ask you to come to the point so that I can return to my packing."

Cathy watched as he picked up a candle and lit a thin cigar with the flame. His profile was harsh, yet infinitely appealing to her, and she only knew that the feeling she had when Raveneau was near was worth more than all the riches at Beechcliff.

"All right then, Cathy." He glanced over at her. "What is it? Why have you come here?"

She cleared her throat. "I've come...to ask you to marry me."

There was a long moment of silence. Cathy's cheeks got pinker as Raveneau poured himself a drink.

"I have noticed," he said with a laugh, "that very wealthy people are prone to making the oddest jokes."

"I'm not joking," she insisted. "Believe me, I wouldn't have risked my mother's wrath and my reputation in Newport to chance coming alone not only to the Whitehorse, but to your very room if I were not dead serious."

"Dead serious," he repeated. "That sounds contagious."

Cathy heaved a sigh, drew off her mobcap, and collapsed in a wing chair near the fireplace. Suddenly, all of it seemed the maddest of dreams. His splendid physical presence told the story, for now she realized that it was folly to imagine such a man could marry someone like her. The grand plan she'd hatched at Beechcliff seemed silly and feeble.

Adam drank his brandy. "If you're so serious, why are gotten up in that costume? I couldn't help assuming that this must be a lark—"

Her chin trembled. "First of all, I've not been allowed to leave Beechcliff, not even permitted to have visitors, so I had to disguise myself in order to slip out. Secondly, you must know that no young lady of breeding could ride a bicycle to visit a man alone at this hour—or any hour—without soiling her good name." Fighting back tears, she added, "If one person recognizes me leaving your room, I'm ruined. It's such a ludicrous world, but I do have to live in it!"

Alarmed, Adam brought her a small goblet of red wine, then leaned against the mantel and watched her sip it. She was like a schoolgirl: charming and mercurial, with an expressive face that was part child, part woman. Perhaps it was a consequence of being raised like a hothouse orchid, with Hermione Parrish as the master gardener. Cathy was a bit awkward in her dealings with the outside world.

When Alice trundled over to lie down on Cathy's feet, Adam softened. "I perceive that you've been beset by more problems back at Beechcliff. Did you imagine that someone like myself, on the outside, might be able to help?"

"Mother has managed to wring a proposal of marriage out of the Duke of Sunderford," she whispered.

He didn't hear at first. "I'm the last person you ought to envision as a knight in shining armor. Not my role at all—" Then her words sank in. "Did you say that Winnie's asked for your hand? He's come up to snuff after all?"

"Winnie? Is that his name?

"It's what his friends call him. You didn't know?"

She shook her head miserably. "I might laugh if it weren't my own future that's at stake. He didn't ask for my hand, but rather mumbled that he'd make me a good husband. He doesn't want it any more than I do, but he needs our money. It's a sickening situation!"

"I couldn't agree more, but surely you realize that it's mad to think that I could intervene somehow, let alone marry you, Cathy!" He laughed again, for emphasis, but she only looked sadder. "You do agree, don't you? I mean, we scarcely know one another. We just met, for God's sake! While I think you're a very nice girl and I sympathize with your plight, I need much better reasons than those to *marry*."

"You say that word as if it meant a lifetime of extreme torture."

"I'm trying to tell you that I'm not husband material. Nor hero material, for that matter." Raveneau strode away toward the four-poster bed then glanced back with one black brow arched. "Quite the contrary. Why the devil did you choose me?"

"You're the only other man in Newport with a proper British title and I thought that Mother might, under duress, accept you as a substitute for the duke. And…" She couldn't tell him how she'd felt the moment he walked into Beechcliff, like a figure from a romantic dream. "I like you. I thought we might deal well together—"

"Cathy, how many men have courted you—or kissed you?" Adam strode back to her, watching her face. "How many men have you even talked with alone, as we have done?"

"I—couldn't say." She curled up in the chair, unable to meet his stirring gaze. "Not…very many, obviously, since Mother has monitored and scheduled every hour of my days."

"And you are twenty-one?"

"Yes."

"I think your mistake has been to wait so long before standing up to your mother. You're backed completely into the corner now—but there must be another way to escape. I hardly think it's fair for you to expect me, a virtual stranger, to solve a problem that more properly rests between you and your mother."

"If you're suggesting that I might reason or argue with her, that's impossible."

There was so much more she wanted to say to him, but Raveneau had erected an invisible barrier. She ought to gather up her tattered pride and go home while he was still speaking to her, but the thought of what awaited her there was worse. Watching him finish his brandy and resume packing, Cathy reached down to stroke Alice's neck.

"There was one other reason I chose you."

"Was there?" he replied, politely distracted.

She took a deep breath. "I hope you won't take offense at this, but I've gotten the idea that you need money. I heard something about your estate in the West Indies needing restoration…"

Unable to help himself, he put down the collars he'd been sorting and looked at her. It was like that moment in the teahouse when she'd mentioned her dowry, and he hated himself for the surge of avarice that swept aside all his other doubts. "A marriage based on money would be flawed at its core, don't you think?"

Just then, the door burst open and Byron Matthews appeared. He was holding an open bottle of wine, and his shirt was untucked.

"I've decided that we can't leave for Connecticut tomorrow without visiting Bailey's Beach first," he exclaimed. "It's—"

"I have a guest," Adam interrupted.

"So I see! Good evening, Miss Parrish!" Byron went straight over to sit in the wing chair facing her, put down his bottle, and reached across to clasp her hand. Alice emitted a low, protective sound. "Is it an emergency that brings you here? It's past midnight, you know." He blinked at the sight of her maid's costume but made no further comment.

"It's a long story," Adam put in.

"My emergency is that the duke of Sunderford has proposed marriage and my mother locked me in the house until I accept, or rather until we've formally announced the engagement at a dinner party."

"And you've come to Adam for help?"

Cathy nodded. "A mistake, as it turns out."

"See here, there's no call for sarcasm!" Raveneau protested. "I'm hardly a villain just because I won't marry you in Sunderford's place." Looking to his friend, he made a dramatic gesture for understanding. "For God's sake, Byron, I just met this young lady, and you of all people know that I am leery of marriage. Tell her that my behavior in this situation is entirely reasonable, and that—" He broke off at the sight of his friend moving to a footstool next to Cathy's chair and holding her hand in earnest.

"Did you choose Adam because of his title?" he was asking her, as if Raveneau were not in the room. "You thought your mother might accept him if she were pressed?"

His kind expression broke the fragile shell of her composure and she began to cry, softly. "I persuaded the duke to withdraw, thank God. I convinced him that we wouldn't suit, and he agreed that there must be another heiress more to his taste who could help restore his castle. But my mother won't give up so easily. The only answer is to let her continue to think we are announcing my betrothal to the duke at our dinner party, and then, suddenly, produce a different fiancé. In that setting, with a proper audience, she won't be able to protest." Accepting Byron's folded handkerchief, Cathy wiped her eyes, dabbed her nose, and added, "I did think that it might soften the blow if the substitute were also a titled Englishman, as she dreamed…"

"Would you consider marrying me?" Byron asked, gazing into her eyes. "My brother-in-law is the Duke of Aylesbury, and we could take your mother for long visits to his estates. We'd be socializing with the king and queen. It wouldn't be quite the same as a title of your own—"

From across the room, Adam Raveneau stared in utter disbelief. "Bloody hell! You can't be serious, Matthews! You aren't actually offering to *marry* her, are you?"

She cried, "Do stop saying that word as if it were an epithet!"

"I would be honored to come to Catherine's aid," Byron said. "And honored to be her husband."

His face dark with outrage, Adam shouted, "And honored, I suppose, to spend her dowry while you play at being an artist! You'll never have to worry about paying the bills again, will you, or being able to afford that suite of rooms you fancy at the Savoy!" For good measure, he added, "And, since you are proposing, you ought to know that she prefers being called Cathy!"

She sat up straight and made the only response she could. "Pay no attention to him," she told Byron. "You are a compassionate, honorable man, and I'd be fortunate to marry you." Leaning over, she kissed his cheek and smiled.

Byron whispered in her ear, "Don't worry. He's coming around already." He stood then. "Adam, I am going to get a taxi and see my fiancée home now, before someone discovers that she's missing from Beechcliff."

"Your *fiancée*?" Adam repeated in acid tones. Watching as his old friend put an arm around Catherine Parrish's slim waist and gazed into her eyes, he thought he would go mad. "You're drunk! How many bottles of that wine have you consumed tonight? If you think that I'm going to let you take this bullet for me, when it's even less of your affair than mine, you are mistaken." He strode toward them, determined to remove Byron's hands from Cathy's person.

"But I want to do it," Byron persisted.

"Has anyone ever told you that you poke your nose into other people's business a bit too readily, old fellow?" He was facing them now, mere inches away, and though Cathy had given him her attention, Byron seemed to be holding her closer than before. Adam glared at him. "You can release her now."

"You don't want her, Raveneau. Cathy asked you to be her husband and you refused. Adamantly. Are you telling her she can't have me, either?"

"No. No, I'm not bloody saying that!" He put a hand on Byron's arm to pry him off her. "Damn you, let go! She asked me and now I'm accepting. She needs a genuine nobleman, not some cursed secondhand brother-in-law. I'm the only one who qualifies." He paused. "I'll do it."

At that, Byron stepped back, leaving Cathy to waver, unsupported. She stared at Adam in disbelief. "You'll do *what?*"

"Marry you. I'll do it." With that, he put his own arm around her. "I mean, I've thought about it and it does make sense. As long as we understand the terms— the basic agreement, and the dowry—and we don't muck it up with a lot of romantic nonsense, we ought to deal rather well together. Hmm?"

Cathy nodded, then indulged herself by resting her cheek against his white shirt and breathing in the male scent of him. It made her giddy for something she didn't understand but craved madly. And now she would have it.

It was a dream come true.

Chapter 7

Hermione Parrish was so consumed with excitement over the impending engagement announcement dinner that she barely noticed her daughter. She spent long hours at her elegant writing table, composing lists and notes. Or she invaded the cavernous kitchen and forced Madge the cook to stop her work and consider menu plans for the party. Everything must be perfect, from the table linens that would contrast with Hodgson's arrangements of pink-edged Nice roses in gold vases, to the iced champagne and Madge's special strawberry meringues.

The duke quickly and quietly announced that he was going to Wyoming, and Hermione thought nothing of this. Hadn't Consuelo Vanderbilt's duke done the same after the announcement of their engagement? English noblemen, it seemed, had a universal yen to explore the Wild West. Secretly, Hermione was glad to be rid of him while they planned the actual wedding, which would of course be held in New York City, at St. Thomas's Church on Fifth Avenue.

By the time Jules Parrish arrived at Beechcliff late in the afternoon, the long dining table had been set and Catherine had just emerged from her bath. Her parents visited her room as she stood in her dressing gown and began to choose between the two dresses Isobel held up.

Cathy kissed her father and mused aloud, "I thought I might wear the pale rose satin."

"Absolutely not!" cried Hermione. "It is far too décolleté, child! You have never had any taste in clothes so you may defer to my wisdom from this moment forward. We will have many choices to make before the wedding and there won't be time for arguments." She pointed a long finger. "The clouded moiré, Isobel, just as I told you earlier. The lace applique on the bodice is ideal."

Pasting on a smile, Cathy exchanged glances with her father. "I'll just be glad to get this evening over with. Mother, I thought I ought to tell you that I've invited Lord Raveneau to join us tonight—and Byron Matthews as well."

"Have you forgotten every lesson you've learned these past years? Have I not made it clear that that man is too roguish to mix well in Newport society? My dear, if you are to give fine dinners of your own one day, you must learn to weed your visiting list. If you do not, it will certainly run to seed!"

"Lord Raveneau and Mr. Matthews leave Newport tomorrow."

"At last." She sighed heavily. "I must go to the kitchen now and have a last consultation with Madge. Since we are having only two dozen guests, it is all the more imperative that each detail be perfect."

As if fearing that his daughter would break down in tears once they were alone, Jules followed Hermione as she went out the door. However, when he glanced back, Cathy was beaming.

"You aren't upset about this engagement?" he queried softly.

"Not a bit." She ran barefoot to his side. "Papa, I must confess—"

"No, don't!" Holding up his hand, wincing, he added, "No confessions. When it comes to matters involving you and your mother, ignorance is bliss."

"Will you trust me?"

"I don't know about that…but I will support you, no matter what scheme you've cooked up. This is one decision you ought to be allowed to make for yourself." Jules started through the door then looked back through his spectacles, wondering at the roses in her cheeks and the adventurous sparkle in her eyes. There was almost an air of carnality about her, and if his wife weren't so caught up in her meaningless planning and posturing, she would have recognized it herself—and realized that it had nothing to do with the Duke of Sunderford.

"Who would have ever thought, just a few nights ago, when we were walking up this drive for the first time," Byron paused for breath, avoiding Adam's stare, "that my jokes about you marrying an American heiress would become reality!"

"Who indeed?" His tone was heavy with irony. "You don't seem to be very downcast about losing out yourself."

Byron stopped. They were just a few dozen yards from the mansion's arched entrance where guests were stepping out of a Mercedes automobile. Beechcliff and its grounds were drenched in the tangerine glow of a summer twilight.

"I have a feeling about you and Cathy," he said in sober tones.

"I don't want to hear it," Raveneau shot back. "The only thing I care about at this moment is whether my tie is straight. The rest is madness."

"She's a good person—"

"She is spoiled, sheltered, and insecure. We don't know each other at all, and you've shoved us together for life. If I think about it for very long, I might throw myself off those cliffs." He arched a black eyebrow.

Sighing, Byron looked him over. There wasn't a man alive who could wear evening dress like Adam Raveneau. His black dress-coat and trousers fit to perfection, and were set off by a cut-away waistcoat and an immaculate expanse of white shirt. The tie was a bit rakish, which made him look even better. The golden light of evening accentuated the lines of Raveneau's physique beneath his civilized clothing, the penetrating gleam of his eyes, and the way his hair swept back from his tanned face.

"Your tie is fine. Let's go inside."

"This is the night they should have hired the dancing monkeys," Raveneau whispered as they mounted the front steps. "Where are they when I need them?"

Inside, the two men were led into a magnificent drawing room where Adam immediately spied Cathy standing with her father. She looked to him like a schoolgirl at her first ball, clad in a demure gown of clouded moiré with lace and crystal trimming. The neckline completely covered any breasts she might possess, which appeared to be modest at best. Still, a part of Adam was drawn to Cathy's lively brown eyes and flushed cheeks. She was not a beauty, but he liked her better for it.

But, one couldn't *marry* every girl one liked! He took a step backward and bumped into Byron.

"It'll be fine," his friend murmured reassuringly. "You're not going to run away from that little charmer, are you? She won't bite."

"Stop whispering in my ear. I begin to think that you engineered this entire fiasco, including your little speech proposing marriage to Cathy. You knew how I would react!"

"You give me far too much credit, my lord." A smile touched the corners of Byron's mouth as he went forward to greet their hostess, who was chatting with Hermann and Theresa Oelrichs.

Adam had no choice but to follow. As they drew near, he heard Hermione Parrish worry aloud about the whereabouts of the Duke of Sunderford.

"I can't imagine what's keeping him," she told Mrs. Oelrichs.

"Have you some special news to cap this little party, Hermione?"

"Let's just say that we'll be making a rather momentous announcement."

Adam took a goblet of champagne from a passing footman and reflected that if Mrs. Parrish looked any more self-satisfied, she would have canary feathers popping from her mouth. "I heard that he's packing for a journey to Wyoming," he remarked.

"Lord Raveneau!" Mrs. Oelrichs exclaimed. "How lovely to see you here."

"His lordship and Mr. Matthews are my invited guests," said Cathy as she came up behind them and slipped her gloved hand through Adam's arm. "Aren't we lucky to have them in Newport?"

"Indeed! Have you seen *our* cottage, my lord? Rosecliff is a replica of the Grand Trianon at Versailles." Mrs. Oelrichs paused momentarily for effect, then continued, "I am planning a truly splendid White Ball for next August, and I do hope that you will attend. It will far outshine any *other* affair Newport has seen!"

While Adam diverted Mrs. Oelrichs with conversation about Versailles, Cathy leaned close to her mother's ear.

"Won't you let Lord Raveneau take me in to dinner?"

"For what purpose?" she whispered, still glancing nervously about in search of the duke. "Oh, I suppose so. It can't do any harm at this point, but you must keep the place on your other side open for the duke when he arrives."

Before Adam could exchange two words with Cathy, dinner was announced and the assembled two dozen guests went into the Venetian-style dining room. The room was dominated by a ceiling-high chimneypiece of agate and green marble, and two magnificent Venetian murals faced each other above the long dining table. Eight footmen waited to quietly guide the guests to their places.

Once they were seated, Cathy felt oddly shy as she removed her gloves and consulted the menu card lying between their place settings. At last, she dared cast a sidelong glance at Adam. How handsome he was! His winged collar was beautifully starched against his brown, chiseled jaw. Had she ventured completely out of her depth by coaxing him into this betrothal?

"When I was at Oxford," Adam remarked, "my mother gave me an amusing book about manners for men. My favorite part had to do with moments like these, when a man wonders what to say to his dinner partner. It suggested that one ought to remark upon the table's floral decorations. Perhaps one might be struck by the colors of the flowers, which would remind one of paintings, which in turn would raise the subject of exhibitions. Have you been to any lately, Miss Parrish?"

She blinked. "You're teasing me."

His eyes twinkled. "Not you, but our situation. We're partners in crime, aren't we?"

Hermione was watching them from her position at one end of the table. "I cannot imagine what has delayed the Duke of Sunderford!" she exclaimed to her guests.

Something in Adam's expression made Cathy's heart soar for a moment. He was relishing the prospect of shocking her mother. Before she could comment, the first course was served, requiring that the guests choose between shrimp bisque and a fresh julienned vegetable soup. From that moment on, there was little chance for Cathy and Adam to converse, for all the other guests were anxious to further their acquaintances with the English viscount.

Wines of every description were consumed and delectable poached salmon was served, drawing sighs of pleasure.

"I don't suppose that your cook, Madge, would consider moving to Rosecliff?" Mrs. Oelrichs wistfully inquired of Mrs. Parrish.

"She couldn't be happier in her current situation," Hermione replied.

Later, when Adam had finished his portion of guinea fowl, he lifted his wineglass, leaned toward Cathy, and whispered, "How is your father going to make the announcement?"

His face was inches from her own, allowing her to breathe in the subtle scent of him. "Father doesn't know."

"You're joking."

"No. I tried to tell him, but he said he'd rather not know. He did assure me that he would support whatever decision I'd made." Other guests were glancing over at the sound of her hushed voice, so she added hurriedly, "We'll have to make the announcement ourselves."

"*We?*"

"You, I suppose…"

It was a turning point. Adam knew that he could still extricate himself from this entire coil if he chose to. No one else knew of his rash promises, not even Jules Parrish.

"Adam." Cathy touched his hand under the table. "Please don't desert me now."

Her plaintively whispered words went straight to his heart. When was the last time anyone had needed him as much as she did? The last few years of his life had held little real meaning beyond standing by his mother's deathbed, but now he had a chance to help someone who was caught in an invisible snare. If he turned his back on her, Hermione would force Cathy to submit to her will, and she might never escape.

Perfectly chilled champagne was being poured and a variety of sweets appeared. Cathy chose the meringues while, down the table, Mrs. Parrish was glaring into space with puckered lips, her thoughts clearly a million miles away. Fearing that Hermione might suddenly go in search of the Duke of Sunderford, Adam stood. All eyes were instantly drawn to him.

"I am woefully uncertain of my manners in your country," he began, looking at each guest as he spoke, "and I hope that you will excuse any missteps. I am simply honored to be among you tonight, and to be sitting beside the exquisite Miss Parrish. Her father has allowed me to propose the first toast on this very special occasion…"

Cathy was gazing up at him, utterly dazzled, and watched as he turned deliberately to look into her mother's outraged eyes.

"Will you join me in raising your glasses?" Adam continued. "I ask that you toast my intended bride, Catherine Parrish, and wish us well as we plan our future."

There were a few soft gasps, then the assembled guests became animated, nodding and smiling and whispering as they drank along with Lord Raveneau. Then, to Cathy's further shock, her father stood and raised his own glass.

"Here, here!" exclaimed Jules Parrish. "A toast to young love and the happiness of my beloved daughter!"

Hermione had no choice. Looking as if the blood had been drained from her body, she willed her face to smile, her hand to lift her glass, and her lips to drink.

When the other guests bid the Parrishes goodnight, Adam stayed to protect Cathy from her mother. Byron went for a stroll along the sea cliffs as the prospective bridegroom stood with his new fiancée and her parents in the south alcove. The room, lifted from an eighteenth century French chateau, opened off the foyer and was a favorite spot for friends to linger during farewells.

To Cathy's surprise, Adam held her hand as he met Hermione's piercing gaze. "I should apologize for proceeding without your consent, Mrs. Parrish, but we really had no choice. If I had asked for Cathy's hand, you would have refused."

"Cathy? You call her *Cathy*? You are very brash, my lord!"

"I am," he agreed.

"My dear," Jules said to his wife," I think that we should surrender to the inevitable and give these young people our blessing. Catherine has a right to seek her own destiny."

"What a lot of hogwash! Catherine doesn't know what's best for her; she never has."

"The duke doesn't want to marry me, Mother," Cathy put in. "If he did, he wouldn't have dithered for weeks before caving in and asking for my hand. In any event, it doesn't matter now. Adam and I have announced our engagement before all your friends, and there's no turning back."

"Your willfulness will be your undoing!"

"I would rather be undone by my own willfulness than yours, Mother."

"How could you be so ungrateful? Your brother would never have treated me so shabbily. I have devoted my life to preparing you for this day, and you have repaid me by defying me in front of all my friends. I could have had a stroke and died during your wretched toasts!"

"My dear, why not concede defeat gracefully?" asked Jules. "Be glad that Catherine is marrying a viscount, after all, and not the chauffeur!"

"I have a sick headache." Hermione pressed a thin-fingered hand to her brow. "I am going to bed." She glanced back at them. "Not that I expect to get any sleep."

Jules trailed after her toward the stairway and Cathy and Adam went into the foyer, stopping near the front door to wait for privacy. When the elder Parrishes had gone up the stairs, Adam looked down at his fiancée and felt a flash of the old panic run through his veins. He bent, intending to kiss her cheek and escape into the night, but then Hermione's voice came echoing from the shadowed landing.

"You will live to regret this night, Catherine Beasley Parrish!"

Once again he rose to Mrs. Parrish's challenge. One taunt from her could destroy a multitude of his doubts. "Don't worry, Cathy," he soothed, and gathered her into his arms.

She melted. Her knees wouldn't support her but his shoulders were hard beneath her soft forearms, and he lifted her as if she were weightless. She was thrilled to feel his male body against hers and drank in the new experience.

"Shh," came his breath on her ear. "You're safe now."

Happy to discover what he wanted from her, Cathy closed her eyes and felt his arms tighten around her back and waist before his mouth came down to cover her own. His lips were warm, firm, and demanding; so utterly and wildly male that she forgot how to breathe.

Adam, meanwhile, couldn't believe that she could be so unschooled. She clung to him stiffly, and her lips were pressed together in response to his kiss. Without Hermione there to horrify, he came back to earth, and Cathy's arms around his neck felt rather like a noose.

How could he have agreed to marry this awkward virgin?

Gently, he set her on her feet and saw her hold onto a chair-back for support. "I'm sorry. I've gone too far."

She tried to speak, but couldn't. Something in his eyes filled her throat with tears.

"I'd better let you get some rest." He smiled politely. "Byron and I have a lot of packing to do before we leave for Dakota. He's taking me to visit his family in Deadwood, you know."

"Don't forget to come back for our wedding," she managed to say.

"Let me assure you," Adam replied drily, "that our impending nuptials will be ever at the forefront of my thoughts…"

Part Two

Chapter 8

New York City
November, 1903

"The high and mighty Viscount Raveneau accepted Catherine's dowry after all," Hermione Parrish said in disparaging tones as she looked around the sitting room that adjoined her daughter's bedroom. "Of course, I knew he would."

The women friends and relatives who had assembled to wish Catherine well on the morning of her wedding fell silent, and the air grew thick with their thoughts. Elysia VanGanburgh leaned toward Cathy to whisper, "He'd be foolish not to take it."

The bride-to-be drew her friend into her nearby dressing room. "You know what they are longing to say? That Adam wouldn't be marrying me this afternoon without the dowry."

"It's a reasonable assumption," Elysia admitted. "You don't know him very well, do you?"

"That's an odd question for my maid of honor to ask!" She began to finger the priceless, lace-trimmed undergarments that Isobel had laid out for her to wear under her Worth-designed wedding gown. "You know how I feel about Adam. I'm absolutely mad for him."

"Perhaps, but that doesn't mean you've passed the acquaintance stage. Have you spoken to him since he arrived in New York?"

"Yes, I saw him last evening. He had a wonderful time in South Dakota."

"How nice." Elysia watched her friend's face. "You may think that Lord Raveneau is divine, and I would agree, but aren't you frightened in the least?"

"Frightened of what? My wedding night?" Cathy looked up then, meeting her gaze unflinchingly. "I do wish that we knew each other better, but I dream of how it will be once we are married. And I am overjoyed to escape my mother's plans to marry me off to the Duke of Sunderford. Any kind of marriage to Adam must be preferable to that!"

"I hope you're right." Embracing her, Elysia sighed. "Barbados is even farther away than England, and it sounds so…exotic!"

None of Adam's relatives from England were coming to the wedding. This created quite a stir among New York society, even though his cousins from Essex, Connecticut were attending. In the view of Hermione and her friends, American cousins were a poor substitute for additional English aristocrats.

The guests who were attracting the most attention were related to Byron Matthews. His sister, Shelby, had been a performer with Buffalo Bill's Wild West Show, and she had made headlines by marrying the handsome Duke of Aylesbury only a few months before. The newlyweds had been traveling in America that autumn and had decided to stop in New York to attend the wedding of Byron's best friend, Adam Raveneau.

When the women who had crowded her sitting room were finally sent off to the church, Catherine let Isobel help her into her underclothes, and then donned a robe and went to sit by the window.

"Isobel, would you allow me a few minutes privacy? I would like to a few moments to gather my thoughts. We don't have to leave for the church for an hour, do we?"

"No, miss." She bobbed her head. "I'll wait outside."

Alone, Cathy looked around her bedroom, waiting for a wave of nostalgia to wash over her. Shouldn't she feel misty-eyed on her wedding day? She had been raised in the most luxurious surrounding, showered with advantages. Yet, although the four homes owned by her parents, in New York, Newport, Long Island, and London, were sumptuous, they were also impersonal. Cathy had read *Little Women* repeatedly since age ten and yearned for that sense of loving family and the camaraderie of a cozy home. She had longed for close, constant friends who liked her for herself, but her mother had kept other children at arm's length and it seemed that each time Cathy made a new friend, Hermione took her off to Europe or to one of their other homes. At least then she'd had Stephen to share her complaints and dreams with, but now she was alone.

Outside, an omnibus crept along Fifth Avenue amid countless hansoms. Then a particularly fine carriage paused partway up the next block, and Cathy watched her father alight. Why had he stopped so far from their residence? Still, it was lovely to see him. He spent nearly every waking moment downtown, working to support their lifestyle, and she couldn't help feeling a pang at the realization that she would be moving away to Barbados without ever getting as close to him as she wished.

Jules Parrish lingered outside the carriage, leaning in, laughing. When he stepped back and made a little bow to an unseen occupant, a pretty young woman with golden hair peeped out and extended her hand to him. To Cathy's utter shock, her father stepped forward again and suddenly took the woman in his arms.

"Papa! What in heaven's name—" she whispered in confusion.

He kissed his companion full on the mouth and then seemed to remember himself and set her back inside, out of sight. Glancing left and right, he bowed to her again, then turned toward their mansion and crossed the street.

Cathy's face was hot with disbelief. What could it mean? Had she misjudged him all her life? Was her darling papa a *cad*?

"Catherine?" Hermione's shrill voice carried easily from the far edge of the sitting room. "Your flowers have come. Do dress now, dear, so that we can go to the church. Your father is due any moment." As she advanced toward the bathroom, searching out her daughter, she continued, "Isobel has finished packing your trunks. Aren't you grateful now that I chose your trousseau? Surely you must agree that my taste is superior and the selections I made are perfect in every way?"

When Cathy met her mother in the doorway of the bathroom, she felt faint and her smile trembled. "Of course, Mother."

"Heavens, but you are so pale, my dear!" She lifted her pince-nez and looked her up and down. "Whatever is the matter? Have you a case of nerves?

"Perhaps...a little. One isn't married every day, after all."

Hermione's mouth puckered as she considered this. "You're thinking about your wedding night, aren't you? Don't be shy, you can confide in your mother, you know. Sit down, Catherine, and listen carefully." She drew her down onto a low stool before the dressing table, then began to pace.

Wildly uncomfortable, Cathy sought a distraction. "Papa is coming. I saw him through the window."

"Feeling shy, hmm? Well, I would be remiss as your mother if I failed to explain a crucial fact of marriage to you." The pearls at her throat gleamed in the sunlight filtering in through the lace curtains. "The...physical aspect is, as you must be aware, the means by which two married people have children. However, there is no way around saying this: it's an ugly business. It's degrading, but no matter how humiliated you may be, you must submit without protest. Do you understand?"

Cathy stared in shock. She had no idea at all what her mother was talking about. "Degrading? Ugly?"

"For the woman, you see. Men enjoy every repulsive moment, I believe." Her penciled brows went up for emphasis. "No doubt that stallion you've insisted upon marrying will be worse than most, but that's the price you'll pay for your headstrong judgment." She came closer and stared into her daughter's stricken eyes. "You must yield to him, Catherine, and not cry out— no matter what! The wedding night is the most traumatic of all; not only painful, but bloody as well."

"Bloody?" she echoed weakly.

"That's right! You are sacrificing your virginity after all. You'll have to endure anything he insists on doing to you, not only that night but for the rest of your marriage. It is your duty as a wife, and that pertains to his behavior outside of the bedroom as well. A man of his appetites is bound to have mistresses!"

Just then, there was a knock at the dressing room door and Julies Parrish peeked in, his face wreathed in smiles. "Ah, there are my girls! How fares the bride-to-be?"

Cathy looked at her philandering father and then at her mother, who had just delivered the most horrifying speech she'd ever heard. Somehow, she pasted on a shaky smile and answered, "I've never been better, Papa."

As Adam Raveneau and Byron Matthews tried to make their way anonymously through the crush outside St. Thomas's Church, people demanded to know their identities.

"Are you royalty? Someone from England?" yelled a reporter.

Byron shouted back, "We're just normal Americans. Nothing special!"

The police intervened at that point, parting the crowds, and the two men ran under the long, striped awning that led into the church, their tailcoats catching the fall breeze. A different kind of madness awaited them there. Never had Raveneau seen and smelled so many hothouse flowers, not even at the grandest balls at Buckingham Palace. Masses of bride roses and orchids trimmed the pews and adorned the alter, where the bishop was pacing to and fro. A symphony orchestra tuned their instruments while a choir of fifty assembled in the chancel.

"Excuse me, sir, are you the Viscount Raveneau?" inquired a soft female voice. "The bridegroom?"

He turned to find a saintly-looking old woman smiling at him. "Yes, madam, I am."

"Let me show you to the rooms we've set aside for you and your best man." She toddled off into the shadows, chattering constantly. "Are you nervous? I suppose so. I must tell you that all of us think it is wonderfully romantic that you are marrying dear Catherine instead of that duke. He wasn't right for her at all. Everyone is saying that this is a love match. Not at all the usual situation with American heiresses, you know. Is that true?"

The trio had reached the dark, stuffy anterooms where Adam would wait to be led to his uncertain future. He went past the old woman, then took a deep breath before turning back to give her a smile of irresistible charm.

"Madam, I can assure you that I am not a fortune hunter."

"How lovely." She beamed at him. "Congratulations, my lord. We'll send someone for you when it's time."

"I appreciate your assistance." As soon as the door closed behind her, his smile vanished. "It sounds as if I'm being taken to the gallows, don't you agree?"

"Condemned men don't wear formal dress," said Byron. "Care for a last smoke?"

"God, yes. You haven't got any champagne, have you?"

"I think you had more than enough last night." Walking over to push the leaded-glass window open, Byron lit a thin cigar for his friend and then one for himself "Why are you so down at the mouth? Your future wife was looking lovely at supper last evening and you two seemed to be getting along very well. If that's the case, you ought to be singing for joy. You're getting a charming bride and, perhaps more importantly, a couple of million pounds."

Raveneau cringed and took two steps backward. "Don't speak of it. The very thought of that money makes me sick. I couldn't have sold my soul any more certainly if Satan himself had been one of the attorneys."

"Would you really walk away now if you could, or are you just behaving this way for effect?"

"I'm being paid an obscene amount of money to marry a woman I barely know. It seemed a lark in the beginning, when we made the announcement and watched her mother turn green, but it's not. This is the only future I've got, and I'm selling it off today as if it were no more valuable than this bloody signet ring." For emphasis, he tried to yank the ring off, but it was stuck. "Yes, I'd damned well walk away if I could!"

"It would break Catherine's heart."

Outside, they could hear carriages and motor cars rolling up in front of the church. Voices began to drift down the corridor as guests spilled into the sanctuary, accompanied by the lilting strains of Mozart.

Raveneau met his old friend's gaze, his own marbled eyes eloquent with regret. "What worries me more is the damage I may do in the years to come…"

Chapter 9

Cathy's heart was banging like a big bass drum as she knelt beside Adam on scarlet velvet cushions. Behind her was spread the entire length of her five-yard train.

"Those whom God hath joined together, let no man put asunder," intoned Bishop Potter. His voice sounded very far away.

In a daze, her eyes drifted down over her exquisite gown. Ordered by Hermione in Paris, before they had even journeyed to England to meet the Duke of Sunderford, it was a dazzling full-skirted Worth creation fashioned of ivory satin trimmed with Brussels lace, pearls, and orange blossoms. Adam was reaching for her hand, which was trembling. His fingers were dark and strong holding hers, prompting her to steal a peek at him through her veil. No fairytale princess had ever married a more devastatingly attractive male than Adam Raveneau—and none had known her prince any less well than she knew hers…

Hundreds of people filled the church, watching them, consumed with curiosity.

When they rose together and he squeezed her hand slightly, she felt her new wedding ring. It was a little too big. Sunlight streamed through the stained-glass windows, burnishing Cathy's gown. They bowed their heads for the blessing as the bishop intoned,

"Forasmuch as Adam and Catherine have consented together in holy wedlock…I pronounce that they be man and wife together."

The strains of the symphony orchestra swelled around them. Cathy felt faint and giddy and numb as her husband turned her toward him and drew back her veil. He gently took her elbows and gave her a dry, proper kiss, and then Elysia put the trailing bouquet of orchids, roses, and lilies into her hands.

"Congratulations, my lady!" she whispered, blushing at the sight of Raveneau, while the other four blue-and-white-clad bridesmaids beamed from a distance. "You're a peeress now!"

The recessional began, and Adam tucked Cathy's free hand into the crook of his arm. She hurried to keep pace with him as they traversed the long aisle, nodding and smiling at the sea of blurred faces. Finally, for a brief moment, they were alone in the narthex and she held her breath, praying that he would reassure her with a private kiss or even a few whispered words or a smile. Instead, he released her hand and went to greet the bishop as he emerged from the nave.

Bishop Potter shook Adam's hand, then turned to Cathy. "So, my dear, how does it feel to be Lady Raveneau?"

The guests had begun to pour into the nave, surrounding them. Speechless for once in her life, Cathy whispered, "It feels…fine."

~ ~ ~

The rest of the Raveneaus' wedding day passed in a blur. Somehow, Cathy managed to make proper replies to all the well-wishers who grasped her hand in the reception line. She and Adam traveled by carriage to Sherry's restaurant for the formal wedding breakfast, but there were so many people calling from the sidewalks that they had little chance to converse.

Suddenly, it all seemed like a mad, mixed-up dream to her. How could she be married to Adam Raveneau? When guests addressed her as "Lady Raveneau," she couldn't take it in.

And Adam behaved nothing like a newlywed husband. At Sherry's, over mousse of lobster with champagne sauce, he stood up to toast his bride.

"No man could be luckier than I am today. God grant me the wisdom to realize just how fortunate I am."

What did he mean by that? she wondered. She'd expected her twinges of uncertainty to be erased by the actual wedding. She'd thought that the sight of her handsome groom, standing beside her at the altar, would banish her doubts, but instead they had multiplied. Had he looked her in the eye since they'd said their vows? Had he touched her since that chaste kiss before the bishop?

Jules Parrish was making another toast. He looked as if he'd drunk a bit too much champagne and Cathy held her breath as he said, "I want to propose a toast to the happiness of my darling daughter, Catherine. I hope that she'll know the marital love that our son Stephen was denied. Life is unpredictable, as we now understand, and love is immensely valuable. Just because we can't put a price on it, that doesn't mean it comes cheaply…"

"My dear, do sit down," Hermione murmured loudly enough for many guests to hear. She tugged at his cutaway coat. "We haven't all day, you know."

"Will it ever end?" Cathy's voice broke the silence that filled the plush carriage and spilled out into the dark evening.

"Hmm?" Adam murmured at length, his tone absent.

"Nothing. I was just speaking to hear my own voice." In the shadows, she tried to measure the distance between them. Half-an-arm's-length, at least. "It's over, isn't it? I thought it would never end."

His eyes found hers, gleaming in a way that made her squirm. "If you are referring to our wedding day, I suppose it's only half over. The public ceremony is finished at last, but the private one must still be gotten through."

She looked away, reddening. One of the last people to hug her and wish her well had been Elysia. She'd whispered, "You must write and tell me if it is terrifying or splendid, Catherine! Perhaps our mothers are only trying to frighten us."

"You're dreading it, aren't you?" Adam asked in a low voice tinged with amusement.

"Of course not." She continued to look out the window into the darkness. "I'm only embarrassed because you are speaking out loud about something that is…very private."

"But you and I are husband and wife now. Surely we can discuss these matters?"

"It's not proper."

"According to whom? Your mother?"

"It just isn't," Cathy insisted. "Please, stop."

Adam obeyed. He reclined against the leather seat and listened to the hoofbeats of the perfectly matched grays as they trotted down the bleak streets. He tried not to think about the events of that day, which seemed like scenes in a play. How could it be that this stranger sitting beside him was his wife?

At length, they were overlooking the water and the coach came to a stop. There was the Parrish steam yacht, the *Free Spirit*, with tiny lights strung all around her deck railings. A uniformed crew stood waiting on the afterdeck with Alice the Labrador among them.

Adam emerged from the carriage before the coachman could open his door. "Alice, old girl!" he cried. When the dog ran up the gangplank to greet her master, he crouched and put his arms around her neck. "You'll never know how good it is to see you. I promised I'd come, didn't I?" He remembered Cathy then, and was about to go around to get her when he saw that she was standing nearby.

"Do you think she'll let me near you?" she asked.

"Alice? He laughed a bit too easily as he rose and came toward her. "I thought you two were already friends."

"That was before, wasn't it, Alice? She's probably used to women petting her and trying to win her over, but they never last." Cathy stroked the dog's head. "Do they, girl?"

"I don't know what you're talking about. Let's go on board."

"It looks lovely, doesn't it?"

"I don't know why I let myself be talked into this floating honeymoon on your parents' yacht, surrounded by their riches and their servants."

"We had to get to Barbados, didn't we?"

"Have you ever heard of passenger ships?"

Soon enough, however, Adam began to soften toward his surroundings. The crew introduced themselves, showed the newlyweds all the food and chilled champagne that awaited them in the main cabin, and reminded them to ring if there was anything they needed. Then, they all vanished, like well-trained ghosts.

"It's much nicer than a passenger ship, don't you think?" Cathy inquired sweetly.

He looked around the cabin, which featured inlaid mahogany paneling, Turkish rugs accented by leopard skins, plush velvet-upholstered furniture, and a grand piano. In one corner there was a large wicker basket with a tapestry pillow in it, and Alice was already curling up to resume her evening nap.

"I feel like a bought man," he said. "But then, that's what I am, so why not live like one?"

She watched as he poured champagne, drank it down, and then refilled the glass. "I would like a glass, too."

"Sorry." He brought the goblet of champagne to her and added, "I tried to warn you that I'm a brute."

Her heart ached for a little tenderness from him, but tonight of all nights he seemed incapable of giving that to her. "I'm so very tired. Would you mind if I changed out of these traveling clothes?"

"Of course not." His eyes followed her as she went into the master stateroom. Then he drank down another glass of champagne, shed his coat, tie, and wing collar, opened the top of his shirt, and went over to sit beside Alice. "This could be a splendid voyage if it were just the two of us, couldn't it, old girl?"

The dog made no response so Adam petted her for a bit. When Cathy came back into the cabin and took a seat at the other end of the sofa, Alice clambered out of her basket and went to sit on her new mistress's feet. She leaned against the silk dressing gown that covered Cathy's legs and rested her white-whiskered chin on her knees.

Adam felt his face coloring. "You don't seem to have any cause to be concerned about Alice, do you? Looks as though if anyone's the outsider, it's me!"

"I think Alice is merely being sensitive to my needs," Cathy ventured.

The dog gazed at her master with expressive brown eyes. He took her hint and moved closer, within touching distance. Now what? He cleared his throat. "I take it that the dressing gown is part of your trousseau?"

"Oh—yes." Her blush deepened. "My mother chose everything. She insisted that my taste is very undeveloped and I must put my trust in her."

"No offense, but it looks like something your mother would choose."

"Indeed, I would have preferred fewer ruffles."

"You can have a new wardrobe made in Barbados." Adam discovered that he was rather curious to see what was under Cathy's wedding night lingerie. "Since we're both feeling tired, perhaps we ought to move into the stateroom?"

Her heart was pounding harder than ever. She'd dreamed endlessly of this night, of being kissed and caressed by Raveneau, but now that it was here all she could think of was her mother's warnings. Was it true that only men enjoyed marital relations? Was that why her own father was having an affair? If only she knew what to expect!

"You're looking rather pale," Adam observed drily. "Are you frightened? I don't think it will be awful, unless I'm completely mistaken about my abilities. I ought to be able to make this experience relatively pleasant for you."

She loved the sight of his kind smile. It meant more than any other reassurance he could offer, and she could feel her own mouth turning up at the corners in response. "I can't believe we're talking about this."

"So you've mentioned." He touched her dimpled cheek. "I like your smile, Lady Raveneau."

"And I like yours."

"That's a start, isn't it?" Adam reached for her fluttering hand and captured it. "Let's go to bed."

"But—what about Alice?"

At the sound of Cathy's panicked voice saying her name, the yellow Labrador lifted her head and opened one eye.

"Alice has a fine bed of her own," Adam said. "I love her, but she is a dog. She understands the rules."

"All right. I'll go. But first, let me drink my champagne." She drained the glass and, blushing, smiled at him. "Perhaps that will help to relax me."

"Believe it or not, I have a few tricks of my own in that area. We'll start by taking down your hair. You weren't planning to keep it pinned up in bed, were you…?"

~ ~ ~

Adam took pity on her and extinguished the lights, but there was a transom above the bed that let in an array of romantic moonbeams. As they stood together in the shadows, Cathy feared she might faint when he reached for the sash on her robe.

"Please—please don't make me expose myself to you here, like this. Can't I get into bed and cover myself?"

He blinked, wondering if such drama could really be authentic. "You know, I won't be shocked if you admit to me now that you aren't a virgin. It wouldn't bother me in the least."

"How dare you? Of course I'm a virgin! Why would I let some man do those things to me if we weren't even married?"

"Have you been living in a convent?" When she didn't smile, Adam took her hand in both of his, then caressed her arm inside the full silken sleeve. "I believe that I detect more of Hermione's brand of education…yes? What's she told you about your wedding night? No doubt you're expecting me to torture you."

"Of course not." Her voice was trembling. "Perhaps—it would help if I had a bit more champagne."

"Relax, Cathy. You have nothing to fear. I promise." His fingers stole into her thick, wavy brown hair and loosed the pins that held it atop her head. "Your hair is like silk. It's beautiful." He bent to inhale the fragrance and was surprised that it stirred him so.

She told herself that Adam had done this a thousand times and that he must be legendary for his lovemaking skills. Such thoughts eased her fears but made her uneasy in other ways. How many women had he held and whispered to in just this way?

"Would you like to sit on the edge of the bed while I undress first?" he asked. "Perhaps that would set you at ease."

"Somehow I doubt it…" She sat, then looked away. "I can close my eyes, can't I?"

He laughed, looking even more piratical than usual in the darkness. "As you wish, my lady." The clothing came off quickly. His brown fingers deftly flicked open the array of studs and buttons, then dropped the waistcoat and crisp white shirt over a rosewood bench.

Cathy stared. Her eyes were accustomed enough to the darkness to make out the sculpted masculine beauty of his chest and the lean, strong lines of his arms. Before she could manage further thought, Adam had stripped off his lower garments and she glimpsed his muscled flanks, narrow hips, and partially roused manhood before gasping aloud and squeezing her eyes shut.

"Adam! Oh my goodness!"

"Are you shocked?" With a soft laugh, he sat down beside her and gave her a mischievous smile. "Disappointed?"

Her face was on fire. "I—I think this is unseemly! We ought to get under the covers so that we can cling to a bit of modesty."

"I'm feeling neither unseemly nor modest, but perhaps that's because I'm a man. If you want to get into bed, you may." He bit back an urge to sigh aloud. If there was one thing worse than being forced into marriage with a mousey heiress one barely knew, it was discovering that said heiress was horrified by the thought of revealing her plain little body to her husband.

Cathy scurried gratefully under the lace-edged sheets, still clad in her nightgown. "Are you angry? Bored?"

"Of course not." The soul of patience, he climbed into bed beside her and managed a smile. "It's your wedding night, my dear, and you're entitled to be skittish."

"We have the rest of our lives to practice at this. Why must we rush?"

"Indeed." Raveneau's earlier throb of arousal had died away and he lay on his back in the luxurious, swaying bed, listening to water lapping at the yacht's hull and wishing he could just go to sleep. This business of deflowering the nervous virgin bride required more energy than he could muster.

Cathy reached over and nervously touched his chest. It was warm and hard, and she could feel his steady heartbeat. A surge of excitement gripped her very core. It felt like the champagne, only much, much better and more dangerous.

"Will you kiss me?" she whispered.

"Are you certain you're ready for that?" His tone was underscored with irony.

"Yes. Quite certain."

He slipped one hand around her waist, turning her toward him, and cupped her chin with the other hand. Cathy began to stiffen, but when his mouth found hers, she gasped at the sensation of pleasure. Slowly he kissed her, exploring the soft terrain of her lips, working them with his own mouth until they grew moister and more responsive. His tongue longed to explore further, but Cathy was untrained in the finer arts of kissing, and there was plenty of time to teach her. It was enough for now that she was relaxing and the cadence of her breathing was changing.

Carefully, while still kissing her, Adam let his hand move over her nightgown. He couldn't remember the last time he'd been with a woman who had been so reserved, and who had not been molding herself to him during these first kisses in bed. Cathy lay awkwardly in his embrace, covered in lace and silk from head to toe, and he felt a bit uncertain himself. Uncertain…yet increasingly aroused.

"Can I help you undress?" he murmured gently.

"What?" There was panic in her voice. "Why must I undress? No one told me about that. I had no idea!"

"Never mind," he soothed, kissing her neck and soaking up the sensation of her curls against his face. "Just relax."

She wanted to—desperately! Part of her was melting with desire each time Adam touched her. He kissed her again, slowly, tenderly, his tongue teasing between her lips, and a warm ache grew inside her. When his hand caressed her cheek, neck, and throat, her breasts seemed to tighten and the mysterious region between her legs tingled, then throbbed. Was something wrong with her? She yearned to press against Adam. He smelled so good to her, and his hair curled crisply in her fingers when she touched it.

But what exactly did he mean to do to her? Images of mating horses came to her on waves of panic. He was so strong and so forceful…and the glimpse Cathy'd had of his male member had been enough to strike fear into her heart. What words had her mother used? *Ugly, degrading, humiliating, repulsive!*

Adam felt her go rigid in his arms. He'd been just about to touch her breasts over the nightgown. "For God's sake, what's wrong? What have I done?"

"Nothing," she replied miserably. "I'm just afraid. I've heard so many terrifying stories…!" Closing her eyes, she saw her own dear, gentle father passionately kissing a strange woman in public. "I'm afraid."

Adam wished he could promise her that he wouldn't hurt her, but even with long, lingering foreplay, there were no guarantees. "Look—it's been a long day for both of us. I want your wedding night to be an experience of pleasure and happiness, not fear. Why don't we get a good night's sleep and perhaps we can try again tomorrow?" It was so much easier to just have a mistress! "Take all the time you need. You can let me know when you're ready, all right?"

"You're very kind."

"Good night, Cathy." Adam patted her shoulder as if she were his sister and rolled away to his own pillow. What a fiasco! He felt like a prisoner on Parrish's steam yacht, floating along on an interminable, sexless honeymoon from which there was no escape.

Behind him in the gathering shadows, Cathy rose up on an elbow and tried to catch a clear glimpse of her husband's profile. He was staring toward the darkened porthole, brooding: eyes open, jaw set, and brow furrowed.

Curling into a little fearful ball, she knew that she had made a terrible mistake by postponing their physical marriage. Cathy had put up a barrier between them that was far higher and thicker than she'd ever guessed, and it seemed to grow more formidable with each passing moment…

Chapter 10

A chilly gray mist enveloped the *Free Spirit* during the second day of the Raveneaus' marriage. As they sailed down the eastern coastline of America, their view was shrouded in fog.

"You don't suppose it's a sign?" Adam remarked to the first mate while he was walking Alice at midday. His tone was only half-amused.

Woodrow, a gangly young man with a pronounced Southern accent, looked shocked. "Oh no, suh—that is, I ought to say, *my lord*." He cleared his throat. "It's November. The weather ought to improve the farther south we go. Ah'm looking forward to the islands myself!" A dreamy smile lit his face, then he remembered himself and stood at attention. "What can I do for y'all, my lord?"

Adam considered this offer. "I suppose you might have some chilled champagne sent to the main cabin below. Perhaps a bit of caviar, sour cream, and toast points to go with it?"

"Yes, my lord. Can I bring something for Alice?"

"She'd like that."

"My lord, will you give my regards to her ladyship? I hope marriage agrees with her." A blush spread over the young man's cheeks.

"Thank you, Woodrow, and yes, I believe my wife is well today." Adam couldn't meet the younger man's eager gaze. He suddenly felt more than a little guilty for his own failure the night before to transport Cathy to a state of wedded bliss. His guilt was compounded by the fact that he knew he wasn't the loving bridegroom she deserved.

With that, Adam mustered the remaining shreds of his good nature and returned belowdecks to his bride. When last he'd seen her, at ten o'clock, she had still been asleep.

During his morning of freedom, he'd perused the books lining the drawing room shelves, read in the glass-enclosed upper saloon, walked Alice several times around the yacht, eaten a light breakfast, and struck up conversations with passing crew members. It was hard enough being on a honeymoon with a wife one barely knew, but harder still being trapped onboard a vessel belonging to her wealthy father. Adam began to ponder the meaning of the word "gigolo." If he didn't fit the exact definition, he was at least bought and paid for…and beginning to understand why such arrangements were seldom as simple as they seemed.

"There you are!" Cathy exclaimed as Adam and Alice entered the spacious cabin. She tied the sash on her dressing gown as she spoke.

Adam glanced toward a polished copper bathtub, still filled with steamy bubbles that scented the air. "You've had a bath, I see."

"Yes. It did feel lovely."

"Perhaps I'll order one myself. Suddenly it seems a very long time since the soak I had before church yesterday."

Brushing her long hair, Cathy tried to look calm, as if they frequently shared such casually intimate scenes; as if they had consummated their new marriage last night after all. When Alice came over and sat down on her toes and gazed up at her, she couldn't help smiling.

Adam did order his bath, and was surprised when Cathy didn't flee the moment he disrobed. Instead, she sat in the main cabin and pretended to read *The Age of Innocence*. When a steward arrived with champagne, caviar, and all the trimmings, she didn't know what to say.

"I didn't order this," she managed at last. "I don't think it's even noon yet, Tilburn!"

"His lordship did the ordering," explained the older man. "And yes, my lady, it's past twelve o'clock."

"I suppose I'll have to allow it then." There was a twinkle in her eye.

From the stateroom, Adam called, "Just what I've been craving!"

"I think I can manage from here, Tilburn." She took the tray from him. "Thank you."

Cathy's heart was racing in a way she'd come to recognize as she poured champagne for her new husband and took the glass to him in his bath. He had just finished soaping his wide, tanned chest, and his hand was dripping water as he took the crystal stem.

"Shall we have another toast?"

She couldn't break away from his gaze. "Perhaps it's bad luck," she whispered with a trace of irony.

"No. Let us toast to new beginnings…and courage."

When they both had swallowed, Cathy stole a glance at him. "Your words are innocent enough, but something in your tone, or perhaps in your eyes, makes me blush."

"Good." He lay back in the tub and stared at her. In the satin dressing gown, her breasts appeared fuller than he remembered. "You really do have beautiful hair. It's a shame to keep it pinned up all day long."

Her cheeks went pinker. "When I was young, I used to read *Little Women* over and over again, and my mother thought it was a terrible influence. All that talk of Jo's independence, you know."

Adam nodded. "It's a wonderful book."

"Have you read it? Truly?"

"I have." He was charmed by her guilelessness.

"When Mother wanted to get under my skin, she would remark that I probably felt close to Jo because we shared one common mark of beauty: our hair." She gave him a wry smile. "Do you remember the scene? When Marmee needs to purchase a train ticket to visit their wounded father and there isn't any money, Jo goes out and sells her hair. I'll never forget the horror I felt when I first read that scene, when she revealed that all her hair had been cut off! And insensitive Amy exclaimed, 'Oh, Jo, your one beauty!'" Sighing, Cathy added, "When my mother compared me to Jo, my heart ached, and yet I wasn't even certain my hair qualified as beautiful. It's only brown, after all. Quite ordinary, just like the rest of me."

Adam listened, transfixed, and noticed that she'd sipped the last drop of champagne from her glass. He reached out of the tub for the bottle that sat on a low stool between them and poured. Cathy made no objection.

"Why shouldn't brown hair be just as rich and glorious as any other color? Yours is anything but ordinary…and hardly your only source of beauty." Before she could protest, he added, "I'm intrigued by all this talk of *Little Women*. I thought that *Wuthering Heights* was your favorite book."

Cathy's cheeks burned. "I—I think I will try the caviar."

"Indeed." He propped a foot on the rim of the tub and washed it slowly. "While you sort out the food, won't you tell me your secret? Clearly you have one. I can't think of a better way to break the ice in this marriage."

Looking at him, Cathy thought that, for her, the ice had melted rather than broken. "I feel foolish."

"We've all felt foolish."

"Well…" She took a deep breath. "The story I told you about *Wuthering Heights* wasn't true. My mother forbade me to read it and she most certainly did not name me after the book's heroine. When Elysia and I became friends during the summer ground was broken for Beechcliff, we had long talks at Bailey's Beach about *Wuthering Heights*. She told me about the great, tragic love affair between Heathcliff and Cathy, and I began to dream about them and imagine that I had been named for her."

"Perfectly understandable," Adam said gently.

"I'll never forget Elysia quoting that Cathy was 'a wild, wicked slip of a girl.' I thought that was the most romantic thing I'd ever heard."

"But, if you'd read the book, I doubt that you would have wanted to be like Cathy," he offered. "It's enough that you share her name. It wouldn't do for you to be wicked."

"But you see, I don't share her name. No one has ever called me Cathy except for you, and you did it only because I told you that story in the teahouse."

"Do you want me to go back to Catherine?"

"No!" she exclaimed. "I love being Cathy now."

Adam soaped and rinsed his dark hair, then lay back in the water, his wet, hard-muscled body gleaming in the soft light. The water was cooler and he rather preferred that, just as he preferred Cathy in her more relaxed state. He found himself surprisingly intrigued by her. The whole "Cathy" situation seemed profoundly meaningful, like a metaphor for her real, freer self— locked inside the proper heiress Hermione Parrish had worked so diligently to create.

"What about your brother?" Adam asked suddenly. "What did he call you?"

"Cat." Her voice was small. "I haven't thought of it for so long! When I was a little girl, Stephen decided that I reminded him of a kitten…" Tears filled her eyes. "Sometimes, it seemed that Stephen was the only person who truly understood me."

"No doubt that was true, since he was your brother and understood the workings of your exceedingly unique family. I've often wished that I had a sibling to share those bonds with, someone who would completely understand all the complexities of our family history—and the feelings."

"You and I are both only children now."

Adam glanced toward Alice, who was stretched out beside the bed, snuffling in her sleep. "Except for that old girl."

"I like this caviar. Mother never let me have more than one bite. She said it was too salty."

"Thank God we're rid of her!" he burst out, and couldn't resist the urge to laugh. "Now we can all do as we please!"

Then, to Cathy's further shock, he stood up in the bathtub, water streaming down his powerful body. Her mouth fell open and she emitted a little peeping gasp. "Adam!"

"Are you afraid I'll drip on the priceless carpets? Get me a towel and dry my back, all right?"

She could sense his amusement but couldn't think of anything to do except obey. His big body was shockingly fascinating and alluring to her; his strong tapering back was brown as an oak tree, and his buttocks reminded her of the magnificent statues she'd seen in Florence.

"I'm going to lie down and finish my champagne," Adam said. Carrying the bottle and his glass, he sat down on the bed and let the sheet casually fall over his genitals. Cathy would never relax if he went too fast.

She trailed after him, still carrying the towel. "I think I missed a place—" She broke off when Adam turned and stared into her eyes. "I mean, I was afraid you'd get your pillows wet."

"Go on, then." He rolled over and lay with one cheek resting on his clasped hands, murmuring for good measure, "We're married, you know. You can touch me as much as you'd like."

"Yes, I know that!" Briskly, Cathy dried him off, from one broad shoulder to the other, then down his back to the base of his spine. It was impossible not to look lower, and what she saw made her feel very nervous.

"That feels good. Would you mind massaging my back a bit? Then I'll do yours in return."

Her heart was pounding so loudly she could scarcely hear herself speak. "Certainly."

The corners of his mouth twitched slightly. "I don't deserve you, Cathy."

"Don't tease me." The sensation of his utterly male back under her small hands made her tingle. Her palms began to perspire as she worked at his muscles. "I've told you a secret, now you'll have to tell me one."

"I don't know if I've got one that awful." Mischief continued to inflect his voice. "All right, I'll think of a secret while I rub your back."

"I don't think—" Panic-stricken, Cathy realized that she was being given an opportunity to restart their marriage, but a wave of terror nearly carried her right out of the stateroom. "I mean—" She could feel Adam's body stiffening under her fingers. His eyes were still closed. Mustering every drop of courage she possessed, Cathy took another gulp of champagne and whispered, "All right. But I expect a very grand secret from you, my lord. I've never let anyone give me a massage before."

As they changed places, Cathy was blushing madly and taking care not to look at her husband. Once she was lying face-down on his pillows, smelling his heady essence in them, Adam slipped his fingers around the neckline of her dressing gown.

"Let's slide this down to your waist, all right?" Before she could protest or even think, he'd loosened the satin, freed her arms, and bared the upper half of her body. "Ah. You're lovely."

She squeezed her eyes shut, certain that she was anything but lovely and that he was merely being polite. Why couldn't it be night? "Tell me your secret."

"I'm trying to think of one horrible enough." Gently, his big hands fit themselves to her upper back, testing the delicate shape of her bones and the texture of her skin. "Try to relax, my lady." He felt slowly down to her waist, then gave a soft laugh. "That's not relaxing. You're tenser by the moment. Don't my hands feel at all good to you?" Then, as he inched up her spine and deftly kneaded her shoulders, Cathy gave a little sigh.

For long minutes, there was nothing but the feeling of his hands on her back, and she succumbed to the sheer pleasure of his touch. He knew just what she would like, and there was no point in resisting. The unthinkable—Adam touching her naked back—became reality.

Slowly his fingertips massaged her shoulders and neck, then caressed her hair and felt its silky richness. Her scalp tingled with each touch. Smiling like a kitten, she emitted a little purring sound.

And then, Adam bent over and touched her neck with his lips. Just once. Before she could turn skittish, he began rubbing her arms, coaxing each muscle to surrender, then felt the landscape of her slim hands.

"That feels wonderful…" she admitted as he gently pinched up and down one of her fingers.

"I'm glad."

His strong fingertips were like butterfly wings on her back before slowly moving to graze the curved sides of her compressed breasts. She caught her breath, but her panic had been replaced by a thrill of anticipation. New sensations were fizzling over her nerves like the bubbles in her champagne glass.

Adam kept touching the outside edges of her breasts, straying away then back again, until she was aching for more. Her nipples puckered with need and her breasts felt taut. He was kissing the tender nape of her neck now, then all down her spine, and Cathy involuntarily arched her back. When he brushed his warm lips along the side of one breast, she turned on her side to welcome him.

Adam was nearly mad with arousal, but couldn't let her know. "Cathy, you are beautiful," he whispered hoarsely. He fit his hands over her lush curves and, to his delight, felt her nipples swell against his palms. "My little mouse turns out to be a goddess."

She suspected he was paying her compliments to be kind, but didn't say so. Instead, as Adam kissed her and drew her into a full-length embrace, she closed her eyes and tried not to be frightened by the feeling of his engorged manhood pressing her tummy through the satin robe still belted around her waist. He tasted so wonderful, and each probe of his tongue increased the tingly sensations that were warmly blossoming in the private parts of her body.

She tried to let her tongue answer his, wrapping her arms around his shoulders. Never had Cathy imagined that such intoxication was possible, and she found herself thinking that she could happily melt into Adam's being.

"Open your eyes, my bride," he murmured.

She obeyed and found herself staring at his roguishly handsome face.

"Look at the rest of me. There's nothing to be frightened of."

Biting her lip, she let her gaze skitter over the muscled planes of his chest, down the hard surface of his belly, and then land for an instant on the threatening-looking proof of his masculinity. Blushing, she protested, "I think it's better if I keep my eyes closed."

"You can touch it…"

Her face was on fire. "Not today, thank you."

He laughed softly at that, then kissed her again, long and passionately, as if to reassure them both that she hadn't lost her nerve. Adam was poised above her, his mouth blazing a trail down her throat to her breasts. Cathy gasped when he leisurely took one nipple into his mouth and began to suckle, for the sensations that followed were like fiery sparks that traveled down to explode between her legs. She heard herself moan, and when his free hand undid the sash and opened her dressing gown, Cathy parted her thighs to him.

"Yes," he whispered encouragingly.

Confused by her own arousal, she started to cover herself with one hand, but Adam got there first. And when he touched her, so gently and skillfully, she nearly sobbed aloud. Who could have dreamed…? She squeezed her eyes shut and tried not to think about what he was doing, how he was touching her, letting the tide of passion carry her away instead.

"Ah, Cathy, your woman's body is more eager for this day than you know," he told her softly.

They shared more long, slow kisses that burned away all her doubts. And while they kissed, Adam continued to touch her, gauging her response. When at last he slipped two fingers inside her and she moved her hips in response, he knew that the moment would never be more right. Kneeling between her thighs, he whispered to her and pushed inside, inch by inch. Soon enough, passion replaced her nervous reticence. Adam was afraid of hurting her and so he held back, but her hips came up to meet his and he tasted sweat on her neck and he knew that there was hope for his starchy little heiress after all…

Cathy, meanwhile, was aware of the burning pain, but her primal instincts were stronger. Her body wanted a release for its need, and most of all, she wanted this union with Adam Raveneau. Everything about him drove her mad. Tasting his mouth, smelling his male scent, feeling his big body against hers and having him inside her satisfied needs she'd never known until today.

"My husband," she whispered and pushed back against his thrust.

At that moment, Adam found his own burning release and he stiffened in her embrace. When he was able to focus, to his surprise, he found that Cathy was looking at him in wonderment.

"It take it you didn't hate it?" he murmured, bemused.

She wished all of it hadn't ended, wished he didn't have to leave her body, wished he wouldn't lie on his back with space between them. But she could scarcely absorb her own feelings, let alone share them with him. "No, I didn't hate it. You were very patient."

Absently, Adam reached for one of his handkerchiefs from the night table and handed it to her. "You may need this," he murmured. Then he patted her thigh, eyelids drooping. "If you'll excuse me, my lady, I'm going to take a nap…"

Rising up on one elbow, she stared at him, frightened by the force of her new-born passions and her sharp craving for her husband. He seemed to be asleep, unaware of her gaze. How could he sleep during this turning point in her life?

She noticed the wetness and pain between her legs then. It felt as if she'd been scorched. Looking down, Cathy saw bright smears of blood on the priceless sheets and was struck by the symbolism. She was bleeding for him and he didn't seem to notice…

Chapter 11

"I've just realized something. You never told me your secret," Cathy said as they looked out over the afterdeck rail and watched a school of dolphins arcing through the ocean near the yacht. "That's cheating."

Adam laughed, his profile set against the sunlight and the bright blue water. "I've been wondering when you'd bring this up."

"I was just waiting for you to lower your guard."

Behind them, a steward appeared with their tea tray, and they went to sit down on new wicker chairs amidst the potted palms and an aviary of exotic birds. A few days into marriage, Cathy knew just how her husband liked his tea, and she fixed it more carefully than he would have done for himself. When they were settled and Alice had trundled over for a bite of biscuit, Adam cleared his throat.

"I was just thinking that you grow lovelier with each passing day. You're getting freckles on your little nose…"

"Horrid!"

"Your hair gets curlier the closer we get to the equator—"

"Unrulier, you mean!"

"And the hotter it gets, the thinner the fabric of your shirtwaists becomes."

"Don't be prurient." She laughed in spite of herself.

"I thought it was my duty to be prurient. Wasn't that part of our wedding vows? No? I could have sworn..."

Cathy watched as he sat back in the chair, balancing cup and saucer, and stretched out his legs. Alice appeared and took up her position beside her master. It seemed that he was growing handsomer as the days at sea slipped gently from their grasp. The sun agreed with Adam, deepening his golden tan and setting his black hair agleam. He wore wonderful clothes: starched white or pin-striped shirts open-necked and folded up at the cuffs, beige linen trousers, and burnished leather belts or braces. Cathy felt euphoric in his presence and leaden when they were parted for more than an hour.

"You're trying to distract me from the real matter at hand," she accused with mock severity. You owe me a secret and I intend to be paid."

"I've been thinking about this and find myself with a dilemma. Men don't have the same sorts of secrets women do. Your secret, about the origin of your name, was charming; quite harmless. All my secrets are..."

"Yes?" Cathy sat forward in her chair.

"Dark. There's no other word for it."

"What does that mean? Criminal?"

He laughed. "Hardly. Come and sit on my lap."

"I shouldn't. You're trying to break your side of our bargain, aren't you?"

Before he could respond, she came to him and he slid both arms around her trim waist. How fresh and soft she was in her long, fitted skirt and thin batiste shirtwaist. Her breasts pushed lightly against him, reminding Adam of the moonlit moments he'd spent kissing them the night before. An exquisite cameo pin was fastened at the base of her high, lace-edged collar.

"Every time I see another piece of your jewelry, I chastise myself for not getting you a proper wedding gift," he said. "I'm a poor excuse for a gentleman."

"Even if I cared for jewels, the only wedding gift I wanted was you. If you hadn't come back from the West, I'd still be bound to my mother, hunting noblemen…" Cathy shuddered and clung to his shoulders. He'd never know how lucky she felt every morning when she opened her eyes and beheld him lying beside her. She was so enamored that her heart hurt, but it wouldn't do for Adam to know that, so she managed a bit of laughter instead. "How can you say that you haven't gotten me a gift when soon we'll be on Barbados and I'll become mistress of Tempest Hall? I'll have the most romantic life imaginable."

One side of his mouth bent sardonically. "You must be joking. Have you forgotten that Tempest Hall is tumbling down and your father is paying for the restoration? It's a wonder I'm able to perform at all in bed, I've so little manhood of my own left."

"Don't say that. Money doesn't make a man. The pursuit of money is just an excuse to avoid the real character-building issues in life, I think." Cathy warmed to her topic. "I've never known one person in my parents' circle who had a character I admired. They're all superficial and judgmental."

"Except for your own father."

She pressed her lips together, trying to block from her mind the image of Jules Parrish kissing his lover. "I suppose so, but who knows what might go on when he isn't at home? That's most of the time, after all. He may have just as many dark secrets as any other man."

"I was afraid you hadn't let go of that subject," he remarked in tones of amused irony. "If you keep pestering me you'll hear something that you'll wish you hadn't."

"Such as? I would like to know what your definition of a dark secret is!"

"What about a mistress?"

Their eyes were inches apart but his were unreadable. Cathy's breath burned in her throat. "Are we speaking of a hypothetical mistress? In England?"

"Perhaps. But, what if she were on Barbados? A woman of color?"

Suddenly, she knew that she had probed too deeply and this was his way of warning her away. Certainly, if it were true that he had a mistress on Barbados, he wouldn't taunt her with it!

Would he? She managed a faltering smile. "I know what you're doing. I apologize for stepping on your privacy. You needn't make up any more hurtful examples to teach me this lesson."

Adam could see that she wanted him to reassure her now but he couldn't. "Look, it's more than my privacy that's at stake. I've sold myself. I'm floating along on this cursed steam-palace with a lot of your parents' servants bowing and scraping before me, and I'm going home with a pocketful of your father's money to rebuild my ancestral home. It's bloody humiliating! Worst of all, it's my own doing. I'm the one who kept gambling long after a more sensible fellow would have stopped. I lost everything, and now I've lost even the choice whether to marry or not." He felt her back off his lap but his words continued to flow, like blood from an angry wound. "Can you imagine how that feels? Have you any idea how it might then feel to have my heiress bride demand that I divulge my darkest secrets? I don't know anymore what I'm doing out of an attempt to show you affection, or out of obligation because your father paid me so damned much money! Do I have the right to refuse you anything?"

Cathy backed up until she almost sat down on a potted palm before finding her way into a rocking chair. "Can't you forget about the money?" She was about to ask why he couldn't pretend that he'd married her for the usual reasons, but lost her nerve. After all, it was ridiculous to imagine that someone like Raveneau would have chosen Cathy if she were poor…

As he read her mind, his expression changed. "Come here."

"No." Her eyes brimmed with hot tears that she was embarrassed for him to see. "I wish that you would leave me alone for a little bit."

"On our honeymoon? You can't get rid of me yet."

He closed the distance between their chairs and knelt before her. The sight of tears, trickling down her cheeks despite her efforts to blot them with a wispy handkerchief, stung his heart. "For God's sake, don't cry. I am a beast."

She shook her head. "Don't look at me."

"You're beautiful."

"Liar."

Unable to bear another moment, he swept her into his arms, murmured "Stay" to Alice, and carried his bride off.

"What are you doing?" Cathy demanded. To her astonishment and secret delight, he had no trouble maneuvering them both down the companionway ladder.

"Clearly, I shall have to solve this problem with deeds, not words." Ignoring the crewmember who watched from a distance, he added, "How many times a day must I make love to you before you'll believe my heart's in it?"

"Once more, at least," she dared to murmur.

In the end, Cathy's nerve failed her, at least when it came to making love in broad daylight. As much as she loved being held, kissed, and caressed by Adam, there was always a moment when she began to feel anxious and wished they were on the other side, lying together in the aftermath. Even though he often dozed off, she was content to remain in his arms, soaking up the warm strength of his naked body.

The next afternoon, Cathy stood in the glass-enclosed upper saloon, watching as the lush mountains of Jamaica faded from view. They'd dropped anchor there that noon, going ashore for luncheon and fresh supplies, and the sight of Adam in his West Indian element made her realize how little she knew about his life in this exotic locale. Perhaps he really had been serious when he'd warned her that life on Barbados wouldn't be the romantic fantasy she imagined.

Wandering over to the piano that dominated the room, Cathy sat down and began to play a Bach sonata. It was soothing to lose herself in the music, and it wasn't until she heard the sound of Alice barking on the afterdeck that she raised her fingers from the keys.

Woodrow appeared. "Sorry to interrupt, my lady—"

"What's upset Alice? I've never heard her make such a fuss, not even when those sea gulls were attacking her!"

"It seems that we have a guest. His lordship spotted a small craft that was taking on water, and he ordered the lifeboat lowered to rescue the occupants. They are coming aboard at this moment."

"Really!" She could scarcely believe her ears. "I suppose I ought to go and greet them."

"Lord Raveneau suggested as much, my lady," Woodrow replied, nodding.

The Caribbean sun was beating down on the yacht's teak decks as Cathy made her way back to join Adam. He stood at the rail, watching as the lifeboat rose to the point where its occupants could disembark. Alice was sitting obediently at her master's side, ears perked, ready to growl if either of their unexpected visitors dared misbehave.

"Ah, there you are," Adam murmured when Cathy touched his crisp white sleeve. A faintly ironic smile played over his mouth. "'Twould seem that the honeymoon is ended."

She felt a pang of alarm. "Please don't say that!"

The two men were clambering onto the deck, shading their eyes against the blinding sun, and looking hopefully toward Adam and Cathy.

"Awfully kind of you to take us on," said the taller of the two. He extended his hand. "My name is Theo Harrismith. I'm on my way from Boston back to Barbados, where I was raised, to take on the management of the Ocean Breeze Hotel in Christ Church." Gesturing toward his companion, Theo continued, "Allow me also to present Sutton O'Leary, my accountant. Are you two bound for Barbados on a pleasure cruise?"

While Adam made introductions and explanations, Cathy surveyed the newcomers. She was drawn to Theo's lively blue eyes, rosy cheeks, and dandified clothing which included white duck trousers, an emerald-green bowtie, and a straw boater. When he removed the hat, she saw that his reddish-gold hair was thinning prematurely. She guessed that he was in his mid-twenties.

Sutton O'Leary looked equally youthful with his head of curly dark hair. Wiry and agile, he had a thin, pale face with a sunburned nose and a sparse mustache. His own white pants were paired with a bright striped vest. When he spoke, his accent told Cathy that he was a native of Boston.

Woodrow appeared along with a pair of stewards bearing trays of cold beverages and a variety of tempting snacks. Adam suggested that they go into the saloon to take refreshment since the two men had probably had enough sunshine for one day. When they were all seated on the lavish sofas and Theo had drunk a tall glass of water and a taller one of champagne, he said,

"Are we dreaming?" He looked around at the grand piano, the beautiful palms and flowering plants, and the bright cushions that filled the sofas were reflected in the room's glass walls. "Perhaps we've drowned, Sutton! Might this be heaven?"

"Have some more champagne," Adam offered. "Are you all right? Were you in trouble long?"

"Only a few minutes," Sutton said.

"But it seemed much longer!" Theo exclaimed, holding out his glass to accept the sparkling wine. "That sun is quite terrifying, I don't mind telling you."

"Won't you please tell us more about yourselves?" Cathy found herself enjoying the fanciful Theo Harrismith. "You couldn't have been sailing on that small boat all the way from Boston, could you?"

"God, no!" cried Theo. "We went to Jamaica in May, intending to merely visit, but so many people invited us to house parties that the months just slipped away." He paused. "And, there was the matter of the smallpox epidemic that was just ending after more than a year. As you know, Barbados was quarantined, and even though that was lifted last April, I must confess to waiting a bit just be certain the danger had passed…"

"Smallpox!" Cathy's brown eyes were open wide. "Quarantine!"

Adam patted her hand. "Yes, but it's over now. The quarantine kept me from sailing to Barbados sooner, and it's one of the reasons I was passing time in America with Byron. Like Mr. Harrismith—"

"Do call me Theo!"

He gave their guest a tentative smile. "Like Theo, I didn't want to rush to Barbados the week the quarantine was lifted. Better to be safe, particularly during the summer, when heat becomes a factor." He reached for the champagne bottle. "And then I met you, my bride, and a few more months have passed. I have it on good authority that Barbados has been completely free of smallpox for more than six months."

"All right. I believe you." Cathy returned her attention to Theo. "Do tell us more."

He grinned. "Well, fate does seem to favor me. I happened to meet Hazel Trotter, the owner of the

Ocean Breeze Hotel and a friend of my parents, while she was visiting her great-uncle's Jamaican plantation. Hazel expressed an interest in acquiring a partner, and as I had just come into a sum of money, I accepted. Sutton and I hired that horrid boat, and now here we are." Tossing back his champagne and rolling his eyes, Theo added, "One minute we were saying our prayers and the next we're on board this magnificent steam yacht, drinking champagne and eating caviar!"

"I hope we're not intruding," said Sutton. "You are on your honeymoon, after all."

Cathy and Adam glanced at each other but before either of them could speak, Theo Harrismith was interjecting, "We'll make ourselves useful, never fear. I'll teach Lady Raveneau all about Barbados. I lived on a sugar cane plantation from birth until I went to Harvard at age eighteen. I may have been away these last seven years, but Barbados is in my blood."

"How exciting!" Cathy said. "I've been anxious to hear about my future home but Adam is very closed-mouthed. Sometimes I think he would rather keep me in the dark!"

"Clearly," her husband pronounced drily, "that is no longer a concern."

Chapter 12

Wearing a summery gown of pineapple gauze that showed off her pretty waist, Cathy stood beside her husband on the *Free Spirit*'s deck and shook hands with each member of the crew. They were anchored in the blue water of Carlisle Bay, within sight of Barbados's largest city, Bridgetown.

"I'm going to miss you, Woodrow," she said, clasping the last man's hand. Unbidden, tears stung her eyes. "I suddenly find that I'm sad, breaking my last tie with Newport and my parents. I didn't expect to feel this way! I rather wish that the yacht could stay right here…"

Adam came up behind her and smiled at the younger man. "Just like a woman. Never depend upon one making up her mind."

Coloring, Woodrow replied, "Her ladyship is a long way from home and Barbados is a far cry from anything she's used to."

She gave him a grateful smile. "Wouldn't you like to work for us at Tempest Hall?"

Adam was about to protest that she couldn't just hire servants for their home without consulting him, but remembered that their money was really all hers in reality. Turning away, he called back, "The lighter is waiting to take us ashore. Are you ready?"

Cathy was still waiting for Woodrow's reply. He gave her a sheepish smile and muttered, "Sorry, my lady, but my family's in Newport. I'd be too homesick if I stayed here."

"I understand." She sighed. "I really do."

Standing in Trafalgar Square with the busy harbor behind her, Cathy looked up winding dirt streets that led deeper into Bridgetown. Nearby stood a tall statue of Lord Nelson, a fountain, and a cabstand comprised of rows of horse-drawn sulkies. Alice lay a few feet away, napping in the shade provided by massive trees.

Adam had gone in search of Simon, the Tempest Hall servant who he'd expected to meet them. Theo and Sutton were waiting for something called a mule tram that Theo said would take them right past the Ocean Breeze Hotel's front door.

"Perhaps we ought to be taking the mule tram ourselves, to Tempest Hall," Cathy mused aloud. The sun was strong, penetrating her silk parasol, and she hadn't expected the humidity. "I don't know how long I can stand here like this."

Theo Harrismith, wearing a boater and a magenta bow tie, came to stand beside her. "It's not what you're used to, is it? Never mind, you can admit the truth to me. You may be putting on a brave front for your prince charming, but I know better."

"If there's one thing I despise, it's a wealthy girl who withers away if she isn't pampered." Cathy raised her little chin determinedly. "I've been needing a good adventure. I chose to come to Barbados; in fact, I begged Adam to bring me, so I can't complain."

"Well, I can," muttered Sutton O'Leary. "This isn't a bit like the paradise Theo described to me."

Together they gazed up the narrow streets that turned off of Trafalgar Square like the spokes of a wheel. Broad Street was the closest and busiest, lined with black carriages and divided up the middle by the tracks for the mule tram. Cathy was reminded of pictures she'd seen of New Orleans, for most of the buildings featured fanciful overhanging balconies enclosed by ironwork railings. The windows had jalousie shutters that pushed out from the bottom rather than swinging sideways on hinges.

Perhaps the biggest difference of all between Bridgetown and Newport, however, was as basic as black and white. Nearly all the people Cathy saw walking on the streets were negroes, with skin colors ranging from creamy beige to gleaming brown-black. The women wore white skirts and blouses, with high necks like her own, and some even sported little straw boaters. Other women had their hair wrapped in kerchiefs and they carried objects on their heads like bundles of sugarcane or trays of handmade pottery. One woman balanced a huge container with a spigot, and passersby paid her to dispense cups of her mysterious liquid.

"That's mauby," Theo explained to Cathy and Sutton. "It's a cold drink made from the bark of a scrubby tree and West Indians love it. The mauby women are fixtures in Bridgetown."

Cathy couldn't help staring at each new sight. Newport had never seemed more far away, and she sighed at the memory of the Casino with its clean sidewalks lined with copper beech trees, its lovely shops, and the immaculate lawns of its courtyard.

"Rather odd to see so many black faces, isn't it?" Theo commented, breaking into her thoughts. "We're in the minority here, you know."

"I didn't imagine..." she admitted, then hastened to add, "Not that I disapprove in any way!"

"Ah, her ladyship has progressive political views!" he exclaimed, chuckling. "I suppose you're a suffragette as well."

"I wasn't allowed to express such views, but of course that's what I believe in."

The mule tram appeared around a bend in Broad Street just as Adam came up behind Cathy. He was carrying his tan linen jacket and had loosened his tie. The effect, she decided, was extremely appealing.

"Couldn't we take Theo and Sutton to the hotel?" she asked.

He shook his head. "There wouldn't be enough space in our carriage. Besides, they are going the opposite direction, and you'll have to say goodbye eventually. Better to get it over with."

Theo's wave caused the tram car to stop near Lord Nelson's statue, and the two mules that were pulling it along the tracks seemed glad for the brief rest. The uniformed conductor wore a collection bag slung over one shoulder.

Cathy followed the two men to the tram car. Its bench seats were half filled with passengers who looked the newcomers over carefully, then offered smiles of greeting. Sutton loaded their belongings while Theo took Cathy's hand.

"Don't worry, you'll see me again soon. I'll do anything I can to help you, so you mustn't hesitate to send word to the hotel if you have need of assistance."

"Thank you. I can't tell you how much your friendship means to me." In spite of her sadness at their parting, Cathy gave him a warm smile.

"That's what I like to see, my lady. You'll charm the entire island."

"Time passing, sir," the conductor prodded. "Climb aboard, please."

"Take care," Theo said.

"Goodbye!" cried Sutton as they rolled away toward the swing bridge that spanned the harbor basin known as the Careenage.

Cathy found that she could only wave at first, for there were tears in her throat. Then, before they were out of earshot, she found her voice. "Good luck! I'll miss you!"

Adam came up and put an arm around her waist. "You've only known them a few days. Is your friendship really so strong?"

"Perhaps it's just that I am in a place where I don't know anyone else, except you, of course." How could she explain to him that not only had Theo felt like an old friend from the moment they met, but also that she was secretly anxious about being left alone with Adam in this utterly foreign place?

"Don't worry," he said, "you'll have plenty to distract you at Tempest Hall. In the meantime, I thought we might go to the Ice House for a bit of refreshment. My inquiries have unearthed the information that Simon isn't here at all. He expects us to take the schooner to north to Speightstown, where he's waiting, but the next one doesn't leave for nearly an hour. Let's have a swizzle."

She smiled up at him. "I have no idea what you're talking about, but it sounds like my cup of tea."

"Swizzles are a far cry from tea," he replied with an ironically arched brow.

The Ice House turned out to be not only the supply source for Bridgetown's domestic ice, but also a popular meeting place by virtue of its downstairs shops and upstairs restaurant.

"Are we going to have a meal?" Cathy inquired, looking around curiously as Adam guided her up to a spacious room with windows open to admit the balmy trade winds. Their table was surrounded by easy chairs, and the sounds of relaxed conversation hummed on the warm air. Alice settled down next to Cathy's chair and resumed her nap.

"The last time I checked, there wasn't anything worth eating here except for flying fish. Are you hungry?"

"Not very." She watched, consumed with curiosity, as he ordered two swizzles and a bowl of iced water for Alice. "I've never heard of flying fish."

"I don't know if you'll find them anywhere except Barbados. They're small, but delicious."

"Swizzles aren't fish, are they?" she asked, but he only laughed in response.

Soon, their waiter brought two drinks on a tray. When Cathy asked what was in hers, he grinned and replied, "Jus' a bit of rum, ma'am. Also lime, sugar, an' some bitters. We whisk wit' de swizzle stick." The waiter demonstrated with the four-pronged stick that protruded from her glass, rolling it between his palms. The drink frothed invitingly. "Do enjoy, ma'am!"

"Thank you," she replied. "It looks very refreshing."

Adam watched as his bride took her first thirsty swallow. "Be careful. It's stronger than it tastes."

"It's delicious! Do we drink these all the time on Barbados?"

"If we do, we don't get anything done." His eyes gleamed with amusement as he watched her nose turn pink.

"What do we have to get done, for heaven's sake? There aren't any tennis courts or polo fields, and I don't see anyone out riding horses, and there certainly isn't anywhere to shop. What else is there to do but sit under a fan, read, and drink swizzles?"

"You might be surprised."

"I suppose I should have realized. I mean, Barbados is an island, after all, and this is the West Indies." Pausing, she sighed. "I haven't seen one motor car. Perhaps that's just as well since the streets are dirt..."

"All right," Adam conceded, "it's true that Barbados is far behind America—and probably miles behind your lifestyle in Newport. If I'd known that you cared for it so much, I might have made a better effort to prepare you. However, I seem to remember you telling me that you despised your old routine—the tennis games, the polo matches, the Worth gowns. Did I misunderstand?"

As he leaned toward her, the cynical tone of his voice cut through the haze created by her swizzle. She tried to focus. "No. I thought that was the way I felt. It was the way I felt. Feel." She hiccupped. "Can I have another swizzle?"

"I don't think that's a good idea."

"I promise not to complain about Barbados. I just felt homesick for a moment, but now it's over."

"Cathy, you're half-drunk already and you still have some left. Just—" He broke off at the sight of one of his island acquaintances bearing down on their table. "Oh, God."

"Well, well, if it isn't the esteemed Viscount Raveneau!" the fellow cried. "Good to see you, old man! When did you get back? Gadzooks, here's your old Labrador. Hard to believe she's still alive."

"Alice doesn't know she's old, Basil, so I'll thank you to mind your manners." After a further exchange of pleasantries, Adam gestured toward Cathy. "Basil Lightfoot, I'd like you to meet my new bride, Catherine Parrish Raveneau."

"Bride, you say?" Wide-eyed, the six-foot-four-inch Lightfoot knelt next to Cathy's chair, giving her her first clear look at him. His horsey, sunburned face wore an expression of utter shock. "My lady, your husband has gotten the better of me this day. I'm honored to make the acquaintance of the woman who brought this notorious stallion into the barn!"

"It's a pleasure to meet you, Mr. Lightfoot." Cathy was relieved to hear that the swizzle had not garbled her speech.

"Basil's ancestor, Xavier Crowe, was a pirate of sorts…and my grandfather's arch enemy," Adam remarked.

"Such a lot of nonsense!" Lightfoot exclaimed with a toss of his big head. "He was only my great-uncle, nothing to me. I'm far too gentle a soul to give any thought to old blood feuds."

"But didn't Crowe's Nest, his estate, pass to you a few years ago?"

"That drafty old pile? I couldn't have cared less! Sold it off last winter. Good riddance!"

Adam glanced over and saw Cathy sway slightly in her chair. "I don't mean to be rude, but we have to be going now. Simon is meeting us with the carriage."

"But, I thought—" She broke off at the sight of his warning look, aimed over the back of Basil Lightfoot's big head.

"We'll have to get together soon, all right?" Struggling to his feet, the fellow thumped Adam on the back. "You know, your marriage is going to be big news on this island. The women are going to be spitting mad that you didn't shop right here at home instead of going to the States for a wife. All they do is complain about how difficult it is to find a husband on Barbados!"

Cathy felt strange, hearing about all the island women who coveted Adam. Lifting her glass, she finished the swizzle. Why had she dreamed for so long of getting away from home? At that moment, she even missed her mother.

Adam was looming in front of her, taking the drink out of her hands. "Are you all right?"

"Of course. I'm fine!" She wished he would kiss her, or simply hold her close in his arms and reassure her that she need never be lonely or afraid as long as they were together.

"Christ, Cathy, pull yourself together. This room is full of Bajan society, and I'd prefer that they not carry tales of my intoxicated bride."

Her eyes stung, but she held her head up. Why had he given her that awful drink? Didn't he know how potent they were? Her head began to throb on one side as they went down the wooden stairs, followed closely by Alice, and emerged onto Broad Street. Everywhere there were new smells, dust, noise, voices speaking a part-English dialect that Cathy couldn't understand, people who looked different than those she'd known all her life, and unrelenting tropical heat. She was struggling to open her parasol when Adam cursed softly beside her.

"Hello, Adam."

The sound of a cultured female voice took Cathy's attention away from her parasol.

"Gemma," Adam said. "I didn't expect to see you. I don't think it's been even an hour since I set foot on Bajan soil."

"We women have a sixth sense when it comes to our men. That's lucky, don't you think, since I didn't receive a letter to tell me you were coming?"

Cathy felt as if she were invisible. Gemma, meanwhile, was very real. Exceedingly graceful and beautiful, the woman had a café-au-lait complexion, striking dark eyes, a full mouth, and elegant bone structure. She wore a crisp, lace-edged shirtwaist with a gold pin over one breast and an unwrinkled skirt. Cathy decided that Gemma possessed all the cool composure that she lacked.

"It's been such a long time," Adam was saying, "because of the quarantine...I'm glad to see that you're all right."

"Of course I am." Her eyes fixed on his. "So is my son."

He went pale under his tan. "Your—son?"

"Yes. You two haven't met. Paul was born a few months after you left Barbados, in 1901."

"Indeed? Well, congratulations. I'm sure he must be a very handsome child." Adam turned to Cathy, who had just slipped her hand through his arm. "There is a new addition to my life as well. Allow me to present Catherine, my wife. Cathy, this is Gemma Hart. She owns the Hart Hotel, located just across the street."

"It's a pleasure to meet you," Cathy said, smiling against her better instincts. "We have a new friend, Theo Harrismith, who has just arrived to manage the Ocean Breeze Hotel. Do you know it?"

Gemma laughed as she lightly took Cathy's hand in greeting. "I not only know that sad excuse for a hotel, but I know Theo as well. I certainly don't fear that competition!" She took a few steps past them, then glanced back at Adam. "My dear, I do hope you will pay me a visit when you can. I should like very much for you to meet little Paul."

His eyes were far away. "Yes. Of course."

Cathy's heart was pounding as never before while a chorus of worries and fears swirled round inside her. "Adam? Did you notice that your friend ignored dear Alice…?"

Chapter 13

"It occurs to me," Cathy finally dared to remark, "that I really don't know much about your past."

For a moment, their eyes met, then he looked away into another endless green cane field. What a long day it had been. From Bridgetown, they had boarded a schooner headed north through the aqua Caribbean Sea to Speightstown, where Simon, the son of an elderly family retainer, had been waiting with an open landau pulled by a pair of thin horses. Then they had started inland, bound for Tempest Hall, with Alice lying on the seat opposite Adam and Cathy. No matter how much Adam talked about various aspects of island life—such as green monkeys, fanciful bearded fig trees, and the fluctuating value of sugar cane—he could sense Cathy's thoughts.

Her worries, he supposed, weren't far off from his own. What the devil had Gemma been implying? Was it that her son was conceived before Adam had left Barbados in 1901, and that Paul was Adam's son, too?

The very thought, however fleeting, made his palms sweat. If it were true, then he was in more trouble than he'd ever imagined during the worst period of his gambling debts in England. Why couldn't Byron have minded his own business? At least, without Cathy on the scene, Adam's problems would be manageable.

"Are you ignoring me," Cathy asked now, "or simply at a loss for words?"

"You asked about my past, wasn't that it? I was just wondering how to begin. Did you want to hear about my childhood in Kent? My father, who was killed in an avalanche when I was twelve? The years I spent studying the law at Oxford?" He shrugged. "To be perfectly honest, my past is rather boring."

"Only to you, I'm sure," she replied with a touch of irony. Alice, who had been dozing with her chin resting on crossed paws, opened her eyes and took stock of the situation. Cathy leaned over to pet her silky head. "I wish Alice could talk to me. I'll wager that she could relate stories from your past that wouldn't be boring in the least."

He had to smile at that. "You must realize that that is exactly why I've had a dog rather than a human companion. I don't have to worry that Alice will have too much to drink one night and tell my secrets, the way Byron might easily do."

"That's why you didn't invite him to come to Barbados!"

Adam only laughed at that, then opened his collar, looking around as the carriage climbed a hill. The soil along the roadside was reddish-coral, the fields of cane plants were pale green, and the sky was a vivid shade of azure punctuated by puffs of clouds. Barely visible to the north were the rolling waves of the Atlantic Ocean, and for a few moments Adam and Cathy could see a village nestled at the base of lush, wind-swept hills.

"Do you see the tiny, bright-colored houses?" Adam asked, pointing.

Cathy nodded. The little cottages were everywhere, marching along the roads, clustered in towns, popping up unexpectedly in cane fields. She thought that they looked too small to be real houses, but often there were goats tied in front and old folks peeking out through half-open shutters. The tiny dwellings were painted fantastic colors like cobalt blue, mango, lime green, hibiscus pink, or turquoise, and they were crowned by roofs of corrugated metal.

"They're called chattel houses," Adam explained, "because when Barbadian slaves were emancipated, they weren't allowed to own land. The chattel houses became their possessions; they can be dismantled and moved by ox-cart to a new location."

"I never dreamed it would be so different here," she murmured again. "It really is a different world from New England."

"I know." A roguish smile lit his face. "I love it. I think that Barbados is the best place on earth."

Looking at Adam, Cathy thought wistfully that if he would draw her into the circle of his embrace, she would feel less lonely and out of place. Finally, she worked up the nerve to whisper, "Don't you ever feel...nervous, being white when nearly everyone else is black? My mother would be quite terrified."

"My feelings and your mother's rarely are the same on any subject," he replied sardonically. "I try to judge the people on this island by their characters."

Suddenly, Simon spoke up from his driver's perch, causing Cathy to jump in surprise and embarrassment. He'd been so quiet, she'd forgotten he might be listening to them. "M'lady, you do get use to we wit' time. We all need patience, I t'ink." Simon turned back then, bestowing an encouraging smile on his mistress and giving Adam a quick, meaningful glance.

"Thank you, Simon," she said. "That was a very understanding observation."

"Change take time, ma'am."

Leaning back in the upholstered seat, Adam propped his feet up by Alice's tail and lit a thin cigar. "Simon's been at Tempest Hall as long as I can remember. How many years is it, Simon?"

"I born dere, sir, in 1845. We do see many t'ing change over all dese year, but Tempest Hall still in de Rav'neau family an' we still dere." His smile faded before he added, "Plantation need work, sir. You goin' to stay dis time?"

"Yes, of course. You know, Simon, I would have returned much sooner if not for the smallpox epidemic. The island was quarantined."

Lips pursed, he nodded slowly and loosened the reins. "I guess I forget why you had to leave at all?"

"As I recall, I had matters to attend to in Kent." Adam fell silent. Somehow he sensed that Simon knew he'd left Barbados simply because he'd grown bored and wanted to return to London for a round of gambling and wenching. Tempest Hall had needed so much care, and Adam had felt weighed down by the responsibility. "I was here only for a visit the last time. I never meant to stay permanently then."

"Tempest Hall need a master to care for it." Simon shook his head again. "Since Mistress Adrienne die, nobody in charge, an' you know de plantation goin' to pieces long ago, even before de money she leave us run out."

Adam wished he had a drink. What a miserable excuse for a man he was! Not only had he gambled away his own estate in England, he hadn't bothered to stay in touch with the servants at Tempest Hall. Of course, he couldn't have sent them any money even if he had written. Until his settlement with Jules Parrish, the only possession of value Adam had left was his title.

Cathy spoke up then. "Was Mistress Adrienne your grandmother, Adam? Didn't you tell me that she came here with your grandfather in 1818? How could she have still been alive so recently?"

"Gran lived to be ninety-nine. I think she died early in 1897." He exhaled cigar smoke, his eyes far away. "She was an amazing lady, wasn't she, Simon?"

"Very, very fine," he confirmed. "We all do miss her. We feel Mistress Adrienne's spirit, wishin' dat you come home and take care of Tempest Hall. She hope dat even when she alive."

"I get your point, Simon," Adam snapped. "I feel every bit as guilty as you'd like, so you needn't say any more about it. I'm home now; home to stay. Better still, I've brought a wife! Even Gran, if she is indeed watching over us in spirit, could not ask more of me."

Simon pressed his lips together and shook the reins. "Mmm hm."

The closer they got to Tempest Hall, the more Cathy felt as if she'd fallen into an exotic, timeless world that had no connection to anything familiar. Passing hot cane fields and abandoned, thatch-roofed slave huts, she shivered. It seemed she could hear a whispered message of blood, gold, and the broken dreams of African people who had once been torn from their homeland and enslaved.

A pair of monkeys capered across the narrow, weed-choked road. "This part of the island isn't very well populated," Adam explained. "We'll have to do some work on the roads. The best ones are paved with crushed coral stone."

Cathy nearly remarked that it was lucky her dowry was large enough to encompass public works, but she bit her tongue instead. It wouldn't improve her shaky marriage if she put her finger on that sore spot. No matter how careful she and Adam both were to avoid talking about money, his outburst that day on the *Free Spirit* was imprinted on her memory.

Something else he'd said that day came back to her then; something she'd discounted and pushed aside. Adam had told her that men had darker secrets than women. Cathy had assumed he was trying to shock her, but now she thought of Gemma Hart and a cold chill swept over her.

"It's time for you to come back from wherever you've gone," he whispered. Something in her eyes caused him to take her chin between his thumb and forefinger and kiss her, slowly and deeply. "We've just turned down the drive to Tempest Hall."

The taste of him and the texture of his tanned cheek replaced her chill with a surge of sensuality. "I'm excited to see our home, Adam." Holding his hand, she leaned forward and looked out. They were emerging from a shadowy mahogany forest onto a hilltop from which they could see the crumbling buildings of the plantation below. There were giant windmills, a sugar boiling house, a water catchment tank, and an empty mule pen. The surrounding fields, which swept all the way to the island's north coast, were barren except for weeds.

"Simon!" Adam barked. "The place looks like the devil!"

"Very true, sir," he agreed. "Since dere no money, we t'ink you lucky that we stay at all."

Cathy squeezed her husband's hand. "He has a point."

His face grew darker as they started down the drive. The hedges of sweet lime that bordered the lane were now so overgrown with vines and wild poinsettias that the landau could scarcely fit. Up ahead, Cathy saw palm trees and a battered stucco wall. When they finally reached the gates leading to the house and gardens, she didn't know whether to laugh or cry.

Tempest Hall looked nothing like the romantic estate she'd imagined. Its Jacobean design featured an arcaded veranda supporting an upstairs balcony, above which towered three curved gables and four chimneys.

"It used to be a splendid place," Adam said, his own voice shadowed by sadness and anger. "It's been standing since 1650, you know."

Cathy's gaze traveled from the broken tile roof to the cracked windows to the last remnants of white paint that clung to the gray coral-stone exterior of the house. "It will be splendid again."

When Adam had climbed down from the landau and lifted Cathy out to stand beside him, he felt waves of rage surge through his body. "My grandmother would be furious with me for allowing this to happen. And my grandfather...I can't even bear to think of him now. This plantation was his life."

Wood doves cooed from nearby tamarind trees. Cathy went ahead, through the broken gates, toward the rectangular gardens that were laid out in front of the house. "Adam, you mustn't be so hard on yourself. At least you are here now, and together we'll put

Tempest Hall back on its feet. Start by telling me what used to be here."

He pointed to the north. "That's the kitchen garden. I see that the servants have kept it up, at least enough to feed themselves." Walking forward, Adam stared at the plots on the other side of the house. "Those were flower gardens, planted lovingly by Gran, and in the distance was the herb garden. She used to call it the Knot Garden because of the designs." He started toward the house then. "There was a rose garden as well, with an arbor where my grandparents were married. I used to play there as a child. It's a strong memory, along with the guinea fowl. Do you hear them, making that squeaky sound? They're still scratching about, in back by the sandbox tree. I would go to sleep listening to them, and that was the first sound I heard when I awoke each morning."

Cathy saw two of the hens on the gravel walkway nearby and stared at them in wonder. "Don't they ever quiet down?"

"You'll get used to it. It's rather like the sound of the waves hitting the cliffs in Newport. One doesn't hear it after a while."

Before she could reply, Simon appeared, carrying Adam's luggage. "I bring a cart for de lady's trunk," he said, then added, "Sir, you go inside. Retta waitin' for you."

Seeing Adam brighten, Cathy feared the worst. Was she about to encounter another woman from his past? "Who is Retta?"

"Come with me and you'll find out." He took her hand and led her through the gallery encircling the house, with Alice following slowly behind. Passing through glass doors, Cathy found herself in a dim, musty sitting room. Her first impression was of faded lime-green paint, wide-board floors that needed cleaning, tall deep windows framed by peeling jalousie shutters, and Georgian furniture.

"It's very…impressive," she said.

"I know it's nothing compared to any of your family's homes, but it does have character. I wish you could have seen it when my grandmother was alive."

"We'll renew its charm. Look at this furniture! It's beautiful!

Adam wandered over and ran his hand along the back of a rocking chair. "It's all made of Barbadian mahogany, and the cane seats and backs have been woven by hand." He gestured toward the adjacent dining room which was furnished with a magnificent Sheraton sideboard, table, and cane-seated chairs. "Those pieces date back to the late eighteenth century. They were here when Grandfather purchased the plantation."

Another voice spoke from the doorway. "Not de sideboard, sir. It does come from family house in Connet'cut."

"Retta! It's wonderful to see you." Wearing a wide smile, Adam went to greet the tiny woman who stood with the aid of a walking stick in each hand. Fluffy bits of white hair showed from under the kerchief tied around her head, and her snowy apron fairly shone in the dim light.

"I t'ink you never come back, sir." Adjusting her spectacles, she smiled up at him. "You look more like Captain Rav'neau than ever. You grown into some fine good looks."

"Flatterer." He kissed her withered cheek. "Retta, I'd like you to meet my new bride, Catherine. She comes from America." Holding out his free hand, Adam welcomed Cathy into their circle and watched as the two women exchanged warm, if uncertain, greetings. "Retta was here on the day my grandparents came together to Tempest Hall. They weren't even married then, were they, Retta? And how old were you?"

"Still a girl. Fourteen? Who can 'member such t'ings?"

Adam laughed and met Cathy's eyes. "That was in 1818!"

"Oh my goodness!"

"You never see a lady so old, hmm?" Retta asked playfully, then looked back at Adam. "Time for dis ole woman to rest. You don't need me to show you 'round."

"No, of course not. Will you let me help you?" He watched as she shook her head proudly and tottered off toward the maid's room at the back of the house. "Retta? I almost forgot to ask—what other servants are still here?"

She glanced back. "Only Simon's gran'daughter, June, come t' help me."

Trying not to betray his shock, Adam said, "No one else?"

"De others do leave last year, during smallpox time. No money to feed dem, an' most have fam'ly sick."

"I had no idea. Is June able to be Cathy's maid?"

Retta pursed her lips doubtfully. "She may try, but she jus' a child."

When they were alone, Adam slammed his fist against the wall. "If I'd known what we were coming home to, I would have encouraged you to bring Isobel."

"I don't think Isobel would have adjusted very well," she said with a wry smile. "I think it's best that we didn't bring anyone else from Beechcliff. I have enough adjustments of my own to make without worrying about them." Seeing the stark look in his eyes, Cathy added, "Don't worry. We're here now, and we can restore Tempest Hall to her former glory. Money isn't an object any longer."

Adam arched a brow as he watched a huge cockroach scurry across the shadowed stairhall. "No…money isn't an object and neither is my pride."

Chapter 14

Cathy stood, dust cloth and furniture polish in hand, and stared at the small portrait of Adrienne Raveneau that hung in Adam's dressing room. June watched her from the doorway.

"That's the old mistress, isn't it?" the girl asked. "I've seen that big portrait of her in the dining room."

"I've been trying not to look at it," Cathy said ruefully.

"Why not?"

"Because she's so much more beautiful than I am."

June made no reply, but stared at her mistress, who was looking remarkably common in her long apron and rolled-up sleeves. Retta had shown her how to fasten the kerchief Bajans called a "headtie," and now Cathy wore one to keep her hair clean when she was working in the house. Rosy-cheeked and bright-eyed, she looked more like a girl June's age than the wife of rakish Lord Raveneau.

"June," she said now with a crooked smile, "you might at least be polite and argue with me."

"Argue?"

"Yes—insist that I am mistaken, that I'm every bit as beautiful as Adrienne was!"

"Oh." The girl's brown skin flushed darker. "I didn't know I was allowed to argue with you, ma'am."

"A very tactful reply!" Laughing, she took another look at Adrienne's sparkling green eyes and chestnut curls, then regarded her own reflection in her husband's shaving mirror. Her turned-up nose was smudged with dirt, her eyes were a traditional brown, and she was too petite to be elegant. No wonder Adam had suggested, upon their arrival a week earlier, that it would be more civilized for them to have separate bedrooms. And no wonder he had made no effort to come to her bed yet.

As if reading Cathy's mind, June came up to peek over her shoulder. "I think you're a very pretty lady, ma'am. My teacher tells us that what's inside is more important, though, and we shouldn't waste time fretting about that package we're wrapped in. She says if a person is happy and kind and brave, that will show through on her face and she'll be better than pretty."

Tears misted her eyes. "Your teacher is a very wise lady."

"I miss school," June replied, nodding. "I've been reading the books in the master's library since I came here, but I worry that I'll fall behind."

"Then we'll have to see to it that other servants come here to work so that you can go back to your family and back to school, at least during the week. How old are you, June?"

"Thirteen. I want to go to college and be a teacher."

"Goodness, I had that same dream! Do you know, I even passed the entrance examinations for Radcliffe College…"

"Why didn't you go, then?"

"My mother had other plans for me," Cathy said with a bittersweet smile.

"She wanted you to go to Tempest Hall instead of Radcliffe? I can hardly believe that!"

"Not exactly. She wanted me to marry a duke, but I met Lord Raveneau and...you might say I upset my mother's applecart." Cathy started dusting again, afraid of what June might ask next. "We'd better get back to work, or we'll be here all day."

It was four o'clock when Adam returned from an overnight excursion to Bridgetown. He'd purchased supplies and ice, new horses and farming equipment, and had arranged for repairs to begin on the roof. Part of him felt relieved to be restoring Tempest Hall's dignity, but it pained him more to be spending Jules Parrish's money.

Adam left his new horse, a stallion he'd christened Lazarus, in the stables. Walking through the yard to the standpipe that was Tempest Hall's source of freshwater, he rolled up his sleeves, opened his collar, and proceeded to wash his hands and face. When he finished, Simon had emerged from the house with a towel.

"Mistress sends me," he said, smiling.

"Did she tell you to make me a rum punch as well?"

"Of course, sir. De rum punch waitin' in de library."

Adam wished Cathy weren't so damned good at taking care of him; it made him feel even angrier. Raking his hands through his wet black hair, he walked up the back steps into the kitchen where Retta was sitting in her rocking chair.

"Tomorrow, there will be a delivery from the Ice House, as well as supplies from Fairchild Street Market," he told her.

"Mistress be pleased to hear it."

"Retta, I know you're not as strong as you used to be, but I'm trusting you to oversee this household. Cathy doesn't know the first thing about running a house. Her family is obscenely wealthy, and she's been badly spoiled. Now then, what's for supper?"

"I tell Mistress how to make ox tail stew and she does put it in de pot. I watching it." She gave him a broad smile. "I don' know if it right or not, but she do try hard."

Adam took the lid off the pot and tasted the contents with a wooden spoon. It was astonishingly good. Feeling Retta's shrewd gaze, he muttered, "It needs salt, and more rum, I think. She has a long way to go to match your cooking skills, Retta."

"But she do try hard," she repeated. "You know, sir, when you come up dose steps, I go back to years when de Captain do look jus' like you, an' he come up steps de same way."

"He was nicer than I am, though."

"I see dat little smile, sir!" She reached out and poked at his booted leg. "An' I can tell you dat you gran'father not always so nice. When he young, he jus' like you." Retta paused for effect. "Take him a long time to admit how much he love he wife."

"Indeed? How odd that you should mention it." He glanced at her, blue-gray eyes narrowed. "This conversation is making me thirsty. I believe I'll drink my rum punch and leave you to watch the pot."

"Mistress do be cleaning, upstairs."

"Did I ask?" Frowning, Adam left the kitchen. The house was cool and quiet, no longer musty but well-aired and scented with island flowers and lemon furniture polish. A slight breeze wafted through the gallery while, through the doors to his library, Adam could see a tall rum punch waiting for him on the table next to his planter's chair. He sat down, pulled off his boots, put up his feet, and drank. Minutes passed. Closing his eyes, Adam soon found himself unable to nap because of a barely audible sound on the floor above. He took his drink and went up the white Chinese Chippendale staircase to investigate.

"Woof!" Tail wagging, Alice came out of his dressing room and crossed the bedroom floor to greet him.

Adam crouched beside her, petted her head, and muttered, "Traitor. You knew I was home, but you couldn't muster the energy to leave Cathy's side." Alice licked his hand. "No, no, don't deny it; I know it's true."

He followed the Labrador then, in his bare feet and riding pants, to the dressing room door. When his eyes adjusted to the dim light, he saw what appeared to be two servants wearing aprons and headties, on their hands and knees in the far corner of the room.

"Excuse me." Adam assumed an authoritative tone. "May I inquire what the devil you two are doing? And who are you? When I left yesterday, June was the only serving girl in the house."

"Hello, Adam."

He stared as his pink-cheeked wife got to her feet. "Cathy! I knew you were insisting on doing work yourself, but not dressed like that!"

"I'm just trying to stay clean in the midst of the dust and grime." She waved a hand dismissively. "Since we don't have indoor plumbing, I get tired of washing my hair. Please don't fuss any more about it. You're scaring June!"

It galled him to be scolded in front of a servant, but Alice had rushed over to Cathy's side, tail wagging, and he felt outnumbered. "May I ask again what is going on? We swept out that corner before I unpacked my shoes."

Her eyes brightened. "I've just found something terribly exciting and I can't wait to show you!" Turning to June, she put a hand on her arm. "Will you please go downstairs and help Retta with supper? And I'd be very grateful if you would set the table."

Adam felt even odder as he recognized the glowing expression on June's face. She adored her new mistress—and she was scared of him. For God's sake, whose house was it? No sooner had the girl hurried from the dressing room than Cathy motioned to him to join her.

"Look what I've found."

"You're not going to get me to crawl around on the floor."

"You've been riding and your trousers are already dirty. Just kneel down here for a moment."

Reluctantly, Adam obeyed, just in time to see a millipede slither by and disappear under the baseboard. Cathy's nearness was also unnerving. She smelled of fresh lavender and when she leaned forward to touch the paneled wall, her breasts swelled against the fabric of her shirtwaist.

"Look." She pressed against the wall until it made a clicking sound, as if a catch had loosened. A panel shifted back slightly and Cathy moved it on a hinge so that a hidden compartment about four feet square was exposed. "Can you believe it?"

He wanted to reprimand her for digging around in his family's secrets but it would be too mean. Wasn't she part of his family now? The thought made his head hurt. "I suppose you've already searched all the contents?"

"No. I waited for you." She gave him a winsome smile. "But it wasn't easy!"

"No doubt."

Ignoring his tone, Cathy reached toward the wall. "May I?"

When she moved farther forward, he saw her tiny feet peek out from under her skirt. "May I ask what you are wearing on your feet?"

"You certainly can think of a lot of silly questions. They're ballet slippers, left over from my dancing class years. Just the thing to wear when one is climbing all over a West Indian plantation house."

Adam heard himself laugh, then bit his lip when she glanced back at him. Together they removed what appeared to be ships' logs imprinted in gold with NR, his grandfather's initials, and a rolled-up sheaf of stained parchment. When they brought the items into his bedroom, he put the logbooks on his desk and Cathy sat down on a nearby mahogany chaise, cradling the tattered roll of paper. Alice stretched out on the Turkish rug and began, gently, to snore in the sunlight that filtered through the shutters behind them.

Adam ran his hand over the dark blue leather of the nearest ship's log. "I recognize these. They're my grandfather's journals, begun during his years at sea. When I was very young, I watched him sit at this very desk and write in the newer one."

"I suppose you'd like to preserve his privacy?"

"For the moment."

"May I untie this string?" She pointed to the rolled paper.

Adam moved over to sit beside her and nodded. In the next moment, they were both looking at an old, handmade map. Attached to one side was a folded piece of writing paper with Adam's name written on it. He took it, turned it from Cathy's view, and read it.

"Well?" She couldn't help herself. "This looks so exciting! What does it say?"

"It's from my grandmother, dated 1895. She writes that the map was purported to have been made by Stede Bonnet."

"Stede Bonnet? The pirate you were meant to be at my ball? What a coincidence!" Cathy pointed to the bottom corner of the map where the words 'Bonnet, 1718' were inscribed. "This is amazing! What else does your grandmother say?"

"She reports that the map came to them from Xavier Crowe in 1818, through someone called Huntsford Harms. Crowe was the arch-enemy of my grandfather, who therefore was convinced that the map was counterfeit. Gran, however, had other suspicions. Crowe apparently told Harms that Bonnet buried this treasure near the time of his capture, when he was trying to elude both Blackbeard, who had been his partner, and the authorities. Gran saved the map, hoping that a descendant would share her curiosity."

Cathy watched him fold the letter in half and get to his feet. "And are you?" she ventured. "Curious?"

"You must be joking." He began to strip off his clothes, walking into the dressing room, and his voice carried out to her. "Before I forget, I wanted to tell you that I found a new housemaid for you who arrives tomorrow. Her name is Liza and she's eighteen. She's been working in one of the hotels in Bridgetown, so she ought to have enough experience to be of some real use."

Reeling from the sight of his lean-muscled legs and tapering back, Cathy fought an urge to go after him and put her arms around him. "I'm glad to hear it, Adam, but what about the treasure map? It's Stede Bonnet, after all—the person you were masquerading as the night we met! Doesn't that map pique your spirit of adventure?"

He reappeared in the doorway, fastening a collarless shirt that was white as snow against his tanned face. "Catherine, do I have to spell this out? The map is counterfeit, a creation of Xavier Crowe. I heard about it from Grandfather when I was a boy. Crowe devised the map to distract his English houseguest, Harms, from the real crimes he was committing. The fellow was soon busy digging holes all over the beach at Cave Bay! I would be as big a fool as he if I wasted one more moment thinking about it, let alone believing that there is treasure to be found!"

Rising, Cathy went past him in search of her own fresh clothing. "I have asked that you not call me Catherine."

"May I make a request of my own? Take off that headtie. Your own hair is much more becoming."

"Has anyone ever told you that you're a brute?"

"Frequently. And as I recall, I warned you of that very fact."

When they came down the Chinese Chippendale staircase for supper, with Alice trundling behind them,

Adam and Cathy appeared to be a comfortably married couple.

"May I pour a glass of sherry for you?" he asked.

"That would be lovely."

Cathy felt very lonely. Her heart ached as she wandered down the long gallery, listening to the tree frogs begin to chirp. Even the air smelled different here: damp, green, and salty. With each passing day, she felt farther from home.

Adam had just come in carrying her sherry and his planter's punch when Cathy spied a horse outside Tempest Hall's gates.

"Oh my goodness! A visitor!" Her face lit up.

"Probably a deadly dull neighbor coming to nose around for gossip."

"I don't think so…" Cathy went to the front of the gallery for a better view. Standing on tiptoe, she saw a man leading a horse into the overgrown garden. "It's Theo!"

"Who the devil is *Theo*?"

"Theo Harrismith. How quickly my ill-tempered husband forgets." With that, Cathy hurried out to meet her friend, ignoring the dust her cream silk skirt threw up as she rushed down the pathway.

At the sight of her, Theo swept off his boater and bowed low, eyes twinkling. "You honor me, my lady."

"Don't talk nonsense. Stop bowing! Oh, Theo, I can't tell you how happy I am to see a friend!"

His face fell. "That bad, eh? I was hoping for a better report, though I confess I feared the worst."

"May I hug you?" She savored the affectionate contact, resting her cheek on his shoulder for a moment before stepping back. Her fingers clung to his. "Tell me what brings you to Tempest Hall."

"Truthfully, I was visiting a friend nearby at Farley Hill and decided to pay you a visit to invite you to the Ocean Breeze Hotel tomorrow for luncheon."

Delighted, Cathy replied, "May I bring my bathing costume? I've been longing to swim in the ocean, but Adam has put me off so far." She made a little moue. "I used to go every day to Bailey's Beach in Newport, you know, and I miss that."

"Absolutely. We have the finest bath houses on the south coast, you know. Hastings is the coming place to holiday." He took a small, hand-drawn map out of his coat pocket. "Can you find someone to bring you? I'd fetch you myself, but I have already missed so much work today."

"Don't worry; I'll be there at noon. I can't wait to see the hotel. And Sutton! How is he?"

"Fine, but counting every penny and worrying as usual—" Theo broke off at the sight of Adam Raveneau emerging from the house and advancing toward them. "Here comes your husband with a storm cloud over his head." His eyes moved on to survey the peeling paint and broken tiles. "Looks to me as if his grand estate leaves a bit to be desired!"

"Catherine," Adam said from a distance, "dinner is being served." In response to her sharp look, he approached and put out his hand to the intruder. "Hello, Harrismith. I'm rather surprised to see you so far from Hastings."

"I was just inviting Cathy—I mean, her ladyship— to pay us a visit at the hotel. I thought the change of scenery might do her good." While shaking the other man's strong hand, Theo called on his better nature. "Of course, you are invited as well, Lord Raveneau. No doubt you two are still on your honeymoon and don't wish to be parted."

"I'm sure," interjected Cathy, "that my husband is far too busy with the plantation."

Adam managed to breathe normally with an effort. "My wife is right. However, I trust that you'll keep her safe for me?"

Pinned under Raveneau's rapier gaze, Theo grinned. "My lord, could you possibly think otherwise?"

Moments later, Adam had dismissed the intruder and was leading Cathy back to the house. "Supper will be cold. There's nothing worse than cold oxtail stew."

She was fuming. "Kindly release my arm!"

Suddenly, Adam was nearly overcome with an urge to press her against the porch wall and have his way with her. Instead, he let go of her arm.

Cathy turned to face him. "You are unpardonably rude! How could you have treated my friend that way?"

"Friend? Friend?" God, how he wanted to brand her with his kiss, to tear away her clothing and possess her. "Never mind. Let's go inside and eat."

Marching after him, she cried, "I'm not finished!"

"I suggest, then, that we continue this conversation—or argument, whichever it is—after supper, in the privacy of our rooms upstairs. All right?"

Her heart began to race and, involuntarily, she raised a hand to her breast. "If you insist, sir."

Chapter 15

"It's good, isn't it?" Cathy challenged in an undertone.

"The stew?" He lifted both brows. "For a first effort, it's not bad."

"That is not what I asked!"

"All right then." Leaning in toward his wife, Adam looked deeply into her eyes. "It's good. You may have talents heretofore unknown to me."

She blushed to the roots of her hair and took a last bite of okra slices mixed with tomatoes. "We're having nut cake for dessert. Retta made it herself."

"Have some more wine."

She stared at his long, handsome fingers as he lifted the bottle. "Thank you."

Candles flickered inside hurricane lamps, illuminating the priceless Coalport china. A bouquet of plumeria lent its exotic fragrance to the air. Adam looked rakishly handsome and Cathy felt the electricity spark between them again. Ever since they'd arrived on the island, it seemed as if he'd turned an inner switch, shutting off that part of himself, but now it had unmistakably flared to life again…

"I don't care for any nut cake," Adam said. "Let's go upstairs."

"To argue?"

A smile touched his mouth. "Perhaps."

As she watched him take the nearly full bottle of wine and gesture for her to precede him up the stairs, Cathy knew that she ought to be glad to sense his passion, but she wasn't. Unsettled and excited, yes, but her pride wanted more from him.

"Adam?"

"Yes...?" Reaching the upper corridor, he steered her into his bedroom.

"You needn't be jealous of Theo, you know."

"Jealous! That's ridiculous. I've never been jealous in my life."

Cathy was sorry to see his light, if slightly smug mood being replaced by more storm clouds. Still, he did look terribly handsome when his brow gathered and the line of his jaw hardened. "You've never been jealous? Aren't you human?"

The cloud passed. A predatory gleam crept into his eyes. "You know better than to ask such a question." Circling around behind her, he flicked open the hooks closing Cathy's dog-collar necklace and kissed the soft, sweet flesh beneath the strands of pearls. "You know very well that I am human."

Shivers ran down her back, and she wanted nothing more than to melt backward into his waiting arms. "But—but, Adam, if you aren't jealous of Theo—"

"I don't want to talk about him anymore."

"What is it, then? Why have you been treating me so badly?"

"I don't know what you're talking about - or why we must talk at all now." His hand crept around her waist, drawing her in. "What have I done that's so terrible?"

"It isn't one thing; it's your attitude toward me. You behave as if I'm a burden, or an annoyance…"

Adam loosened her tortoiseshell hairpins and let down her long curls. "Mmm. Your hair smells lovely. How could I be annoyed by you?"

"You know what I mean." With an effort, she turned her face away from his gently questing lips. "If everything is fine between us, why are we in separate bedrooms, and why haven't you come to me even once since we arrived here?"

"I thought you expected separate bedrooms. Your parents have them, don't they?" His fingers were so deft with the fastenings on her gown that he opened the back before she even knew what was happening. "I've been too busy, too worried about the plantation." His mouth grazed the hollow beneath her ear. "I'm sorry."

When he turned her in his arms, Cathy felt her resolve melting away. Raveneau's face, shadowed in the soft light from oil lamps, was so splendidly male that her heart hurt to look at him.

"I'm sorry," he repeated huskily. "Is that what you need to hear?"

She knew that his excuses were hollow; much more than simple thoughtlessness had come between them since their arrival at Tempest Hall. But her mother's voice echoed in her ears: "You'll have to yield to him— it's your duty as a wife!" And, Cathy did long to be back in his arms again. If she turned him away, it might drive an irretrievable wedge between them.

She let her cheek rest against his chest and nearly sighed aloud. "If you're sorry, will that change matters in the future?"

"You're making this awfully complicated," he replied. "Who can say what the future holds? I do know how I feel tonight. I've missed you, Cath."

"Oh, I've missed you, too." Elated, she stood on tiptoe as he lifted her up to meet his kiss. It was thrilling to open her mouth to him, to taste him again, to feel the hard imprint of his body against her own. "I've felt so alone—"

Adam didn't hear her. He was too busy reclaiming what belonged to him, and realizing how long it had been since they'd been together. What had been wrong with him? At that moment, he couldn't imagine.

In the middle of the night, Cathy sat up in bed, fully awake. Her heart was pounding. Where was she? Moonlight illumined a room of grand proportions, its deep windows wearing shutters that pushed out from the bottom. The humid breeze that stirred the mosquito netting around her bed evoked nothing of Newport, and even the distant ocean had a foreign rhythm.

Barbados.

Yes, she was living in Barbados now. But this wasn't her usual, solitary room. This towering mahogany four-poster bed belonged to Adam.

Her husband.

Glancing down, Cathy saw that she was naked. As she reached to cover herself, her eyes strayed to the next pillow, where Adam Raveneau was sprawled in all his considerable glory, the white sheet twisted around one powerful thigh. His breathing reminded her of the purr of a jungle cat.

Slowly, Cathy's vague sense of alarm was offset by euphoria. Why should she feel out of place? She was in her husband's bed, after lovemaking. It was only right. Perhaps her new life as Lady Raveneau was falling into place at last. Lying back, she regarded Adam's moonlit face and wished it were easier for her to relax with him. Even in sleep he seemed mysterious. Unreachable.

She touched his dark hair with her fingertips. Adam stirred. Her hand moved down to his chest. Cathy loved the crisp, soft hair there that contrasted with the firm warmth of his skin. His body was intoxicating to her, but she was afraid to let him know it, and afraid to let herself explore more freely.

Afraid to open herself completely during lovemaking, for fear she'd lose control...and—what? Shock him? Give him some kind of secret, sexual power over her? Cathy held her breath, heart beating hard. Maybe, she thought, a door might open inside her soul and then only Adam would hold the key...

How could she let that happen when he didn't love her?

"Mmm." He rolled toward her.

She looked at his eyelashes, the shape of his cheekbones, the shadows at the base of his flat belly. There was a line of hair that seemed to point to the most masculine part of him. She heard herself sigh.

Slowly then, his eyes opened just a fraction and he watched her. His hand reached for her wrist, moved it down until her fingers touched him. He was astonishingly erect again.

"Looking for something?" he whispered in a sleep-husky voice.

Cathy nearly protested her innocence, but his gaze was so knowing and so irresistible that she smiled instead and went into his embrace. Oh, he smelled so good. Each time he held her hard against him, she wished she could drink him like water. As it was, her thirst was never quenched. While the mosquito netting whispered in the soft breeze, she soaked up sensation. Adam's kiss was full of heat and urgency and so were his hands as they roamed over her naked body, searching out her pleasure zones. Somehow he understood just what she needed most, although she couldn't have asked herself.

Was it a dream? Cathy closed her eyes, aching. Adam's warm mouth was at her nipple, working the pink crest just so, until waves of bliss carried her up, set her down, and lifted her again. She sank her fingers into his hair, moaning, and he made a low, primitive sound in response. When she looked down, she was struck by the contrast between his tanned, chiseled body and her own pale, moonlit flesh.

"Shh," he murmured, encouraged by her abandon.

Cathy closed her eyes again. He was kissing the hollow of her hip, the soft curve of her tummy, and even though the place between her legs was very warm and swollen, she suddenly felt nervous. Why was he kissing her way down there? Her heart began to race; it was hard to breathe. Embarrassed and panicky, Cathy wrapped her fingers around a lock of his hair.

Adam looked up and saw her eyes, big and worried in the shadows. He lifted himself back to lie over her and gave her a long, calming kiss. And then, gently, he entered her again and their hips were moving in a predictable rhythm. Cathy breathed against his shoulder as if she were excited, but he knew that the tension of arousal had been punctured by her nerves.

Later, when they were lying side-by-side in the big bed, Cathy drew the sheet up over her breasts and looked over to see if Adam's eyes were open. They were; he was looking at the gossamer netting overhead. His hands were folded under the back of his head.

"I hope you don't think I'm a prude," she ventured softly.

"Hmm? Oh, no. Of course not."

"I don't know why I got nervous."

"Don't worry. I don't want you to ever do anything that doesn't feel right."

That made her worry even more. Clearly, if their romance were on course, they'd be in unspoken agreement on all things, especially their displays of physical love…"Perhaps I need time to feel more at ease. It's all so different than I expected it to be. I mean, I never even imagined that one might not wear one's nightgown at all times."

"Is that your mother's idea of married love?" His voice held a note of irony.

"I don't really know. It's not a subject we ever discussed."

"Well…no cause for concern." He turned onto his stomach, preparing for sleep. "Goodnight, then."

Before she could speak again, she saw that his breathing had slowed. He was sleeping, as unconcerned as if they'd been married for years and their intimate relationship had gone stale long ago. Cathy rolled away on her side, then slipped one hand down to touch herself experimentally. Had he really meant to kiss her there? The very thought made her face flame.

And yet, she experienced another hot twinge between her legs as she remembered the way his mouth felt on her own lips, on her nipples, on the sensitive spots of her throat, her nape, her wrists…The possibility of even more heightened pleasure was shocking and tantalizing, almost beyond endurance.

Slipping out of bed, Cathy padded into the dressing room. She used the commode, then took a soft, embroidered cotton nightgown out of her drawer and slipped it over her head. It reminded her of her bedroom in Newport. For good measure, she fastened each button up to the base of her throat before returning to Adam's bed. Moments later, she too was asleep.

"Mistress goin' to Hastings?" Retta inquired in an offhand tone.

Adam was watching through the kitchen window as the men from the Ice House unloaded his order on rollers. The ice was in crocus bags, covered in salt. At first, it seemed that he didn't hear Retta, then he glanced back. "How did you know about that?"

"June tells me."

"June hears too much while she's serving supper." He frowned and sipped his strong coffee. "Tell her to close her ears."

"Mistress goin' to Hastings?" she persisted.

"I don't think so."

"You look please wit' youself, sir. Why you t'ink she change she mind?"

He went past her, looked around in a big bowl of fruit, and chose a ripe papaya. "She might not wish to leave Tempest Hall after all. Perhaps she doesn't want to be parted from her husband!"

"Let me fix dat pawpaw, sir." Retta sliced it in half the long way, scooped out the glistening grayish seeds, and squeezed a piece of lime over the fruit. "It do look good! As for mistress, let she go. She want de sea-bath, and miss she friend—"

Adam made a disparaging sound in reference to Theo Harrismith as he went outside, sat down on the steps, and used a delicate silver spoon to scoop out a bite of yellow-orange papaya. The spoon looked as if it would break in his strong hand, and his face was a study in pleasure as he tasted the perfect, juicy fruit.

"Dey jus' ripe enough now," Retta confirmed with a nod from the doorway. Sensing a movement, she turned around to see Cathy, standing quietly and studying her husband's profile and the line of his thigh in riding breeches. Her big brown eyes, full of wistful wonder, spoke volumes to the old woman.

Feeling Retta's gaze, Cathy roused herself and smiled. "Good morning." She lowered her voice and came closer. "I confess, I was staring. He is an awfully attractive man. Hard to resist."

"You tryin' to resist, Mistress?"

She sighed. "Sometimes—yes. I try not to get too close, like a moth to the flame. I'm a little fearful of the fire…"

"Huh. I do t'ink on dat. Meantime, you have pawpaw. You want biscuit? Eggs?" Leaning on her two walking sticks, she looked Cathy up and down, taking stock of her proper lace-edged white shirtwaist and faded rose skirt. Her heavy brown hair was pinned up in a flawless Gibson Girl pompadour and she was carrying a Gainsborough hat with long silken ribbons. "You want to sit in dining room?"

"Retta, you don't need to wait on me. I don't expect it, honestly! And I'll take my papaya right outside on the steps, with my husband."

Adam looked up when she sat down with her plate. "I thought I heard your voice. Good morning."

Already blushing, Cathy smiled. "It looks like a beautiful day." She gathered her courage and hurried on to say, "You were gone when I woke up. I hope you slept well? I did. I mean, I'm glad that we've moved beyond separate beds."

"Have we?" He looked mildly surprised. "Nothing personal, but I do happen to believe that a little privacy in marriage can be a healthy thing."

Her heart sank. The papaya went tasteless in her mouth. "I see…"

"No need to rush it, is there?"

"Rush what?" She felt little prickles of irritation. "Adam, didn't you mean anything you said last night? You told me you were sorry, that you had missed me—"

"Did I suggest that you move into my bedroom?"

"I thought—I was trying—"

"Oh, for God's sake." He got to his feet. "If you were so devoted to me, you wouldn't want to dash off to Hastings to visit Harrismith."

"Well, it doesn't do me any good to stay here! I don't know if it's me or my money, but whatever the case, you clearly can't bear to have me close by for very long!"

"Go, then!"

"I intend to!"

Adam started into the kitchen just in time to see Cathy's papaya half come sailing over his shoulder. "There!" he shouted at Retta. "Do you see what I have to put up with? She's not the angel you imagine by any means."

The old woman merely looked at him, her eyes impassive under the edge of her headtie. "What you 'fraid of, sir?"

"I don't know what you're talking about."

"You do. You too smart." Nodding slowly, she added. "You know."

"The hell with that!" he shouted, and stormed through the kitchen. "I'm going to Bridgetown."

Out on the steps, Cathy pressed an exquisite Parisian handkerchief against her eyes. Tears soaked the gauzy fabric. Feeling Retta's eyes on her, she glanced back. "I hate him. He is a beast!"

"Dat may be. But you 'don hate him."

Part Three

Chapter 16

Cathy sat squeezed in the middle of the fourth bench on the mule tram and worried again about her own judgment. Had she been wrong to leave Simon, June, and the family horse and carriage behind in Bridgetown? Perhaps her own desire for independence would get her into real trouble...

"Pretty, pretty lady," the old man beside her mumbled approvingly. He was carrying a basket of pungent flying fish.

Cathy was relieved when a woman sitting ahead of them turned and gave him a reproving stare, adding, "Mind your manners, Albert!"

The mule tram was nearing the crest of Garrison Hill, bordering the British regiments' parade grounds, where today a lively cricket match was underway. It had been a slow journey because the tram was filled and the driver had been forced to add a third mule to make it up the hill. Cathy found herself worrying about the animals, but no one else seemed to be concerned. At the top of Garrison Hill, the third mule was unhitched as they rolled down to a long, flat stretch of Hastings Road, the ocean spread out to their right.

"Missus, we comin' to de Ocean Breeze Hotel," the driver called back to her. His friendly face was nearly black against the white, English bobby-style hat that was part of his uniform.

She saw the sign then, arching high above a tall, gated picket fence that shielded the building from the road. The hotel itself was a fanciful creation. Shell-pink trimmed in mist-gray, it featured long windows surrounding the upper story. All the freshly-painted jalousie shutters were pushed out to let in the ocean air. When Cathy alighted from the mule tram, carrying a Louis Vuitton satchel with her bathing costume inside, she saw a white cat watching her from the window nearest the gate.

Theo came around the corner then, beaming, his reddish hair blown this way and that by the breeze. He proceeded to embrace her while the occupants of the departing mule tram looked on with open curiosity.

"I'm glad you came," he said, taking her satchel as they went into the lobby.

"Oh, Theo," she exclaimed, looking around, "it's lovely."

Cocking his head doubtfully, he allowed, "We still have a lot of work to do, but I do love the place already. It has a lot of character. In fact, it reminds me of myself!"

She insisted on a tour but Theo was hungry and anxious for conversation, so he showed her around while the cooks made their lunch. The lobby was decorated in shades of white, ecru, pale gold, and rose. The floor was marble, the walls were thick, and there were folding hurricane shutters, with bolts, on every door and window. The crowning touches were a trio of crystal chandeliers, converted to gas, and a few excellent pieces of mahogany furniture.

"I've been going to estate sales," Theo explained. "These are dark days for sugar cane plantations. I've been told that one-hundred-fifty estates were sold during the last decade to clear debts, and the trend is continuing." He made a sad face, then winked at her. "You wouldn't believe the treasures one can find at those auctions!"

Cathy ran her hand over the frayed silk upholstery of a Sheraton settee. "All you need is the money to have them recovered."

"One thing at a time, darling. We are counting our pennies, I fear."

"Your flowers are exquisite." She buried her nose in a massive arrangement of pink and cream lilies. "How do you manage?"

"I go out and pick them myself. That's one advantage to living on a tropical island. You can have a fortune's worth of flowers in every room if you have the talent to arrange them."

Upstairs, they walked quickly through the handful of guest rooms that were finished. They had varnished pine floors, seventeen-foot coved ceilings, and enormous windows. Only the three suites had private bathrooms; the others offered washstands with basins, ewers, and chamberpots, and shared what Theo called "shower rooms" out in the corridor.

They came down a different staircase than they'd gone up. As they passed the postbox marked HRH, and then the office, Theo stopped at the desk to speak to a pretty woman with a mocha complexion. When she glanced curiously at Cathy, he introduced them.

"Yvette Chambers, this is Lady Catherine Raveneau, wife of Adam Raveneau. You know him, don't you, Yvette?"

"Yes, of course," she said in a soft, cultured voice. "It's a pleasure to meet you, Lady Raveneau."

After the two women chatted for a few moments, Theo steered Cathy away. "Do you know what she's called, in terms of her bloodline?"

"Mulatto?"

"Mustefino," he corrected. "It's very complicated on an island like this, and the blacks are the first to correct you if you get it wrong."

"Mustefino?" she repeated doubtfully.

"Don't you remember when I explained it on the yacht? There's mulatto, which is half black, then quadroon, which is one-fourth. Octoroon is one-eighth and mustefino is one-sixteenth."

"It just doesn't seem right. Is it supposed to be better to have more white blood?"

"Usually, yes." The sound of raised voices coming from the kitchen caused Theo to stop and incline his head. "Perhaps we should investigate. I hope it's not dangerous."

The huge white-washed room was crowded with sinks, wooden preparation tables, great old stoves, and pots hanging overhead. There were young people who were washing dishes and cutting vegetables, but two old women were clearly in charge. Both wore full-length aprons and starched headties, and one was so short that she had to stand on a special stool at the stove. She was stirring a huge pot that gave off a tempting aroma, her hips going round and round in rhythm with her long wooden spoon.

Theo introduced the short woman as Mrs. Ford, and her partner as Effie. Both appeared to be over eighty. When Effie heard that Cathy had come from America, she exclaimed that her husband had gone there forty years before in search of better work to support their eight sons.

Scowling, she shook her head at Cathy. "Where is my Alphonse? I ain' wait' no longer!"

"I don't blame you, ma'am." She tried not to smile.

"No. Not one mo' day!"

Mrs. Ford, meanwhile, continued to rotate her hips. "Makin' a mighty fine cou-cou, Mist' Theo! I jus' wish you get me de salt bread I need." She paused. "An' rice. Might run out de rice."

"No matter how many times I ask you before I go to market, you always need more. You add to the list constantly."

"Kippers, too."

"Why are you using the old stove, Mrs. Ford?" Theo attempted to make eye contact with her. "The gas stove works so much better, and I paid a king's ransom for it!"

She shook her head in forceful disagreement. "No, sir! It'll blow up and kill one o' us! An' who, you t'ink? Me!"

"I give up!" He threw both hands in the air dramatically. "You'll both drive me mad!"

Shaking his head, Theo retreated and Cathy followed him into the dining room.

They passed shelves of new dishes on the way out. Each piece was bordered in gold leaf and gracefully inscribed, "The Ocean Breeze Hotel."

"Unfortunately, those two are the best cooks on the island, and I couldn't do without them," he muttered, scowling. "They're utterly infuriating, though. And Mrs. Ford has a vile temper. She threatens me with knives when we argue."

Before Cathy could respond, they emerged onto a verandah that overlooked the glistening turquoise sea. There were planters' chairs facing the view, tables where elderly men were playing cards, and an assortment of fan palms.

"It's spectacular," Cathy told Theo as she wandered over to the railing and inhaled the sea air. Two shuttered bath houses rose out of the water near the hotel and were attached by a tall pier. A cluster of men emerged from the nearer bath house, wading out into the water in their striped bathing costumes. "Oh, my! How inviting!"

"Those are our famous Hastings Baths. You may not think them so wonderful when I tell you that the women don't have an exit into the sea. They have to take their sea-baths inside the structure…"

"You are teasing me!"

"No. But you'll enjoy it all the same, and I'm sure your big strong husband can find a secluded beach where you can have a proper swim." He gave her a sideways glance and a wink.

A bit of sea spray dampened Cathy's kid slippers. "I already love this place too much to stay angry about your silly bath house rules. There were rules at Bailey's Beach in Newport, too. The women swam until noon, and then a flag was run up and we left so that the men could have the beach."

"All the prudery wasn't *my* idea, I assure you. The island has its share of debauchery, but it waits until the sun has set."

"That's a cryptic remark."

"Ah, our lunch is served." Theo led her back to the dining room where a white-clad waiter had just arrived with a tray filled with exotic dishes.

Cathy soaked up the atmosphere. Surrounding them were palms in brass pots and lacy ferns balancing on mahogany plant stands. Their linen-draped table was set with heirloom silver, a bouquet of coral hibiscus, and intricately folded shell-pink napkins. A bottle of French champagne had been uncorked, and Theo offered a toast.

"Here's to Lady Catherine Raveneau. May she and her fairytale viscount live happily ever after."

As their glasses touched, she ventured, "Do I detect a note of cynicism?"

"Far from it. I do sincerely wish the best for you, darling, but I confess that I have my doubts about fairytales…especially on Barbados."

Steaming bowls of callaloo were served. Cathy had already watched Retta make the soup at Tempest Hall, and she knew that it consisted of a blend of dasheen leaves, crab, okra, and other mysteriously delicious flavors.

"Let's change the subject," she said. "How is Sutton? I was hoping he might join us."

"He may yet appear, but when I last saw him, he was in the back office, trying to make our books balance." He motioned to the waiter to pour more champagne. "I keep telling him it's a hopeless task. He's obsessed."

"Are you worried, Theo?"

"About money? Rather. I'm not sure I can keep the place open, let alone purchase new furniture or make the repairs that are needed. Hazel Trotter behaved as if she had unlimited resources, but I've known enough threadbare aristocrats on Barbados to form an army and they're all superb at putting on a front."

"So are you, from the looks of this luncheon." She watched as dishes of flying fish in lime sauce, Yorkshire pudding, buttered green cristophenes, and oven-browned potatoes were presented.

"Touché." He grinned. "It's a gift, I admit it."

"This hotel needs you." Cathy leaned forward. "You know, my father opened a bank account for me when I married so that I would have my own money. I've been thinking of making an investment…"

"Your husband would wring my neck if I enticed you to put good money into this place. More champagne, my lady?"

"No, thank you." She watched as he happily poured the last of it into his glass before she remarked, "The food is just wonderful. I wish I could get one of your cooks for Tempest Hall. Retta was very accomplished in her day, but she's nearly one hundred now and she tires easily." Cathy sighed, then returned to her meal, savoring a bite. "I love cristophenes. I'd never heard of them before I came to Barbados."

"I'll ask around about a cook for you, but I'd rather talk about the real reason you came today." His eyes sparkled. "Wouldn't you like to unburden yourself? I give you my word that I am the soul of discretion." Pressing his lips together, Theo pretended to turn a key, locking them closed.

Cathy had wanted to confide in someone, especially Theo, and now that he'd encouraged her and she was emboldened by champagne, the words came spilling out. Within minutes, she had told the story of how she and Adam had encountered Gemma Hart on Broad Street. "It was the oddest thing. She told Adam that she had a small son, born since he left the island, and there was such tension in the air, I didn't know what to make of it. I'm certain it's nothing. I'm just insecure, and foolish, and—"

"I wouldn't say that," he broke in gently. "On the contrary, I'd say that your instincts are excellent, my lady."

Her eyes stung. The fork she'd been holding slipped from her fingers. "Are you suggesting that she and Adam were...involved?"

"I've heard those rumors." He put a hand over hers.

"But, Theo—how can that be? Gemma is...colored."

"This isn't your lily-white Newport! Gemma's color wouldn't have dissuaded Lord Raveneau. She's a beautiful woman, and such affairs are extremely common in the West Indies." His eyebrows went up. "For a man like your husband, it makes perfect sense. Gemma wouldn't have expected marriage from him, because of her bloodline and his title, so he could indulge himself without consequence. However, he didn't count on her strength of character—or the chance that another sort of consequence might arise."

"A child?" Her voice was a whisper.

"Quite. I don't know if she'll let him go so easily now. I knew Gemma when we were younger, and she's always been exceptionally strong willed."

Cathy was feeling as if she'd been slapped. A voice came to her from a distance.

"Gadzooks! If it isn't Lady Raveneau!" A tall figure burst through the potted palms to loom over their table. "What're you doing in Hastings?"

It was Adam's friend, Basil Lightfoot. Fortunately, Theo recognized him, and he stood and presented himself and made polite conversation about the Ocean

Breeze until Cathy recovered enough composure to smile and extend her hand.

"How nice to see you again, Mr. Lightfoot." She'd forgotten how tall he was and how much he resembled a horse.

"Better not let Adam's old flames see you having luncheon with another man!" he exclaimed. "They'll have your marriage on the rocks in no time. Lots of disgruntled spinsters about on this island. Every gathering I attend, they ask me about you, since it seems I'm the only one who's met you!"

Cathy felt even more unsettled. "I've been terribly busy, settling in at Tempest Hall."

"Yes, yes, I suppose so! The place must've been falling down around your ears!"

Theo listened with narrowed eyes, then interjected, "Mr. Lightfoot must be an expert on old plantation houses, my lady. He was the heir to one of Barbados's grandest." He looked at Basil. "Too bad you had to auction off so many treasures! I furnished half this hotel at your estate sale."

The older man's lip curled. "How did you and Lady Raveneau become such great chums?"

"Actually," Cathy said, "I'm considering making an investment in the Ocean Breeze."

Theo winced at that and Basil went wide-eyed, but before either of them could speak, Adam Raveneau strode into the dining room with Alice beside him.

"Here you are, my dear. I'm so glad you two didn't wait for me." Smiling and impeccably turned out, he lightly caressed her neck with one strong hand and bent to kiss her cheek. Alice sat down next to Cathy's chair and rested her chin on her mistress's lap. "Basil, what a surprise to see you again." He drew up a chair for himself and pointedly left Lightfoot standing.

"Your wife's just been telling me that she means to invest in this hotel."

"Cathy's been pulling your leg, old fellow. She has a wicked sense of fun."

Theo sent a glance toward the lobby, and an instant later Yvette was there, guiding Basil Lightfoot away to another table where an elderly friend was waiting for him.

"It seems I arrived just in time to salvage our reputation," Adam said to Cathy in cool tones.

She could hardly believe he was there, let alone what he'd said. A scream rose in her throat, but Theo's stare restored her composure. "I wasn't doing anything scandalous, for heaven's sake. Is it a crime for a woman to have lunch, openly, with a male *friend*? And will someone tell me why it would be so unthinkable for me to invest in this hotel?"

Before Adam could speak, Theo leaned toward her. "My lady, I insist that you put this notion out of your mind." He looked at Adam. "I told her it was a ridiculous idea the moment she first mentioned it. I told her that you'd wring my neck—"

"I might like to do so, Harrismith, but in reality I wouldn't dream of infringing upon my wife's right to spend her own money in any way she sees fit. After all, her father has been good enough to bestow some of his fortune on me, and Tempest Hall. What sort of oaf would I be if I interfered with the funds he's given Cathy for her private use?" Adam spoke lightly, but a muscle moved in his jaw. "We just need to reach an understanding about discretion on this island."

She wondered if she could be losing her mind. "Discretion? Yes, do, please, instruct me."

Their eyes met, and he saw fury in hers. Intrigued, he brushed a bit of sand from his white trousers before replying, "My dear, a key element in discretion is learning what not to say in public places. We'll take this up in privacy."

"I don't think I want a sea-bath any longer," Cathy said to Theo. "I'll go and get my things. I am so anxious to hear my husband's speech and to learn the reason for his visit here today! Could he have come all this way just to explain the niceties of feminine discretion to me?"

Her host stood, looking nervous. "I'll show you the way." As the waiter cleared away the remaining dishes, Theo whispered in his ear and the young man hurried off. He then turned to Adam with a smile. "I've ordered a rum swizzle for you, my lord. I hope you approve of our barman, Frederick. If you are hungry and would like luncheon, you need only glance toward Yvette. She keeps a close eye on the dining room."

Adam's face was unreadable. "Nothing, thank you." Alice returned to his side, and he stroked her brow.

Theo led Cathy to a small storeroom off the lobby. Once inside, she shook her fists at him.

"I am going to give that philandering, deceitful hypocrite a gigantic piece of my mind just as soon as we leave here! I don't even care if Simon is driving the buggy and hears every word! It would serve Adam right. How dare he presume to imply that my conduct is wanting in any way?" As the angry words tumbled forth, tears began to gather in her eyes. "What is wrong with men?" She broke off, just before the secret of her own father's betrayal came out. "Are they all false?"

"You're asking a man?"

"Oh, but Theo—you're different."

He made no reply to that. "Look, we can't stay in here forever, or he'll be in an even worse mood. I just wanted to let you be hysterical, then tell you that of course you must *not* let on that you know about Gemma, or the baby, or any of the rest."

Cathy blinked as if she thought she'd heard wrong. "You don't mean that."

"Oh yes, I do. A man like Adam Raveneau requires a much subtler strategy. Unless you really do want a divorce, you can't tell him what you suspect or how you feel about it." Theo opened the door and gestured for her to return to the lobby. "Not yet, anyway."

Chapter 17

During the ride home, Cathy found it galling to swallow her real feelings, and even more impossible to be charming. So, she compromised and merely endured Adam's explanation of Barbadian propriety. All her arguments were suppressed, along with the pain and outrage she felt about Gemma and little Paul.

Reaching the end of his speech, Adam said, "So, I'm not sure it's a good idea for you to be seen alone with other men right now. People are bound to be uncertain because you're an American." Cathy's passive acceptance of every word he uttered took the wind out of his sails. Perhaps he'd been too hard on her. "We just have to be careful, until the islanders realize how kind and fine a person you are."

She gave him a demure smile. "Why Adam, you'll turn my head with those compliments."

"Are you having me on?" Now that he'd negotiated their carriage through the maze of roads in and around Bridgetown, he could relax a bit and let himself study Cathy more closely. Behind them, Alice was lying on an empty passenger seat, napping, as the road dipped through a cool, dark gully lined with fanciful bearded fig trees.

"Did you want me to argue with you?"

"No, but I did expect—from the look in your eyes at the hotel—a bit more resistance."

"Well, Theo reminded me that you have a lot on your mind these days, what with returning home and restoring the plantation and adjusting to our marriage. I ought to be more understanding and—" Pausing, she took a deep breath. "And I should try harder to meet you halfway."

"Theo made those suggestions?"

"I have told you that he and I are only friends and you needn't be jealous of him."

"I am not jealous of him!" His nostrils flared. "Stop saying that!" When she merely obeyed, sitting in silence beside him, Adam tried again. "Do you know the reason I came down to the hotel?"

"I can guess."

"No, it was not because I was jealous!"

"Of course not." She couldn't help smiling and feeling encouraged by his outbursts. So much of the time Adam was cool and indifferent, but it seemed that if he didn't care for her he wouldn't be reacting so heatedly now.

"It was because I encountered Simon and June in Bridgetown, and they told me you'd gone on to Hastings by mule tram! Damn it, Cath, it's just not done, especially without even a maid by your side."

"I was craving a bit of time to myself, a bit of independence, but now I understand that I was rash." She felt his eyes on her and knew he was suspicious of her quick capitulation. Turning, Cathy put a hand on his arm and smiled. "I'm quite sincere."

Arching an eyebrow, he muttered, "Are you sure you're the same woman who was staring daggers at me at the Ocean Breeze Hotel?"

"I just needed time to think about everything and calm down." And then she said some things that were quite true. "Adam, I don't want to quarrel with you, or drive you away from me. We have problems enough as it is. I'm feeling quite alone in a strange place, and you're my husband…"

"I know I'm not doing a very good job at it, but I did warn you from the first—that night you came to my room at the Whitehorse Tavern—" He glanced at her and sighed. "Perhaps I should have let you marry Byron after all. He was better husband material."

"I didn't want to marry Byron. He only offered for me so that you would intervene. Not because you were jealous, of course!"

They both laughed then, and the air between them was sweetened by hope. Alice put her head on the back of their seat and watched approvingly.

A few miles farther north, just before the right turn that would take them east to Tempest Hall, Adam steered the little carriage down a bumpy cart track that led into a grove of cabbage palms. The calm Caribbean Sea that lapped at the shore of the island's west coast made for sublime swimming if one knew the way to certain secret coves.

"What are we doing?" asked Cathy.

"I'm providing your sea-bath. You can have it out in the open sunshine instead of inside that absurd bath house. If you long to do something shocking, my dear, this is your chance."

The horses were nibbling the lush vegetation that edged the beach, and Alice was already climbing down to walk toward the white sand and aqua water.

"Do you mean it?" She clapped her hands and Adam grinned at her show of enthusiasm. "Where shall I change into my bathing costume?"

He looked deep into her eyes and replied, "You don't need one, you know. I've never seen anyone else come to this hidden beach. It was my grandparents' secret place."

She nearly said yes, but too many fears crowded in. "Let me wear my bathing costume this time, and then perhaps I'll get some courage."

"I take it you don't want me to help you undress?"

Oh, she did, so much, and yet the thought of it panicked her. "I don't mean to seem so prim, but I'm not used to being seen in broad daylight…"

He shrugged, and Cathy realized that Gemma Hart wouldn't bother with foolishness like bathing costumes, nor would she miss a chance to have Adam undress her. She probably gloried in the beauty of her own body and all its erotic possibilities.

Adam stripped naked, and soon he and Alice were swimming together in the tranquil sea. It took Cathy longer to get out of her restrictive clothing, then her corset and pantalets, and longer still to get into the blue belted tunic and drawers of her bathing costume.

But it was worth it.

Standing on the sugary sand and looking out at Adam and Alice, she called, "Is it at all chilly?"

"That's right—you're used to the waters off New England," he rejoined, laughing. Perhaps that's why you are so overdressed! No, it's not chilly. I've had baths that were cooler than this."

And he was right. Not only was the Caribbean Sea the loveliest color Cathy had ever seen, but it was soothingly warm and placid.

"It's like a dream," she decided, having waded out until even her shoulders were immersed.

Adam approached with the aged Alice, who now allowed her master to support her underwater so that she could float effortlessly. Her Labrador face wore a smile of utter contentment. "Don't you wish now that you could feel that water on every inch of your body?"

Their eyes met and another layer of her reserve fell away. "Yes."

"You still can."

"Next time," she promised. "I'd drown trying to get all the fastenings undone."

"Next time, then." His blue-gray gaze was brilliant against the sunlit water. "I can hold you just like Alice. Would you like that?"

For a moment, she allowed herself to imagine the joy of swimming naked in this heavenly sea and being held in Adam's hard-muscled arms. She could wrap her legs around his waist and they'd drift together, kissing, tasting salt…

"Cathy?"

Color flooded her face, and she looked up to see that he had read her thoughts. "Yes," she said huskily. "I would like that."

One sultry afternoon nearly a week after their swim, Adam was back in Bridgetown, walking alone down Broad Street toward DaCosta & Co. All around him, the city's black citizens were covered from head to toe; the men in suits and fedoras, the women in high-necked shirtwaists, long skirts, and feminine boaters, carrying umbrellas to ward off the day's unusually punishing heat. A mule tram clattered by on the tracks that bisected the dirt street. Someone onboard waved to Adam, but he pretended not to notice.

Inside the spacious store, which sold everything from dry goods to hardware, Adam took Cathy's list out of his jacket pocket and wandered over to the far wall where the kitchen items were stocked. Looking at her neat script, he thought back to that morning.

They had been sharing breakfast in the sunny dining room when he announced that he was going into Bridgetown. His wife had accused him of running away from her and, remembering now, he supposed it was true.

She'd become so much a part of Tempest Hall in so short a time that he'd begun to see her just as clearly as its mistress as he had his grandmother. When he was at home, every move made by the growing corps of workmen reminded him that Parrish money was paying for the repairs to the home he loved. It was easier to ride off on some errand. One day, he'd told Cathy that he was researching the feasibility of planting sugar beets now that the Brussels Convention had lifted the bounties on the crop replacing sugar cane. And so, Adam had visited other planters who were still solvent. He'd drunk rum punch with them, reminisced about his grandparents and the golden days of plantation life, and then had gone home to find his bride still working alongside the hired help. Even Alice stayed behind with her, loyally following Cathy from room to room.

Last night, when he'd gone off to his room alone and mumbled something about catching up on his reading, Cathy had whispered, "Coward." That one soft word had been like an arrow in his back. And then, this morning, she'd rubbed salt in the wound with the "running away" comment.

"Looking for something for your new bride, my lord?"

Adam turned in surprise, nearly colliding with a portly fellow wearing a bowtie and a walrus mustache. "Have we met?"

"I've overstepped my bounds, no doubt, but of course everyone knows you. How many viscounts have we got on the island, after all?" The fellow's jowls wobbled when he grinned. "I'm George Eliot, manager of kitchen goods. I know what you're thinking, my lord, but I must disappoint you. I am not the author of *Silas Marner*."

Adam waited until Eliot had stopped laughing. "I wasn't thinking that." He cocked an eyebrow at him. "You do know that George Eliot was really a woman, don't you? A woman using a man's pen name?"

"How kind of you to instruct me, my lord. Meantime, what were you looking for?" His tone turned businesslike.

"Nothing I can't find on my own. My wife gave me a short list: a nutmeg grinder, a new wringer for the washtub, a large jooking board." He pointed toward the latter, a thick slab of corrugated wood used to scrub clothes. They were used by Bajans who did washing at standpipes, the sources of freshwater on the island, but Retta insisted on "jookin' out" stains on a board laid on top of their washing tub.

"Would I be overstepping my bounds again if I said that I suspect that you were searching out the perfect Christmas gift for her ladyship?"

"I might be." Warming to the idea, he looked around the store. There were perfume bottles, matching sets of jewelry, gloves, and handkerchief boxes. Christmas! He had forgotten all about it.

"May I suggest one of our newer items?" Eliot gestured with a flourish toward a wooden tub with a crank. "The Shepard's Blizzard Ice Cream Freezer!"

Adam was about to dismiss the fellow when he had a vision of Cathy. He could see her, curls coming down and her lace collar wilting, as she helped mix the cream and eggs, and chip ice. They would turn the crank together until the ice cream was ready. Her eyes would be dancing, and she would laugh when he pulled her onto his lap, kissing her, tasting the sweet cream in her mouth…

"Shall I wrap it up, my lord?"

"Hmm? Oh, yes. Thank you, Mr. Eliot. And, could you assemble the other items for me? Here is my wife's list."

When the man was gone, Adam stood alone and closed his eyes, aware that he'd grown hard with desire for Cathy. The warm rush of emotions that came with that physical clench made his heart pound with uncertainty.

Opening his eyes, he saw Gemma Hart coming toward him with a tiny boy in tow. She stopped halfway across the store and waited for him to meet her. Her hair was drawn up in a perfect pompadour, and her elegant face was set off by skin the color of coffee mixed liberally with warm, rich milk. Everything about Gemma was proper and controlled, yet under the surface ran fierce passions. That blend of intellectual discipline and sensual heat made a potent combination, but Adam now found himself curiously immune to it.

"I would like to talk to you," she said. "Come over to the hotel, where we can be alone."

"I'm actually running late."

Her eyes darkened. "I won't take much of your time. I know how many responsibilities you have now, *my lord*, but I must look after your son's interests."

"All right. I'll be there in a quarter hour."

"How generous you are."

George Eliot tapped Adam on the shoulder. He was holding the ice cream freezer aloft, beaming. "Lord Raveneau, I thought you might like a closer look before I put it in the box. Shall I put a large bow on top? I'll bet that would put a smile on your lovely wife's face, eh?"

"Yes, thank you." When Adam turned back, Gemma was sweeping out of the store and Paul's little legs were struggling to keep up with her. Then, as if Adam didn't have enough to worry about, he saw Basil Lightfoot standing near the linens display and watching with interest.

Gemma sat at her writing desk in the Hart Hotel office, adding up accounts, and didn't look up when Adam entered the room. He cleared his throat.

"Oh, there you are," she murmured, and slipped off the reading glasses that she wore on a ribbon around her neck. "I have a lovely bottle of falernum. Would you care for some over ice?"

"No, thank you. I really can't stay, Gemma."

"Join me on the settee, then, and we'll talk."

When they were seated, the door opened again as if on cue, and Paul appeared, frowning. He was carrying a tiny gray tiger-striped kitten. "Mummy, Stripey scrash me!"

"Sit down next to me and I'll kiss it, dear." Gemma patted the spot between her and her visitor.

Adam stared at the little boy, guessing that he was at least two years old, and Paul stared back, still clutching the wriggling kitten. His big eyes were not brown like his mother's, but blue-gray, flecked with gold. His complexion was the palest shade of mocha and his little mouth was well-shaped.

"Darling Adam, can't you see that he needs to be lifted up here? He can't climb up with the kitten in his arms."

The sensation of his large hands on the child's warm body sent a chill down Adam's spine. He had an urge to hold Paul on his lap, to embrace him and listen to the beating of his miniature heart and examine each of his tiny, busy fingers. As it was, he inhaled the scent of him: a magical blend of soap and baby, fresh air and coconut bread.

"Stripey," Paul announced, thrusting the kitten at Adam.

"So I see." He nodded with grave irony.

"Scrash me." Regarding his own wound, a slight mark on one arm, Paul looked as if he might cry again. "Hurts!" He turned the kitten so that they were face to face. "Bad kitty! No, no!"

Gemma ran one thin hand over his curly hair. "That's enough, Paul. The kitten didn't mean to hurt you. It was an accident. Now then, say hello to your papa."

Adam ignored the word she had so intentionally used, looking again into this child's version of his own eyes. "Hello, Paul."

The child studied him gravely. "I want a lollie."

"Go and ask Suzanne, darling."

With that, Paul and Stripey slid to the floor and rushed out of the room.

"He's beautiful, isn't he?" asked Gemma. "And he's the image of his father."

"Personally, I think he looks like you."

"If you are wondering if someone else might be the father, you needn't. His parentage is perfectly evident, especially in his eyes, and you know it. Your mousey little wife would know it as well."

"Is that a threat? A hint of blackmail?"

"Heavens no! Do you think I want your money or your sexual favors?" She smiled and shook her head. "Of course, I wouldn't say no if you begged to visit my bed, but that's not why we're here. To be honest, I haven't been feeling quite the thing lately, and I can't help worrying about Paul's future. What if something were to happen to me? What would become of him?" She shrugged. "I'd like it if you'd leave the wealthy mouse and marry me, but I know that won't happen. I am realistic, if nothing else. You need her money, and I know you're not heartless enough to desert her now that you've brought her halfway around the world."

Adam listened intently, wondering what she was getting at. "Kindly refrain from calling my wife a mouse."

"Please! She's no match for you. Do I sound bitter? Perhaps I am, a bit. If I were white, I believe you'd have married me." She raised a hand before he could speak. "Please, let me cling to my illusions for the time being. They're all I have, my dear. Did you think I was too strong for such nonsense? Well, that was an act, just a show of bravado. I can assure you, I've always been riddled with weakness where you're concerned—

especially after you left and I learned that I was with child."

"Gemma, there is no point in this now. I'm sorry if you've been hurt, but our circumstances have changed—"

"I don't even want money for Paul. That's what you're going to offer me; I know you too well, Adam." An ethereal smile touched her mouth. "I just want you to give him yourself. Is that a ridiculous request? I want you to spend a little time with your son."

Hearing the child's voice in the next room, Adam felt a twinge in his chest. "Yes. I could do that."

"And you must tell your wife." Gemma leaned over and put her hand on his arm. "Is that too much to ask? For Paul's sake?"

The twinge twisted, like a knife. "Yes, that may be too much to ask. You have no idea. Cathy and I already have enough problems—"

"I will not allow you to refer to our son as a *problem*!" Rising, she marched across the room and turned back to point at him. "You've always had life on your own terms, haven't you? Well, I would say that your chickens are coming home to roost, *my lord*! Tell your little wife the truth...or I will!"

Chapter 18

Sheltered by the heart-shaped leaves of the great old sandbox tree behind Tempest Hall, Cathy paced, oblivious to the afternoon heat. Workmen went in and out of the house, waving to her, and she managed to smile and return their greetings, but her mind was elsewhere.

"Have you seen any sign of his lordship?" she called to Simon when he came out of the sugar boiling house. Lately, he and Adam had begun to restore the tumbledown building.

"No'm. Not see he all day long."

"Did he happen to mention to you what time he would be coming home?"

At this, Simon doffed his hat and shook his head. "Sorry to say, no."

Alice appeared at the back door to the kitchen. When she spied her mistress, she clambered down the steps and trotted anxiously toward her. The guinea fowl who were scratching in the sand flapped out of the dog's way.

"Did you fall asleep and lose me?" Cathy asked as the Labrador reached her side and pushed her nose against her skirts. "Ah, Alice, how lonely I'd be without you!" Tears pricked her eyes as she stroked Alice's broad head. The dog gazed up at her, and Cathy could see in the sunlight that her muzzle had gone completely white.

Just then, the sound of hoofbeats reached their ears. Alice began to cry with excitement and started off out into the open yard. Moments later, Adam rode into view on a magnificent black stallion. He was coatless, his shirt collar open against the deep tan of his sculpted face, his raven hair ruffling back in the wind.

Alice was dancing in place next to Lazarus as her master swung down to the ground. The sound of Adam's voice reminded her of her manners and she sat obediently as he stripped off his riding gloves. Then, his long fingers searched out the secret spots behind her ears, flattening out to caress her back.

"Good girl," he murmured. "I missed you."

Cathy emerged from the pool of shade that spilled round the sandbox tree. Lightly, she called, "Hello, Adam."

The sight of her sent a whole host of emotions scrambling within him. He knew why Gemma found Cathy an unlikely candidate for his mate. At first glance, she was altogether unprepossessing: slight, brown-haired, brown-eyed, and snub-nosed, she was prone to flush in a way that announced her deepest feelings to the world. And yet, Adam found himself craving the light of her smile more than anything else at the end of his long and trying day.

"You've gotten some sun," he remarked, handing Lazarus over to Simon. He met Cathy halfway to the sandbox tree and touched her cheeks. "I think it suits you."

"I have some freckles as well. My mother would be horrified."

"They're charming."

She smiled in a way that made her soft mouth look particularly appealing to him. "Adam, I know you're tired, but there's something I have to tell you. It's important…"

They went into the house together, passing through the kitchen first. A pot of okra soup was simmering on the stove, and Retta was napping in her chair near the doorway.

"Theo sent me a note today," whispered Cathy. "He's found us a cook, he thinks. She's the younger sister of Mrs. Ford, his prize cook at the Ocean Breeze. Her name is Josephine."

"Not a moment too soon."

"Sad but true."

They went on into the library, where one of the new housemaids, Beatrice, was hurriedly swizzling a rum punch for her employer. From the sitting room came the sound of pounding.

"It's the men replacing the floors," Cathy hastened to explain when she saw Adam's frown. "Beatrice, would you go and tell them that they may stop for the day?"

When they were alone, Adam took a long drink and ran a hand through his hair. He sighed resignedly. "You know, Cath, I have something to tell you, too. I don't suppose it does any good to put off difficult news."

"Let me go first, then you can decide if we need more bad news in this one day."

"You're turning pale. There's nothing wrong, I hope?"

"It depends on what you call 'wrong,'" she said with a sigh. Then, reaching into the side pocket of her skirt, Cathy withdrew a telegram. "A boy rode out from the West India and Panama Telegraph Company to bring me this. It's from my mother. She's on her way to Barbados to visit us."

Adam felt as if he'd taken a blow to the chest. "Your…mother? Coming here?" He paused for a deep breath. "When?"

"She's sailing on a yacht with my third cousin, Auggie Chase. She thinks they'll be here by Christmas."

"But that's next week!"

Cathy managed a wan smile. "Yes."

"Tempest Hall isn't fit for houseguests! The whole place is torn apart!"

"We'll just have to finish as much as we can and make due. What other choice do we have?"

"Maybe she'll decide to stay in a hotel. The Marine Hotel is very impressive; nearly grand enough for your mother."

With a firm shake of her head, Cathy insisted, "That's not the reason she's coming all the way down here. I know my mother, and she means to do a very thorough job of inspecting our home and style of living."

"In that case, we're doomed." He sank into his planter's chair and stared up at the paint peeling high on every wall, not just in that room, but in every room in the house. "This place is a disaster. God, Cathy, when I remember Beechcliff, and I compare it to Tempest Hall, I might as well shoot myself!"

"You mustn't think that way." Her heart went out to him, and she bent beside his chair and stroked his hair. On the back of his head, there a wave that swept to the right, thick and glossy. "Mother knows you aren't wealthy, Adam. You made that perfectly clear yourself, long before we were married."

"Even I was shocked by the state of this house, though. And, in some ways it looks even worse now because the place is torn apart."

"I thought you didn't like my mother. Why do you care what she thinks?"

"That's a good question." He turned to look into her eyes. "It must have something to do with you."

A pink flush touched her cheeks. "Then we'll just have to lend our own two hands to those of the workmen. We have five days, I think, before Mother and Auggie arrive. Let's set about completing as much as we possibly can, all right?"

"Are you suggesting that we paint and plaster and varnish alongside the workmen?"

"I am indeed."

An odd lightness stole over Adam. It felt good to think that he and Cathy might be able to have some power of their own to steer clear of certain catastrophe. And the notion of throwing himself into physical labor was heartening for a different reason. It would take his mind off the throbbing problem of Gemma and Paul.

Of course, telling Cathy was out of the question for the moment. He'd send a note to Gemma, explaining, then find some old clothes and a paintbrush.

"It could be fun," Cathy suggested with a wide, radiant smile.

Adam surprised her by returning her smile, although one brow arched a trifle sardonically. "Fun? That's a strong word, don't you think?"

"I like a challenge, sir!"

His smile softened. "In fact, so do I."

~ ~ ~

Adam was awake, thinking about Paul, when the tallcase clock on the landing struck three. Moonbeams slanted through the jalousie shutters, and the sweet fragrance of jasmine rose upward from the garden and seemed to enter the bedroom on silvery shafts of light. And, from a distance, Adam heard the enticing sound of Atlantic rollers breaking on the island's north coast.

Just then, Alice raised her head and muttered, "Woof." She had been lying on a tapestry rug beside the bed and now got up and looked toward the dressing room door. When the door opened very slowly, she uttered a louder warning: "Woof!"

Adam rose on an elbow and looped the mosquito netting around one bedpost. He was nut-brown against the luminously white sheets. "Cathy?" he called softly.

"Yes," she admitted. Emerging into the pale light, she wrapped her arms around her waist. She was wearing a thin batiste nightgown, tucked and pleated across the bodice, that covered her from neck to wrist to ankle. Her hair was brushed back neatly and braided from the nape of her neck to her waist.

"Is something wrong?" He wondered if he might yet have a chance to tell her about Paul. It wasn't wise to postpone it, and God knew that the perfect moment would never arrive.

"No...well, yes—I suppose that everything is wrong!" She knelt to pet Alice. "I've been worrying—about Mother and the house...and the future seems awfully black." She couldn't mention Gemma Hart and her young son, but they were right at the top of her list of sleep-banishing thoughts.

"In that case, I'm glad you paid me a visit." His heart seemed to stop for a moment when she came to stand next to his bed, within touching distance.

"I thought that—since I am your wife—that I might take refuge in your bed tonight. " Her eyes were beautiful in the shadows, and her smile seemed to tremble. "The truth is, I could use a friend."

He lifted the sheet. "Say no more."

She found herself blinking back tears as she hiked up her nightgown and climbed onto the big bed. His sheets were so soft; fragrant with his almond soap, fine cigars, and his own scent that always made her giddy with longing. Better still, the bed was warm from his body. When she curled next to him on her side, Adam covered her with the sheet and drew her against him with one strong arm. Cathy could feel the imprint of his naked, hard-muscled body through the thin stuff of her nightgown, and her heart beat faster.

Holding her near, Adam kissed her hair where the braid began. "Is that better?"

"You'll never know." So many times since the last night she'd slept here, Cathy had wanted to come back, or at least discuss their sleeping arrangements, but Adam's cool dismissal of the subject had stung her to the core. Why was he allowed to have pride but she must not? "Adam, will you be my friend and support while Mother is here? You know how difficult she can be…" The feeling of his arm tightening around her midsection was bliss.

"Your friend? Wouldn't you rather have a husband?" His lips touched her hair again, then strayed to a tender spot behind her ear.

Rolling onto her back, Cathy searched his eyes for the truth. It wasn't there. Something inside of her felt shy and uncertain again. "I don't think the husband and wife part can be solved so easily, but I do know that we can be friends. We've done it before—"

"That's not the only thing we've done before," he whispered. His lean fingers grazed her neck, then the curve of her breast, then the batiste-draped line of her hip and thigh. Pausing for a moment, Adam heard a subtle shift in her breathing. She wanted to surrender, but something was holding her back. She seemed to hold her breath.

When she spoke there was a note of poignant whimsy in her voice. "Are all men the same?"

He knew that he could persuade her yet. But, as much as Adam wanted her and believed that she wanted him, a muted voice from deep within told him to hold back, to give Cathy what she needed tonight without demanding something for himself. Why he should follow a course that might enrich their marriage was a question he wasn't ready to ask himself.

"All men the same?" he repeated. It was his chance to extricate himself. "I take it you are referring to that male tendency to go soft-brained while in passion's grip. Doubtless we all have our moments, and I've just had one of mine. How could I not, with you in my arms, Cath?" Then, cradling her against him, he lay back against the pillows and very gently stroked the fine baby curls at her brow. "Go to sleep, and don't worry. Together we can slay any dragon that appears—even your fire-breathing mother."

"Let me remind you," she warned in tones of mock severity, "that the woman you compare to a dragon is your mother-in-law."

The sound of their laughter, mingling in the moonlight, made Alice drop her chin onto crossed paws and sigh with pleasure.

Chapter 19

"I am ravenous."

Hearing his wife's announcement, Adam looked down from the ladder and waited, paintbrush in midair. "Go on."

"Well, am I the only one who doesn't like going all day without food?" Pointing at herself for emphasis, she stared up at him.

He touched her paint-daubed nose. "You look comical." Softening, he added, "Charmingly so."

After four days of frantic work on the house, they had now scraped the peeling spots on his library walls and were repainting the entire room a shade Cathy called "Lime Juice." They weren't the only ones working. There were men on the roof, men in the sitting room replacing the damaged wood floor, and men outside repainting Tempest Hall's exterior. Oddly enough, the chaos, hard labor, and shared apprehension over Hermione's impending visit had brought Adam and Cathy closer. They'd learned to laugh together to lighten the mood. She wore painting clothes: an old skirt, one of his older shirts, an apron, and a white headtie to cover her hair. The shirt reached her knees, and Adam had folded back the sleeves for her. Her costume was covered with spatters of the three tropical colors of paint they'd used so far in the house.

"You shouldn't call me comical-looking when I'm hungry and crabby," Cathy warned. "You might have a fight on your hands."

Laughing, he came down the ladder to face her, then sketched a bow. "No offense intended, Lady Raveneau."

"That's better. Besides, you look every bit as ridiculous as I do." She touched the flecks of green on his black hair. Adam wore a collarless and cuffless old shirt and a pair of baggy white duck trousers he kept for work in the sugarcane fields. An old Oxford tie served as a belt. His brown feet were bare, and Cathy privately thought that there was something carnal about the sight of them when he was otherwise fully dressed.

"Well," Adam remarked on his way out the door, "even Alice has been baptized, I see."

The Labrador glanced up from her spot in the sunshine, and indeed, she too was paint-smeared. Her soulful eyes implored him to bring her a treat.

"I'll be very surprised," called Cathy, "if Josephine will fix lunch at this late hour. Our new cook may be talented, but she's just as temperamental as everyone else from the Ocean Breeze Hotel!"

"My dear, I have ways with women of which your friend Theo is wholly ignorant."

This made her giggle; she collapsed in the planter's chair. "I hope you're right, because—"

"I know, you are ravenous!" With that, Adam disappeared out the back door. He'd taken only a few steps toward the kitchen when he saw Josephine's unmistakable rotund figure walking outside, past the stables. Guinea fowl scattered before her as she marched purposefully northward.

"Josephine!" he called in a friendly voice. "Where are you going?"

She stopped and waited for him to reach her before replying, "I want de sea-bath. I walkin' to de sea."

He watched as she pointed to the coastline that was visible over the brow of the hill. "Perfectly understandable. However, Lady Raveneau is very hungry. Would you mind, before you go, fixing us a bite of lunch?"

Her brow furrowed as deeply as if he'd just told her that the island was about to burn to a cinder. "It de middle of de aft'noon, sir! I make lunch at noon, not all day lonnng." Wagging her head, Josephine repeated, "I want de sea-bath now."

"I don't suppose you might make an exception this time?" He gave her his most devastating smile, the one that had caused countless women to melt in his arms.

"You take me for a fool?" She guffawed. "Slav'ry done wit' long ago!"

He bit back a harsh reply. With Hermione Parrish arriving in three days, he couldn't afford to alienate their one servant who really did an exceptional job. So, he wished her a pleasant afternoon by the seaside and headed into the kitchen by himself.

A few minutes later, Adam appeared back in the library carrying a large carved tray. "I'm going out on a limb with my next comment, Cathy."

The very sight of him looking like a waiter put a wide smile on her face. "Be brave, my lord."

"Although I abhor slavery as much as anyone, it did make life much more convenient for the plantation owners." He found a place for the tray on a low footstool. "Somehow I can't imagine my grandfather being reduced to *this*."

"But your grandfather freed the slaves here many years before the rest of Bajan slaves were free."

"You've been talking to Retta too much."

"You have no idea." She gave him a secret smile. "Let's see what you've brought me."

"Kindly disabuse yourself of the notion that all of this is for you." With a wry sideways glance, Adam eased the cork out of a bottle of champagne, and it frothed out all over his Kuba rug. "Damn! It's because it's warm. We haven't a piece of ice anywhere. Simon's gone to order some today, along with all the other supplies we're out of. Josephine never seems to notice we're running low on anything until it's gone."

"Theo has that same problem with his brilliant cooks."

"Well, he's a lot closer to the market than we are!" He removed napkins from plates to reveal sliced chunks of cheese, pickled beef imported from Nova Scotia, crispy salt bread, and a quartered mango. "It's not much, but it's yours."

"Oh my goodness, it looks delicious!"

When they were seated close together on a mahogany chaise draped with a holland cover, Adam brought the tray up next to them. As they toasted and sipped warm champagne, Cathy looked around the library. A few more hours and they'd be done.

"Shall we start on Mother's room next?" she asked while layering cheese and beef on top of buttered salt bread. The champagne made her feel as if she might burp.

"God, don't call it that. I don't want anything in Tempest Hall to be christened after your mother," he said with a note of dark humor. "But yes, I suppose that the north bedroom should be our next project.

Then, when these bookshelves have dried, we can return to the library and put all the books back. That should be amusing!"

"Drink your champagne and stop scowling." Cathy's eyes twinkled as she bit into her concoction, and Adam's eyes danced back over the brim of his glass. Suddenly, unexpectedly, a warm tide of happiness rushed over her. Not only was she happy, but, it came to her, so was he.

"You look like the champagne just went to your head," he remarked, squeezing her knee. "Either that or you're having a reaction to the Canadian meat. I've never quite trusted that pickling business."

Alice came over to sit and stare silently at them while they chewed their food, her eyes liquid with longing, and Cathy laughed. "Isn't she adorable? And I find it wonderful that she still craves food at her advanced age."

"She's starting to drool. I despise that."

The dog inched closer. When Adam sent her a dampening look, she quickly lay down, but her gaze was unwavering.

"Such devotion," praised her mistress.

"You've spoiled her. There's nothing worse than a spoiled Labrador retriever. We'll never have a moment's peace again."

Cathy was elated. "I know. Isn't it wonderful?" And then, she put tiny bits of cheese and meat on a napkin and gave Alice the treat.

"She will never forget that you have surrendered to her charm," he said, aware of his own rising euphoria. They were having fun, and it hadn't happened overnight. The days of shared work had gradually brought them close together, and now he looked at his wife's flushed cheeks and soft mouth and paint-tipped nose and had a powerful urge to feel her body against him while they kissed. They ought to be enjoying this bizarre picnic in bed.

"I don't know how to eat this mango," Cathy was saying.

"Try scooping out the flesh with a spoon."

She made a diligent attempt, working out her first bite of juicy fruit. But when it had popped free, it left the spoon, flew across the library, and landed on Adam's account books.

"Oops." Her face went rosy pink.

"I don't think this is the right setting for a spoon," he decided, trying to ignore the splat of mango on his precious books. "Just use your fingers." When she gave him a doubtful look, Adam picked up one of the other pieces and held it in front of her mouth. "Go on, Cath. Take a bite, or suck on it, whichever strikes your fancy."

She obeyed, feeling hedonistic as the juice from the tree-ripened fruit ran down her chin. It was more than her husband could bear. He put the tray on the floor and leaned over to gather her into his embrace. The old shirt of his that she wore had come unfastened, and over the top of her apron he could see the curve of her breast. Instantly, Adam was hard. Her upper lip, juicy and dark-pink was snubbed upward just like her freckle-dusted nose. All of her keenly appealed to him.

"Maybe the paint is making us a little mad," Cathy whispered.

"No, not the paint." He kissed her chin, tasting the mango juice, and then her parted lips. "Christ, but you are delicious."

"I would have shared the mango with you, you know. You didn't have to go to such lengths to get a taste…but I'm glad you did."

She was beaming. Adam started to laugh, which made Alice approach the chaise, barking. The air was light with the joy they were creating together. "I've never known a woman like you, Cathy," he said at last.

"I'm going to take that as a compliment." Her lids were heavy as she gazed up at the magnificent face she loved. Then, daringly, she slid her arms around his neck and drew him down to her. Their lips joined and their tongues met; Adam's mouth slanted hungrily across hers. Cathy could hear two thudding heartbeats in her ears. He was lying fully on top of her now, crushing her breasts, making them ache with longing. The piece of mango had dropped between their bodies, and she could feel the juice soaking through her apron.

"Cathy, Cathy…" There was a catch in his voice as he kissed her cheekbones, the tender parts of her ear, her soft, sweet neck. One of his hands found its way up the shirt she was wearing and cupped her breast over the thin fabric of her chemise. He was burning for her.

She had never felt so swollen and wet, such yearning to have him touch her there. Her skirt was hitched up partway, and she wanted to spread her legs to him and feel his hardness against the most intimate part of her. She made primitive little sounds as they kissed, and her tongue hungrily reached out to his.

Dimly, Cathy noticed a distant sound, like footsteps, and remembered the workmen. With a supreme effort, she managed to turn her mouth from his enough to say, "We should close the door—"

"I'm not moving," he said hoarsely. "Shh."

Alice sat up, staring at them, and bumped the champagne bottle. It toppled over and slowly poured onto the rug.

"But," Cathy protested weakly, "the workmen—"

Adam was kissing the hollow at the base of her throat. "Devil take the workmen. Let them watch!"

From the doorway to the library, a high-pitched, strident voice suddenly exclaimed, "I beg your pardon!?" Then, as Cathy struggled to sit up and see who had spoken, Hermione Parrish gaped in her direction and collapsed against her companion. "Auggie! Auggie? Do catch me! I believe I may faint!"

Cathy felt as if the library were spinning around her. Every time she tried to focus on her mother, her vision blurred. Adam helped her sit up, and she held onto the shell-shaped side of the chaise and surveyed the wreckage of her world.

She sensed that her headtie was askew and curls fell down around her eyes. Overripe mango was smashed into her apron, and lime-tinted paint decorated the rest of her. Food littered the carpet. The champagne bottle lay on its side; Alice was lapping up the fizzy puddle faster than it could soak into the antique rug. Worse yet, the entire house was a scene of chaos, and Cathy's first encounter with her mother in Barbados made her cheeks blaze.

"Catherine, is that really you?" Hermione demanded. "What have you got on your head? It makes you look like a little piccaninny."

Adam stood up to face his mother-in-law, blocking Cathy so that she could adjust her clothing. "I must ask you not to use that word in our home. I won't have our staff insulted." He paused to let his words sink in, then spoke again. "You'll have to forgive us for being a bit surprised to see you here, Mrs. Parrish. We weren't expecting you until early next week; Christmas Eve, if I remember correctly."

"My nephew Auggie is a superb yachtsman. He believes that we may have set a new record during our voyage south." She smoothed the perfectly draped skirts of her violet-gray traveling costume and began to remove her gloves. "Dear heavens, but it is warm in this part of the world. No wonder Americans haven't taken to the West Indies very readily." Then, as if suddenly remembering the tall man standing off to one side, Hermione drew him forward. "I am remiss. This is my great-nephew, August Randolph Chase III. Auggie, say hello to Adam, Viscount Raveneau, my—ah—son-in-law."

The two men shook hands. Adam decided that Chase appeared to be the quintessential Newport gentleman. He was tall and slender, with a deeply tanned complexion, wavy dark hair, and a stylish mustache. His pale blue eyes were heavy-lidded as he languidly returned his host's stare.

"A pleasure, my lord," Chase said.

Adam turned to extend a hand to Cathy, lifting her to her feet. "Join us, darling. It's your own mother, after all." Then he returned his attention Hermione. "I hope you'll both accept our apologies for the state of the house. As you can see, repairs are still very much in progress. When we learned of your unexpected visit, we decided to pick up paintbrushes and join the workmen."

Smoothing her apron, Cathy approached with Alice in tow. The dog's eyes were narrowed suspiciously.

"I find your house deplorable, my lord, and I won't pretend otherwise," Hermione was saying. Taking the pins from her peony-shaped hat, she removed it and gestured grandly in every direction. "I would never have let you bring her here if I had known she'd be living in a pigsty." Her nostrils flared. "It's appalling!"

"Please don't talk that way about Tempest Hall, Mother." Cathy forgot about her own appearance as she spoke. "It is our home, and I happen to love it very much. If you had waited for us to invite you when the repairs were finished, you wouldn't have seen it like this."

"You still like to argue, I see," her mother said sharply. "Remember your breeding, my child, and greet your cousin."

"Hello, Auggie. I was sorry that you couldn't attend our wedding."

He bowed. "Egypt held me in her thrall, I fear. I must say I was shocked to return to Newport and find you gone, Cousin." He paused. "I know your mother won't ask herself, but I will. We are both famished. Could you ring for a late lunch for us?"

"We could," Cathy echoed and glanced up at Adam. "But we haven't any cooking staff at the moment. Our—uhm, butler, is buying supplies in Bridgetown, our old cook is too old and frail to stand very long, and our new cook has gone to the beach."

"How can you live like this?" Hermione wore an expression of icy disgust. "I expect your housekeeper to ride into the room on a unicycle, juggling vegetables. I am thoroughly disappointed in you, Catherine. Do show me to my room so that I may lie down."

Adam squeezed Cathy's hand. "We were just about to start painting your room, Mrs. Parrish—"

"I'll take yours, then, until my own is ready."

It was a bitter pill for Adam to swallow, but he saw that he had no choice. He was the host, and this guest was his wife's mother. "You anticipate me. That was my plan."

Cathy threw him a grateful look. "And we will put Auggie in my bedroom. Let me show you the way. Then, while you both are resting, I'll fix you a light meal. One of our maids will bring you fresh water and towels."

"I'll have your luggage brought up immediately," Adam assured them. Of course, unless the workmen offered to help, he would haul Hermione's trunk up the stairs himself.

Cathy led the way, and when she opened the door to Auggie's room, he stepped inside and declared, "At least there is a balcony. I am ill from this heat and shall lie down without delay." Glancing back at Cathy, he added, "If you would have a servant bring me a tray with food and cold planter's punch, I should like it. I'm terribly thirsty."

She tried to smile. "I'll do my best, but I ought to warn you that we haven't any ice today…"

"I feel as if I've gone back in time," cried her mother. "How can you live like this, Catherine?"

Steering her into Adam's spacious bedroom, Cathy closed the door and met her eyes. "I must ask you to listen to me, Mother. I am very happy in my marriage. I enjoy the work of restoring Tempest Hall and, as you must have realized when you came upon us in the library, I am in love with my husband."

"Neither of you knows the first thing about love. The only perception I gained from that exceedingly common scene was that my daughter has cast her breeding to the wind and her husband is a worse barbarian than I had feared." Hermione walked around the room, assessing Adam's possessions as she spoke. "And it's no wonder your servants have no respect for you, dressed and cavorting like a hoyden. No wonder your cook is at the beach rather than doing her job!"

Cathy went to the washstand and poured water into a simple white ewer. "I realize that Barbados must seem very foreign to you, Mother. It is a far cry from Newport, I know, but I am trying to adapt. I can't behave as if I'm in Newport, or I'll never have any success here."

Hermione sank into the chair by Adam's desk. She stared out the window, appearing not to have heard a word of Cathy's speech. Her bejeweled hand went to a strip of velvet trimming her bodice, and she rubbed it between her fingertips.

Cathy set about washing her face and hands. When her mother still hadn't spoken, she went into the dressing room and changed into a simple tan skirt and thin, lace-edged shirtwaist. Without even looking into a mirror, she piled her mass of hair atop her head and inserted tortoiseshell pins to secure it. Hermione was still staring and rubbing the bit of velvet.

"Mother?" She went to her side and knelt beside the chair. The daughter in her was glad to be reunited with her parent. "Is anything wrong?"

The older woman swiveled, and their eyes locked. "I don't believe you. I don't believe that he loves you."

Cathy felt as if she'd been struck. In the old days, at Beechcliff, she would have been afraid to face her down, but this was new territory and even Hermione seemed altered somehow. "I don't understand why you would say something so unkind and hurtful to me."

"I'm your mother. If I don't speak the truth, who will?"

"Well, you're wrong! Adam does love me. We are *blissfully* happy."

Hermione stared out the window again, over the tops of silvery casuarina trees, over sugar cane fields and reddish dirt roads and mahogany forests that led to the wild Atlantic Ocean. Her fingers found the velvet again. A furrow appeared in her brow.

When had her mother ever looked so stricken over her welfare? In the end, everything had always come back to Hermione, hadn't it? In a gentler voice, Cathy asked, "Mother, why are you here? Why did you decide to visit me so soon after my wedding?" She touched her wrist. "Is anything wrong?"

Hermione Parrish drew a ragged breath. "Everything is wrong." Her proud face turned to her daughter, crumpling as she confessed, "Your father has left me for another woman. He wants a divorce!"

Part Four

Chapter 20

"This is hell." Adam climbed into the narrow bed that dominated the small north bedroom and stretched out, frowning. "Hell!"

"I heard you the first time."

"Even Alice is protesting her new quarters. She's sleeping outside my *true* bedroom door."

"I don't blame her. It's rather stuffy in here."

"My feet hang over the end of this bed."

"I'm sorry to hear it." Cathy was busy trying to puff up her pillow and find a sleeping position that would keep her bottom from coming in contact with a broken spring. "Couldn't your grandparents afford to buy a decent bed?"

"This is an antique." His mouth twitched. "Extremely valuable."

"Extremely impractical, you mean." Propping herself up on an elbow, Cathy looked at the fireplace that had been built into one corner. Its tile interior gleamed in the lamplight. It had never been used in its two-hundred-sixty years of existence. "Only the fireplaces in Tempest Hall are more impractical than this bed!"

"I think your ire is misplaced. Stop blaming my grandparents and this poor house and start blaming your mother." Turning toward her, Adam traced the line of her nightgown-clad waist and hip. He longed to curve his hand over her bottom. "Has she told you yet what in God's name she is doing here? For someone so obsessed with proper etiquette, this impromptu visit is staggeringly rude. I didn't expect to see Hermione here until she'd received an engraved invitation from you, me, and the Queen of England."

"Has she asked you to call her Hermione?"

"You must be joking." He drew her closer. "But why shouldn't I? I'm her son-in-law, after all." A wicked smile played over his mouth. "And, I love the sound of that name, don't you? Her-mi-o-ne. Reminds me of an incantation."

"You're very bad." She was euphoric in his embrace.

"You don't know the half of it." Adam slid his hand into her hair and covered her mouth with his, kissing her with slow, hot deliberation.

Cathy knew she ought to tell him about her parents' separation, but didn't want to break the spell. Instead, she let herself melt in his arms. Slowly, slowly, he was opening the tiny buttons on her nightgown with his long fingers. As each one slipped free, he bent to press his warm mouth against the newly exposed skin. She longed to believe that he really wanted her in this way, that he wasn't just pretending. Each touch of his mouth caused her breathing grow more shallow. Her breasts felt swollen, and the place between her legs had begun to ache with yearning.

Adam wanted to lift the gown over her head, toss it aside, and cover every inch of her starlit body with the most intimate of kisses. He wanted to hold her down and part her legs and teach her just how high she could soar...but he remembered how she had stopped him before, how shocked and embarrassed she'd been. So, instead he opened the last button on her bodice and gently pushed it aside to find her eager breast. The nipple was taut, and when he circled it with his tongue, he heard her whimper. He was so hard; the thought of being inside Cathy made him crazy. But he held back; he waited until she arched closer, urging her breast into his mouth, before he began to suckle. Slowly, lingeringly, he worked at her nipple until she was making soft panting sounds. When his free hand drew her nightgown up and found its way between her legs, she opened to his questing fingers. She was slick and so ready, but Adam took his time and deftly touched her, exploring, stroking. In time, he sensed that she was still too anxious to surrender, and so he let his hand drift away and moved over her, kissing her, letting his erection press between her open legs.

Cathy was coming to love the feeling of his powerful body covering hers, of his hands cupping her bottom, his hardness nudging the place she felt most vulnerable. She responded to the slightly salty, musky, male scent of him, and the play of muscles over his wide back as she clung to him.

When he came into her and she arched up to meet him, Cathy had a moment of gratitude for her mother's visit and their exile to the small, uncomfortable north bedroom.

"I saw an *enormous* creature scurry across my floor last night," Hermione announced as she sipped her breakfast coffee. The dining room had been made as presentable as possible, given the workmen's clutter in the adjoining sitting room, and the Raveneaus and their guests had just taken their seats at the beautiful Sheraton table.

"Was it a lizard?" asked Cathy.

"No. It was shiny and dark."

Adam arched a brow. "A cockroach."

"No, no. It was much too big for that. Not that we have cockroaches at Beechcliff, but I was raised in the South and I do recall seeing one during my childhood."

"We have huge cockroaches here," he persisted. "My grandfather used to call them 'mahogany birds.'"

Hermione shuddered and dropped her pince-nez. "How hideous! What sort of primitive place is this?"

"Mother," Cathy exclaimed, "Barbados is a tropical island!"

"I still cannot get over the fact that Tempest Hall does not have indoor plumbing. It's simply shocking! Catherine, can there ever be a day that you do not pine for your marble bathroom at Beechcliff, with the separate taps for seawater and freshwater?"

Flushing, she lied, "Nothing could be farther from my mind. Such matters are of no consequence to me here."

"If we were closer to Bridgetown we would have indoor plumbing," said Adam. "The more distant locations on the island wait longer for advancements like running water, electricity, and telephone service. However, I must add in our defense that we don't need separate taps for seawater. The ocean is minutes away and astonishingly warm compared to Newport."

Auggie spoke up at last. "I am more shocked that there are no motor cars, even in Bridgetown. We may as well be in Africa. Come to think of it, looking around, sometimes I think we are!"

"Cousin, that is a very poor jest." Cathy broke off at the sight of a servant carrying in a tray of papaya halves, and in the next moment, she recognized the girl. "June, what are you doing here? You're supposed to be at school in Speightstown!"

"We have days off because of Christmas, Mistress," she explained softly while serving the fruit. "I missed my grandfather and Retta…and you."

"I'm delighted to see you, too. June, this is my mother, Mrs. Parrish, and my cousin, Mr. Chase. They are visiting from America."

June bobbed her head, mumbled a greeting, and slipped out of the room.

Hermione wore an expression of utter horror. "Catherine Beasley Parrish! One never, ever converses with one's servants at the table, particularly in a manner that invites them to socialize with the guests! Have you forgotten every lesson I taught you?"

Staring at her papaya, she murmured, "Not yet, but I'm trying."

"I beg your pardon?"

"I said that I'm trying not to forget, but this isn't Beechcliff, you know. Our household is much smaller and friendlier."

Raveneau decided to intervene. "What plans do you have for the day, Cathy?"

"I thought we might take Mother and Auggie down to see that impressive mansion on the southeastern coast that you've told me about. Crowe's Nest, isn't that it?" She turned to her guests. "Barbados has all sorts of legends about this house and its owner, Xavier Crowe. He used to hang lanterns on the palm trees to trick ships into thinking they'd reached Bridgetown's harbor. Then, when they came closer, they'd be caught in the treacherous Atlantic waves and crash on Cobbler's Reef. Crowe's men took whatever valuables they could find…"

"My grandfather, Nathan Raveneau, and Xavier Crowe were bitter enemies," Adam explained. "In the end, it was Grandfather who set the trap that Crowe stepped into. He was captured, tried, and hanged for his crimes."

"What happened to his mansion? Does he have descendants?"

"Crowe's wife and nephew went to England after his arrest. The house resembles a castle, and many claim it's cursed," Adam replied, squeezing more lime over his papaya. "It developed some time ago that the nephew had an heir on the island, Basil Lightfoot, but as I understand it, he couldn't afford to keep the place and it was sold last year to pay his debts. As far as I know, it has been uninhabited since Crowe's death."

"Perhaps we can go inside!" exclaimed Cathy.

"Our family owns fifty acres of land just north of Crowe's Nest and it's one of the most beautiful spots on the island, complete with the ruins of an old plantation house called Victoria Villa. I'll come along to show you; it would be safer for you to explore there."

June and Liza, the new serving maid, appeared with the breakfast trays then. There were dishes of poached haddie, toasted and buttered yams and plantains, coddled eggs, and boiled eggs imported from England. Even Cathy was surprised to see such an extensive array of food and wondered if Adam had sent Simon back to market at dawn. When Liza offered the guests a choice of chocolate, tea, or coffee, Hermione began to look satisfied with her surroundings for the first time.

As they were eating, contentment reigned. When Adam reached under the table to squeeze Cathy's hand, she beamed in reply, drinking in the sight of him. Black hair was casually brushed back from his brow, and she flushed at the memory of her fingers sinking into those locks a few short hours ago. Now, as if reading her mind, Raveneau sent her a wicked smile.

"You do like de food?" inquired a soft voice.

Cathy turned to see Retta in the doorway, a walking stick in each hand. "Retta! How lovely to see you up and about today. Yes, breakfast is delicious! Please, sit with us a moment. Perhaps you can answer some of our questions about Crowe's Nest."

As if sensing Hermione Parrish's disapproval, Retta sank down on a side chair that was pushed against the wall. "I stays here, Mistress."

To the others, Cathy said, "Retta came to work for Adam's grandparents when she was a very young girl, some eighty-five years ago. Isn't that amazing?" Then, to the old woman, she asked, "Did you know Xavier Crowe, Retta?"

A cloud seemed to pass over her withered face. "He do be a bad man. Make slaves do evil deeds."

"Have you seen Crowe's Nest?"

"Mmm-hmm. Rav'neau land by dere. I get chills when I go." She shivered at the memory. "Spirits 'pon dere."

Cathy thought about Stede Bonnet, the gentleman pirate, and the treasure map she'd found hidden in Adrienne Beauvisage's closet wall. How much did Retta know about that? A warning glance from Adam caused her to swallow her other questions. "It does sound as if we'll have an exciting outing!"

"For my part," Hermione rejoined, "I am concerned more with tangible matters, such as our lunch. Retta, can you arrange a picnic?"

"Pic-nic?" she repeated dubiously.

"A lovely outdoor lunch served in a wicker basket. You must pack white linen, crystal, and silver—and a tent, if possible. And of course, we'll need an assortment of delicacies, and champagne and flowers—"

"Ma'am," Retta broke in, "I do be deaf." And with that, she got to her feet and tottered off toward the kitchen door.

Just then, Simon came in. He bowed to all the guests, but it was Raveneau to whom he whispered, "I almos' forget dis letter I bring you from Bridgetown, sir." He extracted a small envelope from his breast pocket and proffered it with a sigh.

"Thank you, Simon. Could you please hitch up the horses? We'll be leaving soon." He gave the others a distracted smile. "I'll just take Alice for a turn in the garden."

Cathy watched him rise, her instincts on alert. "We'll go upstairs and get ready."

Outside, Adam and Alice walked under the rose arbor, and he took the letter out of his breast pocket. While the retriever amused herself by scattering the crowds of noisy guinea fowl, Adam scanned the note written in Gemma's own hand. It read, in part,

I am waiting for word from you, my lord. I trust you have told your wife the truth about me—and our son? Paul waits to visit you, perhaps to spend Christmas in his father's home…

Adam had a fleeting pain in his chest, then he straightened his shoulders and steeled himself to deal with the situation. There was a time when he might have sailed off to America or England and then sought further escape through cards, drink, or women. However, the loss of Thorn Manor had taught him that no problem was ever solved for long by debauchery.

Still, this particular problem could not have come at a worse time. Who could blame him for not telling Cathy about Paul after the sudden arrival of her mother? His heart clenched again at the memory of Cathy sleeping in his arms in the aftermath of their shared passion.

Heading back into the house through the library, Adam paused to wedge the folded note into his desk blotter. Voices drifted down the stairs as his wife and the others prepared to embark on their outing.

"Psst!"

He glanced over and saw Retta standing in the doorway, motioning with one walking stick for him to join her. Raveneau crossed to her side and asked, "Is something wrong?"

"Yessir! De pic-nic!" There was a deep furrow in her brow. "Dat lady want a tent an' caviar an' a wicker basket—"

"No, no." He patted her thin, hunched back. "Don't pay any attention to her."

"She talkin' 'bout de servants wearin' livery, sir! She want we all wearin' blue an' gold."

"Utter nonsense."

"What 'bout tent for de pic-nic?"

"Ignore her. Simply have the girls pack what we have for a lunch and give it to my wife. She is your mistress, not Mrs. Parrish. You've stood up to worse types than her, haven't you, Retta?"

"Maybe," she grumbled, straightening her headtie.

Adam watched her head off to the kitchen before he went to meet Cathy at the foot of the stairs.

"I think someone is coming on horseback, " she said. "I caught a glimpse of a rider from Mother's window."

"Wait." He caught the back of her cream silk suit when she started toward the back door. "I'm afraid I cannot accompany you to Crowe's Nest after all. I find that I must go to Bridgetown on an urgent errand."

"I see." Sensing Gemma Hart's presence between them, Cathy felt a sharp prick of jealousy. "I won't trouble you to invent an errand for my benefit."

He pretended not to understand what she meant. "I think that you ought to travel down the coast on the railroad. Simon can drive you to the station at Bathsheba."

Behind them, Hermione and Auggie were descending the stairs. "There's someone looking for you in the yard, cousin," said Auggie. He pointed out the back door. "Can't you hear him?"

At that moment, Theo Harrismith burst into the back stairhall. "Ah, Lady Raveneau, there you are. I feared you had gone out." He was clad in a natty shadow-striped beige suit and a violet bowtie, and he was carrying a large wicker basket over one arm. Bowing low, he swept off his boater. "You grow lovelier by the week. Island living must agree with you."

She flushed prettily. "Good friends like you agree with me, sir. How kind of you to come all this way, particularly in light of your responsibilities at the hotel."

After performing introductions, her eyes fell on his basket. "Have you got a surprise in there?"

"Yes, indeed. I am paying a Christmas call. This is your first Christmas in Barbados, and you don't know our customs yet."

Cathy felt Adam move close behind her. His hand touched the small of her back and she instinctively leaned toward him. "No doubt my husband would have introduced me to those customs were we not so busy with Tempest Hall…"

"That's where friends come in, hmm?" Laughing, Theo reached into his basket and withdrew a fancy cork-stoppered glass bottle filled with red liquid. "I've brought sorrel, our Bajan Christmas drink that's made from red sorrel seed pods." Next he drew out a fruitcake and a fine smoked ham with a red ribbon around it. "We call these great cakes here, and the ham will be your main course. Josephine will make jug-jug, a mandatory dish on Christmas."

"*Jug-jug!*" cried Hermione. "That sounds simply hideous!"

Laughing, he conceded, "It may be, but no one has Christmas without it. It's made of pigeon peas, bits of pork, and guinea corn flour, all cooked together with stock until it resembles sludge." His eyes twinkled. "Jug-jug is a tradition we Bajans cling to, for better or worse."

Cathy looked up at Adam, expecting to find him amused, but he was not. Instead, he took the basket from Theo and said, "Kind of you to think of us, Mr. Harrismith. However, in the future we'll sort out our own Christmas traditions."

Theo's eyebrows went up. "Sorry—"

"No good deed goes unpunished, eh?" cried Auggie before marching out into the yard. When Hermione followed him, Cathy stepped forward to take Theo's arm and lead him outside, away from her husband.

"I don't know what's wrong with Adam," she whispered after they had stepped into the sunlight.

"I'll wager you have an idea, but far be it for me to interfere. Clearly he feels I've done enough of that."

Cathy glanced back at the house and saw Adam standing in the shadows that fell inside the tall library windows. He was watching her and petting Alice at the same time. "You know, Theo, you ought to accompany us on our outing today since my husband can't. We're going to St. Philip, to have a look at Cave Bay and Victoria Villa, and then to see the notorious Crowe's Nest. Won't you come with us?"

"He won't like it."

"That's all right."

"I could serve as your guide," Theo allowed. "I was raised here, after all."

"And, if you come, we won't have to travel on the railroad." Cathy smiled at him and started toward the buggy that was hitched up a short distance away. "Come on. Isn't it a lovely day?"

Inside the house, Adam watched as his wife and Theo walked past the ancient sandbox tree. Cathy was looking awfully pretty in her cream suit with the brown braid trim. She was carrying a matching wide-brimmed hat with a veil to protect her hair from the dust that already coated the hem of her skirt. Unbidden came the memory of her face in the moonlight at the moment of his release. Her expression had been soft, vulnerable, filled with emotion, and he had kissed her with a tenderness he didn't recognize in himself.

"Alice," he murmured in a husky voice, "why are women's skirts so long that they drag on the ground? Terribly impractical, don't you think?"

It was Retta who answered him from the doorway. "Sir, you mus' go wit' she. Build de bridge." Slowly, she tottered across the room on her two canes to join him at the window. "You jus' like you gran'papa. Stubborn. Hard." The old woman shook her head.

"It's my mother-in-law I can't tolerate. It would be hell to spend the day with her."

"But you do dat to show love to you wife."

He almost flinched. "Ah, Retta, it's so much more complicated than you know. There aren't any easy answers these days."

"Can be," she insisted, then slanted a sly look up at him. "It dat Gemma Hart, hmm? I know some t'ings."

"I can handle Gemma, but I must go to Bridgetown today to talk to her."

"Better talkin' to you wife. Or dat Theo man talk to she." Retta started toward the door, pausing to add, "An' you be smart to visit you land by Cave Bay, sir. Maybe take de map wit' you."

"Map? Do you mean the one Cathy found? The map my grandmother put away?" Turning in anticipation of her response, he discovered that she'd already left the library. Adam's questions seemed to echo in the big room. Glancing down at Alice, he stroked her ears and said, "Retta is very old, you know. One never knows what year she's living in at any given moment…"

Chapter 21

As they traveled down the rugged east coast of Barbados, Cathy realized that she was truly falling in love with her island home. The towns that were bordered by the wild Atlantic Ocean were rocky and weather-beaten and half-civilized, and she found them romantic. The views were spectacular. Hills of vivid green staggered down to meet the sapphire-hued sea. The Atlantic Ocean was thrillingly different from the Caribbean Sea on the west coast, its frothy rollers pounding at the stones and sand while overhead mounds of cottony clouds decorated a cerulean sky.

All along the coastline wound the railroad tracks, past Bathsheba with its prized Atlantis Hotel and cabbage palms and tin-roofed houses, past beaches lined with brightly painted fishing boasts, past vertical cliffs and holiday cottages with jalousie shutters pushed open to receive the ocean breeze.

"Isn't it awfully rustic out here?" wondered Auggie.

"Savage, you mean," Hermione exclaimed. "Even dangerous! One never knows what might lurk around the next bend in the road. That is, if you can call this collection of holes and bumps a road."

Cathy laughed as if her mother were joking, and Theo pretended not to have heard. Before long, they caught a glimpse of the rickety-looking train. The engine was small, with an open cab, and the back cars were massed with freshly cut stalks of bright, light-green sugar cane.

"Some of the eastern plantations have had an early crop," Theo remarked. He had stopped the buggy on the crest of a hill and pointed down to the train chugging southward below them. "They all depend on the railroad to transport their cane now. There are a couple passenger cars behind the engine."

"How quaint," Hermione said, her voice slightly muffled by the gauzy scarf she'd wrapped around her nose and mouth to protect herself from breathing any dust. "My dear Mr. Harrismith, although I appreciate your efforts to enlighten us, I must tell you that Auggie and I have no real interest in your island's rattletrap railroad."

"I am interested," Cathy declared.

"And I am ready for lunch," said Auggie. "Let's move along and have a look at this Crowe's Nest place. Don't suppose the old pirate left any treasure for us?"

Theo snapped the reins to start the horses forward. "No, although there were rumors of treasure years ago. Crowe was said to have found a map made by Stede Bonnet himself, and no one is quite certain what happened to it, or whether the treasure was ever recovered."

Cathy looked up, wide-eyed, while her mother repeated in querulous tones, "Stede Bonnet? Why is that name familiar to me? Was he an American?"

"No, Mrs. Parrish. Bonnet was a Barbadian brethren of the Black Flag who lived in the early 1700's."

"What in the name of heaven is a brethren of the Black Flag?"

Theo raised his eyebrows at her and smiled. "Why, he was a *pirate*! Not only that, but Stede Bonnet was a partner of Blackbeard!"

"Oh my heavens!" She brought her gloved hand to her open mouth. "Why, now I remember. Catherine's husband was dressed as Stede Bonnet at our costume ball!"

"Really!" He glanced at Cathy. "Well, I don't want to bore you, but I will say that Stede Bonnet, the gentleman pirate, was born the son of a Barbadian planter. He married and distinguished himself as a fine citizen, but he must have grown restless, because he bought himself a sloop, arms, and a crew, and went to sea. Eventually, he traveled to the waters near Charleston, North Carolina, and joined forces with Blackbeard. Later, they quarreled and Blackbeard betrayed him." Theo stopped to consult a signpost, made more confusing because of the tall cane fields that made it difficult to get one's bearings. Taking a left turn, he continued, "As the story goes, Bonnet was afraid of Blackbeard, and he hid much of his plunder from him and returned to Barbados to bury it. Then, back in Charleston, Bonnet was captured, tried, and eventually hanged. A man of refinement, he died clutching a bouquet of flowers."

"What a fascinating story!" Cathy exclaimed. She could hardly wait to go home and take a second look at the map, and perhaps at Nathan Raveneau's journals. There had to be a way to make Adam take the map seriously!

"All fairytales are fascinating," sniffed Hermione.

Soon they came out of the cane fields and caught a glimpse of the ocean again, out beyond the scrubby, parched landscape. The clumps of windblown manchineel and whitewood trees were bent in half, their distorted branches pointing inland after years of furious storms. Hermione and Auggie had begun to doze until Cathy spotted the ruins of a great coral-stone manor house silhouetted romantically against the blue sky. From a distance, it was eerily evocative, like a ghostly wedding cake with two square, hollowed-out layers. The bottom was trimmed on all sides with an arcaded verandah while the second layer was a smaller square lined with small hooded windows. Of course, the windows were reduced to gaping holes now and the roof was nearly gone.

"Look!" she cried. "Isn't it beautiful! Oh, Theo, it must be haunted."

Behind them, Hermione was grimacing. "Simply ghastly. Must be overrun with vermin and all manner of hideous insects."

"That's Victoria Villa," Theo explained. "And this is Raveneau land. The villa is very old and many would agree with you that it's haunted."

Soon he had navigated the buggy up a rutted, weed-choked cart track. Auggie declared that this was the perfect spot for their picnic, ghosts and vermin be damned, and Cathy was inclined to agree. It was the most stunning place she had ever been in her life. Hermione wanted to go on to Crowe's Nest, but for once her companions dared to overrule her.

They sat on the blanket Retta had packed, on a green slope with a view of the ocean, and ate lunch. There were two bottles of tepid champagne which Cathy poured freely for her mother, hoping it would soften her mood. The food fell short of Hermione's orders, consisting of pickled beef, prickly green soursops and clumps of sea grapes, coconut bread, cold slices of sweet potatoes, and roasted peanuts. However, the view was spectacular. Palm trees growing on the beach waved above the clifftops, and the color of the ocean beyond seemed too intense to be real. Near the shore, the water was dazzling turquoise that soon melted into a deeper sea of blazing sapphire.

"It's as if we're wearing magic spectacles, don't you think?" Cathy said dreamily. Then, as she finished the last of her grapes, she scrambled to her feet. "I'm going swimming!"

Hermione scolded, "Don't be ludicrous. I would have imagined that marriage would have calmed you down, child."

"I have my bathing costume," she insisted, "and just look at that water! There's a way down to the beach from here, isn't there, Theo?"

"Oh, yes, there are steps of a sort carved into the cliff. Do you see them over there? But it really isn't very safe to be swimming here—"

She had already started back to the ruined villa to change, calling over her shoulder, "Don't worry! I won't go in beyond my waist. Besides, there's no one around, and it will be such fun to go out in the sunshine, which I couldn't do at Hastings Baths!"

Theo distracted Hermione and Auggie with stories about the Ocean Breeze Hotel and the Hastings Baths so that they barely noticed when Cathy passed by in her bathing costume. "You must come down to the hotel for a special lunch, Mrs. Parrish. Perhaps I can convince you that Barbados is not the heathen place you imagine."

"More likely you'll convince me that all men on this island are not like my so-called son-in-law. His behavior is disgraceful. I've never known another British aristocrat to have such deplorable manners."

Auggie opened the second bottle of champagne, and it spurted all over the blanket. "The man's a libertine as far as I can tell. Catherine's father wasn't in his right mind or he'd have sent Raveneau packing."

"Is Mr. Parrish unwell?" Theo inquired, noting the sudden high color in Hermione's powdered cheeks.

"You might say that!" she snapped. "Let us not speak of the universal failings of men."

Seeking a distraction, Theo pointed to Cathy's figure frolicking in the surf. "Goodness, look at your daughter. Isn't she a sight? She certainly does know how to enjoy herself!"

Just then, the sound of hoofbeats reached their ears. Shielding their eyes, the trio looked to the west and saw Adam Raveneau galloping toward the villa on Lazarus, his magnificent black stallion. When he was nearly upon them, he reined in the horse and swung to the ground. He was clad only in a white shirt, open at the neck, and snug tan riding breeches tucked into high boots.

Auggie, who had clambered to his feet in surprise, appeared even more startled when Adam handed him the reins. "What's the matter, my lord?"

"Where is my wife?"

He pointed down to the beach that curved against the cliffs. Seeing Adam's darkening expression, he hastened to add, "We told her it wasn't seemly—"

"That is the least of my concerns." Adam stalked past Hermione and Theo without a word of greeting, then descended the niches that were chiseled into the stone so rapidly that it seemed he knew them by heart. He did. How many afternoons had he spent here during boyhood visits to the island? Victoria Villa and Cave

Bay had been a large part of the reason he'd fallen in love with Barbados. Who could resist such beauty and mystery?

And yet now, the sight of his wife swimming alone in the treacherous Atlantic Ocean made him furious. "Catherine!" he shouted, blood pounding at his temples. "Come here immediately!"

She was standing a few dozen yards out in waist-deep water, and each time a wave rushed toward the beach, she laughed and jumped up to let it carry her up and forward.

"What?" she yelled back to her furious husband. "I can't hear you!"

He seethed, waiting for the ocean's roar to subside for an instant. "It's dangerous! Come in, you little hellion!"

Cathy laughed. "I'm fine! I needed some fun, Adam—" Her voice broke off as a huge wave abruptly surged up behind her. This time, she was caught off guard and the water pounded over her, pushing her down toward the beach with such force she couldn't bring her head up for air. Choking, Cathy panicked, swallowing saltwater and struggling helplessly against the immense force of the ocean.

In the next instant, Adam plucked her out of the sea and carried her to shore. He was dripping from his fine linen shirt to his polished boots and, from the clifftops, the others were shouting fearfully.

Hearing Cathy's watery gasps for breath, Adam lay her down on the hot sand and covered her mouth with his, exhaling. Then he pressed both hands against her chest and pushed, and water spurted out and ran down the side of her sandy cheek. Coughing, she blinked at him and struggled to sit up.

"I—I—I was just fine. You didn't have to do that."

"If you call half-dead just fine."

"I would have popped back up as soon as the wave retreated, or whatever it is that waves do…"

"Are you trying to drive me insane?" Adam got to his feet and made a half-hearted effort to brush the sand from his wet clothes. "I could paddle you right now, easily—"

"Now, there's an adult solution to our problems!" Sopping wet, her hair falling down and trailing tortoiseshell pins, Cathy marched barefoot through the sand. Then, as she passed the entrance to a cave, near the steps that would provide her escape route, she stubbed her toe on something hard. "Ow! What was that?"

As his wife leaned against the cave wall to nurse her throbbing toe, Adam hunkered down, and brushed the sand away from piece of wood that now peeked out ever so slightly. He pulled on it.

"What the devil…" he murmured under his breath when it wouldn't come free.

The thing was egg-shaped, like the top of a walking stick. There was a bit of red glass set into the wooden dome that became more visible as he cleared away more of the sand.

"I'm going up," Cathy announced, suddenly tired.

"Wait." He tugged in vain on the mysterious wooden object. Meanwhile, Hermione, Auggie, and Theo were calling down to Cathy and she was getting to her feet. Rising, he turned his attention back to his wife. "Don't try to climb those steps without me."

"I wonder at your concern for my welfare. Just a few hours ago, you were easily enough distracted from me by your message from Bridgetown." She pushed her wet, sandy hair off her face and started up the steps. She sensed his shadow and knew that his hands were close behind her in case she lost her footing.

"If I weren't concerned about you, I wouldn't be here." Seeing her falter, he caught her hand. "You should be wearing shoes."

"And what of your treatment of my friend? If you had any regard for me, you would have been a more gracious host to Theo."

"You know it's not in my nature to be gracious." He gave a short laugh. No sooner had they gained the top step, and then solid ground, than Adam reached out again for her arm. "Cathy, I don't want you going off alone again. I want to be with you on these little adventures of yours."

"You were invited. You had better things to do!"

Hermione, Auggie, and Theo all rushed over, looking uncertain as Adam shook out the picnic blanket and wrapped it around his wife. "How do you feel?" he asked.

"How should I feel with you badgering me?" Tears threatened. "Honestly, Adam, you can be insufferable. No matter what I do, it's wrong."

"Certainly it's wrong if you go jumping into the Atlantic Ocean alone. For God's sake, Cath, you could have been killed in the blink of an eye! Those currents are not just tricky, they're stronger than a dozen men."

"Now see here, my good fellow—" Auggie interjected.

Adam pretended as if the other man wasn't there. "Cathy, let's go inside, where we can talk privately and you can put on some dry clothes," he said, gesturing toward the skeletal mansion.

"I most certainly don't need to be private with you—"

"Behave yourself." He swept her up in his arms and carried her off, ignoring the others and their outraged protests. When they were out of sight under the colonnaded gallery, he set her on her feet and demanded, "Show me where your clothes are."

"No!" Weeks of emotion boiled up in her. "Leave me alone, Adam."

Her blanket had fallen away, and he could see the curves of her body outlined against the damp bathing costume. All manner of primitive urges suddenly burned inside him. "Jesus, Cath, you don't mean a word of this—"

She took a step back, and he moved against her so that she found herself pinned up against one of the villa's wide, arching columns. His body was sharply arousing: big, gracefully muscular, and warm through his riding clothes. He smelled intoxicating. Cathy's heart began to beat faster against his linen shirt.

"You shouldn't behave this way," she protested weakly. "It's—"

"Yes?" His mouth was inches from hers.

She inhaled his breath and felt faint with longing. When she put a hand on his forearm for support, the warm strength of him made her eyes sting. "I'm furious with you," she managed to murmur at last.

"Is that what you call it?" he parried. Then, sliding his arms around her waist, Adam bent her back and kissed a trail up her throat. By the time he reached her jawline, Cathy's arms had stolen up around his shoulders and her hips were seeking his. Overcome by temptation, he kissed her full on the mouth until she groaned and her tongue met his. She was pressed against the length of him. Adam reached down with his right hand and cupped the hot place between her legs. Cathy jerked away and he smiled, white teeth agleam in the shadows. "I think you're fonder of me than you'll admit."

She pointed at him while pressing her other hand to her thumping heart. "You are a scoundrel! Just go away and leave me alone—"

"Only if you'll heed my advice. If you're going to have outings without me, you've got to use common sense! As a married woman, you can't go frolicking in the Atlantic, and you can't be seen riding around with men who are not your husband."

"Wh—what?" Cathy laughed in disbelief, but tears filled her eyes. "You men are all alike. There's not one whit of difference between you and my father, whom I adored from the day I was born. Papa and you both keep mistresses, and both of you hide your secret lives, lying to protect your reputations. How dare you tell me how to behave? I see no reason to trust another man as long as I live!"

Stunned, Adam could only stare as his wife gathered her clothing and ran off toward her mother. By the time he found his voice, it was too late.

Chapter 22

"Wait!" shouted Adam.

Furiously wiping away tears, Cathy urged her companions to make haste loading the buggy while she quickly changed her clothes behind a clump of bushes. "I can't bear to spend another moment with that arrogant libertine!"

"I tried to warn you," said Hermione as she assisted with the buttons up the back of her daughter's shirtwaist.

Before Cathy could reply, her husband was standing in front of them. "Do me the courtesy of hearing what I have to say."

"It's too late."

"It certainly is *not* too late!" He reached for her arm, and she pulled back as if he'd struck her. "I would have told you the truth long ago if there hadn't been some happiness between us at Tempest Hall. But then, each time I was about to speak, I was afraid of cutting down our marriage when it was just beginning to blossom—"

"Very poetic," she cut in angrily, "but insulting to my intelligence. You were afraid, all right, afraid of not having two women at once, afraid of looking foolish by getting divorced immediately after your wedding, and most of all afraid of losing my *money*!" She made the last thrust with relish and watched him absorb the blow.

"If you would just listen to me," he said through gritted teeth. "Could we have a moment's privacy?"

"Certainly not. And you are the one who needs to listen. I now know that my own father kept a mistress, for years I imagine, and he lied to me every day. That is unforgiveable. And, I know that you have also led a double life—and, I suspect, still are!"

"You are wrong—" he protested.

"No more lies!" More tears spilled down her cheeks. "And no more secrets. Your secrets will poison all of us."

Auggie listened in silence, and Theo looked torn as he loaded the buggy and helped the ladies to board. As Hermione passed Adam, she couldn't resist delivering a few cuts of her own.

"I always knew you were a fraud, *my lord*. You'll never amount to anything, and I hope my daughter has the courage to turn her back on this sham marriage and go back to Newport with me while she has the chance!" Then, holding down her Gainsborough hat in the wind, Hermione let Auggie help her into the buggy and glanced back at her son-in-law with a haughty sniff.

Fury welled inside him as he watched the horses start forward and turn away from the turquoise ocean. Unable to resist, Adam shouted, "I don't blame Jules! Thirty years of marriage to you would be worse than a prison sentence at hard labor!"

Theo bit his lip trying not to smile, and he sensed that Cathy was not completely out of temper with her husband. Chin trembling, she stole a glance back at his solitary figure, then stared at her own lap.

"He can be difficult to resist," Theo whispered kindly.

"Maybe, but I'm getting better at it."

"Are you sure?" He slowed the horses as they came to a fork in the road, then turned north. "I think we ought to save Crowe's Nest for another day. "

Suddenly, from the seat behind them, Hermione declared, "I have decided that the time has come to tell the full, sordid tale of your father's disgrace. Auggie already knows, and I trust Mr. Harrismith to keep our family secret."

Theo shot Cathy a nervous glance. "If you'd rather wait—"

"No, I have kept his secrets too long! Besides, out here I won't have to worry about eavesdropping servants."

With a heavy sigh, Cathy turned halfway to look at her mother. "I don't know how much more I can bear this afternoon. Can you condense this story?"

"I shall try." She paused. "The woman is an actress, like Evelyn Nesbit. From New York."

"An...actress!" This was beyond anything Cathy had imagined when she saw her father with his mistress on the street in New York. She had assumed she was a woman from his circle, perhaps even the widow of an old friend. The image of a woman like the famous and glamorous Evelyn Nesbit was too much to take in.

"Indeed," Hermione confirmed acidly. "Her name is Mae Larkspur, and she is twenty-three years old. She has big blue eyes and curly yellow hair, and she is tall and exceedingly shapely."

A wave of nausea rolled over Cathy, and she nearly asked Theo to stop the buggy. Turning in her seat, she met her mother's eyes and saw anger and pain mixed together in them. Perhaps for the first time in her own life, Cathy's heart truly went out to her.

"Are you certain about all of this?" she asked. "It just doesn't sound at all like Papa! I mean, this Mae person is barely older than I am." Another thought came to her. "Perhaps it's just a brief flight of fancy, Mother. One hears of men, at Papa's stage of life, who go a bit mad and then it passes…"

"It's been going on for months," Hermione replied flatly. "Even before we moved into Beechcliff, he was involved with that floozy. I *toiled* to make that house into a showplace Jules could be proud of, and I stayed behind week after week in Newport while he returned to New York to work. Little did I imagine that, while I was choosing fabric for the draperies, my husband was carousing in dance halls with an *actress!*"

"How did you find out? Did someone tell you? Did you see them together?"

She turned her face away, staring at a passing row of coconut palms. "I suppose his friends knew, but no one told me. I didn't have any idea until after your wedding, when he came to me and told me about her and said he wanted a divorce."

Cathy reached back for her mother's hand and held it fast, overcome with sympathy. How could she have misjudged her own dear father so completely? Were all men handicapped when it came to fidelity and honor?

The journey back to Tempest Hall was broken only by a stop at Farley Hall for poinsettias. The red-flowered bushes grew profusely all around the once-opulent manor house that now stood empty. In the back of the buggy, Theo found a shovel, which he used to dig up a dozen poinsettias.

"These ought to cheer you up a bit on Christmas, hmm?" He gave Cathy a grin. "What do you think of this mansion? You couldn't imagine the parties that were held here years ago, when I was just a sprig. Unfortunately, the owner, Sir Graham Briggs, died some years ago, and it turned out that he was stony broke. His widow had an incredible estate sale before she left Barbados, and my mother brought me along. We bought an entire Crown Derby dinner service for just two guineas!"

Cathy smiled, thinking that Theo had found the perfect line of work at the Ocean Breeze Hotel. "We'll certainly enjoy the poinsettias. If not for you, my friend, we might have overlooked Christmas entirely."

They weren't far from Tempest Hall, and before long the buggy was drawing up under the sandbox tree. Simon came out of the stables to greet them and unhitch the horses as the little quartet disembarked. Theo bade the others goodbye, lingering to show Simon the poinsettias.

"Could you put these in pots for Lady Raveneau? Perhaps you could find a bit of red ribbon to decorate them for Christmas."

"If dey make Mistress smile, I do it gladly."

Halfway to the house, Cathy turned back to wave goodbye to Theo and to smile at Simon, who seemed to blush in response. It was a bittersweet moment as she thought of the people she'd come to care for on the island. It wasn't a perfect life, by any means, but in just a few weeks she felt far more connected to this world than she had to Newport.

"I'm so glad that you have seen the light and will be coming home with us, Catherine," her mother was saying as they entered the back stairhall. "It takes a mature person to admit she's made a mistake, I'll give you that. Only think how lovely it will be to leave this hovel and return to the life of privilege you deserve—"

"I don't know that I am going back with you, Mother," she broke in softly. "And I haven't the strength to argue about it now. Let's leave the subject of my future alone until after Christmas, all right?"

Hermione pretended as if nothing at all had been said. "Where are your so-called servants? I would have expected them to have tea prepared for us. That cook of yours is very nearly worthless! She wouldn't last a day at Beechcliff." And, wheeling around, she went off to look for Josephine.

Starting up the stairs, Cathy heard the sound of muted voices in the library. If Adam were in there, engaged in conversation, she could slip into their cramped little temporary bedroom and wash her face. Perhaps there would even be time for a few minutes of rest.

In the library, August Randolph Chase III stood near Adam's desk while Liza, the new maid, swiped at the furniture with a feather duster.

"Sir, may I ask you an important question?" she whispered.

"Why, certainly."

"Do you want Lord and Lady Raveneau's marriage to be a success?"

"Hmm?" He cocked his angular head in surprise. "Oh, well, if you put it that way, I suppose I would have to say 'no.' But what can I do about it? Her ladyship won't even listen to her own mother."

"You could talk to my mistress," she suggested, dusting faster.

"What do you mean? Lady Raveneau is your mistress."

"No, not really. I just come here, from the Hart Hotel in Bridgetown. I work for Mistress Gemma Hart." Liza waited for a sign of recognition. "She is Lord Raveneau's...other lady."

"Oh." Auggie blinked. "Oh! Good God! Are you a spy?"

She shrugged. "Not really. I just let my mistress know how things go on here. She has a right to know, don't you think so? She has to think of little Paul's welfare, not just her own."

"Paul? Is that the love child?"

"Yes, sir." Liza dusted for a moment, letting her revelations sink in. "Paul is like a little angel. Innocent, you know? Mistress Hart wonders if you would like to come to Bridgetown and talk to her. She says, maybe you're growing bored here and you'd like a bit of diversion on your own? She will serve you a fine supper if you come tonight."

"A lovely thought, but how am I supposed to get there?"

"I could say that I have to visit my mother, and I would show you the way. You could drive me, and we could borrow a buggy." Seeing Auggie's uncertainty, she plucked the note from the corner of the desk blotter and held it out to him. "You can see for yourself how much pain Mistress Hart endures. She sent this note to his lordship this morning but he does not answer. He only shoves it away and forgets about it."

Auggie scanned the contents, then put it in the pocket of his white duck trousers. "How do we know what Lord Raveneau has planned? He may have gone to Bridgetown today to see your mistress, rather than coming with us."

From the doorway, Hermione Parrish spoke. "Auggie, I think you should go. Catherine is wavering. It may be up to you to help deliver the death blow to this horrible marriage."

When Cathy tiptoed into the cramped north bedroom, she was shocked to find Adam lying on the narrow bed, apparently asleep. Almost more startling was the sight of Alice breaking all the rules by napping beside him, her white-whiskered muzzle on Cathy's pillow.

She decided that, if she could just be quiet enough to change her clothes without waking him, everything would be fine. There was a massive Barbadian mahogany wardrobe against one wall. In it were the items of clothing Cathy and Adam wore most often; for the rest, they made furtive trips into their dressing room when Hermione and Auggie were downstairs.

Now, Cathy opened one door and withdrew a thin muslin shirtwaist and her simplest ecru skirt. The window nearby was open, and she was grateful for the fresh air wafting up from the ocean. The pink frangipani tree had just burst into bloom, and its flowers spread their heavy scent on the late-afternoon breeze.

Cathy sighed and let herself relax. The sleeping Adam looked like a dream, so darkly and sinfully handsome that just the sight of him sent frissons of desire over her nerves. His hair was tousled and touchable. Stubble made shadows on his sculpted jaw.

Alice snored, then whimpered slightly, all four paws twitching as if she were dreaming of hunting game during her youth on the grounds of Thorn Manor.

Her heart aching, Cathy looked away from both of them and began to unbutton the jacket of her suit. When she had removed it, along with the blouse and skirt, she turned to reach for the other shirtwaist.

A brown hand captured her wrist in midair. "My lady wife."

He had her in such a grip that Cathy had to sit down or lose her balance. "Let me go."

"I like the look of you in your lacy drawers and corset." He kissed her shoulder and gave her a sleepy grin.

"Have you been drinking? For heaven's sake, that's the last vice I would recommend you take up at this point in your career."

Adam laughed. "I like your way with words."

"I don't want to hear any more about what you like about me. If we weren't married, and we didn't have guests, I wouldn't tolerate being in the same room with you—"

"Now that's a lie." He drew her down until he was looking into her eyes.

"You're the expert on lies. How many must you have told to keep your mistress a secret?"

"I only meant that you care, Cath, whether you'll admit it or not." Holding her thick hair, he brought her mouth to his, ever so softly. "We've been making a marriage these past weeks…"

She wrenched free, bright spots of color flaring on her cheeks to betray her body's response to him. "How can you say that, when everything we have shared has been built on deception?"

"Wait." Clasping her hand, lacing his fingers through hers, he said, "Allow me to make one speech in my own defense, and if you choose not to believe me, then at least I've been heard."

To Cathy's consternation, Alice had awakened and moved over to prop her chin on her master's chest, fixing Cathy with sorrowful, pleading brown eyes. "Oh, all right, but I really don't see any point in it." She was interrupted by a loud snuffling sound from Alice. "I mean, how can I trust anything that you say?"

"That's just my point. I haven't lied to you, though it's true that I haven't told you all. At first, what was the point? You insisted on marrying me no matter what. I probably could have told you that I kept an entire harem right here at Tempest Hall and it wouldn't have deterred you."

"Hardly! But go on."

"I'll freely admit the truth of my relationship with Gemma, adding that I have done nothing requiring an apology. I was not married during our involvement; I had not even met you. In fairness, I should add that Gemma Hart is not the woman of loose morals you and your mother might think. She is independent, intelligent, strong, and successful in business."

Torn and stung, Cathy asked, "Why didn't you marry her, then?"

"I didn't love her, not in that way. I was involved with her because I didn't want to marry anyone yet. You'll recall that I told you that very thing in Newport?" He watched her eyes drop, lashes brushing her cheeks. "Now that I am married to you, I think I'd say that I wouldn't want to be married to Gemma instead because she doesn't laugh enough. She isn't very playful or warm; she's too caught up in the serious matters of life, simply because of her circumstances."

This soothed her a little. "But why didn't you tell me sooner, when you knew that I would find out one day? And…" She took a painful breath. "What about Paul? He is your child, isn't he?"

"I've already explained that I meant to tell you, but the moment was never right—and then your mother arrived! You and I were growing closer, and I didn't want to hurt you, but I was wrong. Wrong. I've told Gemma the same thing."

"You've been meeting with her secretly!" she accused.

"We've talked privately once or twice, but there is no romance between us any longer. I have been faithful to you." His hand tightened around hers. "Cathy, I have a long and eventful past, and if that upsets you, we're going to have trouble."

Her lower lip pushed out a little. "You haven't answered about Paul."

"You haven't given me a chance," Adam protested. He looked directly into her eyes. "Yes, he is probably my child—"

"Oh, Adam!" For all her suspicions, it was a painful shock to hear him say the words.

"You wanted the truth, and there it is. But I had no idea until I returned to Barbados with you. He seems to be a fine little boy, but I can't say that I feel any strong paternal ties to him. Gemma wants me to spend more time with him; that's the demand she keeps making. Bringing all that up to you seemed like setting off an explosion in our shaky new marriage. If I have mixed feelings about Paul, what must yours be?"

"I think—" Eyes burning, she wrested her hand free of his and stood up. "I think that Paul is a problem I shouldn't have to deal with. I think that you have made your bed, with your fancy mistress, and now you'll have to lie in it." Slipping her arms into the fresh shirtwaist, Cathy added, "And I have strong doubts whether there is room for me in that bed!"

Just then, there was a knock at the door. Adam was annoyed, but got up and went to open the door mere inches. He saw Auggie standing there, looking more tanned than ever in the shadows. "Can I do something for you, Chase?"

"Sorry to disturb you, but I wondered if I might borrow your carriage for a few hours?" Before Adam could speak, Auggie rushed on: "I feel a bit restless, and I heard your maid, Liza, saying that she needs to visit her sick mother in Bridgetown. Perhaps I could take her, and she could direct me?"

"I suppose so. We aren't much on road markers in Barbados, but if Liza is along, you'll be fine." He gave him a distracted smile. "Try to come back before dark, though, all right?"

Auggie assured him that he'd be extremely cautious with Adam's horse and carriage, then turned and started back down the corridor. As soon as he heard the door click shut, he stopped, grinning, and rubbed his hands together.

"Here I come, Miss Gemma Hart!" he whispered. "If we succeed in destroying this marriage, I'll never have to work or worry about money again. Aunt Hermione will see to it that I live in high style for the rest of my life!"

Chapter 23

Late Christmas Eve morning, Hermione Parrish was enjoying her usual breakfast in bed when there came a furtive knocking at her dressing room door.

"Who is it?"

Auggie glided in to find her propped up against a mound of pillows in the magnificent mahogany bed with its froth of mosquito netting. She wore a beribboned silk negligee that billowed over her grand bosom, and her hair hung down in two long gray braids.

"What a splendid piece of furniture that is," he remarked cheerfully. "No doubt Catherine and Adam miss it."

"Even this bed is a far cry from what I'm used to. Nothing is right. We may as well be savages, living without indoor plumbing and electricity and motor cars…"

"I came to tell you about my visit to Gemma Hart. Aren't you interested?" He perched on the far edge of the bed and helped himself to a wedge of papaya.

"You're awfully chipper this morning. You must have had a success."

"I think so. I told her everything you suggested—"

"That she should bring the child here and confront Adam in Catherine's presence?"

"Yes. She resisted at first, but I think I finally convinced her that nothing else will work. She says that she doesn't want Raveneau for herself, but I scoffed at that, then insisted that nothing will drive Catherine away from him faster than the presence of that child in the house."

"*And?*" She stared fiercely at him over the rim of her teacup.

"And the two of us worked out a plan that I found quite brilliant. The question is, will Gemma Hart have the courage to go through with it?"

Anxiously, Cathy stood in the kitchen doorway and watched Josephine and Retta quarrel over the recipe for jug-jug.

"You do cut de meat too much," Retta exclaimed, leaning against the work table for support.

"This is the right way t' make it." She chopped the salt meat and pork even finer, then added in stinging tones, "It's the *new* way. Better."

"De old ways best. Look at peas dere," the old woman cautioned, pointing into the great pot where green peas were boiling with the meat. "Dey do be cookin' too long!"

Josephine threw a mutinous glance toward Cathy. "I can't do best job if this old woman be always watching me!" Then, grasping the sides of the pot with folded towels, she poured off the stock and began adding guinea corn flour.

"I do make jug-jug near one hun'red years," cried Retta. "Orchid comes to island from Africa an' she teach me jug-jug when I young as little June." She glared at Josephine, who pretended to ignore her. "You parents not even born when I learn jug-jug!"

Cathy rushed over and put an arm around Retta. The frail old woman was trembling all over with outrage, while Josephine simply continued to stir the flour into the stock. With each turn of the spoon, she made a little noise of disapproval. Although Cathy was aware of the dangers of offending the temperamental new cook, she couldn't be silent.

"Josephine, I would like you to listen to me."

"I am list'ning, but I can't leave the jug-jug."

"Retta has been at Tempest Hall nearly all her life, and we all love and respect her very much." She squeezed her thin shoulder gently as she spoke.

"Mmm-hmm."

"I won't tell you that you should take direction from her. After all, we hired you to be our cook and you must be in charge. However, I will ask that you treat Retta with the respect and kindness she deserves." Then, without waiting for a response, Cathy got Retta's walking sticks and helped her out of the kitchen and back into the main house.

"I jus' sit 'til I feel stronger," murmured Retta as she collapsed in a chair in the little servants' room off the back stairhall. "Chris'mas eve, so much work…"

Cathy's heart ached for her; she'd never seen her looking so lost and empty. "I'm going to check on the rest of the house, but I want you to think about the poinsettia plants and where we should put them. Do you think we should group them all together, to make a huge red mass, or spread them around the sitting room and dining room , one by one?"

Retta stared off into space and sighed.

Tears welled in Cathy's eyes as she walked slowly down the corridor to the dining room. When she came face-to-face with the painting of Adrienne Beauvisage Raveneau that now hung there, she looked into Adam's grandmother's eyes and wished with all her heart that she could talk to her. What advice would Adrienne give her? It gave Cathy chills to think that Retta had been at Tempest Hall to greet Adrienne when she had first come to Barbados from England, in 1818. Retta was Tempest Hall's last live link with the past...

"At the risk of sounding like a sneering cynic, it's going to be awfully difficult to squeeze any Christmas spirit out of this house."

Cathy whirled around in surprise and discovered that Auggie was sitting all alone at the dining room table, eating eggs and kippers. His observation made her take a long look at her home. The workmen had finished laying the new, unvarnished floor just the day before, and against the new wood the rugs looked older and more worn than ever. Now the men were enjoying their holiday, and there was no way to predict when they would return.

As for Christmas spirit, one did have to use one's imagination. The poinsettia plants helped, but they were a bit straggly and wild-looking, and a far cry from the abundant blooms they'd had at Beechcliff. Worse yet, they didn't have a towering evergreen Christmas tree. The best Simon and Adam had been able to do was a dwarf orange tree that they'd potted and brought into the sitting room. However, without tinsel and ornaments, it didn't seem to have anything to do with Christmas.

"Can you even imagine what it must be like in New York City right now?" Auggie said in dreamy tones.

She tried to block the images from her mind, but it was too late; they'd burst into full color the moment he'd spoken. Cathy thought of snowy sleigh rides down Fifth Avenue, bells jingling on the horses' harnesses, while every shop was decorated with pine garlands and plump holly-sprigged wreaths. The tree in their mansion ballroom was always too big and overdecorated for Cathy's taste, but she did have some ornaments from her childhood that meant the world to her. When she'd begged her mother to allow them to hang on the tree among their new, more lavish counterparts, Jules had taken her part and together father and daughter had prevailed. Remembering those good-natured debates and the way her father's eyes had twinkled so lovingly, Cathy now felt as if her heart had broken. Had she meant so little to him after all, that he would risk losing his daughter's love for an *actress*?

She turned to Auggie, and her eyes grew misty again. "No, I'll agree that Tempest Hall doesn't look the way I might wish on Christmas Eve…but perhaps it's better that I'm here rather than in New York. If I were in the Fifth Avenue house, I'd only miss Papa more."

"If we were in New York," he rejoined sourly, "we wouldn't be treated to such Christmas specialties as jug-jug or that horrid red drink they make from *pods*. What's it called?"

"Sorrel," she replied, gazing off into the distance.

"I took a peek at the jug-jug, and if you ask me, it looks and smells like discarded stomach contents."

"Auggie! That's a revolting thing to say."

"Not as revolting as *jug-jug*."

Cathy wandered over to look out at the still-overgrown front gardens, yearning for the sight of just one snowflake and the sound of just one caroler. Instead, she saw a large iguana propelling itself across a pathway and into a tangle of bougainvillea. "Perhaps by next year I'll be able to import a few things to make us feel more at home during the holidays. Ribbons and candles, and an Italian nativity scene. By then, everything will have fallen into place and the house will be finished, and Adam and I will laugh about all the calamities that befell us during my first Christmas on Barbados."

"Well, that's a nice *dream*, anyway."

She wanted to sit down on the old settee and have a good cry, but just then Alice came trotting into the room. The old Lab's gait might have been a trifle unsteady, but her tail was high in the air and wagging happily. She went straight to her mistress and pushed at her hand with her moist nose.

"Hello, darling." Cathy hitched up her skirts and knelt to put her arms around Alice. "What would I do without you?"

"Now that's true love," remarked Adam as he came in carrying a big box. His presence lit the room. "You risk getting a big whiff of old Alice's breath, and even I don't love her that much."

As determined as she was not to surrender to her husband's potent appeal, Cathy couldn't help smiling. "Poor Alice." She covered the dog's ears. "Don't listen to a word he says. I'll bet you've smelled his breath on many mornings-after without complaint."

He laughed. "I've brought you a package that's just come up from Bridgetown. It had a New York postmark."

Her heart began to pound; her palms went damp in that instant. She sat down on a mahogany settee near the window. When he put the big parcel on the rug before her, Cathy saw that it had been addressed in her father's own hand. Her mouth was dry. "It's from Papa."

"But that's wonderful. Just what you've needed." Adam glanced at her face expectantly and was taken aback by the conflict in her eyes. More softly, he said, "Surely you aren't going to pretend that you love him any less because of what your mother has told you?"

"How can it ever be the same again?" Her voice broke. "He isn't the person I looked up to since birth. Everyone else in the world has let me down, but never Papa."

"Cathy, just because he's human—" He broke off when he saw that she was near tears. "Just open the package. Give the poor fellow a chance."

She shot him a pained glance. Could he be so obtuse, not to realize that she might as well be talking about her husband as well as her father? But then Alice sat down and rested her head against Cathy's knee, and she began to tear away the brown paper. In the shadowed dining room, not far away, Auggie pretended to read a book.

She gasped when she saw the golden box. "Oh, look—isn't it lovely?" Her fingers worked at the lid, and then she found a creamy envelope on top of a dense nest of wood shavings. Part of her didn't want to open it, sensing that its contents would make her hurt more than ever, but the urge to have communication from her father was too strong. She slipped her thumb under the seal and took out the folded paper. It was covered with Jules's neat handwriting:

Dearest Catherine,

I am missing you terribly this Christmas, our first apart. Are you missing me? I will always love you with my whole heart, you know. However, now you are married and far away and my life would have been emptier than ever if I'd kept on as before. You know your mother. Can you find it in your kind heart to forgive me for wanting a bit of love for myself?

Merry Christmas, angel.

Your Papa

Slowly, the hot tears began to spill at last from her eyes and run down her cheeks. She covered her face with her hands. Sitting down beside her on the settee, Adam put his arm around her and gave her his handkerchief.

"It's all right to love him, you know. No one's perfect."

When at last Cathy had calmed herself, he watched as she put her hands into the nest of wood shavings. Her guileless face was pale except for a smudge of color on each cheek. After a moment, she made a discovery and withdrew a small, blown-glass Christmas ornament. It was slightly garish: a little dancing bear, painted orange-gold, with a green ruff, a silver face, and a red nose. Cathy's tears began again.

"For God's sake, what is it?" Adam asked, looking askance at the rather ugly decoration.

"Papa gave me this for the first Christmas tree I can remember," she managed at last. "I was four, I think. We were at our little townhouse, downtown in New York City, before we had much money." Reaching into the box, she took out another object. This one seemed to be a slightly worn, homemade Santa Claus ornament, with an angel hair beard glued onto the globe and a face and hat painted above it. "Oh—it's Stephen's ornament! He made it for me that same year in New York, and I was forever picking at the angel hair. The Christmas before he died, he glued on a new beard, but this one hasn't fared much better. Isn't it sweet?"

His eyes stung as he nodded. "Yes, it is sweet."

One by one, Cathy found all the ornaments that had marked the early years of her childhood and the memories of her dearest Christmases past. "I'll put them on the little orange tree," she decided.

"A splendid plan," Adam agreed.

Now that she had opened the door of her heart to her father, it was easier to let down her guard with Adam a bit, too. After all, it was Christmas Eve. Couldn't they have peace and harmony for the holidays? She turned a little on the settee and smiled at him. "Would you like to help me?"

"Why don't we do it a bit later, after supper? I'll open a bottle of our best wine—"

"And we'll light candles all around the sitting room!" Just then, Cathy saw her mother entering the room. Jumping up, she went to her, arms outstretched. One of the gilded bird ornaments hung from a hook on her fingertip. "Mother, you're looking well today. Merry Christmas!"

Hermione stopped and stared in surprise. "What's that dreadful object?"

"Oh." Flushing, she looked back at Adam, then at the package. "Well, it just arrived by post." She swallowed. "Papa sent my ornaments."

"How dare he?" Grabbing the little bird, she smashed it on the new floor. "Get rid of the rest. I won't have anything around you that reminds me of that philandering jackass."

"Mother!" Cathy felt the blood rushing to her face, but in spite of her anger, she couldn't bring herself to respond in kind. After all, her mother had been betrayed and had no idea how to properly express her pain.

Adam stood up, longing to protect Cathy from Hermione, to tell the woman exactly what he thought of her. However, when he looked at his wife, he realized that it wasn't his place to get involved. This was her battle to fight.

"Please, try to understand," Cathy was saying. "Those ornaments are all I have here in Barbados of my childhood—"

"Then it's time you grow up like the rest of us." Halfway to the dining room table, she paused, watching Simon as he hurried in with a brush and dust pan to clean up the shattered glass. "Furthermore, we had much better decorations than those. Why, you were only six when we moved up Fifth Avenue to the mansion. And, as I recall, that's when I wanted to pitch those old things away." She paused to sharpen her point: "Those gaudy ornaments look like ones that Mae Larkspur would choose!"

Adam watched Cathy gasp softly, then turn pinker. With an effort, he turned away, calling to Auggie, "Come outside with me, old fellow, and I'll show you the iguana that's been prowling around. We haven't many left on Barbados."

Looking dubious, the younger man followed him. Adam was just opening the verandah doors when Liza appeared with a tray.

"Here's your coffee, Mrs. Parrish," she said. "I tried to get Josephine to make it the way you say."

"It can't be any worse than that mud you usually serve," Hermione grumbled.

Adam paused in the doorway. "Liza, I am missing a small, folded note that was here on my desk yesterday. Did you happen to see it when you were dusting? On the floor, perhaps?"

She blinked, backing out of the room. "No, sir."

"How curious." He paused at Cathy's side and touched her warm cheek. "I'll leave you now."

Hermione sipped the fresh coffee and her face puckered. "Honestly. Are they slow-witted in that kitchen? This coffee tastes as if it's two days old."

"Mother, kindly remember that you are in my home."

"Don't be ridiculous. This isn't your home, you're just passing through until you come to your senses."

"You are wrong." With a supreme effort, Cathy managed to keep her tone even.

"Do not speak to your mother that way."

"What about the way you speak to me? Shouldn't mothers treat daughters with respect as well?"

"You are being nonsensical."

"It's not just the coffee, Mother. I understand that you have been hurt badly by Papa, and I want very much to be close to you now that I am a married woman, but you seem to be determined to tear down my new life rather than building it up."

Hermione nervously fingered the pearl choker at her throat. "I have only spoken the truth for your own good. Who will do it if not your own mother?"

"No, that's not the way it is," Cathy said firmly. Leaning forward, she held the older woman's eyes. "When you denigrate Adam and our home, you denigrate my choices. When you mock my childhood ornaments, you are also belittling the sweetest emotions of my heart."

"Catherine, if you allow yourself to get caught up in that sort of sticky sentiment, you will only be hurt more in the end. A healthy dose of harshness will keep you safer." It was Hermione's turn to lean forward. "As your mother, I would be failing you if I encouraged you to love your husband. You'd be far better off learning to love material goods."

"That's a terrible thing to say!"

"Is it?" She paused, sipped more coffee, and grimaced. "Your possessions won't betray you the way a man always does. And believe me, if your father could be unfaithful, the devilish Lord Raveneau is capable of much, much worse…"

Chapter 24

Hermione's ominous words left a dark spot on Cathy's fragile heart, but she tried to erase it. A long bath helped, and June washed her hair, then rinsed by pouring buckets of fresh water from the standpipe over her head. By the time Cathy had dressed in an elegant gown of cream lace over palest mint-green silk, it was time to go down and oversee dinner preparations.

Retta's withered face lit up at the sight of her mistress. "Pretty, pretty lady tonight," she exclaimed, reaching out from her rocking chair to touch the ribbons that wound through Cathy's upswept curls.

She beamed back at Retta. It was a relief to see that no one was fighting. The jug-jug was finished, along with turtle soup. The ham Theo had brought was now baked and maple-glazed, and there were dishes of cornmeal cou cou, string beans, boiled cristophenes, and sweet potatoes. For dessert, there were thin slices of great cake, tamarind balls, and sautéed plantains. June was at the table, pouring ruby-red sorrel into the etched crystal goblets.

"Ah, there you are."

Cathy whirled around at the sound of Adam's voice, rich and warm with affection. "Oh - don't you look nice!"

"I dressed while you were having your bath."

"I know, I saw your shirt lying on the bed." She colored, thinking of the moment she had pressed the snow-white fabric to her face. When he took her hand now, the warmth of his skin sent a delicious shiver down her spine. Had any man ever been more indecently handsome?

Retta spoke. "Happy Chris'mas, sir."

He bent to kiss her cheek. "Happy Christmas, Retta. How are you feeling this evening? Why don't I make you a little rum punch to celebrate the holiday?" Glancing back at his wife, he winked almost imperceptibly. "Shall we all have one?"

Cathy was feeling a bit giddy by the time they sat down for dinner. Even Hermione and Auggie looked friendlier to her, and their faces were softened by the flickering hurricane lamps.

"Have you ever seen anything more disgusting?" Hermione muttered to her young relative as they both poked at the jug-jug with their forks.

"What's that, Mother?" Cathy inquired from across the table.

She put on a tortured smile. "I was just saying, dear, that this china is exquisite. I've been meaning to mention it."

"Aren't you kind," said Adam, sardonically polite. "It's Imari. Chinese. My great-grandmother Devon gave it to her son when he bought Tempest Hall, before he married."

"Simply lovely."

Auggie spoke up: "I saw a similar pattern at the most memorable dinner party of Newport's last Season. Do you remember, Catherine? The Henrys had a stream running down the middle of the table, with fish in it! And, there was an enormous sand pile filled with priceless jewels. We were encouraged to dig them out between courses and keep them as party favors…"

Adam looked at his mother-in-law. "More wine?"

"Anything would be preferable to this odd-tasting scarlet beverage."

"The sorrel? I suppose it's an acquired taste. Still, it was kind of Harrismith to bring it." Smiling with a trace of bemusement, Adam poured her wine, then reached under the table to find his wife's soft hand.

Cathy felt a shock of arousal at his touch. She stared at the lock of black hair that curled over his crisp white collar, then let her gaze slide down to his fingers that held an antique fork. The thought of those beautifully-shaped hands touching her intimately sent a flood of warmth to the very core of her being. He turned his head and looked at her then, smiling as if he could read her thoughts.

"Happy Christmas, Cath."

"Yes," she whispered, nodding. "I believe it may be, after all."

When the meal was finished, Hermione and Auggie took their wine and found seats near an open window. They could hear waves breaking on the nearby north coast. Alice followed Adam as he went around the room and lit candles of all sizes that he'd put in place just before dinner. The golden candle flames wavered in the island breeze, creating an atmosphere that overlaid the traditional Christmas images with the heady essence of the tropics. Alice stared at a nearby candle until she appeared to be hypnotized, and after a few minutes, she lay down beside the orange tree and dozed.

One by one, Cathy withdrew the ornaments from the box her father had packed for her, and she and Adam hung them on the little orange tree. The air between them was heavy with deeper meaning and the heat of yearning.

"It's odd, isn't it, that this present means more to me than something a hundred times more costly." She spoke softly, just to Adam, and gave him a gentle smile over her shoulder. "Papa has always been at a loss when it's come to buying gifts for me; usually he let Mother do it for him. But now he seems to understand what I need most."

"It does seem significant. Do you wish him happiness?"

She nodded wistfully. "Now that you say it, I do. He found a hidden door to my heart today, and now that I've let him partway in, I can't seem to go back. I have always loved Papa so much…"

Hermione walked out of the sitting room and stood alone in the gallery, staring out at the moonlit garden. The tree frogs had begun their whistling "coqui" song from the folds of the banana trees' broad leaves. In the distance, a nightjar called and the ocean crashed in response.

Adam kissed his wife's hair and slid an arm around her waist. The last ornament found a place on the tree. "I think it's a good sign that you've thawed toward your father. His love for you was one of the few honest sentiments I witnessed at Beechcliff."

From across the room, Auggie's voice rose with a note of desperation. "I am having a devil of a time whipping up Christmas spirit, aren't you? Oughtn't we be able to jump into a sleigh and race up Fifth Avenue at breakneck speed, bells jingling on the horses' bridles? And I've been craving a *genuine* Christmas meal at Sherry's restaurant. Molasses-glazed roast goose with chestnut stuffing, acorn squash, and mincemeat pie…"

"Honestly, Auggie," Cathy exclaimed, "I can't see why you came to the West Indies for Christmas if you're going to complain so! What good is it to moan and groan about New York? We are in Barbados this Christmas; it is my new home, and I don't want to hear any more of your lamentations!"

With thinned lips, the young man rose and went to join Hermione in the gallery.

"Shall we make our escape while we can?" Adam asked bluntly.

She blushed. "Yes. I think we should."

"Oh—I almost forgot." He led her under a sprig of sea-grape leaves that had been attached to the arched doorway. "Look: Bajan mistletoe."

Cathy laughed and went happily into his embrace. They kissed with more euphoric pleasure than they'd shared in a long time, and she dared to hope that it was more than Christmas spirit.

Watching her master and mistress go upstairs arm-in-arm, Alice seemed to weigh her own options. Finally, with an effort, she rose and tottered off after Adam and Cathy. A few minutes later, she arrived at their bedroom to discover that the door was closed tight and her dog bed had been moved outside on the floor. Heaving a sigh, Alice circled several times and finally lay down.

"Isn't it a glorious night?"

Adam paused in the midst of stripping off his clothes and looked at her. She'd pushed out the jalousie shutters and flung the window open to its limit. The tiny bedroom was awash with silver-white moonlight and the tangy deep breeze from the ocean. Cathy leaned out, hands braced on the sill, and thirstily inhaled the night as if she were drinking the finest champagne.

"Isn't it glorious?" she repeated. "Dear God, I love this place so much."

Something about her was so juicily unguarded that Adam dropped his shirt and went over to embrace her from behind. "So it's Tempest Hall that's put that glow in your eyes?" he murmured before bending his head and kissing Cathy's neck. Her fragrance went straight to the core of him.

"I'm afraid to say it, but it's more than the house." She turned slowly in his arms and glanced at him through her lashes. The intimacy of his broad, muscled chest against her, when she was still fully dressed and standing, sent a current of heat over her nerves. "It's everything." Cathy longed to tell Adam that Tempest Hall was special because of him, but lost her nerve. "It's beginning to feel like…home."

"It will feel more like home when we're back in our own bed."

"Is it going to be *our* bed after Mother leaves?" A winsome smile lit her face.

"Perhaps it should be, my sly little minx." His lips grazed her ear. "Aren't you hot in that gown?" Reaching around her slender back, he found the tiny buttons and flicked them open.

"You certainly are good at that."

"I've had a bit of practice, in preparation for this night."

She laughed softly as the gown came away from her body.

"Something amuses you?" He held her close, and the sight of her lacy camisole, molded to the swell of her breasts above her corset, made his groin clench.

Cathy's brown eyes widened. "No." Her voice was faint. "Nothing at all."

He stepped back to gently pull her gown from her arms, and it puddled on the floor around her feet. Quickly, his fingers undid the laces of her corset and it too was discarded. "Oh, Cath, you are so beautiful; I ache with wanting you."

She blushed. "You're just saying that."

His strong arms drew her firmly against him, her breasts flattening under the pressure of his chest. His fingers tangled in her curls that had come loose as he kissed her throat with such deft tenderness that Cathy moaned aloud. "Don't ever think that," he whispered when his mouth was poised over her own. "I don't have to say anything at all."

The tide of desire rose higher and higher. He captured her mouth in a scorching, plundering kiss that left her weak-kneed and breathless. In the next moment, he had drawn her with him onto the bed and they were lying together, feasting on kisses. Cathy could feel the heat of him through the fabric of his fawn trousers, and the power of his masculinity was almost frightening.

"I'm burning," he muttered, his glance flicking downward. Capturing her hand, he pressed it over his crotch. "Do you feel what you do to me?"

Her own face flamed in response.

"Don't let yourself be embarrassed," Adam chided softly. "That's just holding you back from real pleasure." Opening her camisole, he touched warm lips to the secret places all around her breasts, watching as her nipples grew more and more erect and listening to the heightened cadence of her breathing. "That's right, let go."

Her heart raced at the prospect of surrendering completely to her husband, of following willingly wherever he wanted to take her. And yet, the passion was swelling as never before. It carried her higher and higher, like the dangerous ocean waves she longed to swim toward. Why not take Adam's hand and go with him tonight?

Lightly, he licked her nipple, then took it into his mouth. She exhaled the last of her doubts in a long groan and sank her fingers into his hair. "Oh—oh!" Moonlight splashed over the bed. In the distance, she heard the sound of the Atlantic rollers booming as they broke against the sand. Cathy pretended the waves themselves were picking her up and carrying her out into the night.

Adam's tongue swirled over the surface of her nipple as his lips tugged gently, just enough to fill her with concentrated sensation beyond anything she'd ever imagined. He hooked a thumb into the waistband of her cambric drawers and drew them down. His palm fit itself to the hollow of her hipbone before his big, beautifully shaped hands began to explore the curves of her bottom, then her thighs, touching her in unexpected places. Cathy opened her eyes. She could see him in the starlight, sitting back on his heels, the tapering lines of his chest like a sculpture. Gazing into her eyes through the shadows, he brought her foot to his mouth and slowly kissed her instep.

"Adam—" She was shocked by the erotic sensations radiating from her foot, the last place she had expected to be capable of arousal.

"You're ravishing, Cath."

"So are you." Her feet curved around his neck, urging him back to her, and soon he was kissing her again, hungrily, and she was lifting her hips against his. She could feel the hot length of him like a brand against her own aching need and helplessly opened her thighs further. "Adam…"

"I love the sound of my name on your lips," he muttered against her hair. Swiftly, he stripped of the rest of his clothing, aching to be inside her but forcing himself to hold back. He kissed her belly, the backs of her knees, then her soft inner thighs, and felt her tremble against his face.

Cathy could scarcely breathe. The smoldering heat between her legs was consuming her; it was as if every nerve in her body was there, swollen with need. Then, for an instant, she felt Adam exhale. The warm pulse of his breath sent a mad tingling sensation over her womanhood. The ache heightened.

Somehow she trusted him to make it better. In the past, she'd had glimpses of what she needed with Adam, but could never abandon herself to passion. Now, she saw his brilliant eyes focus on her in the moonlit shadows. His hands cupped her bottom. He trailed kisses over her tummy and she let her head drop back, closing her eyes, and laced her fingers through his hair.

"Please," Cathy breathed, consumed by a mixture of shame and liberation. As she guided his mouth to the hot, swollen bud, she pictured herself being lifted by the waves.

He touched her there with only the tip of his tongue, and when she jerked, he clasped her hips and began to kiss her in earnest. Slowly, seriously, Adam made love to his wife, listening to her breathing as he brought her to the brink with his skillful mouth. When she was on the precipice of release, he would retreat slightly, then slowly begin again. It was exquisite torture. Finally, Cathy made a soft, involuntary panting sound and he changed the motion of his tongue.

Suddenly, feeling as if she were falling from the highest wave down, down, down toward the beach, Cathy lay back and held her breath as the scalding tide rushed over her. Sheer physical bliss rolled up and out, over and over again, until even her fingertips were tingling. And Adam wouldn't stop. Weakly, she pulled at him. At last he covered her body with his own and entered her to feel the last contractions.

"Ohh!" she cried. Her eyes stung as she buried her face in his strong neck. "That feels—so good." He filled her to the hilt, and she pushed up to meet his thrusts.

"That's my girl."

Cathy wrapped her arms around her husband's shoulders and held on for dear life, wishing that she never had to return to the real world.

Chapter 25

When she opened her eyes, Cathy saw bars of sunlight filtering through the shutters. One of Adam's lean brown arms crossed her naked midriff, imprisoning her. His face was half on her pillow, his mouth inches from her ear. When she tried to move, he made a low sound in his sleep, and she felt him stir and stiffen against her thigh.

Memories of everything that had happened the night before began to march to and fro across her mind. Waves of shame brought hot blood to her cheeks. The forbidden things she'd let him do, encouraged him to do…things she'd never imagined.

Heart pounding, she lifted Adam's heavy arm and turned away on her side until there was a little space between them. Carefully, she drew up the sheet to cover herself.

Shameless. Indecent! *Lewd.* Brazen! Her mother's voice seemed to shout the words in her mind as images of what they had shared taunted her. Turning her head, she peeked at Adam's sleeping profile. Could she ever meet his frank stare again?

Under a spell cast by moonlight and ocean waves, she'd opened her very soul, but in the morning light, everything felt different. It seemed that no other proper woman could have ever done the things she had done or reveled in the sensations Adam's lovemaking had evoked. She had been brought up in complete ignorance, constantly instructed not to grant any suitor even a kiss for fear of losing his respect.

Cathy had never felt more confused as a lifetime's worth of her mother's rigid morals collided with the erotic feelings she'd let Adam draw forth. And she was afraid. Afraid that she'd let him see how much she loved him, and now that he'd conquered her inhibitions, he'd lose interest and look elsewhere to satisfy his male urges. If her own wonderful father could do that, what not Adam?

Slowly, silently, Cathy drew back the sheet and crept out of bed, mortified by her own nakedness. It took only a moment to pull a full-length nightgown over her head and to slip her arms into a silk dressing gown with a sash that tied securely around her waist. Her slippers were near the door, but before she made her escape, she stole another glance at her husband. He'd thrown one lean-muscled arm over his head, and the sheet barely covered his narrow hips. Sleep did not make him seem more vulnerable. Like a big jungle cat, his muscles were coiled under the sleek, warm surface of his flesh as if he might awaken at any moment and spring.

Backing out of the room, Cathy nearly fell over Alice, who had dragged her bed directly in front of the door and now scrambled to avoid being sat upon by her mistress. Somehow, Cathy kept her balance and got the door closed without rousing Adam.

"Poor doggie," she whispered guiltily.

A voice spoke from the other end of the corridor. "You look as if you've had too much sun. Or perhaps you are blushing, Catherine?"

"Merry Christmas, Mother."

"Would you care to dress in my room?" Hermione, perfectly turned out in lavender crepe, lifted her pince-nez and surveyed Cathy from head to toe. "Surely you don't intend to present yourself downstairs like *that*?"

"I will make use of the dressing room, thank you." She kept her head up as she passed her mother. "I didn't want to disturb Adam. He's still sleeping…"

Hermione was leaning forward, squinting through the pince-nez. "What in heaven's name is that on your neck?"

She took the bait and stopped in front of Adam's shaving mirror. There, just below the curve of her jaw, on the spot where her pulse beat, was a tiny, mauve-tinted smudge. "Perhaps it's an insect bite," she mumbled, then flushed.

"Hmmm. I'll see you downstairs."

As mistress of the house, Cathy felt obligated to be present on Christmas morning. She could smell the breakfast cooking that she and Josephine had planned, and she wanted to distribute wrapped presents to the servants before they went off to spend the holiday with their families. At least there was plenty to keep her mind off Adam and her own mortifying behavior of the night before…

Freshly gowned in raspberry-and-white-striped silk, Cathy went down with Alice to greet the day. Over fried flying fish with lime, eggs, melon, scalloped breadfruit, and biscuits, she chatted with her mother and Auggie. Assembled on a nearby chair were the gifts the trio had chosen for one another. Knowing that all the presents had been chosen out of obligation took the pleasure out of opening them, and she postponed that ritual as long as possible.

Auggie had just finished tearing the wrapping off his new cufflinks when Adam appeared, carrying a cup of coffee. Simon was a few steps behind, his arms filled with an enormous box. He looked expectantly at his employer.

"Just set that down by Lady Raveneau, Simon." Adam gestured with his free hand. Alice hurried straight to his side, tail wagging.

Cathy felt herself coloring anew at the sight of him, and yet she couldn't help staring. Adam had gone coatless and wore a cream vest over linen trousers, and her favorite tie: dark blue silk with a narrow yellow stripe. It was knotted expertly round a starched white collar that made a perfect foil for his dangerously handsome face.

"Good morning, my lady," he said softly as he drew up a chair next to Cathy's.

"Wouldn't you prefer to sit at the table like the rest of us?" queried Auggie.

"I'm not hungry. I'd simply like to watch Cathy open her gift."

She tore away the paper and came to a big brown box that smelled faintly of mildew. Blue letters emblazoned on the sides proclaimed: Shepard's Blizzard Ice Cream Freezer.

"What an unusual gift for a man to give his new bride!" declared Auggie, wrinkling his nose. "Hardly romantic, if you don't mind me saying so. But then, nothing on this island is what one might expect."

Feeling everyone's eyes on her, Cathy put on her brightest smile. "Adam is so creative. He's just fooling me. There's no telling what's really inside this carton!" And, heart pounding, she opened the flaps and looked inside.

"What is it, Catherine?" asked her mother.

"Well, it does look like…an ice cream freezer."

"I got it at DaCosta's. I thought—" Adam broke off when he saw that his wife was appalled by his choice. She went from pale uncertainty as she looked at her relatives, to hot-cheeked speechlessness when she turned toward him. Unable to meet his eyes, she mumbled words of thanks and rushed off to the kitchen.

"Perhaps something's burning," Auggie suggested archly.

It came to Raveneau that he should have gotten something daringly extravagant and romantic, like diamonds. The ice cream freezer would have been a lighthearted afterthought, if he were the right kind of husband. But of course he wasn't, and he certainly hadn't been the day he'd made that purchase.

Standing up, he faced his mother-in-law. "I meant well. I thought we'd make ice cream together on hot afternoons…" The explanation sounded hollow even to his own ears.

"My dear boy, you are speaking to the wrong woman about such rustic pastimes. Don't you know that someone of Catherine's background would be insulted by such a present?"

Her tone struck like scalding water, but he took it unflinchingly. "Perhaps you and your daughter have both forgotten that I can't afford to give jewels. The only money I have to spend has the Parrish name on it."

"You don't seem to have a problem using our money to pay off your colored mistress!"

"Mrs. Parrish, for a woman of so-called breeding, you have the manners of—"

Just then, he was interrupted by the sound of male voices singing Christmas carols outside. As they launched into "Silent Night," Adam called for Cathy. Stepping into the gallery, he had a clear view of the garden where five men stood, singing as loudly as they could. When Cathy came in with Retta, he gave her an impatient glance.

"I had to make you come. They're scrubbers and they won't go until they've seen the mistress of the house."

Cathy could scarcely bear to be near Adam. It had been hard enough to look at him after her unbridled abandon the night before, but his unromantic Christmas gift had distanced her even more. "What are scrubbers?" she managed to ask, glancing back hopefully toward Retta.

"Dey sing," the old woman said derisively, "den make beggin' speech!"

"It's an old Bajan Christmas tradition," Adam added. "They're hoping for some money and some food."

"Huh!" Retta snorted. "I go wrap up de food and sorrel for dem." As she turned to go, she caught Raveneau's eye and muttered, "Why you don' give de mis'ress a nice jookin' board fer Chris'mas?"

"Very amusing."

Outside, one of the scrubbers had stepped forward to proclaim, "Mistress and Master, I neither come to boast or to brag, nor to tek down de flag! But tellin' you bout de mornin' our Lord Savior was born, and wishin' you a happy Christmas morn."

Cathy smiled back at them, uncertain whether or not to respond. "Is that all?" she whispered to Adam.

"If only it were," came his acerbic reply.

They resumed singing, and after a bit the leader exclaimed, "Hark the herald angel sing, Open de larduh and give we somet'ing; Peace on earth an' mercy mile, Two rums for a man an' one for a chile!"

Just then, Simon appeared outside with Christmas gifts of coins, a basket of food, and a bottle of red sorrel. Adam led Cathy out the front door to shake hands with the men.

"Take this food and money home to your families," he said. "And wish them a happy Christmas."

The quartet broke into one last verse: "Goodbye to the Mistress an' Master, too. Thank you very much an' God bless you!"

As they went on their way to the next house down the road, Cathy looked uncertainly up at Adam. "I still don't understand. Why are they called *scrubbers*?"

His mind remained on the unfinished argument with Hermione. "Hmm? Oh, I don't know. My grandmother used to say that it must be another butchered Bajan variation on an English word. Since they seem to fancy themselves poets, perhaps they meant to call themselves 'scribers.'"

"Sir?" Simon spoke up from a few feet away. "Josephine ask you to come to de kitchen an' see 'bout Christmas food for de field hands."

"Certainly." He turned to Cathy. "I'm glad for the respite from your mother. Will you excuse me for a while?"

"But, shouldn't I come, too?" Her heart ached as she longed for him to take her hand or show in some way that he didn't think less of her after last night.

"No, you go back to the dining room and finish exchanging gifts with your relatives. No doubt you'll receive something that will make up for my offering."

As she watched Adam stride off into the garden, his wide shoulders set, Cathy felt heartsick.

"Auggie and I have decided to go this afternoon," Hermione told her daughter. "We'll pay Theo Harrismith a brief visit at his hotel, then set sail for America as soon as possible. I have never felt welcomed by your husband, and today he made his feelings crystal clear. I won't stay under the same roof with that libertine for one more day."

Cathy stared at the table covered with Christmas wrappings and plates of half-eaten food. More tears welled up from her heart. Had her mother been right all along? Were men so different from women?

"I won't ask you to come with us," Hermione said. She glanced at Auggie, then leaned forward and patted her daughter's hand. "But do remember that, with all our faults, we are your family. I will never betray you the way your father and your husband do."

Auggie stood up. "I for one will be glad to get off this godforsaken island and return to civilization. I can't imagine being anywhere else but New York for the Opera season!"

"And there will be a spring collection from Worth," sighed Hermione. "In fact, I wonder if it might be a good idea to go to Paris to do our shopping. Paris in the spring would be the perfect tonic, don't you think?" She peeked at her daughter from the corners of her eyes.

"Why, someone is approaching the front door," Auggie exclaimed. "I'll answer it, since the entire meager staff is in the kitchen."

Cathy was feeling too forlorn to even look up until she heard a chillingly familiar voice calling, "Lady Raveneau, you remember me, don't you? My name is Gemma Hart."

In a fog, Cathy stood up and extended her hand to the visitor. To her dismay, Alice approached Gemma, tail wagging. "Happy Christmas, Miss Hart," she heard herself saying in cordial tones. "What brings you to Tempest Hall today?"

"Adam's—and my—*son*, Paul."

It was then that Cathy saw the little boy. He'd been hiding behind his mother's skirts, but now he peeked out with big, blue-gray eyes in a mocha-hued face. With shock, she realized that she was looking into eyes that mirrored Adam's own. Was her heart still beating? All of Cathy's world seemed to be contained in Paul's innocent gaze and the more knowing one of his mother.

"H'lo," said Paul.

Her heart thumped to life, filling her chest. "Hello, Paul." Bending down to his level, she reached out a hand to him. "My name is Cathy."

When he stepped out from behind his mother, she saw that he was wearing a little brown checked suit with short pants and a tiny bow tie. He clutched the handle of a lidded basket with both hands. "I got Stripey in here."

Alice, who was usually so gentle, nearly pushed Paul over in her curiosity to smell the basket. "Who or what is Stripey?" Cathy asked.

"My kitty," he confided, then lifted the lid so that she could see the little gray face and hear its mew. Aghast, Alice began to bark.

Auggie came up beside them. "Paul, why don't we take Stripey into the gallery so that your mummy can talk to Lady Raveneau?"

Although Cathy didn't know what to make of that, she had more pressing worries. She saw the fire in Gemma's eyes and recognized her jealousy.

"You have made yourself at home, I see," Gemma said, looking around the inviting room.

"Of course. This *is* my home."

"Perhaps, but you are just a substitute."

Cathy was taken aback by the soft, cultured tone of the woman's voice. It was at odds with her message. "Look, Miss Hart, I understand that you resent me—"

"I believe I would have been mistress of Tempest Hall if not for my race. He would have married me if only I were light-skinned. It just isn't done, though, not even by a rebel like Raveneau."

"Perhaps that was true once, but—"

"Have you been lulled into trusting him? How foolish! Do you imagine that he has fallen in love? Adam Raveneau will never change. He is too much a male; he thrives on his conquests!"

All the blood drained from Cathy's face, and for a moment she thought she might faint. "Why have you come here? Why do you wish to hurt me?"

"I am here for my son, not myself, and certainly not for you." Suddenly, Gemma looked exhausted. "I am ill. I must leave the island to get proper medical treatment, and it is time for Adam to face his responsibilities as a parent." Her lovely mouth tightened. "I am here to tell you that your honeymoon, such as it may have been, is over."

Hermione came up beside her. "Are you quite all right, Miss Hart? Can I call for a glass of water?"

"My driver is waiting outside; I must go. I've left Paul's little trunk on the steps." She started through the sitting room, toward the door. "I don't want to see Adam. I don't have the strength."

Just then, Paul burst back into the room, clutching the mewing Stripey in his chubby hands. "Mummy! Don't leave me!"

"I've explained already, darling. You're going to stay with your papa until I'm well enough to return." And with that, Gemma kissed him, put him from her, and hurried out the door. Moments later, they heard the sulky roll away down the drive.

Paul began to wail, tears streaming down his face. "I want Mummy!" he cried over and over again. Stripey slipped from his grasp and darted between Alice's legs. The aging Labrador gave chase, barking, and the two circled the room before Stripey jumped over the ornament-laden orange tree. Alice plowed straight into it, the tree crashed to the floor, and shattered bits of blown glass scattered across the sitting room.

Auggie picked up the sobbing Paul before he could cut himself on one of the broken ornaments, and Cathy managed to coax Alice safely out of danger before she realized that her own cheeks were wet with tears.

"Will someone tell me what the devil is going on around here?" shouted Adam. He stood in the sitting room entrance, staring at the wreckage with angry dark eyes. Slowly, he focused first on Alice, whose ears were down, and then on the striped kitten who was clinging to a branch of the toppled orange tree.

"Papa!" wailed Paul. He stretched out his arms, leaning wildly out of Auggie's grasp.

Adam blinked. "Oh, God. Paul." He took the child and wiped his wet, smeared face with a snowy handkerchief. Next, he looked at his wife. "I still need an explanation."

"Do you indeed?" Chin trembling, Cathy willed herself to walk by him, pausing only to add, "I am going upstairs to pack, my lord. This marriage has been impossible from the first, just as you warned me in Newport. Finally, I have faced facts."

Part Five

Chapter 26

Stunned, Adam watched his wife walk away, her head high and her pretty raspberry-striped skirt swishing from side to side. The room seemed to be whirling as he tried to absorb her words.

"Mummy!" cried Paul.

He focused on the little boy. "It's all right," he told him firmly. "Don't cry. You're safe with me."

Paul stared for a moment, into eyes that were identical to his own, and stopped crying. Tentatively, he rested his head on Adam's chest and sighed.

"Auggie, we must pack as well," Hermione was saying loudly. She did not deign to glance at her son-in-law as she swept past.

He would not play the old woman's game. "No. You both will stay here until I return. Sit down and wait." When his eyes flicked over to the contrite Alice, she immediately went to her usual spot on the rug and lay down. Meanwhile, Hermione and Auggie obeyed as well, frowning to express their displeasure.

Unfortunately, Adam seemed to have no choice but to take Paul along as he went up the stairs two at a time. He found his wife in what had once been his bedroom, pulling a large trunk out of the dressing room. She opened it and went back to fetch a selection of skirts.

"I won't have time to pack everything, I'm afraid," she said without looking into his eyes.

"Cathy, this is madness. For God's sake, I know you're upset—"

"On the contrary." She kept her face averted. "I am quite calm. It's actually a relief to face the truth at last."

"What the devil are you talking about? What truth?" He shifted Paul in his arms and went closer.

"Please don't shout. Your son has enough to contend with right now, don't you think?" She managed to glance up, but his stunned expression was too unsettling to bear. Unbidden, an image came to her of Adam and Gemma, naked together, creating this child in his arms. She pulled nightgowns out of a drawer and re-folded them. "Really, there is no point in this discussion. You were not prepared to marry, but I virtually forced you into it, didn't I? I refused to listen to your protestations. There was no sound basis for this marriage on either side, so why should we be surprised that it is tumbling down around us?"

Paul had lifted his head from Adam's chest and began to squirm. His father held him fast, staring at Cathy. "Do you mean to say that you are just going to give up and walk away?"

"Yes, I suppose I do." Her heart hurt when she tried to breathe, but she refused to let him see her tears. "To be perfectly honest, I have had enough of men and the pain you inflict so casually."

"This is your mother's doing. She has poisoned your mind!" He let the struggling Paul down, barely noticing when he went running with tiny steps toward the doorway. "Cathy, for God's sake, let's sit down and talk about this—"

"I'm afraid it's too late." She pointed toward the corridor. "You have other matters to attend to, primarily the well-being of that innocent child. Go and get your son, Adam, before he wanders too close to the stairs. You're responsible for his safety now."

Hours later, Cathy found herself alone in one of the Ocean Breeze Hotel's finest rooms. Her mother and Auggie had adjoining suites across the corridor and, after the journey south and a fine meal with the surprised but welcoming Theo, they had all pleaded fatigue and retired early.

Through her open window, Cathy saw that the last fragment of sun had disappeared into the ocean and darkness was wrapping the hotel in its balmy embrace. She unpacked her trunk to the sound of the tree frogs across Hastings Road and the waves lapping against the bathhouses.

In a side compartment of the trunk, she glimpsed the slim volume of Emily Dickinson's poetry that her brother had given her for Christmas five years before. When she touched it, she saw his face as he had been in their happiest moments, carefree and charming, her one ally in the bizarre world their mother had constructed around them. Tentatively, Cathy opened the cover and saw the inscription in his familiar hand: *"To Cat."*

It was too much pain. She pushed it back in the compartment until it was out of sight.

When all the drawers in the mahogany tall chest were filled, Cathy took out a nightgown and looked over at the bed. A maid had drawn back the counterpane on one side to reveal a single pillow. Since the moment they had left Tempest Hall, she had been numb. The sight of Adam standing in front of the manor house, holding Paul in his arms while Alice sat next to him, had been heart wrenching. As the carriage, driven by Simon, started down the lane, Paul had raised his pudgy hand and called, "Bye-bye!" Adam's expression had been stony with disbelief.

She replaced the nightgown in the drawer, dimmed the light at her bedside, and went out into the corridor. The hotel was completely quiet. Perhaps because it was Christmas day, there were only a handful of other guests, and it seemed that they had all retired for the night. A clock on the landing struck ten.

Downstairs, she saw a light burning in the small office that opened off the lobby. Inside, Theo sat at the desk with its assortment of pigeonholes, laboring over a ledger. On the wall beside the desk was a reference board with a wooden slot for each room.

"Couldn't sleep?" he inquired without looking up. "I'm not surprised."

"I couldn't even get into my bedclothes," she admitted. Her heart began to thump again at the mere thought of lying alone in the dark room for the whole long night.

He glanced at her, lips pursed, and shook his head. "What have you done, darling? What were you thinking?" The sight of her looking so forlorn caused him to put down his fountain pen and stand up. "Let's go in the kitchen and have a bit of port, shall we? That sounds like just the thing for you."

When they were sitting at one of the big, rustic work tables, now cleared of food and scrubbed clean, Theo raised his glass to her. "Here's to the future."

"Are you being ironic? Yes, of course you are."

"Well, I must say that I'm surprised. What has Lord Raveneau done that's so appalling? I had the distinct notion that you were in love with him."

Her forefinger found a long curl that had escaped and twisted it round and round. "I love him so much it hurts," she said softly. "But I'm convinced it can never work."

"Because of the child? No matter what shocked pronouncements your mother might make, you could still work it out. I know that your heart is big enough."

Cathy gave a great sigh and sipped her port. "I think that Paul was just the straw that broke the camel's back. I see now that the whole arrangement was flawed at its core. Adam doesn't love me, and he hates the fact he needs my money. Our marriage makes him feel like a bought man, and he's far too proud for that."

"You're quite certain he doesn't love you? As a somewhat impartial observer, I can assure you that he is far from indifferent!"

She flushed. "Perhaps, but you are referring to flashes of jealousy, not real love. I've decided I will never understand men. Their primitive emotions always seem to trump tenderness…or loyalty."

"I surmise that we are also speaking of your father?"

Cathy looked away, her eyes agleam with unshed tears. "It's very hard to open one's heart only to have it treated so casually. You said that my heart is big enough to forgive Adam, but it has been battered from many sides and I am very weary."

"Perhaps you merely need a respite, then, though the rest of the island will gossip about your presence in my hotel."

"I would like to stay for the time being, and I don't care what anyone says. I'm going to help you with the hotel and be your silent investor. Perhaps, if you had a backer, you could buy the Ocean Breeze from Hazel Trotter one day!"

"I think the port is going to your head." Theo's eyes twinkled. "And, my dear, you know that this isn't the place for you, don't you?"

"I'm not certain of anything right now, except that I will never live with my mother again, no matter how she may coerce me. It's been wrenching to accept the fact that I can never be close to her if I want to be strong and happy, but it's true." She gave him a pensive smile. "I'm thinking about buying a house of my own, and I then I could engage in some sort of meaningful work. Tutoring students, perhaps! I have put my foolish dreams about love and marriage behind me. And Adam…deserves another kind of woman, one who can—"

After a moment, he touched her averted cheek and prompted, "Yes?"

"Who can…match his passions. Someone who is as magnificent as he is, rather than a—a shrinking violet like me."

"I see." He saw a tear escape and held out a handkerchief. "Cathy, you are hardly a shrinking violet! As for your husband's passions—"

"I don't want to talk about this anymore." She drank the small amount of port that remained in her glass and stood up. "My heart hurts. I should go to sleep. You do understand, don't you?" Then, reaching out, Cathy took his hand. "I am so grateful for your friendship, Theo. Thank you."

~ ~ ~

"Look, Paul," Adam coaxed the tiny boy. "It's a special bed, just for you."

Clad in a miniature nightshirt and clutching a tattered stuffed monkey, Paul stared at the crib with distrust. It had belonged to Adam's father when he was a baby. Crafted of mahogany with turned spindles, it featured a tiny support for mosquito netting.

"Stripey?" Paul asked. He turned his curly dark head and looked around the spacious bedroom.

Adam's head began to throb again as memories of his extremely taxing day flooded back. After the horrific scene of Cathy's departure, how many hours had Paul, Stripey, and Alice spent chasing each other around Tempest Hall, leaving a trail of mayhem in their wake? It wasn't that Paul paid no attention to his father's command to behave; on the contrary, when Adam gave him a quelling stare or raised his voice, the little boy burst into tears and begged for his mother in pitiful tones. It was Retta who had finally taken him in hand, cleaned him up, fed him, and instructed Adam to bring the crib out. To his utter dismay, she had insisted that he put it in his own bedroom.

"Stripey is sleeping," Adam now told Paul. He laid a forefinger over his mouth. "Shh."

With a furrow of suspicion in his tiny brow, the child repeated, "Sleeping where?"

"He's very cozy and happy; don't worry!" He didn't care where the kitten was as long as it was quiet. "Now let's get into your fine new bed—"

He suddenly clung to Adam's neck, sobbing. "Mummy, Mummy!"

Feeling as if he were losing his mind, Adam looked around and saw the cane rocker where Cathy liked to sit and read. Holding the boy close, he sat down in it and began to rock, hoping that the delicate piece of furniture didn't collapse under his weight. "Don't cry, Paul. It's going to be all right. Shh." As he rocked, he inhaled the child's scent and felt the heat of his little body. Slowly, Paul loosened his grasp and his sobs turned to sniffles. "We'll be all right, don't worry."

The rhythm of the rocking chair was soothing to Adam, too. And perhaps he was holding on to Paul for reasons of his own. They rocked long after the little boy fell asleep, until Adam finally stood and gently bent to put him in the crib. Sprawled on his back, his mouth open, the nightshirt tangled in his pudgy legs, Paul's dependence upon him suddenly struck home.

It seemed impossible that his life could have changed so radically in one day's time, that only last night he had brought his wife to a state of complete abandon, in a bed in this very house. Now she was gone and he was left to contend with a child he barely knew, who missed his mother and needed a parent's love.

What did he know about being a parent? He had buried all feelings for his own father and mother years ago, while still a boy; the only person to whom he could talk about them had been Gran Adrienne, but even she couldn't completely break through the shell he'd erected.

A bottle of brandy stared at him from his desk across the room. Raveneau stared back at it, longing to accept its invitation to take away his pain.

"Cathy," he whispered and wondered how it all could have gone so horribly wrong. Unable to stay alone in the bedchamber another moment, he went out into the corridor, then down the back stairway in search of Retta. He found her in the little serving room near the back door, sitting in a straight-back chair and mending socks by the light of an oil lamp.

"I do t'ink you come," she murmured. "But where de baby?"

"He's sound asleep. Finally." Adam sank into a chair across from her and propped his elbows on his knees. "Retta, I feel as if I'm going mad. One moment my wife was here and everything seemed to be fine - " At the sight of her white eyebrows suddenly arching up, he paused. "All right, perhaps I haven't been a perfect husband. But was I so bad that she had to leave? How did this happen?"

"You know how." She nodded twice for emphasis.

"I should have listened to you. You tried to warn me."

Shrugging, she peered at him through her spectacles. "Not so much. Jus' do say you should not be 'fraid of love, sir. You push you pretty wife away 'cause you do fear love."

Adam wanted to protest, but the fight had gone out of him. Instead, he gave a harsh sigh and leaned back in his chair, waiting.

Nodding, Retta continued, "An' I say you build de bridge, an' you try, sir, but den you do break it." She gestured toward the ice cream freezer that now stood in the shadows near her chair. "Foolish man."

He winced at the sight of it. "I meant well."

"I tell you again, you gran'ma do leave everyt'ing you need to woo a wife." After a telling pause, she added, "If you want dat."

It came to him then, through the mist of pain and denial, how keenly he did want it. The possibility that he might have lost Cathy forever, that she would never turn her radiant smile on him or oversee Tempest Hall with him or stand on tiptoe in his embrace again, was too terrible to contemplate. "How can I bring her home, Retta?" Closing his eyes for a moment, Adam said the words that had hidden inside him for so long, bolted inside a secret room he hadn't been able to enter. "I love her."

"Good. Now, sir, first you mus' fix you."

Before he could reply, Adam heard a faint cry in the moment of silence.

"Papa! Papa!"

Everything else was forgotten as he jumped to his feet and ran up the back stairs, his heart clenching with terror and guilt. What if Paul had climbed out of the crib and started off toward those front stairs Cathy had warned him about? What if he'd fallen or discovered a sharp object and cut himself? He could be bleeding, pinned under a piece of furniture, burned by a kerosene lamp…

"Papa!" The tiny voice grew more urgent, threatening tears.

Adam burst into the bedroom, scanning the dimly-lit interior for the child he was now responsible to protect. "Paul!"

Just as he'd feared, the boy was not in the crib. He tore aside the mosquito netting and the blanket, but uncovered only the stuffed monkey. Just then, the mingled sounds of panting and sniffling came to him from the corner behind his desk. Adam was there in two strides. First he saw Alice, standing close to the darkened corner, looking up with an urgent expression.

Her body blocked the shape of little Paul, who was patting her even as he struggled to escape.

"Woof," said Alice.

"Oh, thank God." Adam knelt beside them and put an arm around the dog's neck. "Good girl. You're the most magnificent girl."

She began to pant again and licked his cheek. This made Paul laugh; he came closer and pressed his own sleep-warm mouth to his father's face. Just when Adam was beginning to relax, and had slipped an arm around the little boy to draw him onto his knee, something furry came flying through the air and landed on Alice's back.

"Stripey!" squealed Paul.

When Alice reared back to dislodge the attacker, Stripey leaped onto Adam's arm instead, claws extended. In the next instant, the kitten sprang into the air again, landing on the bed. To Adam's horror, Alice attempted to go after him but was too arthritic to jump that high. Instead, she stood up with her front paws on the mattress and barked at the hissing cat.

"Woof! Woof!" Alice threatened. A moment later, Stripey launched himself again, this time into the corridor, and the elderly Labrador gave chase.

Paul was giggling and trying to run after the animals, but Adam held fast to his nightshirt. "Oh, no you don't. It's well past your bedtime."

When he stood and began to carry him toward the crib, Paul sobbed, "No! Papa's bed!"

Too tired to argue or endure another bout of tears, Adam turned toward the big testered bed and set him down. The little boy sat looking at him, wide-eyed, until he drew back the covers, pulled off his riding boots, and lay down beside him. Paul came closer. Adam scooped him up so that his curly head was tucked into the crook of his shoulder.

"Mummy?" he asked with a little sigh.

"Mummy had to go away for a bit, little one, but Papa will take care of you. Now, go to sleep." Glancing down, he saw that the child's eyes were open and they shone with tears. "Did you know that when I was a little boy like you I had a pony? The pony's name was Esmerelda and she had one blue eye and one brown eye." Encouraged by Paul's soft chortle of delight, Adam continued, "Esmerelda loved sugar cubes and she had her own pet kitten, just like Stripey." He went on with the story until he heard his son's breathing soften and he knew he was asleep.

Alice was sitting next to the bed, staring at them, her eyes filled with questions.

"Ah, girl, you are probably confused," Adam whispered. With his free hand, he reached over and stroked her brow. "I am confused as well. Your mistress has gone away, and I have realized that I shall have to formulate a brilliant plan to win her back."

Alice appeared to nod in the shadows, then inclined her head meaningfully toward the bed.

"You too? You're all taking advantage of me. I shouldn't allow it, you know." He made no protest, however, as she went immediately to the bedsteps and managed to negotiate them. Moments later, the big dog was settling down beside him, sighing loudly with pleasure.

"You may have to help me execute my plan, Alice. Lady Raveneau is fonder of you than she is of me right now." A smile touched his mouth before he remembered Retta's advice that first he must fix himself. "Fix myself? Bloody hell, that's the last thing I want to do."

Just then, a massive wave of fatigue swept over him and carried him away.

Chapter 27

From a distance, Adam heard knocking. He attempted to open his eyes without success. "Mmph?"

"Good God, what's happening here?" cried Byron Matthews as he entered the bedchamber with a breakfast tray. "Are you all right?"

Adam squinted at him. "I must be dreaming."

"That was my line, old fellow." He set the tray, laden with coffee and cups, down on the little tea table Cathy had installed in the bedroom. Turning, Byron surveyed the rumpled bed. His friend was fully clothed except for his boots, which were haphazardly discarded on the floor. He wore riding breeches and a wrinkled linen shirt, and locks of his black hair stuck out rather comically. Alice lay snoring against his right leg and a sleeping curly-headed toddler in a nightshirt was sprawled across Adam's chest, preventing him from sitting up. In the middle of the other, empty pillow curled a gray tiger-striped kitten. Ribbons of sunlight tried to find their way through the shutters with limited success. "This was hardly the scene of domestic bliss I expected to encounter at Tempest Hall."

"Believe me, none of this was my idea." His head hurt, though he was quite certain he hadn't drunk any of the brandy that had been enticing him the night before. "Where the devil did you come from?"

"I sent you a telegram yesterday. Didn't you get it?"

"Yesterday? Are you referring to Christmas, the worst day of my life?"

Byron poured himself a cup of coffee and added two lumps of sugar. "What's happened? I'm almost afraid to ask the identity of that child."

Just then, Paul sat up and looked around at the two men and the strange room. His chin began to quiver. "Mummy. Want my mummy!"

Alice suddenly shook herself awake and indulged in a long, loud yawn. However, one look at her master sent her clambering off the bed and out of the room to find her breakfast.

"Paul," Adam said firmly, "please don't cry. Let's get you up and dressed—"

The child was already climbing down and bending to look under the bed. Moments later, he dragged out the chamber pot, lifted his nightshirt, and aimed with mixed success. Looking on, Byron laughed.

"You might need a lesson or two from your..." he sent a questioning glance toward his friend, who gave a reluctant nod. "Father."

Pointing at Adam, Paul corrected, "Papa."

"You've clearly been very busy since I last saw you," Byron remarked as he handed Raveneau a cup of coffee.

Between them, the men got Paul dressed and the three of them went down the corridor to the back stairs. Paul was carrying his stuffed monkey and Stripey capered behind them, chasing a centipede that eventually darted under a cracked baseboard. When they came into the sunlit dining room, June was there, spreading covered dishes on the long table.

"Can I please take the little boy and feed him, sir?" she asked. "He's very handsome! Josephine has made a special breakfast."

Adam thought back to the day when he had come home and discovered Cathy wearing a headtie, working alongside June in the dressing room. The girl had clearly adored her mistress but had appeared to be somewhat intimidated by him. Perhaps it wasn't too late to change her opinion.

"That's very kind of you, June," he told her now, smiling. "You know that Lady Raveneau isn't here, so I appreciate any extra assistance you can offer."

"Is it true that she is going home to America?" she asked in hushed tones.

Her words were a shock to him. "Not if I have anything to say about it."

Paul was reluctant at first to leave his father, but June smiled at him so brightly that he finally went off with her.

"Does your monkey have a name?" she inquired as they left the dining room.

He looked at it for a moment, pondering, and answered, imitating the throaty chatter of a monkey, "Ooh-ah!"

Adam glanced at Byron and smiled. "Brilliant child, isn't he?"

Filling their plates with eggs, coconut bread, and papaya drizzled with lime, the two men went out into the gallery. They took planters' chairs overlooking the gardens Cathy had been laboring to restore and ate for a few minutes in silence.

"That's better," Adam said at length. "I don't remember having any food yesterday."

Byron blinked. "No food on Christmas Day? This is all very mysterious. Are you going to enlighten me?"

"Perhaps. I would rather you tell me first what the devil you're doing in Barbados and how you came to turn up in my bedroom at the break of dawn!"

"It's ten o'clock." After a pause, he continued, "All right then. I decided to take you up on your invitation and come to Barbados to paint."

"What invitation?"

"The one you extended after your wedding, just before you and Catherine left Sherry's restaurant to board the yacht. You practically begged me to come." Byron finished his coconut bread with a look of pleasure.

"You must be joking. Do you imagine that I can remember anything I said that day?"

"And on which day *have* you been in your right mind?"

For a moment, Adam longed to lift him out of the chair by his lapels and toss him off the steps, but realization dawned that he was actually quite grateful for the abrupt arrival of his old friend. "You're infuriating, you know, but I am glad to see you."

"Of course you are! Would you care for more coconut bread?" Byron's auburn hair glinted in the sunlight as he went back into the dining room and returned with the entire dish. "I think I'm going to like the food here! It's quite exotic."

"Were you planning to stay at Tempest Hall and eat my food during your entire visit?"

"Ha! I know you don't mean to be rude. Of course I'm staying here. I could barely afford passage. Now that I've arrived, I confess that I'm counting on the benevolence of you and your beautiful bride."

Adam was beginning to enjoy himself. "Naturally. And, I may ask you to help me with a project or two while you're here."

"Of course. I'm not very handy, but—"

"Not that sort of project. More in the line of helping me deal with the son I've just been given to raise, and perhaps assisting with the recovery of my runaway wife." He gave him a dark smile. "Easy enough, eh?"

It was Byron's turn to look pained. "I was hoping my worst fears were unfounded. I've witnessed many of your past…adventures, but I dared hope that once you were married to that charmer, you'd be safe from yourself. For God's sake, Raveneau, it's only been a few weeks!"

"I hate it when you turn judgmental." He drained his coffee and ran a hand through sleep-mussed hair. "Did I ever happen to mention Gemma Hart to you?"

"Yes…" Byron squinted. "I'd forgotten she lived on Barbados. You didn't—"

"Quite right, I did *not*. Though you may find it difficult to believe, I've been faithful to Cathy. However, it seems that there is a bit of leftover business from the last time I visited the island, three years ago…"

"Paul."

"I was completely unaware. There was a smallpox epidemic, so Barbados has been quarantined, and as you know, I've been traveling." Adam paused, and the only sound was the creaky chatter of the guinea fowl as they scratched under the sandbox tree. He took a deep breath. "But, to be honest, it's not just Paul. Cathy could have probably dealt with that situation if she were happy in our marriage."

Leaning forward in his planter's chair, Adam recounted the series of events that had led to this impasse. Talking about it helped him see even more clearly where he had gone wrong, but finding a solution was another matter.

When he concluded with Retta's admonition to fix himself first, Byron exclaimed, "Good God! And to think that Hermione Parrish has been here! No wonder it all began to go off the rails."

"It was only a few days, but it felt like years. You know, Cathy was badly abused by that woman when she was growing up. Her mother tried to train her like a pet, with just one goal in mind: a duchess's coronet. I could sense her feeling freer the farther we traveled from Newport, but after her mother and cousin turned up here, it all started going wrong again. God only knows what that tyrant told her about men and marriage." He took a breath. "And of course, discovering that her father has a mistress young enough to be his daughter hasn't improved Cathy's opinion of men."

"But it doesn't sound as if you've exactly been a model husband."

Adam sprang up then and began to pace. "You don't know how it felt to have no real say in the running of my own home. The money has all come from Jules Parrish. Even as I've been working to restore the plantation, I've felt as if I've sold myself, been gutted of my manhood." His voice was raw as he turned to gaze at Byron. "Knowing that I had gambled away my own fortune hasn't helped."

"And Cathy? Did she lord it over you that it was her money and not yours?"

"No. Of course not. But in the end, if she wanted to do something and I didn't agree immediately, she could go right ahead and do it anyway. Her father set up a private account for her so that she would always have her own funds. She brought in more staff and arranged for work to be done in Tempest Hall. Admirable endeavors, but reminders that our marriage was based on my need for her dowry—"

"Well, that's common enough among you aristocrats!"

"I would like to think that I am bloody different from the rest of those weasels. But the humiliating truth was here every day to remind me of my flawed character. I've been a kept man from the moment I agreed to this marriage, and every fiber of my being rebels against that!"

Byron stared, realizing that his friend was expressing feelings that had been suppressed for too long. "I understand."

Adam stared back at him for a long moment, then went down the steps into the garden where Cathy's new plantings of flowers and herbs were beginning to grow. It came to him that if he didn't see to it that they had water, they would die.

Byron followed along, helping as they filled buckets at the standpipe and carried them back to water the plants. After repeating the process three times, Raveneau watched the ground soak up the moisture and sighed. "She worked so hard on this garden."

"You have feelings for her, then?" Knowing his friend, it seemed best to stop short of the word "love."

Adam's reply was interrupted by a clatter on the verandah, followed by the sight of Alice bursting into the garden and running past them with something in her mouth. Paul chased after her, laughing, and Stripey brought up the rear.

"Alice!" thundered Adam. "Come here this instant! If you touch one paw to your mistress's new plants, you will be sent to the ravine to live with the monkeys!"

The old Labrador put her ears down and returned to stand before him. When Raveneau made a gesture with his hand, she sat and dropped the large dark object from her mouth. He bent to retrieve it while Byron looked on.

"It's my tricorne hat, the one I wore to the costume ball at Beechcliff the night Cathy and I met. Paul has clearly been playing in my dressing room." Pensively, he unpinned the crumpled cockade from the brim and studied it. "My grandmother gave this to me, you know, when I was very young. She believed that it belonged to Stede Bonnet, the pirate."

"The one you were masquerading as that night? How did she come to have it?"

"She was always interested in him. When I was visiting one summer, she and my grandfather took me along to an estate sale at the plantation reputed to have once been Bonnet's, and that's where she came into possession of this hat. They told us that this was the pirate's unique cockade: white with a blood-red center." Raveneau glanced absently at his friend, his thoughts far away. "I've always been skeptical of my grandmother's notions, but perhaps I should reconsider. At the moment, however, there are other matters to deal with. No doubt Paul takes a nap after lunch. Would you mind watching him for a bit while I have a wash-up and go in search of my wife? There's a chance that she means to leave the island with her mother, and I can't let that happen."

Byron blinked again. "Of course. What are friends for?"

Cathy sat in the office at the Ocean Breeze Hotel, staring at the big reservation book on the desk before her. The words seemed to spin in front of her eyes; it was impossible to concentrate.

"We're leaving now," Theo said, popping his head through the arched opening that joined the office to the lobby. "I wish you wouldn't worry about all that nonsense yet. I'll explain it to you later on."

She stood up and smoothed her dove gray skirt. "I need something to occupy myself today."

"We aren't very organized; it's a system only Yvette and I understand, I'm afraid."

"Oh yes, Miss Chambers! Is she with her family for Christmas?"

"Yes. Her father lives in Speightstown, but she'll be back soon."

"I'm looking forward to being a help to her when she returns." Cathy followed Theo out into the lobby, where he had already arranged a large vase filled with pink hibiscus. "Will you be away all day?"

"As long as it takes to get your mother and cousin loaded onto their yacht and on their way." He donned a straw boater and cocked his head at her. "You're certain you'd rather stay here? No, never mind, don't answer that. I don't want you to come. You've had quite enough exposure to your mother…and speaking of Her Majesty, here she comes!"

The sight of Hermione and Auggie descending the stairs made Cathy feel unexpectedly emotional. Her mother had dressed with care in violet crepe trimmed with ivory lace and wore a silk hat adorned with a violet bow and feathers.

"I am desperately anxious to get back to New York," Auggie was saying as he paused to check his reflection in a mirror trimmed with shells. "I have had quite enough of life in the hinterlands!"

Cathy stood up a little straighter as she approached her mother. Crossing the lobby, she noticed for the first time that their matching trunks were piled near the hotel's entrance and servants from the yacht were waiting nearby. "It looks like a lovely day for a sea voyage, Mother."

Surveying her daughter, Hermione gave her head a haughty little shake. "My dear, you simply *must* come with us. I don't know if I can bear to leave you behind in this appalling wilderness."

"I've already explained that I won't go." Cathy refrained from telling her mother that she was resolved to remain at a distance from her, but her firm tone underscored the words she did speak. "I intend to remain here on Barbados."

"Don't worry, Mrs. Parrish, I'll look after your daughter," said Theo, stepping between them. "We'll hire a maid and a respectable companion for her, so that her reputation won't be compromised. I'll see to it that she has a lovely rest here, with plenty of sea air, and then when she is stronger, she can face the future."

Hermione peered at him through her pince-nez. "I suppose I shall have to trust you, Mr. Harrismith, but this situation is extremely improper. My only consolation is that we've gotten rid of that horrid man."

A shadow passed over Cathy's face. "I'll say good bye then, Mother." She leaned forward so that their cheeks brushed, then they went outside in search of her cousin.

Auggie was standing next to the carriages, talking to Basil Lightfoot, but he broke off abruptly at the sight of Cathy. "Mr. Lightfoot was just passing by and I was saying that he must visit Newport one day!"

When more farewells had been made and the little procession of carriages had started off toward Bridgetown, Cathy felt as if an enormous weight had been lifted. The air was sweeter, and she inhaled deeply.

Walking onto the verandah, Cathy gazed out at the white-frilled waves rolling in across the deep turquoise ocean. The departure of her mother and cousin removed an enormous obstacle from her future, but it still hurt to think about what might lie ahead. Raveneau was like a ghost, haunting her night and day…

"Hello, Cathy."

The sound of his voice was so real! She spun around to see him standing just a few feet away, tall and sun-darkened and strong in his fresh, tailored clothes. Her heart leaped, so powerful was the urge to run into his arms, and yet she resisted.

"You shouldn't have come here," she heard herself say.

"Should I not? You are my wife."

Dazzled as always by his physical presence, she reached to her upswept locks, relieved to find them all in place.

"You're lovely," he said, walking toward her.

"Adam—"

His dark gaze devoured her, lingering on her wide eyes, her full lower lip, the high curve of her breasts and tiny circle of her waist. "There are shadows under your eyes. Are you ill?"

"Of course not. You just saw me yesterday." Walking away to a corner of the verandah that was sheltered by a row of potted fan palms, she perched on the edge of a cane settee. Of course he followed and sat beside her, so close that she felt her palms grow damp. "Adam, I have left you. You mustn't come here like this, do you understand? If it's the money that concerns you, you needn't worry. It is yours now; my leaving won't change that—"

"Stop that!" He was so furious at her words that he nearly covered her mouth with his hand. "Devil take it, Cath, you can't mean it! Not about the money, I don't give a damn about the money, but about our marriage. I won't allow you to walk away from our marriage."

"I've done it, though." Tears pricked her eyes but she quickly blinked them back. "We can't have this conversation every day. I told you when I left Tempest Hall how I felt."

"I don't accept it. Where is your blasted mother?"

"They are sailing for America today. Theo's taken them to Bridgetown, to the yacht."

"But you have stayed." He closed his eyes for a moment as a wave of sheer relief swept over him. Every fiber of his being ached to take her in his arms, to bend her back and kiss her until he felt her surrender and respond.

Her endearing blush deepened. "I have stayed, but not because of you. I am investing in the Ocean Breeze—"

"Not that nonsense again!"

"It is not nonsense! You insult me, but of course it is not the first time. Remarks like that only serve to strengthen my resolve." Glancing down, she was distracted by the sight of thigh muscles flexing through his trousers. She prayed he wouldn't touch her. "I mean to buy a house of my own, and find rewarding work. I know I could contribute to improve life on Barbados, perhaps by tutoring students or helping in a hospital. You, meanwhile, have a son who needs you, and a plantation to restore."

"A house of your *own*? What about Tempest Hall?" He wanted to throw her over his shoulder and carry her off. "Cathy, for God's sake, come home with me."

"You only want me now because I've left. When I was there, you held me at arm's length—unless you were laying claim to me in your bed." Emotions surged up in her that were so strong, she almost felt faint. Her face was very warm, and when she instinctively raised her hand to one cheek, her fingers trembled. "Please, Adam. Go home."

Her simple words were like arrows, and they found their mark. Still, he sensed her vulnerability, knowing that she would be powerless to resist if he touched her. He burned to kiss the pulse that beat at her throat and to cup her breast over the sheer lace of her shirtwaist, yet realized that, in the end, it would only drive her farther away.

"I'll go because you have asked me." His voice was hoarse. "Cathy, will you take my hand to say goodbye?"

How could she refuse so plain a request? To do so would betray the extent of her weakness. She looked at his hands, at once strong and elegant, with long, deft fingers that could make her melt with a touch.

"Goodbye, Adam."

It seemed a good strategy to reach toward him first. When her small hand touched his, she felt a current of arousal that was shocking, even though she had expected it. His skin was cool and dry against her damp palm. For a moment, his fingers flexed as they held hers, caressing, and Cathy yearned to go into his arms.

A voice inside reminded her that nothing had changed, and that to return to Raveneau would only mean more pain. She managed somehow to stand up and slip her hand free.

Adam rose too, and looked down at her, searching her expressive face for a sign.

"Until we meet again," he said, and walked away.

Chapter 28

"And here, my lord, is your new home." Herbert Stoute stopped in front of a very old building on Roebuck Street and jangled the ancient keys at Raveneau. He nearly had to shout over the noise of carriages, drays, vendors with pushcarts, and passersby.

When the door had opened and they were inside, Adam told him, "This will not be my home, Mr. Stoute, but my law office." He cast a dubious glance up the dark and dusty stairway. "Perhaps, if work keeps me in town, I may sleep here on occasion."

"There's a splendid view from the upstairs balcony, my lord! You can see the ships in the Careenage from there. It would be a fine enough home for any man."

He watched the bent old man, who was scarcely taller than Cathy, rush about throwing open windows to let in what sunlight could be found on the narrow street with its tall buildings. Had he lost his mind, returning to the law?

"This room would be an excellent office, don't you agree, my lord?" Mr. Stoute wore an ill-fitting black suit and a pearl tie pin. Standing in the center of the parlor that opened off the stairhall, he gestured with both arms thrown wide. "The previous owner has even left you some very serviceable bookcases!"

"Indeed?" With a derisive arch of his brow, Adam crossed to the collection of rickety bookshelves and touched them. "You have a flair for exaggeration, sir."

"Well, perhaps the house needs a woman's touch. Your little wife should put it all to rights in no time." He began to back toward the door. "I won't keep you from your work, my lord. If you would be so kind as to make the final payment…"

"Before I do that, I would like to make a closer inspection." Raveneau shrugged out of his lightweight suit coat and loosened his four-in-hand tie before reentering the stairhall and heading toward the back of the building.

"I can promise you that you have made a fine bargain with this purchase, my lord!" cried Stoute as he trotted along in his wake. "In fact, I should like to show you something."

He led him into a darkened, musty chamber that opened onto a tiny, overgrown garden, then turned, smiling triumphantly. "Did I mention that this building comes with a pedigree?"

"No, you didn't," he replied ironically, glancing up at the peeling paint. "However, I would prefer a workman to a pedigree."

The little man pretended not to hear. "Yes, yes, indeed, the famous gentleman pirate, Stede Bonnet, lived here during the months he spent outfitting his sloop, the Revenge, to become a pirate ship! It was his last home before he went to sea, never to live on this island again."

Adam wondered if he were hearing things. "You must be in jest."

"Jest? Why should I jest? Have you not heard of Stede Bonnet? He was married, you know, and came from a fine family, with a prosperous plantation just east of Bridgetown. It will always be a mystery, what made him give up his respectable existence on Barbados and turn in secret to the life of a pirate!"

"How do you know so much about him?"

"I'm descended from a Bonnet family slave; in fact, my mother's maiden name was Bonnet, taken originally by one of his slaves because he came from Africa with no surname of his own."

Adam inclined his dark head. "Interesting."

"Grandfather Bonnet knew lots of stories, passed down through the years, and when he made his way in the world as a free man, he was able to purchase this building , already knowing its history. I was fascinated hearing the tales as a child, imagining Stede Bonnet living here in secret while preparing his sloop and assembling his pirate crew. He was the only pirate I know of who paid for his own ship and crew, rather than simply stealing them in a sea battle!" Stoute stared off dreamily into space for a moment. "Of course, he had no knowledge of the seafaring life. The venture didn't go very well for him."

Adam stared around the tiny room at the assortment of dusty and broken old furniture. "That's a fascinating story, however—"

"Wait! I brought you here to show you this…" Stoute threw open the door to a heavy old-fashioned mahogany armoire. Malodorous old coats were piled inside, and he dug behind them to expose a wooden box. "My lord, might I request your assistance?"

"Stand aside and I'll lift it out."

The small carved chest was made of thick wood, decorated with tarnished brass fittings, and set with a broken lock. Adam placed it on a nearby chair and glanced over at Stoute with a mixture of impatience and curiosity.

"My lord," the old man confided, "I realize that this property needs more work than you realized when you agreed to buy it. However, we must see our agreement through, for my wife is very ill and I have no funds to seek medical care for her. I promise you, I am selling you not only this building, but also its very unique contents—"

Glancing around again at the piles of filthy, broken furniture, he wondered, "How can I imagine that that you are doing me a favor, sir?"

His voice dropped to a whisper. "I speak of this box, my lord. I have guarded it all my life, but what use is it to me now? But I give you my word that is owner was none other than Major Stede Bonnet, the gentleman pirate!"

Raveneau wanted to exclaim, "Him again?" He nearly explained that he already had a trove of worthless Stede Bonnet memorabilia, but something stopped him. After all, Stoute meant well, and his wife needed medical attention. "All right, then. I'll deal with all of this on my own." He reached into his vest pocket and withdrew a bank draft. "Here is your payment. I wish you and your wife well, sir."

"Ah, thank you, my lord! You're a fine man after all!" He went backing out the door until he had disappeared.

When Adam was alone and contemplating the tasks that lay before him, he thought of Cathy and how she had cleaned alongside June at Tempest Hall, wearing a head-tie like one of the servants. How charming and filled with enthusiasm she had been. When she'd shown him the hidden panel in his dressing room, her excitement had been contagious—yet he had refused to be infected. Now, remembering how he had glanced over his grandmother's letter while refusing to share it with Cathy, a wave of angry regret swept over him.

"No wonder she could not love me," he whispered. "I pushed her aside each time she came near." Abruptly came the sharp memory of her words to him at the Ocean Breeze Hotel: *"You held me at arm's length—unless you were laying claim to me in your bed."*

"Adam? Are you here?" A male voice traveled down the corridor to him, followed by the sound of a child's feet running on the uneven wooden floor. Paul burst into the room first, followed by Byron and Simon.

"Papa!" cried the little boy and jumped into the air, trusting his father to catch him. He lay his head against Adam's chest in a now-familiar gesture. "Hello, Papa."

He held him close for a moment, inhaling the spicy scent of his curly hair and feeling the humid warmth of his small body. "Hello, Paul. Have you and Uncle Byron come to help me?"

"We bringed books," he replied proudly.

Adam gave Byron and Simon a weary smile. "Thank you. As you both can see, I have a bit more work to do here before I can open my office and begin practicing law…"

As Simon went off to direct the two field hands who were unloading the wagon and Paul wandered into the corridor to play with his wooden top, Byron joined his friend. "What on earth inspired you to choose this building? Why isn't it cleaned out? God, I hate to think what sort of vermin could be living amid all this debris."

Adam wished there were a place to sit down, but every chair in the room was broken. Briefly, he related the events of the morning, ending with Mr. Stoute's gift of the wooden box.

"Do you believe him?" asked Byron. "About Stede Bonnet, I mean? For a man who lived two centuries ago, he is certainly turning up in your life a great deal."

"Agreed. I've decided that this is either a wild coincidence or an outrageous hoax. In any event, I already have more Stede Bonnet artifacts than I have time to deal with, even though Retta goes on at me almost daily to delve into the things my grandmother set aside for me."

"Oh, right; no time. Remind me why you decided to buy this building and take up the law again?" As Byron spoke, his gaze wandered around the room, from the peeling paint to the jumble of useless furniture.

"You know why." Raveneau began to fiddle with the lock on the carved box. "I'm fixing myself." Before Byron could reply, he had pulled the latch free and opened the lid. Both men leaned forward and peered into the small chest. On the top of a lot of papers lay one item of interest: a white cockade with a blood-red center.

Two days later, Adam sat at a very old desk in his freshly-scrubbed and painted law office. Leather-bound books lined the repaired shelves while his new blotter, pens, ink, and rosewood stationery box were arranged on the desk before him. He was dressed in fawn-colored linen trousers and coat, a cream-colored vest, a fine white shirt, and a dotted navy tie. Every hair was in place, he had shaved with extra care that morning, and his shoes were polished.

Also on the desk was the battered chest supposedly owned by Stede Bonnet. After he and Byron had their first glimpse of the cockade, Adam had closed the lid and put it away. The fact that the cockade had been identical to the one his grandmother had given him seemed to prove that the connection to Stede Bonnet was real. But beyond that, what did it matter? Wasn't it all a lot of nonsense designed to distract him from the real business of winning his wife back?

Adam looked at the tallcase clock, a treasure unearthed from one of the heaps of junk, ticking quietly against a beeswax-colored wall. In a half-hour, his first potential client was due to arrive, so there was no time to waste. Opening the musty-smelling box, he removed the soiled cockade, and a little chill ran down his back as he looked at it, imagining Stede Bonnet himself placing it in the little chest. Under the cockade was a stack of yellowed, mildew-spotted papers.

One by one, he studied them. In a document dated January of 1716, Major Stede Bonnet of the island militia was named a Justice of the Peace. Under that were hand-drawn plans for the construction of a sixty-ton Bermuda-style sloop-of-war, including the addition of ten cannons. At the bottom of the last page was a handwritten note requesting that the shipwrights build bookshelves all around the bunk in the captain's cabin; the note was initialed *S.B. September, 1717*. Next were legal documents, drawn up by Bonnet's solicitor, that gave power to Stede's wife Mary Allamby Bonnet, along with two gentlemen, to tend to his affairs while he was away from Barbados.

At the bottom of the pile were two more hand-drawn images. The first one was a circle with lines radiating out from a dark center. From across the page, a line pointed back to the center, with the printed word, "RUBY?" It came to Adam that this must be the design for Bonnet's cockade; he had apparently intended to fasten a real ruby at the center. The final image was a sketch of a large rectangle. In its center was a skull above a long bone, flanked by a heart and a dagger. When he turned the last page over, he saw some scrawled numbers and signs that made no sense: R ~ 3...7 X 2...3 X 4...9 XX.

Finally, at the bottom of the box lay a large, ornate key covered with patches of dirt and rust.

Adam rubbed his jaw as he took it all in. Although the discolored, crumbling paper and the faded quality of the ink testified to the authenticity of the documents, and they were surely fascinating, of what use were they to him?

"Ah-hem! Sir, do you be de solicitor?"

Calmly, he closed the box, pushed it off to the back corner of his desk, and stood up. "I am." Extending a hand, Raveneau went to meet the tall black man who waited near the doorway. "Please, come in, sir, and take a chair. I take it that you are George Farnsworth? It's good to meet you."

The older man did as he was bade, twisting his hat in his lap. "I askin' you to make de last will an' testament. Goin' to Panama to work on de canal."

This was a frequently-heard story in Bridgetown of late. The United States was eager to take over the canal project, and Barbadian workers were eager for work. Other countries had tried to build a canal across Panama, but past efforts had been plagued by a high death toll from disease and engineering challenges that at times seemed insurmountable.

As Raveneau talked to Mr. Farnsworth, he learned that the man was newly married and had a child on the way. He was afraid that, if he died, his many feuding relatives would lay claim to his property, and he wanted to be certain that a legal will was drawn up.

This sort of task was child's play for Raveneau, but it felt good to have a real client. There had to be a beginning, and today was it.

After luncheon at the Ice House, there were two more appointments in the afternoon. One was a prosperous ship owner named Asa Forester who needed a solicitor to draw up documents for a series of future projects. Near the end of the long appointment, Forester confided that he had planned to interview other lawyers, but he was so impressed with Raveneau that he would look no further.

By the time he made the long ride home to Tempest Hall, the sun had nearly set. Cantering down the lane lined with hedges of sweet lime, Adam knew an unexpected sense of contentment when he saw the manor house come into view. Green monkeys capered in and out of the mahogany forest, and the wood doves made their last soft calls of the day.

There were lights in the windows of the manor house, and enticing spicy smells drifted out on the breeze. As Adam continued toward the stables, Simon emerged from the house holding Paul's hand. Alice came behind them, limping slightly.

"Papa!" cried the little boy.

At the sight of his son running toward him on stocky little legs, Adam drew back on the reins. Reaching down, he scooped Paul up and held him close with one arm. "How's my little monkey?"

Laughing, Paul revealed the tattered stuffed toy he'd been clutching against his tummy. "Monkey. Ooh-ah!" Then, pointing to Lazarus's proud head, he cried, "Him a horse!"

Smiling, Adam looked into his eyes, and something sweet and inexpressible passed through him. He handed the reins to Simon and dismounted, then stood for a long moment, cuddling Paul closer, his rough cheek turned against a headful of soft baby curls.

If only Cathy were there! He longed to hold her in his arms and share all the news of his day over a leisurely meal. For a moment, Adam imagined her as she had been in the past, waiting for him under the sandbox tree when he'd ridden up after an absence. The memory of her hesitant smile and fresh, unembellished beauty sent a stinging pain through his heart.

Where the devil had he gone all those days he'd been away from Tempest Hall? What had ever possessed him to leave when she had been here? Her presence had been like a soft, warm light, spreading over the house, the gardens, and all the people who lived and worked here. Only he had been stubborn enough to attempt resistance.

"Little one, are you aware that your father is a fool?" he murmured as he started toward the house, the child still safe in his arms. Alice came to meet them, and Adam bent to pet her. "This old girl already knows I'm a fool. If you could talk, you would have warned me that I was going to lose her, wouldn't you?" It was then that he noticed something protruding from one side of her mouth. "What's this?"

The Labrador cocked her head at her master. Her brown eyes spoke volumes, and then she gave an eloquent sigh and released one of Cathy's gardening gloves into Adam's open hand.

"Oh, God. You're killing me." His eyes stung for a moment. "I should have put you in charge. Clearly you could do a better job managing my life than I have."

"Sir," came Retta's voice from the kitchen steps. "Come inside now. I do make you a fine cou-cou for you supper."

"It smells incredible. Where is Byron? I thought he would be watching Paul today."

June poked her head out of the door, and the little boy broke into a big smile. "Mr. Matthews went to Bathsheba to paint. Little Paul has been with me today. We found some old toys in the nursery and made a beautiful block tower."

Climbing the steps to the kitchen, Adam set his son down and watched him go to June and cling to her skirt. "I should have remembered those toys. I played with them myself when I was young." He paused at the hot stove and dipped a spoon into the mixture of cornmeal and okra, stealing a taste. "Ah, Retta, it's perfect! Not a lump in the entire pan."

"Lump?" she repeated, incredulous that he would even speak the word. "No, sir! An' mind yo' hand outa my way."

"But where is Josephine? Shouldn't she be doing the cooking?"

June replied, "She says that there isn't enough work for her here now, so she went to visit her auntie in Speightstown. I think only the mistress could deal with Josephine's tempers."

"Couldn't everything just go smoothly for a few days at a time?" He shook his head. "I can't think about all this right now. I'm going to wash up and eat, and maybe then I'll have a clearer head."

Retta glanced at him through narrowed eyes as he went toward the door. "Not easy fo' man to do all t'ing alone. Dis house do miss…someone."

"Do you think I don't know it?" Adam had to duck to go through the low doorway. Outside again, he took a deep breath.

Next to him, a soft voice encouraged, "You can do it, sir."

Glancing down, he saw that June had followed him, holding Paul's tiny hand. "Yes. I intend to," he replied with a grim smile. As the trio walked toward the main house, he had another thought. "June, you shouldn't be here taking care of Paul; you are supposed to be in school during the week!"

A shadow crossed her face, and she looked down. "My teacher died. "

"I'm sorry to hear that. How many students are in your class?"

"Twelve girls. We have no school until a teacher can be found, and very few want to teach young girls like us."

"We'll have to find a solution to this problem."

"Is it possible, my lord?"

His only response was a dashing smile that caused her to stand up taller and take hope.

After dinner, Adam bathed Paul, then sat with him in Cathy's rocker and told him a story, this one about a frog named Paulywog who wore a coat and learned to fasten the buttons all by himself. The last thing the little boy did before falling asleep was touch the front of his nightshirt and mumble, "Paul's but-ton."

Together they rocked in the candlelit silence. Adam looked down to see his son's little hand splayed trustingly on the hard curve of his shoulder, clinging to the fine linen of his shirt. A fleeting memory came to him of similar moments on the lap of his own father, but he had learned long ago how to turn his thoughts away from such painful images. Gathering up his son, he stood up.

So far, Paul had rebelled each night against sleeping alone in his crib, and each night his father had relented and brought him into his bed. This time, he gently lay him in the crib, tucked Ooh-Ah near, and put out the candle that guttered low beside the rocker. He longed for nothing more than to climb into bed himself and sleep deeply until morning, but he hadn't had a good night's sleep since Cathy left…and there was too much work to be done.

Without making a sound, Adam carried an oil lamp into the dressing room, uncovered the hidden panel, and brought out his grandfather's log books and his grandmother's keepsakes. He brought all of it back to his desk and began to look through them with a much altered attitude than he'd had the last time.

This time, when he studied the map, he saw clues that seemed to fit together with the documents in the carved box at his law office. There were very faint numbers: 3, 2, and 4, written in flowing script alongside the dotted lines that led between a series of three X's, one of them with an "R" beside it. Adam reached for his coat, draped negligently across the bottom of the bed, and found the paper that he'd had the foresight to bring with him.

Unfolding it, he held it nearer the lamp and read: "R ~ 3…7 X 2…3 X 4…9 XX." He looked back to the map again. The first numbers in the sequences were the same, and in one place, instead of one X, there were two! His heart began to pound as he recalled the paper in the box at the law office. Could it be a code?

Out of the corner of his eye, Raveneau noticed that Alice was creeping up the bed steps to snuggle into her place on Cathy's side of the bed. She froze for a moment, glancing his way, but he pretended not to see her. Now that he was alone, he found that he was grateful for the persistent love of a tiny child and a dog. It was a long way from the life he'd led in London, gambling and wenching to his heart's content, seemingly unaware that he deeply needed more. Sometimes at night when he held Paul and they rocked together in the silence, his heart would swell and it would come to him how lonely he'd been he'd been since his boyhood. It was pain he'd never wanted to feel again.

Only now did Raveneau pour himself a small glass of brandy and prop his feet up on a cane stool. He sipped once, twice, then finally took his grandmother's letter in his hands. When he'd read it in Cathy's presence, he'd erected a barrier around his heart. This time was different.

Dearest Adam,

I am writing this letter and putting away these secret treasures against the day you will need them, when I trust you will discover this box and all it contains. I ask you to open your heart and your mind, pretending that I am there with you, talking on the verandah as we have done so often.

He skimmed over the next passage about his grandmother's acquisition of the map and its supposed ties to Stede Bonnet. This was the part he had related to Cathy the day she'd discovered the secret panel.

My dear Adam, you are a Raveneau through and through, and I understand that better than anyone. You should have been born in the eighteenth century, when you could have been a privateer like your great-grandfather Andre Raveneau, or fought duels like my father, Nicholai Beauvisage.

You remind me so much of Andre. He was the ultimate rakehell—irresistible, and impervious to true love until he met Devon. Even your great-grandmother needed a lot of patience and faith to wait for him to open his heart, but of course, eventually he did.

I know, too, that when your mother betrayed her family and then your father died, you locked your heart away. Perhaps you felt that love and grief were too closely entwined? If you are reading this letter, the time has come to begin to trust again. True love is not a sign of weakness, but of strength. The men from whom you descend learned that lesson, and now it is your turn.

Here are the clues to a treasure that will secure your future, and which you may share with the woman you love. But remember, darling Adam, that love is the greatest treasure of all.

Forever, I remain, your Gran Adrienne.

His heart pounded as he read the last words. It truly was as if Gran were sitting across from him, gazing at him with her sparkling, perceptive green eyes. It hurt to think about his parents, and it had been a shock that Gran had mentioned them and the tragedy in his family. But then, she had never been one to mince words.

Longing to fill his glass with brandy and drink it down, Adam instead sat back in his chair and let himself absorb her message. It still felt to him that love and pain went hand-in-hand, but was he going to be a coward? That's what she was saying, it seemed: that men who closed their hearts to love might appear to be dashing rogues on the outside, but underneath they were merely afraid, running away from life's finest gift.

Folding the letter, Adam thought back to the days after he and Cathy had come to Tempest Hall, when he'd done his best to avoid his bride and yet she had waited for him, braver than he as she attempted to bridge the gulf between them.

Little Paul made a soft sound in his sleep and clutched Ooh-ah closer. Alice lifted her head, watching the little boy, until she was satisfied that he was all right.

His grandfather's journals were still there waiting for him, but when Raveneau opened the first one, he made a new discovery: its center had been hollowed out to serve as a container for a rather large case covered in threadbare tapestry. After fetching a second oil lamp from his bedside chest, he lit it and opened the case. Inside was an exquisite diamond-and-sapphire necklace and a smaller, worn velvet case containing what appeared to be a very old fan.

There was another message from his grandmother, inside a tiny envelope with his name inscribed on it in her neat script. This time she was brief, explaining that the necklace had been a gift from Andre to Devon on their wedding day, and it had been passed down to her. The fan, Adrienne wrote, had been the cause of her own first meeting with Nathan Raveneau. *It was reputed to belong to Queen Marie Antoinette, and I had to have it, even if it meant quarreling with your grandfather on Oxford Street!*

As Adam unfurled the delicate, hand-painted fan, it seemed that he could hear her laughter and see her as she had been eighty-five years earlier on that day in London, fresh and lovely and impudent.

Next he opened his grandfather's log books. The sight of the initials, *NR*, embossed in gold on the front of each volume, brought back sharp childhood memories. Nathan Raveneau had been a handsome, vigorous man, even in old age, and Adam had loved to sit on his lap as he paged through the logs, recounting sea adventures to his grandson.

Now, reading them for himself in the dim light, Adam felt a new sense of kinship with his ancestor. To his surprise, he discovered that Nathan had also written long passages in 1818 about the masquerade that had begun his relationship with Adrienne, and the way his true identity had been exposed the night he abducted her from Harms Castle and took her to his ship.

Finally, Adam heard the clock on the landing strike midnight. It was tempting to read on through the night, but soon enough Paul and Alice would both be awake and insisting that he greet the morning with them. With a sigh, he rose and put away the newfound treasures.

When he had stripped off his clothes and stretched out on the testered bed, Adam was grateful for the soft caress of the night breeze. Next to him, Alice snorted contentedly in her sleep while the sounds of Paul's quicker breaths came from his spindled crib.

Closing his own eyes, he thought again of the hours he had just spent with his grandparents. Their words seemed to provide the missing pieces for his future and, as he surrendered to sleep, he felt a sense of peace for the first time since he had watched Cathy leave Tempest Hall.

Chapter 29

"What more could you ask for?"

Cathy looked up from the ledgers and gave Sutton O'Leary a radiant smile. "We truly are in paradise, aren't we?"

They were sitting at a table on the verandah, the remains of their breakfast on plates stacked to one side. Account books were open before them, but the turquoise ocean, glittering like a carpet of diamonds in the morning sun, was a powerful distraction.

"If it weren't for those shadows under your eyes, I might think that you were happy!"

She wrinkled her nose. "I'm doing my best to be happy, Sutton. I have a lot to be grateful for, don't I?"

Just then a tall figure appeared in the doorway and boomed, "Aha! I have found the lovely Lady Raveneau!" Basil Lightfoot approached the table, seemingly oblivious to the other guests who looked up from their breakfasts. "May I join you, my lady?"

Sutton gathered his books and stood. "I was just leaving. You are welcome to my chair, Mr. Lightfoot." His lips twitched as he perceived Cathy's accusatory sidelong glance. "May I order you breakfast?"

"Just tea, thank you." Basil made a show of taking Cathy's hand and kissing it before he sat down. "May I say that you grow lovelier in your unattached state?"

"Why do you say that?"

"I have seen Lord Raveneau numerous times in Bridgetown. Rumor has it that he is living there now, on Roebuck Street. He is frequently carrying Gemma Hart's baby son; it's quite a touching sight." Pausing, he watched her face. "'Twould seem that your situation has altered?"

"Sir, you overstep your bounds."

"Ah, my lady, I beg your pardon. I felt the need to be blunt because of time constraints. You see, I have traveled out of my way this morning to invite you to come out with me for a carriage ride."

She blinked. "Out? With you?" As comprehension dawned, Cathy felt her cheeks getting hot. "Mr. Lightfoot, you have mistaken—" Just then, Theo began to wave wildly at her from the entrance to the dining room. Secretly relieved by the interruption, Cathy said, "Apparently, I am being called away by an urgent matter. If you will excuse me, sir…"

He was on his feet in an instant to pull out her chair for her, but before she could rise, there was another commotion behind them. Cathy turned, with Basil Lightfoot close behind her, and beheld Adam striding out onto the verandah with an anxious-looking Theo trotting in his wake. Adam was carrying Paul, who clung to his father with one hand and a stuffed monkey with the other.

Cathy sighed involuntarily. In spite of the long hours she had lain awake at night, conjuring up images of his eyes, his mouth, the shape of his fingers, her memory did not do Raveneau justice. He seemed taller, his shoulders wider, his face more sinfully handsome than even she, who loved him to the point of pain, had remembered. And his marbled blue-gray eyes seemed to blaze straight to the core of her heart.

"Adam!"

"None other." Clad in a tan linen suit and a brown striped tie, he shifted Paul in his arms as if he'd been carrying the toddler since birth. "Lightfoot, I'm sorry you have to leave now."

"But, I don't! Nothing of the sort!" Basil spluttered, and then made the mistake of stepping in front of Cathy as if to shield her from her husband.

Raveneau inclined his head ever so slightly, a dangerous glint in his eyes. "I insist. Goodbye."

"All right, I'll go, but you really ought to make up your mind, my lord. D'you want a wife, or not? Because—"

"Stop talking," he said as his entire body tensed. "Immediately."

Before Basil could do something even more foolish, Theo darted forward, gestured for the taller man to precede him into the hotel, and hurried him away.

"What the devil was that buffoon doing here?" Adam demanded. "Were you encouraging him?"

"If I was, it is none of your affair," she whispered heatedly. "You have no right to storm in here and order people around."

The hotel guests were looking up from their breakfasts, and Paul appeared to be on the verge of tears. Lowering his voice, Adam said,"Kindly join me in the lobby where we may converse with more privacy."

Feeling suddenly and intensely alive, Cathy led the way. Her mind listed all the reasons she should keep him and his illicit child at arm's length, but her heart was singing. Upon entering the lobby, she was surprised to see Byron Matthews and June sitting on one of Theo's prized settees.

"Byron's come to Barbados to paint," Adam explained.

His friend grinned at Cathy. "Of course, there's more to it than that. Hello, Lady Raveneau; it's splendid to see you again." Standing, he lifted her hand and kissed it.

"I'm so happy you are here, Mr. Matthews!" And indeed, she was pleased not only because she liked him, but also because Adam now had companionship at Tempest Hall. Cathy then greeted June with a warm embrace and allowed Adam to guide her onto a second settee. When they were all seated, Byron held out a lollipop to Paul. "Come and join me, Mr. Button."

The child climbed down from his father's lap and went to get it but then came right back. Gazing soberly at Cathy, he touched a fastening on his short pants and explained, "But-ton."

Her heart seemed to melt under the spell of his eyes, which were so much like Adam's. "That's a fine button, Paul. Do you know how to work it yourself?"

He nodded and tasted the lollipop, lounging back against his father's chest. "Papa taught me."

"Well, it's a skill in progress," Adam amended with a wry smile. Turning to Cathy, he continued, "I know you are very busy, so we will be brief. June's teacher has died and her class is unable to attend school until another can be found. I thought that you—"

"Oh, yes!" she cried. "June, you and your classmates must come to me for your lessons. There is nothing I would enjoy more."

Adam arched an eyebrow. "You anticipate me, my lady."

She ignored him. "The only problem is that I have some duties here at the hotel and I cannot leave during the day. Would it be a terrible inconvenience for you girls to come to me and have your lessons here?"

"Most of us live in Bridgetown, ma'am," June replied, beaming. "We can travel to Hastings on the mule tram."

"What a splendid plan!" exclaimed Byron.

"We couldn't dream of having a better teacher," said June. "I am so happy!"

"If you will make a list of the books you want the class to have, I'll provide them," Adam told his wife.

She nearly waved away his offer with the assurance that she would purchase them herself, but something in his expression stopped her. "All right. Thank you."

"Good. That's settled then." He glanced pointedly at Byron, who immediately got to his feet.

"We'll be on our way. Come on, Mr. Button, your Uncle Byron will give you a ride." Byron held out his arms to Paul, who reluctantly complied. They went first, out into the sunlight, and soon the child had been hoisted onto Byron's shoulders and was giggling with excitement as they walked toward the open landau.

Simon, who had stayed outside to water the horses, came forward now to greet Cathy.

"Ma'am, we do miss you."

"It's so nice to see you, Simon. Please give my best wishes to Retta, won't you? I hope that she and Josephine are getting along."

He only shook his head and looked heavenward, then bade her farewell. When Cathy turned to Adam, her heart began to pound again. "I'll say goodbye, then. Thank you for bringing June and suggesting this arrangement."

"You're welcome, but I'm not leaving." Shielding his eyes against the sun, he looked toward the carriage, which was rolling out onto Hastings Road. Little Paul was waving and crying, and Adam waved back, calling, "I'll see you tonight! Be good for Uncle Byron."

She felt a pang of unexpected emotion at the sight of Paul's tears and Adam's fatherly response. "I don't understand. Didn't you come with them?"

"No." He pointed to Lazarus, standing in the shade of a stout, jug-shaped baobab tree. "I rode down on my own. I have other business to attend to today."

She felt more nervous by the moment. "Well, I won't keep you from it, then…"

"Cathy." Gazing into her eyes, he said simply, "It's *you*. You are my business."

Her nervousness gave way to a tingly melting feeling that started in her heart and traveled down between her thighs. "If you are worried that I am seeing other men so soon after our…separation—"

"Oh, God." His expression told her that he was holding himself in check. "Will you walk with me for a bit?"

She let him lead her down to the beach, where they took off their shoes. Adam hung his suit coat on a tree branch and loosened his tie as they started off, away from the hotel and the bathhouses. Glancing over, Cathy drank in the sight of him, coatless, his tapering chest and narrow waist accentuated by the fitted vest. "I really can't be away very long," she said. "Mrs. Ford, the cook, is expecting me for our little pre-luncheon meeting. Tomorrow is the outdoor market in Bridgetown and I want to discuss her list…"

Adam started to reach for her hand, then stopped himself. "I perceive that you are making yourself quite indispensable here."

"I like it very much. Theo has been exceptionally kind to me."

"I'm glad."

"Are you? Truly?" Cathy glanced down at the hem of her skirt, which was now edged with sand, and shook it slightly with both hands.

Stopping to wait for her, Raveneau listened to the sound of the ocean for a few moments. "That's what I want to tell you. In spite of my behavior on the verandah, I didn't come here today to challenge any of your would-be suitors to a duel and then attempt to reclaim you myself."

The dry, honest tone of his voice struck a chord deep inside her. "No?"

"Cathy, I am here to tell you that I have done you an injustice. You deserved a man who would woo you properly and not be afraid to let you love him, and to show his love in return." He rubbed his jaw with long fingers. "Everything you said about me the day you left Tempest Hall was true. I didn't deserve you."

The strange melting feeling intensified inside her. It was hard to breathe. What was he trying to say? "Adam, we can't go back and change the past. I begged you to marry me, knowing how you felt, so I can hardly blame you for not being transformed into a romantic lover after we recited marriage vows."

"And is this what you want? To remain separate from me, here at the Ocean Breeze?"

His tone was even, but the passion in his gaze made Cathy look away, and perspiration dampened her delicate shirtwaist. "At the moment, I can only contend with today. What I know is that I have been controlled all my life by my mother—until the day I broke free and married you. What did I know about men, or real love, or marriage? Everything I had witnessed growing up turned out to be hollow. And my feelings for you have only confused me more." To her horror, tears sprang to her eyes, and Adam offered a handkerchief from his vest pocket. Lifting the snowy linen to her face, Cathy felt a shock of arousal as she breathed in the scent of him. "We should go back, I think."

As they turned and started in the direction of the hotel, he cupped her elbow protectively. "You're right, Cath. We were both quite unfit for marriage."

She was grateful he didn't argue with her or tell her again why she should return to Tempest Hall with him. "I've never been on my own until now. I hate to say this, but all my life Mother was like my jailer."

His arm moved naturally around her waist, drawing her against the hard length of his body in unspoken understanding. "Thank God she's gone."

"I would say that you and I both need to sort out our lives. You are a father now, and that is a very demanding role. It's plain that Paul loves you very much. As for the two of us, I simply don't know what the future holds…"

He wanted to tell her that he didn't intend to lose her, by God, that he would kill any other man who tried to touch her. He burned to take her in his arms and bend her back and kiss her deeply until she was moaning in surrender and he could feel her melt and her hips arch against his. Yet, somehow he managed to suppress all of these primitive urges.

Instead, Raveneau merely reached out to gently brush back tendrils of her hair that had come loose in the sea breeze. "You are even lovelier than when I last saw you."

"That's very kind of you, but we both know that I am no beauty—"

"I know nothing of the kind. I am utterly sincere." His strong hand shaped itself to the fragile curve of her jaw. "Clearly, life here agrees with you, and I want you to be happy. I have just one request."

She ached to feel his lips on hers. "I'm listening."

"Give me a chance to court you as you deserve." When she didn't protest immediately, he continued, "Will you have dinner with me two nights from now?"

"But, how—where?"

"Let me surprise you. May I call for you at seven o'clock?" Seeing her hesitant expression, he gave a rueful laugh. "Don't worry, I promise not to abduct you and ravish you against your will."

Cathy blinked, slightly disappointed by his words. "Well, then, how can I refuse?"

"Exactly so," Adam replied with a rakish smile. He caught her delicate hand and lifted it to his mouth, aware of the quickening of her pulse. "I shall look forward our evening together."

Letting herself enjoy the thrill of anticipation, she smiled back at him. "Yes, my lord, so shall I."

It was midday by the time Raveneau walked from Trafalgar Square onto the Chamberlain Bridge which separated the inner and outer basins of the Careenage. To the east of the swinging bridge, exposed hulls were being scraped, painted, and repaired. To the west, the outer basin and Carlisle Bay were lined with tall-masted schooners and other ships from every corner of the Caribbean. Adam paused for a moment to watch cargoes of plantains, mangoes, and lumber being unloaded and transported to nearby warehouses.

Asa Forester was waving to him. The rotund older man stood halfway down a set of wide steps that led from a landing to the water. Adam remembered his grandfather explaining that the Wellington Stairs were often used by visiting dignitaries and royals when they disembarked from their ships.

"There's nothing like it, is there, Raveneau?" Forester called in robust tones, spreading his arms wide to gesture at all the activity in the port.

Adam met him on the broad landing and extended his hand. "I take it business is going well, sir?"

"Do you see the bags of sugar and casks of molasses and rum that are arriving at the wharf? That's my lighter that they'll be loaded onto, and then transported to that magnificent ship out in the bay." He pointed to the northwest.

"Could that be the *Patriot*, your latest acquisition?" Drawing up the bill of sale and other papers had been the first of many tasks for him as Forester's lawyer. "A handsome ship indeed."

"I'm grateful to have found a solicitor I can trust, Raveneau, so that I continue to attend to the matters of true importance, like building my fortune!" He threw back his curly white head and laughed. "I trust I haven't kept you too busy?"

"I share your sense of gratitude, sir. I have a fortune of my own to build." A dry smile touched Adam's mouth.

"And I understand you asked me to meet you because you need a favor?"

"I do. However, if you agree, perhaps I could earn it with a few hours of my professional services at no cost."

"Very interesting!" Forester waggled his bushy eyebrows. "There is a tavern just a stone's throw from here on Bay Street. I propose that we sit down and discuss this matter over a cold glass of ale."

It was time Adam didn't have, but on the other hand, the man was his best client and this conversation could save his marriage. So, he went along to the Pelican House, dodging puncheons of molasses being rolled haphazardly toward the waterfront via two-wheeled carts called spiders.

"Someone should find a way to put brakes on those contraptions!" Forester barked after nearly being run down.

Once they were safely settled at a table by the window and had been served, Adam leaned forward. "Sir, as you know I have access to all your records—"

"Of course! I had a good feeling about you or I wouldn't have hired you, Raveneau."

Adam smiled, thinking how pleasant it was that Forester seemed to know nothing of his title. It was a welcome respite from being called "my lord" at every turn. "Thank you, sir. In your records, I saw a bill of sale for a brigantine called The *Golden Eagle*. Do you still own it?"

Forester drained his glass. "Another hot day in paradise. I really longed for a swizzle, but my wife would say that it's much too early…isn't it?" He tugged at his celluloid collar. "The *Golden Eagle*, you say? Yes, yes, I own her. Older than the devil, but quite beautiful. She's just returned yesterday from Venezuela. Why do you ask?"

"The *Golden Eagle* was my grandfather's ship."

"Ah! So that's where I'd heard that name Raveneau before! My memory's not what it used to be; too much rum, my wife would say." He paused to chuckle and signaled for another ale. "She's a beauty, just old fashioned. Why did he sell her?"

"I think, by the time he was eighty, he realized that the ship needed to be in more regular use, and his children couldn't take it. My own father was hopelessly landlocked, and my aunt had married a Frenchman."

"Hmm! I'm only the second owner since Nathan Raveneau, as I recall. I heard that she had quite a colorful past!"

Adam gave him a jaunty smile, remembering some of the passages in his grandfather's log books. "You might say that. And I would like to give her one more adventure, if you'll consent to letting me borrow her for a few days."

"That's quite a request!" Forester exclaimed, his eyes widening. "Are you experienced with a vessel of that size? I wouldn't have imagined a solicitor on the deck of an eighteenth century brigantine!"

"My great-grandfather was a famous French privateer captain, and I have cousins who are still building and sailing ships in Essex, Connecticut. I suppose it's in my blood. Actually, more so than the law, to tell you the truth." Leaning back in his chair, he took a long sip of ale and added, "In any event, I would need another captain because I will be…otherwise occupied part of the time we are at sea. I was hoping that you might lend me a skeleton crew along with the ship. A discreet skeleton crew."

"You're a brash one, Raveneau!" Forester's eyes sparkled. "I like that! Yes, I'll help you. How soon do you need the *Golden Eagle*?"

"In two days." He finished his own ale and took some money out of his pocket to pay for them both. "I'm very grateful. Thank you, Mr. Forester."

"I don't suppose you'd be interested in coming to our house for dinner…and meeting my daughter? She's quite a charmer!"

"Although I'm sure your daughter is lovely, I'm afraid that I'm married." Counting coins onto the table, he shifted his hand to make his wedding ring more visible.

"Are you? That's not what Basil Lightfoot's been telling people. If you'll take a piece of advice from me, I would tell you that it's not a good policy to let your wife live apart from you. People begin to gossip."

Adam felt a familiar surge of frustration and a possessive white heat when he thought of Basil Lightfoot or any other man believing that Cathy was available. "I appreciate your advice, Mr. Forester, and I agree. My advice for you, if anyone should mention my wife to you again, is to suggest that they mind their own business."

The other man blinked. "I can see that I've touched a sore spot!"

"Not at all." Standing, he flicked a bit of dust from his sleeve. "The important thing is that we have a bargain. I'll be in touch to settle the details."

"Of course. And let this favor be my gift to you. I intend that we shall have a long and prosperous working relationship, and perhaps this will set the seal on it."

A smile flickered at the corners of Raveneau's mouth. "No doubt it will."

Chapter 30

"How many of you can tell me the name of the President of the United States?" Cathy asked the twelve adolescent girls seated before her. When several hands went up at once, she beamed and gestured toward a student in the back row. "How smart you all are! Frances?"

"Theodore Roosevelt, Miss Cathy," she answered in a small voice.

"Very impressive! I'd like you all to write his name, as you think it is spelled. I'll write it, too, and then we'll talk about it."

As all twelve dark heads bent and they went to work, Cathy felt a surge of happiness. It was immensely satisfying to have put together a classroom here in the hotel's sunny music room, with three rows of long tables, a dozen matching chairs, and a small desk for her in the front. The day before, she had had her doubts that the girls would really come, but all twelve of them had arrived on the mule tram, just as June had promised. They wore freshly laundered and pressed white dresses and bows on the ends of their braids, and each one carried a pencil case and an essay book. On that first day, Cathy had used some of her own books, holding them up to show illustrations and then passing them around. Before planning lessons, she had decided to spend a day or two quizzing them on various subjects to discover how far they had come with their previous teacher.

One of the hardest decisions had concerned her own name. She felt strange about asking them to call her Mrs. Raveneau, since she lived apart from her husband and the marriage could well be over. Yet, it didn't feel right to introduce herself as Miss Parrish, either. So, for the time being, she said that they might call her Miss Cathy.

The girls had begun putting their pencils down when suddenly Theo appeared in the doorway, walked past the tables, and whispered in her ear.

"Oh, dear," she told her students with a bemused smile, "it seems that I'll have to step out for a few moments. But Mr. Harrismith will teach you in the meantime. He is very interested in the recent success of a flying machine built by the Wright Brothers, and I know he would enjoy sharing his knowledge!"

The sound of them buzzing behind her as she walked toward the door made Cathy pause. "And I know that you will show him your best manners. We are all here today because of Mr. Harrismith's kindness. If there is any misbehavior, he has my permission to drill you on sums."

She pretended not to see the slightly panicky expression on Theo's face before she went out the door. His news that Byron had arrived with schoolbooks was exciting, but she felt a twinge of disappointment that Adam had not come himself. Just in case, though, Cathy paused in the corridor to peek into a shell-edged mirror. Her hair was pinned up into a soft pouf, and she looked pretty yet studious in a high-necked shirtwaist of lace-trimmed batiste paired with a long, fitted gray skirt. Hurrying into the lobby, she saw Byron coming through the main door.

"Hello!" He set a large crate of books on a marble-topped table and expelled an exaggerated sigh of relief. "Someone has sent you a very heavy gift."

"How lovely! It's kind of you to deliver it."

As she reached out her hands to him, Byron's eyes swept over her delicate form, lingering on her big brown eyes and warm smile. "I should have fought harder to marry you myself," he murmured with a rueful smile. "Would I have had a chance?"

Her smile softened. "Although I completely adore you, dear Byron, I'm afraid the answer is no. And I think you know the reason why."

Cathy could see him wondering if he should ask more questions about her reasons for being at the Ocean Breeze, but before he could speak, she lifted the lid from the crate and began to take the books out. There were several copies of *A Course in Spelling* and a full dozen *Geographical Readers*. She counted six arithmetic books, and then, on the bottom, there were twelve new leather-bound volumes of *Little Women*, including Cathy's own which she had inadvertently left behind at Tempest Hall. An envelope was tucked inside that book, and she opened it.

Cathy, I know I should wait for your list, but I've discovered it's bloody difficult to find texts for this age level on the island. The search continues. I hope it's not too much to ask that your students share some of these.

How fortunate they will be to read Little Women with you as their teacher.

Until this evening, I remain – Yours, etc., Raveneau

She felt herself blush helplessly, and longed to touch the pad of her thumb to the signature which he had scrawled with careless elegance.

After a moment, Byron cleared his throat. "I have something else in the carriage. Adam has sent you a blackboard and easel."

"Indeed?" Reluctantly, she slipped the note back into the book and followed him outside. There was a large, flat rectangle wrapped in brown paper on the seat of the open landau. And, to her surprise, Cathy saw both little Paul and Alice, crouching together under the hulking baobab tree. Paul was scratching with a twig among some rocks and leaves while Alice watched him protectively.

The sight of Paul always stirred up her emotions. She couldn't help thinking back to the very first day they'd arrived on the island, when Adam had been rather cool to her and they had encountered Gemma Hart in Bridgetown. Just the memory of Gemma's knowing gaze could still make her feel sick inside. And, too often, lying awake in the middle of the night, she relived every horrible, humiliating moment of their encounter at Tempest Hall. The image of Paul, coming out from behind his mother's skirts, was seared into her memory.

Repeatedly, Cathy had told herself that he was an innocent victim in this drama, but just the thought of him caused a visceral reaction. Why was he here again? Why wasn't his father looking after him? Before she could put these questions to Byron, Alice turned and saw her mistress.

"Woof!" she cried joyfully and trundled toward her.

"Ah, girl, it is so good to see you," Cathy said with feeling. She bent and began to pet the old Labrador as Byron started toward the carriage.

Just then, Paul screamed in fear and pain. Trembling, he struggled to his feet and held out his arm, shrieking and crying at the same time. Alice was the first one at his side, closely followed by the two adults.

"What happened, Paul? Was it a thorn?" Byron hoisted him into his arms and wiped the child's tear-soaked face with a handkerchief.

Suddenly, Alice began to bark urgently at the base of the tree and Cathy hurried over. "What is it, girl? What do you see?"

The dog reached out with one paw and gingerly touched a few leaves just enough to expose a wriggling wormlike creature perhaps six inches long. Byron came, too, still carrying Paul.

"It looks like a centipede," he said, bending closer. Alice continued to bark and Paul's shrieks grew louder.

"Why, it's enormous! Adam warned me about them at Tempest Hall," Cathy said, trying to get a closer look. "He said the Bajans call them 'forty legs,' and although their bites sting and can make you sick, they're not fatal."

"It bite me!" Paul sobbed.

They could see it then, two tiny marks on his pudgy wrist. It was already beginning to swell around the edges of the bite. Something inside of Cathy stiffened up, and she took charge. "Byron, follow me. We'll take him up to my room."

Paul's cries were subsiding as Byron followed her up the back stairs with Alice laboring in his wake. When they reached Cathy's suite, she opened the door and quickly drew back the counterpane on her bed. The windows were open, and a soft, warm breeze lapped at the mosquito netting.

"Just set him down right here, and then I want you to go and ask Mrs. Ford, the cook, what to do for a centipede bite." She turned to Paul and sat down beside him on the edge of the bed. "I don't want you to worry about a thing, darling. You're going to be just fine."

"Ooh-ah," he whimpered.

"That's his monkey," Byron said from the doorway. "I'll fetch him from the carriage while I'm downstairs."

When they were alone, Paul looked around the testered bed and the pretty room, and his tears began to flow again. "I want Papa!"

Cathy instinctively learned toward him with her arms open, and to her surprise, he came immediately into her embrace, resting the weight of his damp curly head on her breasts. His little hands clung to her. Although her restrictive upbringing had allowed her very little experience with babies or small children, she felt something warm and sweet blossom deep inside her heart. Tightening her arms around him, she turned her cheek against his brow, inhaled the sweaty-baby scent of him, and rocked slowly back and forth.

Just as they both began to relax, Byron burst back into the room with Ooh-Ah in one hand and a basin with supplies in the other. "Is he all right? Good God, Adam will murder me if he's not all right!"

It seemed that Mrs. Ford had matter-of-factly prescribed soap and water, followed by cold compresses to be changed every few minutes. She had even sent some of her precious ice to chill the wet towels. While Cathy proceeded to administer first aid,

Paul refused to leave her lap, and he even kept his face turned against the fresh bodice of her shirtwaist.

At one point, seeing Byron's distraught expression, Cathy whispered, "Your friend cannot blame you for anything that happened today. If he is so attached to this child, perhaps he should look after him himself rather than relegating his care to you."

He blinked. "He's been an amazing father, but he can't be in two places at once."

"What in the world does that mean?"

"Nothing. Never mind. But I'm his best friend, and I would lay down my life for this child." Pausing, he bit his lip. "Perhaps I should place a telephone call to him. You have a telephone here, don't you?"

"Yes, but there isn't one at Tempest Hall, so it won't do you any good."

Byron's eyebrows went up. "Oh, right. Well, I was thinking he might be in Bridgetown."

"Byron, unless you have an itinerary of his movements, I hardly see how you could reach him there by telephone." Cathy's face softened as she looked down at her tiny patient. Drawing the icy towel back, she examined the wound. "I think it's better already!" she told Paul. "The swelling is nearly gone. I'll bet it barely hurts at all now!"

He stared at it, too, then snuggled back against her. "Caffy?"

"Yes, darling."

"Will you be my mummy?"

Suddenly there seemed to be a lump in her throat. "But you already have a mummy, sweetheart, and she loves you very much."

"Mummy sick, Papa say." Gravely, he looked up at her face and experimentally patted her cheek.

Slowly, she nodded, then began to rock back and forth again. Byron put Ooh-ah into the crook of his little elbow, but Paul didn't seem to notice. Soon, he was asleep.

A little while later, Byron took the sleeping Paul from Cathy's arms and carried him down to the landau. Alice sat next to the child, guarding him and gazing sadly at her mistress as the carriage rolled away from the hotel.

Feeling emotional, Cathy sent her class home a bit early and had a long bath. The realization that Adam was going to arrive to take her out for dinner soon was a bit surreal. Reclining in the warm water, she began to shiver with nerves as she thought of being alone with him and the possibility that he might touch her or even attempt to kiss her. As memories flooded back of their wild nights in his bed at Tempest Hall, her nipples tightened and the pulse between her thighs throbbed. For a long moment, she lay still, her eyes closed against the feelings that she seemed powerless to control. Then, with a sigh, she sat up and began to wash with lavender-scented soap purchased long ago in Paris. The sooner she put some clothes on, the better off she'd be!

Since she didn't have a lady's maid at the Ocean Breeze, Cathy usually asked one of the chamber maids to help with her corset when she dressed in the morning. Tonight, they had all gone home, so she pushed the buzzer for the kitchen and waited to see who would turn up.

"You rang, my lady?" came Theo's voice from the corridor.

"Oh, Theo! Isn't there a female in the hotel?"

"They're all occupied with dinner preparations, I'm afraid. Do you need help with your corset? I have sisters, you know. I can do it."

"Wait!" She stepped into her gown and drew it around her so that it only gapped open in back, where the corset laces waited for him. "All right, come in."

He wore a bemused expression as he approached her. "God help me if your husband turns up. He'd surely challenge me to a duel and carve my heart out with his rapier."

"Don't be silly. He's not that terrifying, is he?"

Theo waggled his eyebrows and laughed. "Oh, yes, completely." He took the laces in his hands and instructed, "Inhale, my lady."

Cathy braced herself against the bureau as the corset tightened around her, and then she felt him fastening the tiny hooks that marched down the back of her gown of cream silk embroidered with fragile seed pearls. "But Theo, he knows better, don't you think? About you, I mean."

"I doubt it. The fact is, I am sure that Raveneau realizes I would have fallen in love with you long ago if it weren't impossible. Men sense these things."

She felt her cheeks grow warm and was grateful that she was turned away from him. "You're just being kind. You and I have been friends from the moment we met, and that's often a more durable relationship, don't you think so?"

"I do. That's why I've settled for it so happily." He straightened the seams of her gown and patted both of her shoulders. "There you go. You look exquisite."

"It's kind of you to say so." Turning, she looked at her reflection in the mirror and realized that she scarcely recognized the woman gazing back at her. She was slender yet shapely, with beautifully expressive brown eyes and delicate features. It seemed that the former roundness of her face had been gradually replaced by finely etched bone structure. Her upswept hair, always uncooperative in Newport, was fuller and wavier in this tropical climate, and there were tendrils curling softly around her face. The Worth silk gown, with its fragile batiste overlay and trails of seed pearls, clung almost provocatively to her curves.

"You know it's true, don't you?" Theo prompted gently.

A rosy glow spread across her cheekbones. "You have no idea the things my mother has said to me all my life about my looks. I am so used to seeing her shaking her head hopelessly at the sight of me, instructing me to stand up straighter or smile differently or eat less in an effort to improve my shape. Do you know she made me wear a rod at home for my posture?" Sighing, she shook her head a little. "Now, I've realized that it's up to me to create my own opinion of myself, and I'm working on that."

"Good girl. There's a man waiting for you tonight who clearly adores you."

"Well, I must confess that I'm still afraid to believe that…"

"Give him a second chance. Don't we all deserve that?"

Cathy had a sudden memory of sitting with Adam on Christmas Eve, opening the unexpected gift from her father. What had Adam said to her then? "Give the poor fellow a chance…No one's perfect." As she stared into space, reliving the moment with new meaning, a shiver ran down her back.

"I'm going then," Theo called brightly as he made his exit. "I'm afraid you're on your own from now on tonight!"

Chapter 31

Standing on a broad stone terrace that overlooked the Atlantic Ocean, Adam Raveneau listened to the rhythmic pounding of the waves and enjoyed a moment of keen anticipation. Palm trees swayed above the beach and, in the distance, the tall-masted *Golden Eagle* was silhouetted against a silvery full moon as it rested at anchor beyond Cobbler's Reef.

The sun, a magenta ball of fire, was just sinking into the ocean. It was a magical evening.

All his plans were now in motion. Glass hurricane lamps were lit, the intimate round table was set with fine linens and crystal, and Josephine and her helpers were working in the kitchen. Adam waited, aching to see Cathy, to look into her eyes, to touch her fingers.

When the landau came into sight in the distance, his heart leaped. The carriage kept to the coast road, hugging the cliffs, leaving a cloud of coral dust in its wake.

Entering the mansion, Adam descended the hand-carved mahogany staircase and glanced around the grand entrance hall. When he'd decided that Crowe's Nest would be the site of his romantic evening with Cathy, he hadn't counted on the effect that years of emptiness would have on the mansion. There had been almost as much cleaning to do as in his law office in

Bridgetown, but he'd done it gladly. Making the entry hall and verandah presentable for this evening had been a labor of love.

Now the landau was drawing up the semicircular drive to the front entrance. As it came to a stop and Simon climbed down to open the door for Cathy, Adam went out to greet her.

She peeked out of the carriage door, wide-eyed and more beautiful than he could have dreamed. Unable to help himself, he let his gaze roam from her softly upswept hair, down over her expressively radiant face and the gossamer gown that blew softly against her form, to the glimmer of seed pearls that embroidered the hem of her petticoat. Closing the distance between them as Simon stepped back, Adam held out a dark, strong hand to her.

"Welcome to Crowe's Nest, Lady Raveneau."

Cathy's heart swelled as she met his tender gaze. This was the sort of fantasy that she always had imagined happening to other girls, but never to her. In his black and white evening clothes, he looked more like a character from a romantic novel than someone from her very own life. "I've been wondering where Simon was taking me," she admitted, putting her hand in his. "I had envisioned a simple dinner...perhaps at a hotel—"

"Simple? For you? Nothing of the kind, Cathy. You had told me that you wanted to come here..."

As they walked up the steps, she murmured, "I didn't imagine anything quite so special."

"Nothing I could possibly do would be special enough for you."

His penetrating eyes sent a tremor of arousal through her. "Adam, do you remember the night we met…when we talked in the Chinese teahouse at Beechcliff?"

"Remember? I have relived every moment of that night more times than I can count."

The corners of her mouth turned up. "Sometimes I remember it, too. From the moment you called me Cathy, I think I was under your spell."

Torches were lit on either side of the doorway, flickering in the soft evening breeze, and they paused there. Adam restrained himself from gathering her into his arms and covering her mouth with his. Instead, he continued to hold her hand, caressing her tender palm with his thumb. "And now?" he whispered. "Have I broken the spell beyond repair?"

"Well, the notion of a spell isn't quite right for a marriage, is it?"

"Cathy, you must know what I mean."

She stood up a little straighter, her eyes clear. "I suppose I wouldn't be here tonight if I'd given up all hope…"

"Good." He nodded slowly, letting her words sink in. "Let's go upstairs, and have dinner, shall we? I think it's time we became reacquainted."

Cathy looked around as they entered the mansion, taking in the arrangement of freshly cut hibiscus, peacock flowers, lilies, and red lobster-claws. "You have been busy! Hasn't Crowe's Nest been uninhabited?"

"I wanted this evening to be perfect."

"Adam, before I forget, I must thank you for the schoolbooks that Byron brought today. I can't tell you how much I appreciate them…and your thoughtfulness."

"It was a small gesture compared to what you are doing for June and her friends." He took her arm as they went up the wide stairway. "But, while we are speaking of gratitude, I owe a huge debt to you for your kind treatment of Paul today. I know that it can't have been easy, given the circumstances, and I apologize for not being present. You shouldn't have been put in that position."

When she looked up, she saw that he was watching her expression with deceptively keen eyes. What did he hope—or fear—to see? "Don't apologize. He is a little boy and quite innocent in the tangle of our adult lives. Is he better?"

"Yes, just a bit sleepy, still." He paused, considering for a moment whether to say more. "Actually, since I was busy with these preparations, Byron brought him here this afternoon. They're upstairs."

Cathy brightened. "May I see him, please? I should feel so much better to see for myself that he is all right."

This wasn't part of the romantic, intimate evening Adam had planned, but he nodded. It was difficult for him to forget the shadow in Cathy's eyes when she had been in Paul's presence in the past. He had been hoping that, if he could win her love again, the situation with Paul could be slowly resolved over time. "How can I refuse?"

So they went up the stairs, past the landing that opened onto the terrace where their dinner would be served, continuing to a long, candlelit corridor that smelled faintly of mildew. Adam paused before a door, tapped once, and opened it. Inside, Cathy beheld a grand bedchamber lit by hurricane lamps, while moonlight spilled through full-length windows opening onto a balcony. In the center of the room, Paul rested in a massive mahogany four-poster bed.

Byron got up from a wing chair and put down his book while Alice struggled to her feet, tail wagging at the sight of Cathy. "I was just about to take this old girl outside. She's been giving me rather urgent signals. Could I leave Paul with the two of you?"

When they were alone, Adam and Cathy went to look at Paul, who was sprawled across a pillow. He still wore the same clothing he'd had on at the Ocean Breeze Hotel, and his stubby fingers clutched Ooh-Ah, the stuffed monkey. Cathy felt a surge of emotion as she remembered the way he had snuggled against her that afternoon.

It was Adam who reached out with one lean hand and gently caressed his son's dark curls. "His head is always like a furnace," he remarked. "If I didn't know better, I would think that he has a perpetual fever."

"I don't know much about children," she murmured. "My mother kept me away from babies."

"I must admit that, although I've known a few, I never paid much attention until now. It's amazing the instincts that come to life when you're responsible for a child who looks to you for love and protection."

She leaned against him for an instant, touched by his words. "Yes." Taking a deep breath, she added, "I felt that myself today."

Adam regarded her with tender bemusement. "Did you indeed? I appreciate that you've shared that with me."

Just then, Paul's long lashes fluttered and he opened his eyes. "Papa? I firsty."

Glancing around, he saw the glass of coconut water that Byron had left on the bedside table. "Here you go." He picked him up with one strong arm and lifted the glass with the other.

Paul drank it down, then focused on Cathy. "Hi. Hi, Caffy." He gave her a shy smile.

Pleased, she beamed back at him. "Hello, Paul. How are you feeling tonight? I've been worried about you."

He looked at the place on his wrist where the centipede had bitten him. "All gone." Then he extended his wrist toward her for proof.

"Indeed, sweetheart. I'm so glad. And you were such a brave boy; your papa must be very proud of you." To her surprise he leaned toward her, arms outstretched, and she took him from his father and felt his warm little arms hold onto her as they had that afternoon. Heat emanated from his dark head, just as Adam had observed. "You're a beauty, Paul."

He had turned his cheek against the soft hollow next to her shoulder and whispered, "Caffy. Caffy."

Adam gave a snort of mock jealousy. "Clearly the youngest Raveneau male is trying to steal your affections. Paul, I must insist that you release Cathy. Papa has other plans for her tonight."

She held him closer. "It's true; he does have the Raveneau charm."

Just then, Byron and Alice came back into the room. "Not a moment too soon!" Adam exclaimed.

Byron couldn't help smiling at the sight of what appeared to be a loving little family, and he knew that his friend was trying to hide his own pleasure at the growing bond between Cathy and Paul. "I was just about to tell Paul another story about that frog—"

"Paulywog," Adam corrected.

"Right. Come on, Mr. Button. I've brought you a sliced mango as well."

This was enough to lure Paul from Cathy's arms. Before the couple could leave, however, Alice approached the tall set of bedsteps and began to bark. She nudged at the top step with her nose.

"Now what?" Adam demanded. "By the time I get Cathy alone for dinner, it will be midnight!" He bent to look at the step, and Alice nudged it again. When he pulled it upward, the top lifted on a hidden hinge. His heart beat harder.

"How exciting!" said Cathy, crouching beside him. "A hidden compartment! I wonder what it means?"

Adam exchanged glances with Byron. "As I understand it, this bedchamber belonged to Xavier Crowe, my grandfather's arch enemy. He's the one who owned that map Gran Adrienne hid in the dressing room."

"The map you had no interest in when I showed it to you?"

"Yes, that one," he replied ironically. Reaching into the deep stairstep-box, Adam brought out first one handsome three-barreled flintlock pistol, and then another with one barrel.

"Clearly Xavier Crowe was prepared to be attacked in his bed!"

"Is there anything else?"

Adam felt around in the dark box. "No, that's all, and while these pistols are very interesting—" He was interrupted in the midst of closing the step by more barking from Alice. "For God's sake, what now?"

She pushed her nose into the opening and came back with something white and crumpled in her mouth. Triumphantly, she dropped it into Adam's hand. It was a soiled white cockade with a blood-red ruby center.

~ ~ ~

"How ever did you manage this?" Cathy asked as they sat facing each other across the table on the stone terrace, enjoying their first course of carrot and ginger soup. "You couldn't just walk in and have your way with Crowe's Nest, could you? Doesn't someone own it?"

He gave her an enigmatic smile, remembering the connections that he'd unraveled through Asa Forester. "I found the new owner and rented it for this evening."

"And Basil? Have you found any signs of him here?"

"Not one. Nothing's been done for years; in fact, if I didn't know better, I would have thought I was the first person to come through the door since 1818, when Crowe was arrested and hanged, and his family went to England."

"How curious. I wonder why the new owner hasn't done something with it."

"He is a ship's captain from North Carolina. One day he hopes to retire from the sea and refurbish the place, but for now he was happy to have us clear out the cobwebs and use it.."

"It's eerie being here." Lifting her head, she looked past the tops of the palm trees to the moonlit beach below. "Isn't that the spot where his slaves hung lights so that approaching ships would think they had reached Bridgetown?"

"Yes. And when the ships struck Cobbler's Reef, his crew would attack." He watched her troubled face and took a breath. "But that was long ago, and you and I have too much to talk about to dwell upon the distant past."

Slowly, Cathy turned back, feeling the pull of his gaze. "Did you have a particular subject in mind?"

"I have a long list," he replied with a rueful smile. "The truth is, I have longed, every day since you left Tempest Hall, to talk to you, if only to tell you about my day and to hear about yours. Now that you are here, I don't know where to begin."

"That doesn't sound like you. You are usually so forthright!"

"Indeed, I'm not used to feeling this way." He leaned forward, his darkly handsome face set off by a snowy starched collar. "Nor am I used to talking about such feelings, but I've realized that I must."

His words touched her, but she also remembered that when she had lived at Tempest Hall, he'd shared very little with her unless he was tearing back the veil on her hidden passions. "You'll understand if I am wary, won't you?"

In the flickering glow of the hurricane lamps, a shadow passed his eyes. "Of course I understand. Tell me then, Cath, about you. Are you enjoying your new role as a teacher?"

Instantly, her face was alight. "Oh, yes!" Stories of the lessons she had taught and her plans for the new books spilled out. She related anecdotes about the girls, lingering over the moments when she had seen them feel excited about something they had learned. "I really can't explain the wonderful feeling I have at day's end. It's an immense, deep satisfaction."

"I'm not surprised that you are a gifted teacher. You must continue. Perhaps we could build a school?"

She blinked. "I don't want to rush into that. We're doing just fine for now."

Adam waited as their soup bowls were cleared and a course of baked flying fish with breadfruit cou cou was served. There were side dishes of curried green bananas, beet salad, and spinach soufflé. Raising his glass, he made a toast. "Here's to the pleasure of honest work." Watching her over the rim as they both sampled the cold wine, he added, "I've been discovering that satisfaction myself."

"You have?"

"I've opened a law office in Bridgetown."

"What? I—I am shocked! How is that possible?"

He raised a hand and rubbed his eyes with long fingers. "I made it possible. I found a building that was inexpensive, I worked to make it presentable, I opened my office, and now I have clients and a growing income."

Suddenly, Cathy found it hard to breathe. "That's amazing. What brought about this ambitious undertaking?"

"You did, when you left me. It's always bothered me that I needed your father's money to save Tempest Hall. It's been the flawed motive at the heart of our marriage. When you left, I finally realized, with Retta's advice, that I needed to change myself before I could become a husband worthy of you."

Cathy saw his strong brown hand move toward hers on the tablecloth. Nothing in her life had prepared her for such a scene with so splendid a man. As tears crowded her throat, she reached toward Adam's hand and touched him, releasing an inner tide of suppressed yearning.

"I am not without hope," she murmured.

He closed his eyes, took a breath, and his mouth bent in a charmingly lopsided smile. "Good. That's good."

For a moment, gazing at him in the candlelight, Cathy saw him again as he had been in their bed. Naked, hard-muscled, graceful and sensual. She remembered the feeling of her fingers in the black hair that now was brushed back so neatly from his brow, the firm warmth of his skin against her own. As memories of his fiery, intimate kisses crept in, she began to blush and forced herself back to the present.

Adam, watching her, slowly arched a brow. "I too am not without hope, my darling. Shall we have our dessert on the beach?"

Before she could speak, he was behind her, pulling out her chair. His fingers grazed her waist as she rose and turned to face him. Impulsively, Cathy touched his cheek. "Yes, I should like that."

"Have I told you how beautiful you look in that gown?"

"It was one of those Mother ordered for me from Worth last Season. It always seemed too elegant for me, but now I find that it suits me." Her smile widened.

"You are like a new butterfly, growing ever comfortable with your beauty."

She thought Adam might take her in his arms and kiss her then, but instead he gathered into one hand the two small dishes of guava mousse that the servants had brought. The coffee and brandy were left behind as he dropped spoons into a coat pocket and took her elbow with his free hand. There were steps leading from the terrace down to the lawn, and then a pathway to the beach. They walked together in emotion-charged silence, enveloped by moonlight and the sound of the waves crashing on the beach.

When they reached the white sand, Adam gestured to a large flat rock that made an ideal bench. He held her hand as she perched on the edge, then joined her, sitting so that their shoulders and hips touched. The contact with his male body stirred her deepest and most fragile longings.

Adam put a spoon and the little ramekin of mousse into her hand. "It's one of Retta's specialties. Did you know that she came here tonight, to help cook this meal for us? She's been quite strict with me since you left."

Glancing up, she saw the smile that flickered at the corners of his mouth. "She loves you."

"Yes. I'm very grateful for her presence. She reminds me of my grandparents, who provided the most stable part of my past." He took a bite of the flavorful mousse and considered his next words. "Cathy, you asked me once about my family, and I brushed you aside. I'd like to remedy that now."

She nodded slowly. "Please."

"I had a relatively normal childhood. My father was a university professor, and we divided the year between Oxford and Thorn Manor in Kent. My grandparents visited occasionally from Barbados. I had a pony and a dog like Alice. Then, when I was twelve, everything changed. My father wasn't a very approachable person; I think he was closer to his books, and he also began to go on mountain climbing expeditions, which took him away from home for long periods of time. Mother grew lonely, I think. She took a lover, a baron from a neighboring estate, and one day I walked in on them."

"Oh, Adam!" Immediately, Cathy thought of her own pain when she had seen her father kissing his lover on the morning of her wedding.

He looked away, then met her eyes. "I've never talked about this to anyone except Gran. I hate it."

"I understand. You don't have to go on."

"But I do. I can't continue to keep parts of me locked away from you." He took a deep breath. "My father came home that same day, and I was so angry and confused that I told him what I'd seen. That was the worst mistake of my life. My parents had a terrible row...I will never forget the sound of their shouts and Father throwing things. Truthfully, I thought he was going to murder her. Father returned to Switzerland the next day and was soon killed in an avalanche. One couldn't help wondering what risks he had taken in his state of shock and rage."

Horrified, Cathy held fast to his hand. "I am so sorry." She sensed he must have blamed himself, but couldn't bring herself to say the words.

Adam was silent for a long moment, during which old feelings of guilt flared in his eyes. Then, he drew a harsh sigh and continued, "My mother fell ill after that and was never the same. She sent me farther away to school, and I spent holidays with her brother's family, who weren't particularly welcoming."

"I begin to understand you," she murmured.

"Well, I'm a grown man now, and I am determined not to remain a prisoner of the past. Thank God for my grandparents, who brought me to Barbados for summers and who showed me that it was possible for two people to love each other."

"What happened to your mother?"

Adam rubbed his jaw, lost in memories. "She died a few years ago. We had an opportunity to become closer in the months before her death...and Alice was Mother's dog, you may recall. Also, during the years I was at university, Mother became involved in caring for orphans in the village of Thorncliff. That's how I came to later give our manor house to the village for use as an orphanage." Pausing, he gave her a bleak smile. "That is, after I gambled away every shilling I had for its upkeep."

"Oh, Adam, I am grateful to you for sharing your story with me. My heart aches for you, for the boy whose life was turned upside down by the betrayal and flawed judgment of adults." Her eyes gleamed with tears. "You and I have suffered some of the same hurts."

Raveneau set his dessert aside and turned toward her. Again, she expected him to take her in his arms and kiss her, but instead he simply reached for her small hand and brought it to his chest. Through the starched fabric of his shirt, she felt the powerful thump of his heart.

"That's what you do to me," he said in a rough whisper. "I ache for you."

She could only nod, unable to trust her own voice.

"I have a gift for you." From his other coat pocket, he brought out a slim case covered in threadbare velvet.

Cathy accepted it and gently pushed the tiny ruby button that opened the box. Inside was a fragile-looking fan. "Oh, it's beautiful! I'm afraid to touch it."

"Don't be. It's Gran Adrienne's fan, and she meant you to have it." Watching as she unfurled the confection of ivory, embroidered silk, and lace, Adam added, "The silk was embroidered in the fifteenth century. Legend has it that Marie Antoinette had the fan made after receiving the silk as a gift."

She turned wide eyes up to him. "It's the most exquisite thing I've ever seen."

"It actually caused the meeting between my grandparents. My spirited Gran saw it in a London shop window and ordered her carriage driver to stop. Grandfather's phaeton was in the way, and she mistook him for a coachman and said some things she shouldn't have." Adam grinned at the memory of the two of them relating the story to him during his childhood. "When he later realized that she had caused that scene in the middle of Oxford Street over a *fan*, he wasn't very gentlemanly in his treatment of her."

"How romantic!"

He laughed, shaking his head. "I may never understand women."

"I adore the fan. Thank you so much. I shall cherish and protect it." Reverently, she returned it to the velvet case.

"And I shall envy it, being so close to you." He slipped both hands around her small waist. "Ah, Cath, what a fool I've been."

She gazed up at his sculpted face, savoring each moment as at last he gathered her into his embrace and slowly covered her mouth with his. Helplessly, Cathy wrapped her arms around his wide shoulders, touching his collar and the crisp curls that brushed it. Everything about him felt like coming home. She couldn't suppress a soft moan as he parted her lips and deepened their kiss, his tongue tasting hers, at first gently and then ardently. His heart was beating against her through the thin silk of her bodice. Her breasts were tightening and the place between her legs was moist, longing, tingling.

As his mouth moved to scorch the side of her jaw and find the pulse below her ear, every nerve in her body was alive with arousal. She waited for him to mold his hand to her breast, to lean back with her so that her hips could make contact with his.

But instead he seemed to be gently disengaging from her.

"My darling," he murmured. "You'll never know how much I've missed you in my arms."

"Aren't you…"

"Yes?" He held her slightly away and smoothed soft tendrils back from her brow.

"Aren't you going to…ravish me?"

An irresistible smile spread slowly over his face, and he drew her against him, whispering into her ear, "Is that what you'd like?"

The wetness increased between her legs. "Yes, I think I would."

"I'm delighted to hear it. But there'll be no ravishing tonight. I promised you a proper wooing, and that is what I mean to give you." His mouth trailed fiery little kisses over her cheekbones. "Tonight I had something else in mind."

Drugged with passion, she tipped her head back. "Something else?"

"Yes. There's something I must tell you." Adam held both her hands, pressed his mouth to them, and gazed directly into her eyes. "Cathy, I love you."

They were the words that, long ago, she'd stopped hoping he would speak, and even now she questioned her hearing. "Adam…are you certain?"

"I've never been more certain about anything. I love you with all my heart." When he lifted her onto his lap so that she could lean against his chest, he felt her tears on his shirt front. "You don't have to say anything yet. Just let me hold you."

Over the top of her head, Raveneau thought he saw a shadow move in the grove of coconut palms. However, his impulse to investigate was overridden by the sweetness of the moment with Cathy. Perhaps it was a green monkey that had strayed over to the coast. How could it be a person? He had no enemies, after all...

Chapter 32

Retta sat in a rocker on the sunny stone terrace at Crowe's Nest, her purple-striped headtie bobbing with each movement of the chair. "How long we do be stayin' in dis house?"

Adam glanced up from the papers he had spread over the same table where he and Cathy had dined two nights before. "Retta, how can you be out of sorts? It's a beautiful day. Just look at the ocean; aren't you enjoying the change of scenery?" He threw her a disarming smile. "The end is in sight. We'll be back at Tempest Hall soon."

She sniffed and turned her attention to Paul, who was playing quietly with his wooden Noah's Ark. "Mind you stay 'way from dat wall, child."

"Don't worry," Adam assured her. "We've already had a long conversation about the rules if he is going to be out here. He understands, don't you, Button? And Alice is standing guard."

The little boy nodded soberly at his father and returned to the task of lining up the animals on the deck of the ark while the old Lab sat up a little straighter, her gaze fixed on Paul.

"I love it here!" called Byron's cheerful voice as he emerged onto the terrace carrying a plate of eggs, coconut bread, and warmed-over flying fish. "It's a real holiday. Ah, listen to the ocean…And look, there's a pirate ship anchored in the distance!"

"Papa's ship," Paul informed him.

"That's right; I almost forgot that your papa is a pirate at heart!"

Raveneau moved a paper aside to make room for Byron's plate. "Can you be serious for a moment? I've been waiting to go over my plans with you."

"'Bout time," Retta declared.

He ignored her, speaking instead to Byron. "I have everything arranged. The rest of the crew for the *Golden Eagle* will arrive after lunch today, and they'll be rowed out to the ship. We aren't sailing that far, so I've asked Forester to supply only a skeleton crew." He slanted a look at his friend. "Of course, you'll be onboard."

Between bites of coconut bread, Byron remarked, "Why does that not surprise me? And what about Paul?"

"Simon is going to fetch June when her classes are finished today. Tomorrow is Saturday, so she is free to stay here overnight and help Retta with Paul. She is very excited to be playing a part in this adventure."

"It seems that the only person who is not aware of your plot is Cathy. What if she declines to be abducted by you, Lord Pirate?"

A slow, secret smile touched Raveneau's mouth as he remembered her whispered confession that she longed for him to ravish her. "I don't think she'll decline. Quite the opposite." Looking down, he pointed to the various Stede Bonnet papers arranged on the table next to the faded treasure map. "I've worked out the code for how many steps to pace off, and the map shows the angle to follow. This morning, I'd like to go up to Cave Bay again and see if I can narrow down the treasure site. I need to locate the mysterious ruby that appears to be one of the keys to the map. I can't take Cathy there and then be digging all night."

"Has it not occurred to you that the sands have shifted tremendously since Bonnet buried that treasure...*if* he buried a treasure?"

"Yes, I've thought of that, but I am determined to find it. I'd be a fool not to try."

"De ruby do be on a peg," Retta said suddenly. "Orchid say dat old pirate trick, to mark stepping-off place."

Raveneau's heart jumped as he remembered the day he'd dragged Cathy out of the surf at Cave Bay and she'd tripped near the cave on an immovable egg-shaped object with a red center, barely peeking from the sand. At the time, he'd been so preoccupied with the argument they were having, and with the infuriating presence of his mother-in-law and Auggie, that he hadn't given it any further thought.

"Retta! That's the key! You are a genius!" he cried, and went to lift her off her feet and embrace her. "What would I do without you?"

Paul began to jump up and down beside them, a carved wooden giraffe in each pudgy hand. "Yay, yay, Retta!"

"Sir! Put me down. Squeeze too hard, dis ole woman can break!" Fondly, she reached up to pat his cheek. "You do be such a Rav'neau. Watch out for danger."

"What danger could there be? It's not as if Stede Bonnet, or even Xavier Crowe, can intervene tonight. It's 1904! I am only creating this adventure for Cathy's sake, because she deserves pleasure and excitement on a grand scale. Otherwise, I'd just go over to Cave Bay and dig the bloody thing up right now."

Byron looked pensive as he popped the last bite of papaya into his mouth. "Speaking of danger, I've been meaning to mention to you that I think saw someone outside the night that Cathy was here. When you two were with Paul, and I took Alice outside to do her business, I swore I saw a figure moving on the beach. Alice saw it, too, and barked, but…perhaps it was one of the servants, or a crewmember from the *Golden Eagle*."

Remembering the shadow he'd glimpsed in the palm trees, Adam frowned. "Right. After all, who would want to spy on us?"

The twilight sky was streaked with hibiscus pink, and a soft, salty breeze filtered through the jalousie flaps as Cathy finished going over the week's menu with Mrs. Ford. Under one arm was a folder containing her students' first essays, and she was anxious to retreat to her room and read them.

"Aren't you glad that Yvette will return from Speightstown on Sunday?" asked Theo when she emerged from the kitchen.

She considered his question. "Yes, I suppose I will be. I've been grateful to feel useful here, but now I have more than enough work with my students."

"You've been a tremendous asset to the Ocean Breeze. I don't know if I could have kept going without all your assistance and advice."

"I could say the same thing to you, my friend." She held up the folder of essays. "Would you mind if I eat in my room? I'm longing to read these. I think I'll have a bath and go to bed early."

"That's an excellent idea." Just then, someone coughed, and they both looked up to see Basil Lightfoot advancing toward them. He wore a frock coat, and his hair was neatly parted in the center above his horsey face.

"Ah! Just the person I was hoping to see," he announced, ignoring Theo. "Catherine, would you do me the honor of having dinner with me? I've been longing to see you, to talk to you…"

Her eyes danced toward Theo, who had raised both brows. "It's very kind of you to ask, Mr. Lightfoot—"

"I beg you to call me Basil."

"I'm not sure that would be proper, since I am a married woman—"

"What sort of married woman lives apart from her husband in a *common* hotel?"

"Now just a minute," cried Theo. "The Ocean Breeze is hardly common!"

Basil gave him a scornful glance. "If you had any knowledge of true refinement, Harrismith, you would know just how common it is. Hardly the sort of proper environment Miss Parrish was raised to enjoy, but then neither is Tempest Hall!"

"Excuse me, sir," she interjected. "I have tried to be polite, but you go too far. If you can't behave like a gentleman toward me and Mr. Harrismith, I will have to ask you to leave us."

When Lightfoot had turned on his heel and stormed away, Cathy gave Theo a big smile. "What an insufferable snob. Good riddance to him!"

~ ~ ~

After the sun had set and she had finished her dinner of potato and plantain casserole, Cathy indulged in a hot bath, then drew on a thin lace-trimmed batiste nightgown and got into bed. There were some comforts at the hotel that she appreciated; running water in a proper bathroom and modern gas lighting were among them. Now, with plenty of light and a view of the sea through her balcony's shuttered doors, Cathy snuggled into her bed and took out the folder of essays.

All week she had found it difficult to concentrate, but the problem had worsened considerably since her evening at Crowe's Nest with Adam. How many times had she relived each word they had spoken, each shared touch, each tender moment? Sometimes it was still difficult for her to realize it hadn't been a dream.

"Cathy, I love you."

Adam had spoken those words to her. Truly. It seemed that the imprint of his lips remained on her fingers where he had pressed his mouth to them. And perhaps most meaningful of all had been his manner. Never had she known him to speak to her with such unfettered sincerity. In the past, he had thrown up his guard whenever she attempted to know him more deeply, but at Crowe's Nest, he had been a changed man.

Still, wasn't it just a lot of words?

Lying back against her pillow, she set the folder aside and plucked the volume of Emily Dickinson's poetry from her bedside table. There was Stephen's writing on the frontispiece: *To Cat,* and she went on to read, *Live! Don't waste a moment, precious sister.*

When she had read that inscription years ago, he had still been alive himself, and she had understood so little of the world outside Newport and Fifth Avenue that most of his meaning had been lost on her. No more. As she listened to the rhythm of the ocean, Cathy lost herself in the eloquent poems until one stopped her.

Wild nights! Wild nights!
Were I with thee,
Wild nights should be
Our luxury!

Futile the winds
To a heart in port,
Done with the compass,
Done with the chart.

Rowing in Eden!
Ah! The sea!
Might I but moor
To-night in thee...

Her heart swelled as she read the words again and again, immersing herself in memories of Adam. Yes, Stephen was right; it was time to *live* in a way she had never dared before...

"I look ridiculous," Byron complained as he climbed onto the *Golden Eagle*'s quarterdeck where Raveneau was gazing out at the coastline. The molten orange sun had nearly disappeared into the Caribbean Sea to their west.

Adam glanced at his friend, who wore a striped head scarf, a white shirt, petticoat breeches, and buckled shoes. A gold hoop dangled from one ear. "Where is your spirit of adventure? You look exactly like a pirate!"

"No. I look ridiculous. *You* look like a pirate! Even more than you did at the Parrishes' costume party. It's uncanny."

It was true, for tonight Raveneau embraced the part with relish. He was clad in the same black breeches and jackboots he'd worn at Beechcliff, but tonight he had left off the heavy coat and instead wore a loose shirt of fine white linen with lace cuffs that fell over the backs of his dark hands.

"Do you think so?" His fingers grazed the flintlock pistol, borrowed from Xavier Crowe's bedsteps, that was thrust into the blood-red silk sash knotted around his waist. "This is a nice touch, I think," he admitted. "I have my grandfather's sword as well, but I'll save that for later."

"I have never known a man to go to greater lengths to win a woman. And you've got a whole crew of us backing you up! If it were any other woman but Cathy—"

Suddenly his wicked grin softened. "I know. She deserves all this and much more. I would do anything to make her happy."

"Well, your chance is at hand," Byron remarked. "I can see the Ocean Breeze Hotel now, in the distance…"

When Raveneau left his longboat on the beach and approached the hotel, he was grateful for the darkness. If anyone saw him, they'd think he was an apparition.

Lightly, he climbed the back steps to the verandah. The evening was well advanced now, and the guests had retreated to their rooms. Through the jalousie flaps, he saw a light flash in the kitchen: Theo's signal that it was safe for him to proceed.

Using the verandah railing and a sturdy trellis blanketed in bougainvillea, Adam climbed to Cathy's balcony. The shuttered doors were open slightly, and through them he saw her immediately, like an angel sleeping in her gauze-draped bed. There was a light burning softly on the table beside her, and a small book lay open on her breast.

Stepping into the room, Raveneau was suddenly conscious of the risk he ran with this bold scheme. He knew a moment of doubt, but it passed like the cloud gliding past the moon. Silently, he came up beside the bed. Cathy's hair spilled over the pillows, her lips were slightly parted, and her delicate fingers clung to the book. Glancing at the page, he saw the poem she had been reading and smiled.

"Rowing in Eden indeed," he said under his breath. His eyes shifted to the swell of her breasts, their rosy nipples visible through the sheer batiste of her nightgown. Instantly aroused, he momentarily imagined himself in bed with her, touching those breasts that had so long been hidden from him, taking a nipple into his mouth…

Not yet!

He took a sharp breath, willing his erection to subside, and reached out to turn down the gaslight to a tiny, wavering flame. Then, before he could decide how to wake Cathy, her eyes opened. She blinked, twice.

Her voice was a whisper of disbelief. "Are you real?"

"I am, my lady." Raveneau's smile flashed white in the shadows. He swept off the tricorne hat set with Stede Bonnet's cockade, bowing low before her. "I've come to take you with me. We're going to sea in search of pirate treasure."

She shook her head, smiling now. "No, I am dreaming. I'm going to close my eyes again."

Suddenly, he was kneeling at the edge of her bed, his face just inches from hers, and she could feel the warm pulse of his breath on her cheek.

"I am no dream. I have never been more real, and I mean to give you a night better than any dream you could imagine." He took her hands and brought them to his rakishly chiseled face, kissing her tender palms. "Come with me, Cathy, or I'll take you by force."

Now she was fully awake, her heart pounding hard with excitement and arousal. "You are very bold!"

"Indeed. And this is just the beginning." He leaned close, his mouth hovering near hers, and felt her tremble. "Say you'll come."

"Yes." She nearly panted the word. "Yes, I'll come!"

Chapter 33

It was a perfect night to be a pirate, Cathy thought with a giddy smile. The ocean was calm and silvery, the air was soft and warm, and clouds continued to drift past the moon as Adam brought the longboat alongside the *Golden Eagle*.

Although she was bursting with curiosity, she said little, watching as one of the dark shapes on the deck of the romantic-looking sailing ship threw a rope ladder down to them. Thank goodness she had donned trousers and a shirt before they climbed down from her balcony at the Ocean Breeze. It seemed that Adam had thought of everything; when she got out of bed, he'd retrieved a bundle of boy's clothing from the corridor and told her to get dressed.

"There'll be none of your corsets tonight," he had promised with a grin. "I hereby liberate you."

Now, climbing the precarious ladder ahead of Adam, then throwing her trousered legs over the rail, she thought for an instant that she had never done such things, not even as a little girl. Her mother's rules had been oppressive.

"I can't believe this is happening," she said to him as he leaped lightly over the rail to stand beside her.

"But are you happy?"

"Will you be shocked if I say yes?"

He laughed, looking more like a pirate than ever. "Hardly, my sweet. Now, come with me."

Cathy looked all around as they crossed the polished deck, fascinated by the colorfully-dressed crew who were busy now getting the brigantine underway. Above them, a sinister-looking flag fluttered from the top of the mainmast.

"Look! What's that black flag? It has a skull on it!"

"Oh, that's a pirate flag." He guided her toward the hatch. "Stede Bonnet's flag, actually."

"Where on earth did you get that? He lived nearly two hundred years ago!"

"But we've gone back in time, or hadn't you noticed?" As they went down the ladder into the darkness, Raveneau plucked a lantern from the bulkhead and held it aloft as they traversed the gangway. At length, he opened a paneled door and ushered her inside. "Welcome to my cabin."

Cathy watched as he lit the lanterns hanging from beams until a handsomely-furnished captain's cabin was revealed. There was a table built into the bulkhead, flanked by two chairs, and it held a covered tray that emitted delicious smells. Suddenly, it came to her that she was very hungry, for it had been hours since her light supper.

"I'm ravenous!"

"I thought you might be. Hunger is a consequence of high adventure." His eyes were agleam with amusement as he joined her at the table and took the cover from the tray. There was a loaf of crusty bread with butter, a bowl of sliced mango and pineapple, and a dish of pepperpot, still warm and fragrant. "Retta made this just for you. She claims it is the pepperpot recipe handed down to her by Orchid, my grandparents' housekeeper."

Cathy served herself but waited to begin until he had poured glasses of cold white wine. "I miss Retta…"

"And she misses you. Everyone at Tempest Hall misses you." Watching her over the rim of his raised glass, he added, "Here's to you, Cath."

"And to you, my lord." After they had toasted and begun to eat, she gazed around the cabin. There was a large, comfortable-looking bunk attached to the bulkhead across from them. Above it, starlight streamed through a narrow transom. The realization that she and Adam were alone together in the same room with a bed made her blush. "Won't you tell me about this ship? Have you become a sea captain as well as a lawyer since my departure from Tempest Hall?"

He arched a dark brow and lounged back in his chair. "Actually, the *Golden Eagle* was my grandfather's ship, built in Essex, Connecticut. He and Gran Adrienne sailed her from England to Barbados in 1818, and I imagine that they shared adventures of their own in this very cabin…" He reached out to lace his fingers through hers. "As for the rest, let's just say that I am a sea captain for this night. A night out of time."

"Yes." Staring at the fine lace spilling across the back of his hand, Cathy felt as if she had fallen into an eighteenth century novel. "Will you enlighten me further about the pirate treasure? Is it real? The same one on your grandmother's map?"

"Yes, and I have come to believe that it's quite real. When this night is over, I'll answer all your questions, but for now I ask only that you give yourself over to the adventure…and trust me."

He looked wickedly handsome in the lanternlight, every inch a pirate in his loose shirt. The old flintlock pistol and a sword in an engraved scabbard were stuck in the red sash knotted round his waist, and hard-muscled, booted legs stretched out to graze her own small feet. Cathy closed her eyes for a moment, nearly overcome by the power of her feelings for him and the magical night they were sharing.

Slowly nodding, she whispered, "Yes. I can do that."

Raveneau sat up at that, leaning forward to touch the backs of his fingers to her soft cheek. "You won't regret it, love. I mean to make all your dreams come true tonight."

"Well then…I surrender."

"Do you indeed?" Passion flared in his eyes. "We'll see, my beauty."

In the hours before dawn, when the air was hazy with moonlight, Adam sat across from Cathy in the longboat as he rowed them toward the reef that protected Cave Bay. The *Golden Eagle* was anchored to the east, strung with lanterns that bobbed with the ship. The glittering, choppy Atlantic Ocean was spread out around them, sometimes splashing into the boat. It would require all his skill to bring them safely through the currents and surf.

It would have been prudent to bring other crewmembers in the longboat, but Adam wanted to be alone with Cathy on the beach tonight. This was their adventure, and the magic depended on their solitude.

Pulling back on the oars, he watched her as she looked excitedly toward the shore. Her beautiful hair tumbled down her back, and she had added a head scarf fastened pirate-style to her costume. He adored the line of her profile: her big brown eyes, the delicate snub of her nose, the lips he dreamed of tasting, and her proud chin. It was maddening, the way he hungered for her night and day. He hadn't felt anything like this since his youth, when he'd been ruled by lust. This aching need went much deeper, however, because it was intimately connected to his heart.

"What a wonderful adventure this is," Cathy exclaimed suddenly.

"Yes…" As the sea spray showered them, he gave her a devilish grin. "Rowing in Eden, so to speak."

She narrowed her eyes. "You! You looked at the poem I was reading when I was sleeping tonight!"

"How could I help it? It was open on your breast. I was mesmerized."

"You are a wicked man, to take advantage of me in such a vulnerable state. Just like a real pirate!" Then, Cathy sat up straighter and pointed toward land. "I can see the cave! Adam, it's the beach where I went swimming that day and you saved me from drowning!"

Laughing, he shook his head. "No, that wasn't me. That was someone else, a brute who didn't deserve you."

Their eyes met for a long moment, her own suffused with answering laughter and something richer that gave him hope. Just then, a great wave lifted the boat and sent it plunging down with alarming speed. Water surged over the sides, but Cathy had the presence of mind to cling to her wooden bench seat. Adam used all his strength to maneuver the oars so that the boat would not capsize, and moments later they were riding high on a new wave toward the beach.

When the boat skidded forcefully onto the sand, Adam leaped out and pulled it to safety before the tide could yank them back into the surf. Next, he reached for Cathy, lifting her into his arms and bringing her out of the boat.

"I'm sorry. Were you frightened?" He held her fast against him.

"With you as my protector? How could I be?"

"You're all wet—"

"This is Barbados! It's warm, and my clothes will dry quickly." Before he could protest again, she put a finger over his mouth. "This is an adventure, remember?"

His hand came up to hold hers there, and he kissed her palm for a long moment, closing his eyes to hold back the unfamiliar tide of emotions. At length, he shifted her hand to his jaw. "We should get on with the treasure hunt before I start kissing you and become impossibly distracted."

"Kissing…?" she repeated, lips slightly parted.

"Yes, kissing. Have I told you that I love the way you look in pirate clothes?" He gave a husky laugh and held her away from him. The wet shirt clung to her uncorseted breasts, and her legs were artfully displayed in trousers. "You're entirely too alluring."

"And my mother thinks that only a Paris gown and Tiffany jewels will attract a man!"

"Your mother is wholly ignorant of the ways of men. And I won't have her on this beach with us tonight, even in spirit!"

"Yes, my lord," she replied meekly, then tapped his chest. "What's that you have under your shirt?"

Raveneau drew out a leather pouch and led her to a large, flat rock a few yards away. "Wait here." He put the pouch in her hands before going to fetch the shovel and lantern he'd stowed under the boat seats.

When he returned, he produced matches to light the lantern. Cathy watched as he unfurled some papers from the pouch and studied the markings on the old piece of parchment, explaining, "This is Gran's map. Do you see this spot where the dotted lines begin? That's just outside the cave, where you tripped the day we quarreled here on the beach."

"What? Do you mean that object I tripped over was put there by Stede Bonnet?"

He nodded, still studying the map. "I do."

"But that was nearly two centuries ago! How could it still be there in the sand? Wouldn't it have shifted with time?"

"Bonnet had the foresight to use a long peg, wedged inside a crack in the cliff wall." Smiling, Adam pointed to the numbers on the faded sheet of parchment. "He was crafty, that's why no one else who had this map over the years was able to find the bloody treasure. None of these numbers is the right one. He left the code hidden in his Bridgetown house, which fortuitously became my law office."

Looking around the sandy cove with its cave, cliffs, and the eerie skeleton of Victoria Villa looming in the distance above them, Cathy shivered again with excitement. "I am reminded of *Treasure Island*, my brother's favorite book. Stephen used to make me hunt for the 'treasure' that he hid on the grounds of our estate in Long Island."

"You must miss him very much."

"He would have loved this night..." Her eyes misted before she came back to the present. "I must say that none of the pirates in *Treasure Island* were half as splendid as you, my lord."

"Are you comparing me to Long John Silver?" Adam handed the leather pouch to Cathy and gathered up the shovel and lantern. He wanted to tell her that he wasn't her blasted lord, he was her husband, but he kept his own counsel. After all, she hadn't come home yet. "Follow me, my beauty. You will be my assistant."

Happily, she clutched the pouch to her breasts and ran along through the sand at his side. It was low tide, and the cave yawned open ahead of them, its entrance shrouded in clumps of sea grapes. The notion that two centuries ago Stede Bonnet himself had been here before them and they were walking in his footsteps was thrilling beyond measure.

Reaching the entrance to the cave, Adam pointed to a place he had marked that morning with a shell wedged between the rocks. "This is where the peg is buried. I'm certain it's our starting point for the search."

"You have already been here to set the stage?" Her face fell. "Are we just going through the motions?"

"Absolutely not! I just stopped by this morning to get my bearings so that we wouldn't be flailing around in the dark. I'm sure you have noticed that everything looks different by moonlight." Raveneau hunkered down, muscles flexing in his thighs as he held the lantern closer to the stone cliff. Then, he began to dig gently with his hands. "I just covered it with a few inches of sand…"

"It's very exciting!"

He continued to push the sand away, perplexed. The ruby-set knob should have appeared by now. Could the tide have shifted the sand so much in less than one day? When it became clear that the ruby wasn't where he expected it to be, he began to explore all along the stony entrance to the cave until he located his quarry nearly a foot away. And this time, when he pulled on the egg-shaped knob, the peg easily slipped free from the sand.

"I don't understand." Raking a hand through his black hair, he stared at the erstwhile walking stick that had been sharpened to a point. "It doesn't make sense."

"Do you mean it has moved? How could that happen?"

"I haven't the faintest idea." His eyes scanned the clifftops as he thought. "It doesn't really matter, since I know where the thing was and we can work from that point. I just don't like this."

Cathy watched him carry his tricorne hat and the lantern to the water's edge, facing in the direction of the *Golden Eagle*. He lifted the light and passed the tricorne in front of it twice, then paused and repeated the motion.

After a few moments, there was a signal from the ship. Her heart began to pound harder. "Do you think we are in danger?"

"No." Raveneau flashed a reassuring smile. "Not a bit. But I believe in caution, especially when you are involved. Now then, let's get back to work. You take the lantern and keep the map open so that I can see it."

And so they began. He took a compass from the pouch, studied the map and the other papers, oriented himself where the peg had originally been, and began to walk in measured steps.

"One, two, three, four, five, six, seven." He stopped. "Bring the map and the lantern."

As she approached, Cathy said, "The number on the map is three, Adam. Why are you walking seven steps?"

"Trust me." Smiling, he cupped her chin, kissed her briefly, and groaned. "When this is over…"

"You're going to kiss me some more?"

"You have become quite the temptress! Indeed, that is my intention. Would you welcome such a plan?"

Cathy cheeks warmed under his suggestive gaze. "I might be persuaded," she murmured. "You are a wickedly handsome pirate."

Raveneau's hand fit itself to the curve of her waist, and he brought her flush against him just long enough to let her feel the proof of his desire. "It must wait until we've found this treasure. Now stand back so I can think!"

She held the lantern as he used the compass, turned, and walked again, counting off three more steps. Another turn directed him back toward the cliffs, and he measured off nine steps until he was inside the cave. Then, after setting the compass down to mark the spot, Adam got the shovel and beckoned to Cathy.

"This should be it." His voice was low, and he laid a finger over her lips. "Let's be very quiet, all right? Just in case…"

Broken clouds streamed across the night sky, and the moon was revealed again, slanting white light into the cave. Cathy stood to one side, holding the lantern as Raveneau dug the hole, deeper and deeper. At length there was a sharp noise as the shovel struck something hard, and he looked up from the waist-deep hole and grinned.

"Success!"

Soon he had widened the pit so that the entire chest came into view. It was a brass-bound rectangular iron box with a handle at each end and a great lock on the front. Without an invitation, Cathy jumped down beside him and stared in wonder.

"I can hardly believe it," she whispered.

"Nearly two hundred years after Bonnet put it here…" Adam reflected. "I would say the time has come, wouldn't you?"

"But that lock is enormous! How in the world will we open it?"

"One thing at a time, Cath. Let's bring it out first."

Together they got the heavy chest up onto the floor of the cave. Then, he reached into the leather pouch and brought out a large, ornate key. "I have a feeling this is going to fit."

And it did.

When Raveneau turned the rusty key and lifted the lid, the sight that met their eyes was more wondrous than either of them could have imagined.

Chapter 34

Nestled in a golden cloth was a mass of silver and gold coins, gleaming in the moonlight and mixed chaotically with jewels of every description. There were necklaces and bracelets of rubies and sapphires, rings and trinkets set with sparkling gems ranging from amethysts to diamonds, and small leather bags that held dozens of uncut emeralds.

"I can hardly believe my eyes," Cathy whispered. "What are those coins? I've never seen anything like them!"

Adam held a few up to the flickering lantern. "The silver ones are 'pieces of eight,' and the others are gold Spanish doubloons. They're worth a small fortune, I'll wager. It's amazing to think what stories are connected to the contents of this chest, stories we can only imagine."

As he returned the coins to the chest, he noticed a black cloth wedged into one side. Removing it and shaking it open, Adam made a low sound of wonder. "Look at this. It's Bonnet's own flag, the same one I found the drawing of in Bridgetown. That flag flying on the Golden Eagle is just a replica I had made, but this is the real thing. It's our proof that this chest was buried by Stede Bonnet."

Before Cathy could reply, a loud howling sound startled them both. "What was that? An animal?" she exclaimed.

"Devil if I know." Immediately, he closed the chest, locked it, and buried the key. "Wait here. Don't move; do you understand?"

No sooner had he stepped out of the cave, sword drawn, than the howling commenced again, followed this time by an eerie voice calling, *"Leeeave my treasure! Leeeave my treasure!"*

"Who's there?" Raveneau demanded.

"I am Steeeede Bonnnnet! I demand that you leeeeave my treasure!"

"Ah, I see. Are you a ghost, Major Bonnet?"

"Yesssss!"

"Well then, I'm not worried. If you're only a spirit, you can't harm us." With that, he turned and went back into the cave. Reaching Cathy's side, he touched a fingertip to his mouth and shook his dark head. "Shh. Wait."

There was a long silence, then the howling commenced again, this time seeming to be closer. Raveneau went to look outside the cave again.

"You're becoming a bore, Major Bonnet. Since you clearly have no earthly use for your treasure, and it is on my land, I suggest that you go back where you came from."

"I willlll not!" cried the voice.

Looking overhead, Adam side-stepped as a tall figure came leaping down from high up the steps that were carved into the cliff. The intruder, who was elaborately dressed as a pirate captain, nearly fell forward, but managed to recover and hastily drew his own sword. His tightly-curled gray wig and tricorne hat were askew, and he wore a black silk mask with large holes cut for his eyes.

"Why, you're not a ghost at all, but quite human," Adam remarked in mock surprise. Stepping effortlessly into the *en garde* position, he leaned forward and flicked at a gold button on the intruder's velvet coat. "Put down your sword, sir, and save your own life."

"Never! That treasure is mine! *En garde!*"

Glancing over, Adam saw that Cathy had flattened herself against the cave wall. And over his opponent's shoulder, he spied Byron rowing toward them from the *Golden Eagle* in response to the lantern signal he had sent.

As they circled each other on the moonlit beach, Adam's practiced eyes picked out clues to the attacker's identity. "What right have you to the treasure? Clearly you are not Bonnet's ghost."

The man made a clumsy attempt to advance and lunge, but Raveneau easily deflected his blade. "I am the heir!" he screamed in frustration.

"I don't want to kill you, but you are leaving me no choice." He circled again until his opponent's back was to the cave. Quickly then, Raveneau's blade glided over the other sword until, in a split-second movement, he flicked at the man's velvet coat sleeve. Moments later, the torn velvet was crimson with blood.

"Urgh! How dare you?" He gaped at the sight of his own blood. "How dare you?"

"How? Quite easily, or do you need another demonstration?" Laughing, Adam effortlessly parried and riposted but stopped short of drawing more blood, his blade merely resting against his opponent's throat. "It's Lightfoot, isn't it? Perhaps you didn't know that I was one of the founding members of the fencing club at Oxford."

Cathy was suddenly next to them, brandishing the shovel like a weapon. "Do as my husband says and drop your sword."

Sweat dripped down his face as he obeyed. When Raveneau stepped forward and pulled down the black silk mask, he discovered Basil Lightfoot on the verge of tears.

"You have wounded me, my lord! I shall visit the magistrate and see to it that you are charged!"

"Indeed? I would remind you that you attacked me. I could have killed you in self-defense." Using the black scarf, he tied Lightfoot's wrists together in front of him. "Besides, you aren't really hurt. I just grazed you. Ah, here comes Byron to take you to the ship, where you won't be able to disrupt our night any further. But first, tell me what the devil you have been up to with this ill-conceived charade!"

He sniffed and looked away. "I was the heir to Crowe's Nest, as you know. That map was a legend in our family. It belonged to my great-great uncle Xavier and should never have fallen into the hands of the Raveneaus! I always knew that once you returned to Barbados, you would eventually track down the treasure *for* me, so I've just waited for this day."

"Your ancestor was a criminal," Raveneau said coolly. "He stole that map; neither of you had any right to Bonnet's treasure. May I remind you again that this is Raveneau land?"

"It was my only chance to have the funds to regain Crowe's Nest, to restore my good name on the island—"

"Mr. Lightfoot, did you have any help with this scheme?" Cathy asked suddenly.

His eyes narrowed in her direction. "How perceptive of you, my dear. Have you guessed that your cousin August joined forces with me when he was on the island and has continued to consult with me since his departure? We shared a common interest in crushing Lord Raveneau."

"And, more to the point, a common interest in the treasure?" She shook her head in disgust. "Auggie has spent his whole life searching for an easy route to lasting wealth."

Byron had landed on the beach in the other longboat and was approaching the trio. "I see you've had a visitor!"

he shouted to Adam. "Who knew your little treasure hunt would become so fraught with peril?"

"This pirate business is exhausting. No wonder they all died young! Do you think you can take him to the ship and put him in the hold? But have someone clean and bandage his arm first. It seems that my rapier drew blood."

"Aye, aye, Captain!" came his cheerful reply.

"Byron, look at you!" Cathy exclaimed. "How dashing you are in your buccaneer costume. I didn't know you were on the ship tonight."

"What would become of Lord Raveneau without me? I would dare to suggest that he wouldn't even have you if I had not intervened in Newport."

"No one *has* me," she protested.

"Not yet," Raveneau murmured under his breath, then pricked Basil's chest with his sword point. "Go along with Byron, old fellow, and be grateful you're alive."

He followed them to the longboat and pushed it off into the surf, watching as his old friend negotiated the current with his oars. A bit of light was beginning to show behind the eastern sky's cloak of night, a sign that the sun was preparing to creep up over the horizon.

"Are we going to have to load that chest into our longboat?" Cathy asked when Adam returned to her side.

"I think I will put it back and return later today with a carriage. Aside from the unwieldy weight of that box, I'd rather not have the entire crew of the *Golden Eagle* see it."

"Oh, that's a good idea." She made a little sound of relief. "I confess I'm feeling a little tired now that all the excitement is over…"

Adam put his arm around her, and together they went back into the cave. Retrieving the key, he opened the box once again. "Choose something that you like as a keepsake of this night."

Cathy's eyes roamed over the assortment of magnificent gems. "It's a bit overwhelming, I think." At last she reached in and plucked out a relatively simple ring featuring a rich, round cabochon ruby set in a flat band of yellow gold. It looked very old. "May I wear it?"

"I hope that you will, my love."

As he slid it onto the ring finger of her right hand, she ventured, "You must realize that you are very wealthy in your own right now. You needn't think about my dowry any longer."

"Why do you think I have been so driven to find the treasure? I needed to find it to build a new foundation for our marriage...that is, if you decide to give it another chance. I've been doing quite well as a lawyer, but I don't want to keep those long hours in the future. I would rather be present with my family and focus on transforming Tempest Hall into a profitable plantation again." Drawing a deep breath, he reached for her hand and gazed into her eyes. "I once had wealth, but I was careless with it. I didn't realize that money meant freedom until it was gone. And I was also careless with love, but I am now committed to a different path ."

Tears welled in her eyes as emotions rolled through her like the waves on the nearby beach. "Adam..."

"No, don't say anything now." Rising, he set about returning the chest to the bottom of the pit. When the hole was filled and the cave bore no signs of their discovery, Raveneau replaced the contents of the leather pouch, gathered up the shovel, and put an arm around Cathy's slim shoulders. "Let's go. I have other adventures in mind, but first I think we both need a bath and a nap."

Standing on tip-toe, she whispered into his ear, "Other adventures?"

"Indeed." His smile was at once wicked and loving. "Will you come with me willingly, my beauty, or must I toss you over my shoulder?"

Soft raindrops danced against the transom window above Raveneau's cabin as he lay in the bunk next to Cathy and gazed at her sleeping face. Although the morning was advancing, the light outside was dim.

He told himself that he should sleep, but it was impossible. All his senses were attuned to Cathy, to her breathing, the gleam of her tumbled curls, the way her lashes made tiny shadows on her soft cheeks, and the faintest glimpse of her breast that peeked above her partially unbuttoned shirt. Under the blankets, her legs were bare. Just the thought of them made him hard. How he ached for her...

"Mmm." She licked her lips in her sleep, smiling slightly. Raveneau clenched his teeth. Bloody hell, hadn't she slept long enough?

Reaching out, he tentatively let the pad of his thumb graze the place where her shirt covered her right nipple. Instantly, he could feel it behind the fine fabric, puckering in response to his touch. His own arousal was almost more than he could bear. Just when he thought he might have to go out to the gangway and pace, Cathy's eyes fluttered open.

For a moment, she thought she must be dreaming. Lying next to her was Adam, the impossibly splendid pirate, his black hair tousled, his skin brown against the white sheets, and his blue-gray eyes gazing at her with heart-melting longing.

Slowly, her bearings returned. In the dim light, she saw the warm, paneled outlines of the captain's cabin and felt the coziness of the bunk. The hip bath, where she had washed in blessedly hot, soapy water before getting into bed, stood in one corner.

"I don't remember…"

One side of his mouth quirked upward. "I think you were asleep the moment your head touched the pillow. You missed the spectacle of my bath."

Blushing prettily, she confessed, "I'm sorry."

His eyes never left hers. "Can I get you something? Are you hungry?"

"Only—" The pulse had commenced again between her legs. "Only for you."

He reached over and took her delicate face between his two strong hands, gently kissing her brow, her eyes, her cheekbones, and finally, her parted lips. The sound of her low moan nearly put him over the edge.

"Ah, Cathy, I'm dying I want you so…"

"Please, not that," she whispered with an impudent smile. Her hand reached up to touch his wide shoulder and caress his tapering back over the fabric of his unlaced shirt.

Adam took her in his arms and pressed her back into the pillows, kissing her with all the passion he'd suppressed for weeks. His tongue plundered the softness of her mouth and, as her arms twined around his neck, it came to him that she was kissing him back with frank sensuality. Gone was the inhibited hothouse heiress who had so often gone rigid in his arms.

Raising his head for a moment, he searched her brown eyes. "Where did you learn how to do that?"

"From you!"

"Oh, right. But you never did it before."

She sighed. "I think I was…afraid of surrendering to you."

For a moment, he could scarcely take it in. He buried his face in her neck, pressing burning kisses from her ear down to the top of her shoulder, all the while keenly aware of her ardent response.

"Cathy, let me love you."

"Yes." Her voice was choked.

Quickly, he pulled the shirt over his head to reveal the tapering, hard-muscled chest she had dreamed about at night. Then, lifting his hips, he yanked off the half-buttoned breeches and he was naked. His potent masculinity gave her a moment of anxiety, but it was swept away on a tide of desire, love, and trust.

She watched as Adam's long fingers deftly unfastened the buttons on her shirt. When he drew the two sides apart and her breasts were revealed to his gaze, Cathy felt the hot ache building between her legs. They kissed again, ravenously, for long minutes. Her shirt came off and now they were both naked, fitting together as they embraced like two pieces of a perfect whole. His hands explored her delicate curves and she gloried in his touch; it seemed that all her nerves were on fire for him. When, at last, he held her near and kissed his way down to her breast, she thought she might faint with pleasure as his warm mouth found her nipple.

"Oh…"

As Adam suckled, his tongue working at the ruched nipple, his free hand drifted over her hipbone to the curls at the apex of her thighs. One touch and she opened to him. Ever so softly, his fingertips explored until she was writhing against them and holding his face to her breast. He, meanwhile, pushed his throbbing erection against her thigh. It took all his powers of self-control to hold himself back.

Cathy's muffled moans encouraged him to leave her taut breasts and kiss lower, across the hollows of her belly. This was the moment when, in the past, she had gone stiff with shock and resistance. Now, however, she opened her thighs even more, arching up against him. Her fingers were tangled in his hair.

"Adam." Her plea was barely audible.

"Let me love you, Cath. Tell me what you want," he said hoarsely, then touched the tip of his tongue to the bud of her desire and felt her shudder. "This?"

"Yes!" Congested and wet with arousal, the shocking sensation of his tongue was almost more than she could bear, and yet she wanted more, more.

Adam held onto her hips and moved his tongue in a leisurely circle, leaving and then returning to the spot where he knew all her nerves were concentrated. "And this?"

Cathy felt the hot tingling become a great surging tide, building, building. "Yes, yes."

Finally, his mouth fastened on the swollen nub and tugged gently while his tongue continued to swirl, and she held onto his hair, whimpering, as the wave crested at last and seemed to explode deep inside her, spreading quivering warmth to every nerve in her body.

Just then, when she longed for it most, his powerful body was covering hers again and he was holding her, kissing her. She kissed him back with abandon and felt his erection nudging at her still-pulsing core. When he entered her, pushing in gradually to the hilt, Cathy knew a sense of bliss beyond anything she had ever imagined. She lifted her hips to meet him, and for a moment he drew back to look at her.

"I love you, more than you can ever know."

Any lingering doubts were washed away. "I love you, too, Adam."

He rose up, partially withdrawing from her, then slowly entered again, savoring every moment of being held so snugly inside her. Cathy's head arched on the pillow as she met his increasingly powerful thrusts, and the sound of their breathing filled the cabin, sweat mingling with their kisses. Then, to her surprise, he braced her hips with his hands and rolled over so that she was lying on top of him.

"It's all right, Cath, you can do it," he murmured.

She sat up straighter, knees on either side of his powerful body, and tentatively moved back and forth. He was deeper inside her than ever, and the sensations became even more sharply arousing. Her own nakedness was forgotten as Adam's hands came up to cup her breasts, and he bent his knees and met her movements with his thrusts. Her hair spilled in wild waves down her back as she rode him, letting herself be carried away on the waves of their passion.

At the end, as her own climax built again, she leaned forward and kissed him, panting, and he cupped her bottom with his hands. He was driving up inside of her one more time, and she felt him at her very core when the moment of his release came.

Adam held her in his arms, still pulsing, his heart pounding against hers. The air was musky with the mingled scents of sweat and sex.

"You are amazing, love." Turning with her on his side, he kissed her damp brow.

For long minutes, they lay thus, in a state of complete fulfillment, and Cathy drowsed with her cheek against his chest. "I am so happy," she whispered at last.

"You won't be embarrassed to face me in the sunlight?"

"No. Never again. In fact…"

"Yes?" Adam caressed the line of her hip and derriere. "Tell me, my beauty."

She gave him a demure smile. "I am looking forward to kissing you…more intimately."

"Good God, you are wicked. I feel certain that can be arranged," he teased, "but at a later date. We'll sight the Ocean Breeze soon, and you and I must dress."

Cathy clung to his warm strength, dreading the moment when he would withdraw from her. "I don't want this to end."

"Neither do I. I would prefer to have the ship sail around the island again while you and I make love for hours, but I'm afraid that's not possible. My client, who is also the *Golden Eagle*'s owner, is waiting for her in Bridgetown…and I must deal with Lightfoot and fetch the treasure."

"Are you going to offer to buy the *Golden Eagle*?"

He looked bemused. "You know me too well, love."

"And what of Basil?"

"I'll have to release him. What crime has he committed, after all? In fact, I find I have some sympathy for him. I may give him a few gold doubloons to help him get on his feet, and then he may be more inclined to leave us alone in the future." Gently, he separated from her and rose up on an elbow. There was a damp cloth nearby, left from his bath, and he used it to blot the wetness between her legs.

"This night has been magical. I wish we could stay here…"

"We have the rest of our lives to make magic, Cath. Look at me now; I have something to ask you." He tipped her chin up with his forefinger. "Will you marry me?"

She felt giddy. "But we are already married."

"Are we? I don't think any of it was done properly, from the courtship to the wedding. Let's make it all new.

Let's have a ceremony at Tempest Hall with just a few guests…"

"Yes, oh, yes!"

He laughed as she pressed kisses to his chest. "You might want to think about it before you agree. What about Paul? We don't know if Gemma will come back, and I'll never forget your face the day she brought him to Tempest Hall…"

"Paul is innocent. I love him more each time I see him, and whatever the future holds, I will care for him." Her gaze softened. "He's your son, Adam."

Tears stung his own eyes as he held her in his arms. "Ah, darling Cathy, you have made me so happy. I only hope I can be worthy of your love."

"You already are," she murmured before losing herself in the wonder of his kiss.

Epilogue

"My feets cryin'!" Retta exclaimed when she saw Raveneau and Alice enter the kitchen.

"Would you rather have Josephine finish the callaloo?" he asked before dipping a spoon into the fragrant soup rich with okra, crab, coconut milk, and dasheen leaves.

"On de weddin' day? No! Now, mind yo' hand outta my pot, sir." Glancing over at the younger woman, who was putting the finishing touches on a coconut cake, she muttered, "Jos'phine make de callaloo? No!"

Josephine looked up and replied, "Hmph!"

It was up to him to smooth their ruffled feathers. "The callaloo is delicious, and the cake looks splendid!"

Softening, Retta reached up to pat his cheek, still slightly damp from his bath. "Take dat dog and go now!"

Standing outside under the sandbox tree with Alice by his side, Adam listened to the guinea fowl scratching and watched Simon direct the preparations that were underway beside the rose arbor. As a boy, he had helped Gran Adrienne prune the roses and had listened to her stories about her wedding to his grandfather on that very spot.

"He really didn't want me then," she had confided, smiling radiantly in spite of her words. "He didn't know then that he loved me. Fortunately for both of us, love finds a way."

The sight of Paul chasing Stripey around the arbor brought Adam back to the present. "Hey there, Button, come with me and let's get you dressed."

The little boy ran to his father and jumped up as he always did, trusting that Adam would reach out and catch him. As they went into the house through the gallery entrance, Byron appeared, dressed in a pale gray morning coat over a single-breasted vest and a cravat.

"You should be getting dressed yourself," he told Adam, falling into step beside him.

"We aren't at bloody St. Thomas's Church this time, you know. We're supposed to enjoy this day."

"Yes, but—"

"A surprise guest is due to arrive at any moment, so there will be no ceremony until then."

Byron stared, wide-eyed. "You can't tell me who it is?"

"No. Exciting, isn't it? It may overshadow the wedding as the highlight of the day." He glanced over at his friend and added, "I have been meaning to ask if you're planning to stay here on Barbados? We both hope that you will. I'm not quite sure what I would do without you!"

He laughed. "That's kind of you, but I have one more painting to finish, then I'm going back to Europe. It's time for me to get on with my own life. Do you suppose there is another girl out there who can hold a candle to Cathy?"

Raveneau's eyes softened. "If there is, I've no doubt that you will find her. However, take a piece of advice from me and avoid heiresses. All that money only complicates matters!" The trio had reached the upstairs and went into the north bedroom where Adam turned his attention to his son. "June gave you a bath this morning, didn't she?"

"Yes, Papa." There were newly built shelves lined with brightly colored toys, and Paul reached for Ooh-Ah as they passed by. When they reached the bed, he stood still as Adam stripped off his rather dusty play clothes.

After Cathy had come home, she insisted that Paul continue to sleep in their bedroom for a few days. Then, very gently, she'd transitioned him into the north bedroom, praising him for being big enough to have his own bed and assuring him that he could climb out and come to them during the night if he needed to. Soon, with Alice stationed nearby in her new cushioned basket, he was sleeping happily in his own room.

Over the weeks, as Adam watched Cathy with the little boy who had done so much to help him open his own heart, he found himself falling even more deeply in love.

"Will you please unfasten your buttons so we can get you undressed?" A blue broadcloth sailor suit had been laid out at the foot of the bed. While Paul worked soberly at the buttons with Alice watching, Adam went to join Byron at the window overlooking the garden.

"I shouldn't be surprised that everything has come to rights, knowing you," his friend remarked.

"Knowing me? Are you referring to the dissolute, bored, detached libertine I was when I met Cathy?"

Glancing over, Byron saw the smile that flickered over Adam's mouth. "You may have been flawed, and you doubtless still are, but there was always something inside of you that gave me hope. Something…fine."

He looked at him through slightly narrowed eyes. "Have you been talking to my bride? Those are the sorts of things she likes to say."

"You may pretend to be sardonic about it all, but look at what you've done since you found the treasure. You've helped Basil recover and restore Crowe's Nest—"

"Well, he's not really such a bad sort, and I didn't want him lurking about as our enemy. I rather like the notion of a descendant of Xavier Crowe living there, don't you?"

"You shared a portion of the treasure with Herbert Stoute and many other descendants of Stede Bonnet's slaves. As a result, Mr. Stoute was able to get medical care for his wife and take care of his family."

Adam shrugged. "What's the use of money if you can't do something good with it? If anyone deserved to benefit from Bonnet's piracy, those families did."

"You also started a new school, not only for June and her classmates, but also for other girls, and you gave over more than half the building your law office is in!"

"Did I have a choice? I took Cathy away from the south side of the island when she came home, but she wouldn't live here if we didn't make arrangements for her students. Besides, that building was far too quiet with just my office in it, and I'm not there often enough. Too many rooms were going to waste." He flicked a speck of lint from his sleeve. "After the wedding, it might be more convenient to spend part of the week in Bridgetown. Cathy can teach again, and I won't have to travel back and forth."

"You're not fooling me, you know."

He laughed. "I'm damned if I will start spouting off about my virtues, so save your breath."

"Papa!" called Paul.

Byron caught his sleeve as he turned away and said softly, "*And*, you made burial arrangements for Gemma last month."

"Even my old libertine self would have done that much. She was Paul's mother."

Soon, Paul was dressed in the sailor suit and broad-brimmed straw hat that Cathy had chosen. Adam took him over to see his reflection in the mirror, and he beamed. "I the Ring Bear."

"That's right, Button, and it's a very important task. Now, take Alice and Uncle Byron down to the garden. Your uncle Theo and his friends have just arrived, and I know he's waiting to see you."

Alone in the north bedroom with its freshly painted blue walls, Adam indulged in a moment's reflection on the past, when he and Cathy had shared this narrow bed while her mother held court in his bedroom. Even then, he had loved her, but the barrier he'd erected between himself and the world had prevented him from understanding such a delicately complex emotion…and what it required in order to thrive.

He dressed with efficient care in a tailored frock coat, vest, striped trousers, and cravat. A starched white wing collar stood out in contrast to his tanned face. After quickly brushing his dark, silver-flecked hair back from his brow, Adam adjusted his cravat and went out into the corridor. The door to the bedchamber he shared with Cathy was closed.

He knocked.

The door opened just enough for June's nose and one shocked eye to appear. "Sir! You can't come in; you know you can't. It's bad luck."

"That's nonsense, June. I have a gift for my bride, and it's something that she must wear during our wedding, so you'll have to let me in." He looked over her head. "Cathy! Don't make me break the door down. It wouldn't be pretty."

Her laughter carried into the corridor. "Come in then, darling brute." She opened the door herself, and the sight of her made his heart turn over.

"June," he told the girl, "I have a very important task for you. Go downstairs and watch for the landau. Let me know the moment it arrives."

"The landau?" Cathy repeated as June hurried away. "I don't understand."

"It's not your job to understand anything today, my love. All you have to do is look beautiful, which you can do even in your sleep, and say 'I do' when the parson asks you if you'll have me."

She shook her head, noting the way his dark eyes roved over her. "You are being nonsensical. Nonsensical and prurient."

"I suppose I should save my prurience for later, hmm? You do look exquisite, Cath. So much more beautiful than in New York last autumn."

Turning to survey her reflection in the mirror, she knew he was right. Today, she wore a lovely but simple gown of ivory silk overlaid with lace-trimmed silk muslin and banded with satin at the fitted waist. The low, square neckline was draped simply so that just the tops of her breasts peeked enticingly above the fine silk. There was no train, no veil, no crystals or pearls, only Adrienne Raveneau's antique fan hanging from a delicate chain around her waist.

"I certainly feel more beautiful, and that's what counts, isn't it? Goodness, when I think back to that day…I was so nervous, and so foolish."

"Let's not waste time thinking back when this moment is so perfect." Raveneau stood behind her at the mirror. Her rich hair was massed on top of her head, and he kissed one of the escaping tendrils that brushed her temple. "Close your eyes."

Her heart was beating fast as she obeyed, feeling his fingers on the nape of her neck and then the coolness of jewels. When Cathy opened her eyes and saw a glittering collarette of sapphires and diamonds around her neck, she drew a breath in wonder.

"It's a Raveneau family piece," Adam explained, "given by my great-grandfather Andre to his bride, and then passed down to Gran Adrienne." Turning her in his arms, he murmured, "She would be very happy to know you are wearing it today."

"I love it. Really, there aren't words." Standing on tiptoe, she kissed him, shaping her small hand to his jaw. "I almost wish we didn't have to go downstairs…"

"You have become quite insatiable, my beauty! And, I confess that I would agree with you if Paul weren't waiting for us in the garden. He's very proud to be the 'Ring Bear.'"

Cathy giggled softly, but before she could reply, a harried-looking June appeared at the door. "My lord, the landau is here!" Pausing, she looked over her shoulder. "And, a *guest* is coming up the stairs right now!"

Before the last word was out of June's mouth, a slender bespectacled man appeared and stepped inside the bedroom. He took off his Panama hat and stared straight at Cathy with pleading eyes.

"Angel?"

With a sound of disbelief, she ran to meet her father and held fast to him. "Papa—how—how can this be?"

"I had a letter weeks ago from Adam, urging me to travel to Barbados for today's ceremony," he said, patting her back. "I am so grateful to him for affording me this opportunity to be part of your life again."

"And are you…alone?" The word caught in her throat. Once again, Cathy saw the carriage on Fifth Avenue and the young woman her father had kissed in broad daylight. "Papa, did you bring *her* here?"

He took a deep breath. "No. I am alone. That, uh, interlude is ended. I woke up one day and realized that I was behaving like a fool, carrying on with a girl young enough to be my daughter!"

Cathy's heart softened further. "Well, who could really blame you after decades with Mother? You deserved to be a bit foolish, even to be in love."

"The crime lay in keeping such a secret for so long. I deceived everyone around me."

Adam came closer and caught his father-in-law's eye. "We are all human, sir."

"Yes, yes, so very true, and it's kind of you to say so."

"Not at all," he replied with a self-deprecating smile. "I've become rather an expert on the subject of human flaws. In your case, sir, I believe that you were a very good man caught in a web of unbearable circumstances."

Jules continued to hold his daughter while his eyes grew misty. "After our dear Stephen died, it finally dawned on me how brief our time on this earth is. The largest fortune in the world can't change that."

"I couldn't agree more, Papa," Cathy exclaimed. "It finally came to me that, no matter how much I might wish it, Mother will never understand that."

"I won't speak ill of your mother, but we know that she will not change. My only chance for some real love and happiness, apart from being your father, was to separate from her. I am just so sorry to have hurt you in the process."

For a moment, she closed her eyes, happy to join him in letting go of the past. "Yes, I understand." Touching his cheek, she added, "I am so grateful that you are here with us today. Let's make a new start."

"Ah, good. Good." Jules blinked back tears behind his spectacles. "I can't express how much that means to me. Also, I am looking forward to meeting my new grandson."

His tone was so simple and honest that Adam reached out to pat his arm. "That's very generous of you, sir."

"Not at all. I am grateful to be included as member of your family, and to have an opportunity to meet that beautiful child I saw running past outside. Do you think he will like the rocking horse I brought for him?"

"Oh, Papa, how wonderful. Paul will love it!" Cathy hugged her father again and exchanged glances with Adam, who wore the heart-melting smile she adored. "What a splendid day it is!"

"Indeed," her husband agreed. "A splendid day to be married."

The wedding was performed under the rose arbor with only two dozen guests, including Cathy's original class of students. When was time for Paul to produce the ring, it slipped out of his pudgy fingers and rolled into the rose bushes. It was Alice who braved the thorns, pressing her nose to the gold band, and crying, "Woof!"

Adam bent down to retrieve the ruby ring Cathy had chosen from the treasure chest. After their adventure, he had taken it to the jeweler to be sized and had the man engrave *"Rowing in Eden"* inside the band. Now, slipping it onto his unsuspecting bride's wedding finger, he smiled at the sight of her tears.

"With this ring," he murmured, "I thee wed."

In the end, Adam was holding Paul in his arms and Alice was sitting on the hem of Cathy's gown as they kissed and the minister pronounced them husband and wife.

Everyone was hungry. The guests moved to the arcaded verandah to eat Retta's callaloo, flying fish with spices, baked yams, rice, and thinly sliced fried plantains. Josephine's special coconut cake was delicious, but the best part of the afternoon came when Cathy announced that they would make ice cream. Out came the ice cream freezer that had been banished to the storage room since Christmas. Byron and Theo chipped a block of ice while the cream and eggs and vanilla warmed on the stove. When the freezer was filled and packed with ice, everyone began to take turns at the crank.

"Is it ice cream yet?" cried Paul as he tried out his new carved wooden rocking horse on the verandah.

Jules bent near him and asked, "Would you like to help me make the ice cream?"

Moments later, watching her father guide Paul's little hand on the crank, Cathy felt as if her heart would overflow with joy.

"I couldn't understand it at the time," she told Adam, looking back at him with a radiant smile, "but that ice cream maker was an absolutely perfect gift."

He wrapped his arms around her waist, and she leaned into his strength as they stood together, surveying the party and basking in the glow of their hard-won love.

The End

I sincerely hope that you have enjoyed TEMPEST, my first all-new novel in seventeen years!

TEMPEST really began around 1980, during frequent visits to Newport, Rhode Island, while I lived nearby on the Connecticut coast. Touring the opulent "cottages" and reading books about the families who had lived in them, I was fascinated. I always knew that one day I would tell a story about a Newport heiress like Consuelo Vanderbilt.

Then, in the mid-1990's, near the end of my two-decade-long publishing career with Ballantine Books, I paid another visit to Barbados (already featured in SILVER SEA) and the magical, pink Ocean View Hotel, and was inspired to set a novel there during the Edwardian era. TEMPEST was born. The book was partially written when I decided to take a break from writing. I put it away... and somehow, fifteen years passed! The e-book revolution prompted me to re-publish my twelve historical romances, with fresh edits and gorgeous covers. I was hooked again, and couldn't wait to get TEMPEST out of the drawer and re-discover the world of Adam and Cathy!

You can read more about the real settings on Barbados in the Author's Note at the end of SILVER SEA, but I would like to again thank John Chandler and his staff at the Ocean View Hotel for doing so much to help me with my research. I am especially grateful to John for his colorful stories, which are woven into the fabric of TEMPEST! The Ocean View is closed now, but I like to think that it lives on in spirit as the "Ocean Breeze." John has also gone on, with his wife Raine, to create another magical destination in the seventeenth-century-era Fisherpond Great House. Don't miss it if you visit Barbados!

I feel that TEMPEST is more richly layered than most of my other books, and I hope you do, too. It's been exciting and nerve-wracking to write it, then assemble my own team of professionals to edit, proofread, design the beautiful cover, and format the book. I'm proud of the result and so grateful to each person who added their skills to the process.

In the fall of 2012, I traveled to Cornwall with my dear friend, the historical novelist, Ciji Ware. I am currently writing the first volume of a trilogy set in Cornwall around 1800, and I plan to have SMUGGLER'S MOON ready for you to enjoy in 2013! (You can expect to reunite with many members of the Raveneau family!) In the meantime, I hope you will read my other novels, all available now as e-books, and I'd love to hear all your thoughts.

I love to hear from readers—it's all about YOU!—and I hope that you'll be in touch! Here are some ways to contact me: **http://cynthiawrightauthor.com/contact.html**. I promise to reply!

Warmest appreciative wishes to each one of you—

Cynthia Wright

Meet Cynthia Wright

My career as a novelist began when I was twenty-three, with a phone call from New York announcing that CAROLINE would be published by Ballantine Books. Can you imagine my excitement? I went on to write 12 more bestselling historical romances set in Colonial America, Regency England & America, Medieval England & France, and the American West.

My novels have won many awards over the years, but what means most are readers' messages like this one: "When I read your books, I can't wait to turn the page, but never want the story to end." It's been a thrill to have all my novels published as e-books (newly edited, with gorgeous new covers!). The icing on the cake is my all-new Raveneau novel, TEMPEST, in late 2012! Next, I'll be working on the first volume of a trilogy set in Cornwall around 1800.

Today I live in northern California with my husband, Alvaro, in a 1930's Spanish cottage. When we aren't riding our tandem road bike or traveling in our vintage airstream, I love spending time with family, especially my two young grandsons. I also recently received a degree as a Physical Therapist Assistant and feel blessed to have two rewarding careers!

I'd love to have you join me at my website:
http://cynthiawrightauthor.com/

And on Facebook :
http://www.facebook.com/cynthiawrightauthor

And on Pinterest:
http://pinterest.com/cynthiawright77/

P.S. Many of you have asked, "In what order should I read the Beauvisage & Raveneau books?"
Although the titles stand alone, these two series intertwine with some characters crossing over, and many readers enjoy them in chronological order:
1781 - SILVER STORM
1783 - CAROLINE
1789 - TOUCH THE SUN
1793 - SPRING FIRES (A Beauvisage/Raveneau Novel)
1814 - SURRENDER THE STARS
1814 - NATALYA
1818 - SILVER SEA (A Raveneau/Beauvisage Novel)
1903 - TEMPEST

Novels by Cynthia Wright

CAROLINE
Beauvisage Novel #1

~

TOUCH THE SUN
Beauvisage Novel #2

~

SPRING FIRES
Beauvisage Novel #3
(A Beauvisage/Raveneau Novel)

~

NATALYA
Beauvisage Novel #3

~

SILVER STORM
Raveneau Novel #1

~

SURRENDER THE STARS
Raveneau Novel #2

~

SILVER SEA
(previously published as BARBADOS)
Raveneau Novel #3
(A Raveneau/Beauvisage Novel)

~

TEMPEST
Raveneau Novel #4

~

YOU AND NO OTHER
St. Briac Novel #1

~

OF ONE HEART
(previously published as A BATTLE FOR LOVE)
St. Briac Novel #2

~
BRIGHTER THAN GOLD
Western Novels #1
~
FIREBLOSSOM
Western Novels #2
~
WILDBLOSSOM
Western Novels #3
~
CRIMSON INTRIGUE
(Not yet released)

View all of Cynthia Wright's unforgettable novels here:
http://cynthiawrightauthor.com/books.html

Made in the USA
San Bernardino, CA
27 July 2017